Possession Of My Heart

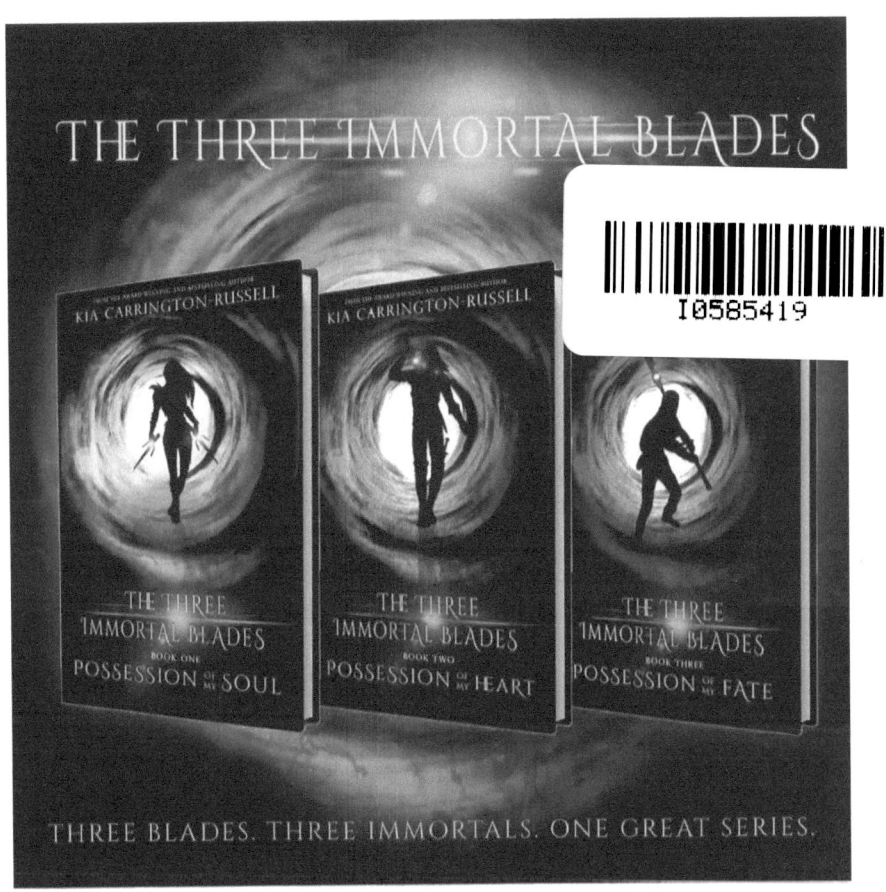

Possession Of My Heart

The Three Immortal Blades

Kia Carrington-Russell

Crystal Publishing

CRYSTAL PUBLISHING
Published by Crystal Publishing (Australia)

Copyright © Kia Carrington-Russell 2014

The moral right of the author has been asserted.

Cover Design: © Angela M Hudson
All Images Used Under Licence by Shutterstock.com

ISBN 978-0-6483370-8-9

CRYSTAL
PUBLISHING

Dedication

A huge thank you to my family and friends for all their support! I can never thank you enough for all the kind words, gestures, and support you have given me. I am glad to be surrounded by such loving people who allow me to dwell in my fantasy worlds and then read every part of it. I love you all and thank you all for your contributions in my life and writing.

Thank you to all my fans and supporters, who, whether you realise it or not, impact me greatly. Your purchase, reviews, messages and excitement for the next book gives me an overwhelming happiness and sense of achievement. I am glad you enjoyed reading about my fantasy worlds as much as I did writing them.

Thank you everyone; you are all truly magical.

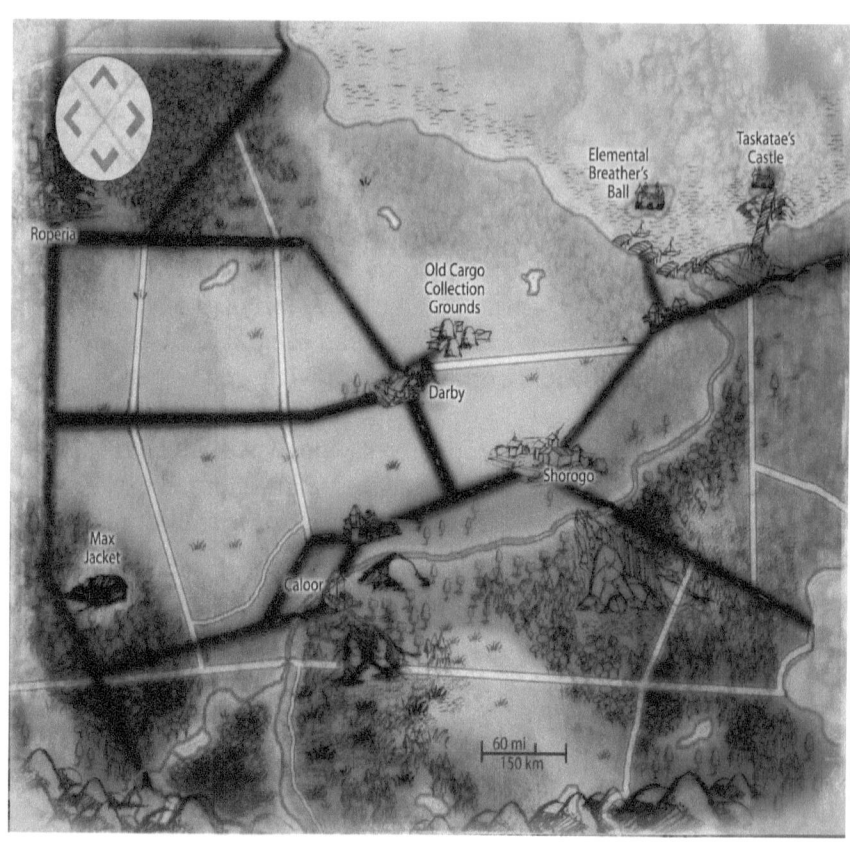

Prologue

They're after the blades, I realized to myself, searching for where Aeisha once was. I looked down at her paired blade in my hand, summoning the energy it possessed. I could sense her partnered blade — it was not that far from here. Was the girl a distraction?

As if hearing my annoyance, Ashley ran over to me as the Starkorfs all began to flee behind the small girl that took Paul's knife, which held no significant power to it, why run away with it? Plus, they had Aeisha's other blade.

"They're here for the Immortal Blades. Chase them and find that girl, find out who sent them," I shouted.

I felt Aeisha's pulse once more from whoever held it and ran with my blade. The girl that had taken Paul's knife must have been a distraction. I ran to the direction where Aeisha called to me. It did not take me long to run past only eight houses until I found the four Starkorfs that ran from me. The one in front was holding Aeisha.

They quickly turned to face me as another arrow shot for me, this time breaking through my Shield and into my shoulder. I winced from it, holding my hand firmly to the injury. *How did it get through my Shield?* I felt the pulse of Tyran and then the shiver of Misfeata coming to the surface. *But how is Tyran close, does that mean Nathanial is behind this ambush and close by? Have they been following us this whole time or is Lucas working with him, telling him of our location?*

"Get out!" I screamed ripping at the arrow and tearing it from my shoulder. Pain stirred in my wound more than usual. *What does this mean? Is Nathanial absent, but still leading this ambush?*

I projected my Shield once again as orange ripples swirled around me, only to be broken by another arrow that shot into my leg. I screamed once more in anger as I felt my face twist, trying to compose Misfeata. *Where are these arrows coming from and how are they penetrating my Shield?*

Anger swelled within me as I faced the Starkorfs, running for them.

"Give me Aeisha!" I raged, angered by my attackers, annoyed they thought they could steal Aeisha from me successfully.

I cut the first Starkorf's stomach quickly, catching it as it fell forward and using its body as a shield, noticing another arrow coming for me. The arrow pierced into the Starkorf's body as I dropped it, leaping for the other.

I caught its wrist and swung him in front of me as another arrow shot for me. Another Starkorf's burnt face caught the corner of my eye as it tried to use Aeisha against me, trying to strike me down with her.

I crouched, using the Starkorf I had hold of as the shield to my back. I elbowed the oncoming attacker in the stomach and quickly slashed Aeisha across his knees. He staggered and dropped as I pierced his leg, catching Aeisha's partnered blade as his grotesque figure screamed on the ground.

I jumped over a fence and hid against the side of a house, firming my back to the wall to hide from the archer. I searched for the archer, noticing the other Starkorf who now ran in the opposite direction, away from me. An arrow hit her back and she dropped to the ground as another caved into the side of her head. The archer is killing their own kind.

Perhaps the archer was no ally of the Starkorfs either? Or maybe because they hadn't killed me or stolen Aeisha and the archer was displeased. I stared for a little longer, hearing a sob behind me. I turned with blades in hand ready to confront my attacker, only to find a small child in front of me with tears running down her face.

My eyes widened. *Is it human? Or is it a trick?* I briefly searched behind: a trampoline, a few toys on the ground, and a vegetable garden at the back. No hiding places for any others to attack from. I stared back into the child's face as emptiness filled it and shock echoed through such innocent eyes. *There is no evil in this girl. This is only a mere human child.* I looked away in disbelief. *She would have seen everything.* The reality of this other world made me nostalgic. *I have taken the innocence of this girl away, opening such a horrific nightmare in front of her.*

I will now be the memory of her greatest fear.

1

My Heart

When my eyes bleed red and I find myself to be crying
once again,
I push you away.
For your own protection and to deter my condescending
taunts,
I will try to push you away.
I can feel that my heart skips a beat when your skin touches
my own;
but I must push you away.
I need you to be safe, a memory of my redeeming qualities;
I must lock you away.
And as I try to lock my heart away from you and you look into
my eyes, and I yours;
I know: I cannot push you away.
As you hug me and kiss my forehead and tell me it's okay,
I cry, because I cannot push you away when I cling so tightly
to you.
My heart resides within you, no matter what death may await
us.

Chapter One- Restlessness

"*A*re you ready?" I questioned Paul as we both looked at the entrance of the hospital in front of us. We were only in a small town this time, one that stated 'Darby Welcomes You' as we drove in.

"Yea." Paul reached into the back of the car and grabbed a small backpack. His green eyes turned almost gray in the thundery weather, and the dark lighting only emphasized the dark bags that were under his eyes from lack of sleep.

"Okay," I said. "Let's go." I jumped out of the car and slowly closed the door as two nurses came out of the hospital entrance for their lunch. I scurried to the side of Paul's door and opened it. I quickly retrieved the bag he gave me and threw it over my shoulder, giving him a glance that prompted him to nod in confidence.

He quickly stumbled into my arms, feigning weakness. I held his weight with my shoulders and half-carried him to the hospital entrance. As the two doors opened, Paul kissed the top of my head and whispered into my ear: "Good luck, Karlz." I could feel a smile pull at my lips but I somehow managed to keep my face expressionless.

As soon as I saw the first doctor I kicked my acting skills into gear, as did Paul.

"Please!" I yelled over the tranquil music that played in the waiting room. "Someone help!"

Paul started coughing violently into my shoulder, and within seconds the first nurse had rushed to our side.

"I don't know what happened," I exclaimed. "He just all of a sudden—..." I started to tremble. "He just got sick! Please you have to help him!"

"We will," the nurse confirmed, before she called over her shoulder for reinforcement.

I let Paul fall into the doctor's arms. "I'm sorry, but I can't do this anymore!" I said dramatically, running away toward the toilets. The doctors made little fuss over me, as I had hoped. I paused at the entrance to the toilets, quickly glancing back at the small huddle of nurses bent over Paul. One nurse turned to look at where I had been standing until Paul grabbed her arm, distracting her from searching for me. *This is my chance.*

Instead of entering the toilets, I scurried down the hall, searching for some form of medical room. A small room that matched the criteria came into sight. I quickly ran to it, using my powerful sense of sight to see where everything was. I couldn't switch on the light because that would draw too much attention.

I fumbled through the labels until I finally found the one I was after: Adrenaline. The heavy door opened slowly behind me, leaving me with just enough time to jump to the roof and plunge my hands and feet into the side of the walls. I forcefully projected my Shield to keep myself in place, pushing against the walls so I didn't fall.

The bottle I was holding fell to the floor. I quickly strained to project a small Shield over the spot it fell to. With a little pulse from my shield it bounced back up toward the ceiling, where I quickly caught it with my mouth. After my confrontation with Tyran I was now able to project my Shield within a short physical range... *another* new skill I had to learn how to control.

The light flickered on and a nurse walked in and began searching over the labels. Her hands tightened over what she was after and she walked out just as quickly as she had come in. When the light was switched off at last and the door was closed I quietly dropped to my feet, retrieving the bottle out of my mouth. I opened the zipper on my backpack and placed the bottle in the bag. When I went to retrieve the other bottles also labeled 'Adrenaline', I found to my dismay, only another three. Indeed it was a small hospital but this would only last me a few weeks, maybe two at the most.

Soon Paul and I would have to go to another hospital and steal more bottles just so I could sustain life. Pumping myself with adrenaline was the only way to keep myself alive when my body next had a fit and shut down. *At least I now know it shuts down because it is trying to fight the Shielder blood that runs through my veins that continues to curse me,* I thought, thinking of Misfeata's blood inside me.

I checked the corridor to make sure nobody was around and then ran down to the toilets near where I had left Paul fumbling and coughing in a show of sickness. When I finally drew his attention he nodded and pulled a tight face, causing the doctors to look up at him in concern.

Paul let a huge fart out. I looked away in embarrassment. How men found it so easy to fart at any time was beyond me. The doctors took a few steps back before searching over Paul, who simply patted his belly. I held my breath and ran in to hug Paul.

"Oh baby, you're alright!" I smiled happily.

"Sorry guys." He scratched his head, messing up his dark brown hair. "Guess I shouldn't have eaten all that cheese, huh?" I couldn't hold my breath any longer and started tugging Paul out the door as he wrapped his hands around my waist.

"Oh, you're alright!" I cried out again. My voice was high-pitched and false. To be honest, it was annoying. Paul and I both kept walking to the car, not bothering to look back at the nurses as they looked at each other in confusion. Finally, we got into the car where I could breathe normally again.

"That one stunk bad," Paul said, smiling as he put the key in to start the engine.

"Don't they always?" I joked, carefully putting the bag down at my feet and catching a glimpse of myself in the review mirror. I adjusted it, disgusted at the sight. I looked the same as I always did: fair skin, green eyes, and light brown hair—which I noticed had lengthened over the last few months. Now my body was fitter, more toned, and adapting well to the training Paul and I did together. But regardless of what others might see, I saw a hideous beast.

I hardly dared look at myself in the mirror now in case it was Misfeata who looked back. I stopped myself from getting angry to avoid allowing Misfeata to stir within me. I hated myself and avoided acknowledging my existence, for if I thought of it for too long, I would question how my existence could be good for anyone. *I am now a thief; stealing from hospitals.* It was Paul's idea after Max Jacket had told us that injecting my body with adrenaline would keep me alive, but now I questioned how far he was willing to go to save me at the cost of his own sense of morality.

Paul's hair had also grown over the last two months, giving it a wild, messy, untamed look. His olive-colored skin now had a lot more pink scars; the worst being the three scratch marks ingrained in his chest. I caught his eye. His expression was hard and his green eyes flickered in the storm. *How far will Paul go for me? Does this make me a terrible person to let him destroy himself for me? Is he really happy with all this running, stealing, training, and searching for my parents? Is this a reality anyone can come back from?*

"How many did you get this time?" Paul quietly asked, looking back at the hospital as he reversed into the dimly lit street.

"Only three," I sighed. I couldn't take them all. I had to leave at least one just in case someone needed it more than I did. It was hard to steal from hospitals as it weighed heavily on our conscience. We always looked out for cameras, at any moment we could have a criminal record on our hands. I couldn't walk up to a doctor and say: "Hey, can you prescribe me adrenaline as this is the only way forward? Sorry, no, I can't explain." We now constantly played with a double-edged sword. In trying to keep myself alive, I risked a future for us both of running from the law. *How selfish of me to let Paul do this.*

Projecting my Shield still strained me after my confrontation with Tyran. Although I was the victor, I had survived with much physical and mental damage. Slowly my Shield was regaining its strength, but only because I worked on it tirelessly every day. I had nowhere near the power that Misfeata had, but I was slowly building myself up to have enough strength to at least defend Paul.

I lifted my long black shirt and looked over the scabby marks on my elbows. It only projected the memory of the green shards piercing out of them. *If Misfeata ever tried to possess my body like that again, I wonder how far she would go. These wounds are taking too long to heal and I have them all over my body. It's been two months now. They should have already completely healed.*

"You had to use your Shield didn't you?" Paul asked, looking over my stomach. I searched over his face as the flash of lightning behind him flickered the night with color, turning his hair from dark brown to silvery gray. He looked across at me with saddened eyes. A depressing sight; I recalled the ghost of the cheeky smile that had once stretched over a face that was now stricken with worry. I slid my long shirt over my knees and looked out the window at the rain that had now started to pour.

Paul turned into a large driveway, before stopping the car outside a derelict looking building. We bought this car for $460. It was old and rusted, with paint scratched off, leaving patches of white all over the two-door car. I didn't know what type of car it was. I didn't even care; all that mattered was that it got us from place to place.

"We will stay here tonight. The hospital shouldn't know anything is missing for another day or so. We can afford to stay here one night." Paul left the car running as he grabbed his wallet and walked into the small office on the right to book a room. The light flashed on and off, stating there were rooms available. No doubt there were. The roof was rusted with clumps of brown and the pool had taken a green tinge to the water.

The hotel room was only tiny, freezing as well. Paul and I slept in our separate single beds next to one another as the lightning flashed color through the room. Rain beat relentlessly against the windows.

There weren't any curtains for privacy—only brick walls surrounding us. With only the one blanket to keep me warm, my teeth chattered as I tried to fall asleep.

I quietly tiptoed to the small cupboard that was in the corner of the room. I opened it, hoping to find at least another blanket, but was greeted only with an ironing board. I clutched my body as I shook uncontrollably in the cold. I looked at the small gap that came between Paul's bed and my own. Not even a thirty-centimeter ruler would come between. I grabbed the thin blanket off my bed and wedged myself next to Paul in his. His body heat was so much warmer than mine—like a hot water bottle. I fiddled with the blanket until Paul fidgeted and rolled over so he was facing my back.

"I wondered how long it would take you," he said with what I could imagine was a sluggish smile. He lifted his blanket and I squeezed under it, fumbling with my blanket so it wrapped around me. He moved his arm around my stomach. I allowed that small comfort and his gentle snoring to soothe me to sleep.

I woke up to the smell of scrambled eggs, finding myself to be alone in the small single bed. A trail of fresh blood soaked the pillow I laid next to; droplets and splatters of blood crossed the floor, tracing around the corner and into the kitchen. I instinctively clutched at my waist in search of Aeisha—she wasn't in her usual spot. Where are my blades? I searched around the room, finding the lantern next to me to be the closest thing to a weapon. Slowly walking to the edge of the wall dividing the kitchen and bedroom, I strained to hear what was around the corner. I stopped, holding the lamp tightly. Taking a deep breath, I leapt across the room in a roll, holding the lamp above me and landing in a crouched position. To my dismay nobody stood in the kitchen. Only a bloody figure lay on the floor, and dull green eyes stared up at me.

Paul.

I froze as I scanned over his body—all the cuts and stabbings—my eyes finally resting on Aeisha. My very own blade was now embedded in Paul's stomach. I only had time to cough out a shocked cry before I turned around and was confronted with Lucas. He raised Aeisha's other blade to my throat. I only had a brief second to look into Lucas's cold face: his angular jaw, his tight lips, his dark golden hair—all stained with blood. Lucas stared at me with piercing brown eyes that I no longer recognized. He looked at me with the same contempt I felt for myself — as though I were a beast. As Lucas's eyes tormented me, I felt the cold ooze of life pouring out of me. Slowly, I looked down to see Borac gliding out of my chest, causing me to slump onto my knees, struggling for breath. A flash of green gem streaked past my sight as I heard Misfeata's laugh echo through the room. I screamed as green shards pierced through my skin, breaking apart the shell that kept my soul intact.

My head flung to my knees as I panted, choking for air. Perspiration covered my whole body as I searched over the blanket that concealed my feet. I heard a creak and opened my eyes to find a pair of piercing blue eyes staring back at me.

"Another nightmare, ey?"

A familiar voice. Ashley stood still as he looked over me.

I straightened myself, forcing my hard face to slightly soften as I looked over the single bed beside me where Paul loudly snored. Thank goodness. It was just a dream.

"It's been a while, Ashley," I said. He leaned against the wall with one leg bent back, arms crossed against his chest.

"Still carrying around your little pet?" Ashley slowly took one of his legs off the wall, as he stood strong before me. "I wonder what he dreams of as you perish in your own nightmares," he said contemplatively as he glanced over Paul. "I imagine his obsession with you actually is returned in his dreams. Instead, in reality he walks around with someone who isn't willing to show him a quarter of the affection he displays.... I imagine."

"You speak out of line. If you came to die, say one more thing of the journey I have chosen to take," I spat.

Ashley let out an exhausted sigh. "Come, I have someone I need you to meet. Someone whom I think will benefit your cause." He walked out the front door that he had easily broken into. As I grabbed Aeisha, I winced and clutched my stomach, finding red on my hand as I retrieved it. My wound had reopened. I grabbed my jacket that hung on the end of my bed, slowly getting up to put it on to cover the visible signs of my bleeding stomach. I quietly closed the door behind me, casting one quick glance at Paul who was still sleeping peacefully.

After hearing the click of the door behind me, I looked up to see Ashley standing beside a man I had not yet met. The first thing that captured my attention was his dominant features—starting with his florescent pink eyes. His smooth baby-soft skin, white hair, plump lips, and thick eyelashes, gave the impression of a man in his mid-twenties. I squinted at him, quickly glancing over his bold red suit that certainly condemned him to be out of place at a cheap motel like this. Then I recognized the detail in the material — the little ripples.

"Material of an Elemental Breather," I said hesitantly, straightening my back in preparation for conflict. The man simply laughed at me maliciously, forcing a hand over his mouth until his mirth lightened into a giggle. I met Ashley's eyes to see him roll them in exasperation.

"Oh my," the stranger said. "We are certainly paranoid."

15

I searched Ashley's eyes once more, annoyed at being mocked. I resented this meeting with the stranger he had presented. "Are you serious?" I questioned Ashley. Ashley sighed, letting the awkward silence roll on.

I peered over the stranger once again, waiting. "Who are you and why are you here?"

"Oh how you have changed, young one," he said, his piercing eyes looking through me.

"I've never met you," I said coldly.

"In truth, you have," he said. The man before me shrunk into a wolf within seconds. Although there was not much shrinking to be done, the wolf was enormous. I stared at the wolf in front of me, recalling the same thick fur and features of the one at Max Jacket's home. This was the same wolf.

"Sam?" I asked in astonishment. Sam was the pet wolf of Max Jacket. The animal and I had bonded before the ambush Max Jacket had organized against us. I gazed at him in amazement as he transformed again into the young man that previously stood in front of me.

"Actually, my name is Scott," he said as he made a funny face and a clicking noise. He waved his arms in the air dramatically. "You know, code names, secret names… Awkward," he proclaimed flamboyantly.

"I don't understand," I admitted, still astonished.

Ashley stepped forward to speak: "Max Jacket and Trish abandoned their home not too long after the encounter with Tyran. Scott came in search of you, coming across me instead. Mum's still in hiding with Chris and Suzumiya, but Kurt hasn't been found. He's just vanished. Everyone is staying quiet until we find Kurt again, but Scott found our hiding place and demanded to see you."

I nodded at Ashley, taking in what he had stated and then looking over at Scott once more. "And you've come to me, why?"

"I wanna help your little group thing that you've got going here. It seems like a little bit of fun and, well, my father hasn't much time for me, even if I did find him." He sighed to himself with a small giggle. "Wasn't quite accepting of his own son, but balderdash, I'm a free man now," he said, glowing as he gazed at nothing in particular. I glanced up at Ashley, who was looking the other way. This man before me had literally stunned me; I didn't know what to say.

I heard the click of the door and looked behind me as Paul came out shirtless, rubbing his eyes as he looked at us all sleepily. Scott only took a second to start giggling to himself and then he clicked his fingers. "And aren't you cute!" he said, absolutely beaming.

Chapter Two- Appearance

*I*t has been a few months now since Paul and I have left the others, and much has changed since the betrayal Lucas had cast over all of us. I had previously thought so well of Lucas — unsuspecting of his true identity as a Starkorf. I was once naïve, so fond of him. Now, I was confused by how I felt after my reunion with Paul, who then followed to protect me. It was Lucas's betrayal that lead to Paul's injury as we were ambushed by his brother, Nathanial, in the old warehouse near my town, Roperia. That was the reason why I had to face all my fears to obtain both of Misfeata's Immortal Blades, Aeisha, and also Borac. I sighed as I recalled how I had used Tyran's Immortal Blade to bargain with Max Jacket and Trish so that they would heal Paul.

That very same day was when Ashley became the cold, uncompassionate person he was now. Because of this war, Ashley's father Seth, was killed in front of us all, by Lucas's brother. He had very little interest in others' safety anymore, and was constantly trying to throw himself into fights as everyone else quelled their actions. The others were in hiding, confused as to why Kurt never returned to lead them.

Nathanial was now the descendant of the Elder, Tyran — Misfeata's brother — and therefore my life rival. I had defeated him once through their father's body, Praytar. The lack of control Misfeata had exercised as she possessed my body, led me to near death. Her Immortal Blades Aeisha began changing my form and piercing my skin with shards of green gems. If I hadn't taken control of my body, I think I would be dead, or a beast roaming with no recollection of myself.

After everything I have learned — and with deceit still stinging me so bitterly — Paul and I left in search of my parents, hoping that I would soon be reunited with them. They had been kidnapped during my time away from Roperia. It had taken me a while to control my own ability of Shielding, but with the ability now to do so, I had to contend with the new challenge of finding a cure for my body. Misfeata's Elder blood mingling with my own caused my body to shut down at every assault. My largest threat was Misfeata herself who tried to possess my mind, body, and soul, whenever she saw a chance. Upon success she would be able to properly rein over the war again against her brother. This war had raged for many centuries — a world we humans were unaware of.

Ashley often found us, I never understood how, but he would always do: to check up on us, to see whether the Starkorfs have already found us, to scout for new information. He was just as hunted as I was. He was always restless, and I told him the same thing every time he came: that I was not interested in fighting any longer. No matter how many times I told Ashley, he was always hopeful to fight once again — to avenge his father by finding Nathanial and Lucas and killing them. It was a very dark world we lived in, and with distasteful motives for survival. Such a war has led Ashley to have hatred in his heart. I could not muster his thrill for the fight, and yet he still followed as if he were lost.

"Karla, read this," Paul instructed quietly, still trying to avoid eye contact with Scott, who did nothing but ogle him under the pretense of manicuring his nails. I had told both him and Ashley I didn't need their help, but the Element Breather would just not leave. I thought infatuation with Paul was the reason more than any other.

I directed my attention toward what Paul offered. It was a news article in the local paper that seemed odd. Many people had been found murdered near an old cargo collection grounds. Although police thought it to be murder, there were no physical signs of violence, poison, or anything of that sort.

"Starkorfs," Ashley said bluntly, leaning up against the wall in the small motel room that we stayed in.

"It seems odd though. They only attack small towns, not one as large as this," I said in reply.

"Those Starkorf beasties are quite the feral dogs." Scott crossed his legs and gazed between his nails and Paul, who still had his head down in discomfort. "If you'd have seen as many as I have, you would be mortified; the majority of them can't even sustain the feasting and go all mutated and disgusting. Like a bunch of feral animals."

We all stared at him as he spoke; he was unfazed by his intrusion into our conversation. Scott still seemed out of place in conversation. I recalled our time together when I knew him as the great big wolf I was so fond of. Max Jacket kept him as a pet who couldn't say anything. Now he was partaking in a conversation in a light-hearted way that mocked the seriousness of the situation. It was almost provoking.

"What was the point of that? We already know, that's not useful," Ashley spat angrily.

"Point of what?" Scott asked slowly, breaking his attention away from his nails to Ashley. He searched over his angry face before cackling loudly. "Oh my. Me and my big mouth again." He barked in hysterics and out of the corner of my eye I could see both Ashley and Paul cringe simultaneously.

"We could always check it out, perhaps tonight when it is dark, so we will be unseen. I will stay for it." Ashley pushed himself from the wall and stared at me questioningly. "If you don't mind?"

"We were going to leave town tonight," Paul interrupted, his eyes almost pleading when I searched them. "We are searching for your parents, remember, Karlz?"

"We are," I reinforced. Ashley's mocking smile proved he thought himself proven right. I continued nonetheless. "But we can leave tomorrow. We will search over this place tonight." With that, the decision was made, and silence fell upon the group.

I gazed up at the moon that blazed strongly in the night sky. Even if it were midnight, the moon shone so brightly, it suggested it were day. To my tormented mind, the glare stood as a potential spotlight for a bloody battle. Although this town was not overly big, it was not overly small either, which complicated the issue of why Starkorfs would be preying here. The Starkorf only usually hit towns if they were small enough to wipe away in one brutal blow: a feasting that would maintain them for a solid month or so, I've heard.

A rustling noise was made and we all froze where we stood. We looked into the old, fenced grounds through the barbed wire to find nothing there. I looked over to Ashley, who looked back at me, then shot a glance at the tense Paul. We all eyed the well-lit ship grounds. Scott seemed skittish as he glanced at everything around us. His chest was rising and falling frantically with every pinch of noise that could be heard.

"Have you never dealt with Starkorfs?" I provoked. He quickly glanced over my face and then the surroundings once more.

"I... I... " All of a sudden he let out a wild cackle and bellowed in a high-pitched tone: "I have taken on the world. Don't—..."

Within those short few seconds Ashley had grabbed his mouth and pulled him close to the ground. "Are you an utter idiot?" he quietly spat, his blue eyes piercing like daggers. Ashley's grip was suddenly lost as a little pigeon hovered above his hand. I grabbed at Scott's new form.

"A pigeon, really?" Paul mocked. He froze and dropped his gaze as I gave him an effective look.

"If you want to leave us then leave, but don't be so stupid as to expose us," I lectured Scott. Slowly Scott's feathered chest slowed down and he retained his usual form, pulling on his red suit to straighten it out.

I felt a cold grip on my hand. I turned around to see a wolf with yellow eyes growling at us savagely only five meters away. Ashley let his grip leave mine and he stood up slowly as we stared at the abnormally shaped wolf. Slowly, I glanced over its whole body to find it had a snake's tail.

Leaving us not enough time to take in its deformities, the deformed beast howled and then barked savagely, before running straight toward us. Instead of fighting, we all started to run. It had been a long time since I allowed myself to cower away from a fight of any kind. But this creature instinctively made me just run. We all ran around a corner as Scott let out some weird, feline scream. I quickly glanced at him thinking he was changing into some form of bird with his squawk, but no, he was still running as the man he was, simply screaming.

My feet met a rock and I tripped, grazing my hands and face along the gravel. I tried forcing my arms to lift myself, only to have my body reject the movement. Paul quickly noticed my disappearance, and between us we only needed one quick look to realize what was happening. I concentrated on projecting my Shield around me, but I was vulnerable. I tried to croak out for Paul to stop, but he brushed past my slumped figure, standing in front of me protectively with a knife. As slow as everything was, my eyes fixated on the advancing wolf — how close and large it looked near Paul and me.

As the giant deformed wolf leapt for Paul, he clenched the knife in a protective stance, ready to fight it off. Another wolf jumped over my figure and lunged for the other, intervening in what might have been a fatal encounter for Paul.

Yelping pierced the air and the wolves bared fangs as they bit into the necks of one another. A reflection of discolored eyes grabbed my attention and I realized the newest wolf amongst us was Scott. My body started to convulse and I felt my hearing ring. Fire started to swarm through my body as death bestowed its grip on my every function.

Scott was thrown across the gravel as the other wolf lunged at him once again. He quickly plunged his back paws into the beast's stomach and threw him off, before charging at the beast once again. They continued to lunge into one another's thick fur.

My eyesight started to blur as I felt a cool serum spread through my figure. The pinched pain in my skin slowly began to subside. I was rolled over onto my back. Ashley now stood in front of me protectively and Paul held the syringe that had just been injected into my blood stream. My head rested on his knees as my sight quickly found its balance again. His hand was numb against my face yet subtle, so I could still feel his slow stroke around my lips and cheek to rid me of the froth or blood I had choked up.

Quickly I felt my system kick in and my hearing reawakened to the growling and yelping of the two fighting wolves. Slowly Paul raised me up as Ashley glanced down at me with saddened eyes. The expression quickly left as he retracted his protective stance, making me question if he did have such a caring look to begin with.

I looked over to see Scott's fangs plunge down on the wolf's throat. Then he began throwing it around like a rag doll. Scott threw the wolf to the side and it scraped over the gravel. It released a low, whimpering noise. As its eyes slowly opened and closed, Scott changed to his human form, wiping away the blood that was smeared around his mouth. He impatiently tugged out a silk napkin out of his bloodied suit and wiped at his mouth with it in a gentlemanly fashion. Somehow he all of a sudden looked much older than usual. I noticed a deep bite mark in his neck that continued down to his collarbone. He caught my staring eyes and adjusted his suit to cover the wound.

He walked over to me, seeming somewhat angry and yet at the same time upset. We froze when we all heard a cracking noise. We looked back at the fowl wolf that lay on the cement, as its jaw slowly broke open. The cracking went in beat with what I imagine the ticking of a bomb would be like. We all stared at it, knowing something was about to rise from the corpse. Along with the cracking of the beast's jaw, its stomach slowly started to swell and then quickly began to shrink. The cracking of its jaw had stopped and its mouth extended wide.

We all stared at it in unison, hearing our own breaths being swallowed by the stilted atmosphere. A choking noise was heard and then a pile of colored snakes poured out of its mouth. Paul quickly helped me onto my feet and once again we all started running as a wild bunch of snakes slithered over one another toward us at an alarming pace.

We ran around a corner before being blocked off by a dead-end. We frantically looked back at the snakes, searching over the fence for an opening. Scrambling on our hands and feet we climbed over the fence, flinging ourselves over into the deserted grounds that contained the large cargo ships. They looked as though they had been sitting there for years abandoned, perhaps it was only a storage area now? Little movement was made as a light breeze brushed past us, whistling dauntingly between the empty cargo ships. Some doors swung open lightly with an eerie screeching movement. There were large tunnels that had been dug into the ground on the right side of the cargo ships. They were surrounded by a tall wire fence. The tunnels seemed to lead into an underground area, which quickly faded into darkness, as the moonlight could no longer reach its shadowed depths. Two figures ran out of one of the manmade holes. Instantly, my heart plunged and I felt a slight stir of Misfeata. I fell to the ground as something triggered her to rouse violently within me.

"Karla?" Paul dropped himself down to my level as I held my chest. I concentrated on forcing Misfeata back down into where she lay dormant. Surprisingly, I was able to condemn her quickly back to her long sleep.

Misfeata had stirred from within because of the familiar person who now stood in front of me. The last person I wanted to see, only looking at him squeezed my heart.

"Karla?"

He had changed a lot since I had last seen him: scragglier than before, his eyes more tired, his sandy-blonde hair longer.

"What are you doing here?" Ashley protectively stood in front of Paul and me before either of us could think of the answer. Or worse, take action ourselves. I was surprised that Ashley had not tried killing Lucas already. Lucas was a traitor, and Ashley's beautiful father Seth, died because of it.

A pretty girl not much younger than me, who had long honeycomb hair and green eyes that shone brightly in the moon's blaze, accompanied Lucas. She shuffled slightly under the awkward tension. She wore white pants with a white shirt that covered her entirely, almost as if she were wearing a dress over the long pants. Her look of innocence was deceiving as I saw the crossbow in her hand and yet no arrows were strapped to her body. I frowned; I did not understand the point of carrying a bow if she had no arrows.

Lucas pulled himself straight and stood tall once again. Businessman-like, unsure if Ashley was still the enemy or like before, his brother. Before answering he had one more look down at me, making me realize I was still on the floor, and, steadily, I brought myself up from the ground behind Ashley, glaring at the both of them.

"I was summoned here," Lucas replied strongly.

"By whom?" Ashley raised the knife and tensed. I now knew he had not forgotten and his father's face was flashing in front of him. As if hearing my thoughts, Ashley went to pounce on Lucas with anger. The young girl next to Lucas raised her bow and shot an arrow past both Ashley's face and mine, cutting a few strands of my hair that was tightly pinned up. The strands released and fell gently over my face, into my eyes. Ashley turned to see where the arrow had shot from. There was a small trickle of blood from his cheekbone.

I realized then that it was not Ashley she was shooting at, but one of the snakes that had folded over the large wire fence behind us. The pile of snakes had quickly risen over the fence and her arrow landed into the first that poured over the top. Somehow amongst our confrontation with Lucas we had forgotten the other danger at hand.

"Run!"

We all ran, glancing wearily over the large mass of snakes that plunged themselves over the edge of the fence. We poured into the open field, looking over the grounds and then up at the old cargos. I gestured for all of us to reach the high cargos, noticing that we had all been split up. Ashley and I ran away from the fast-striking pile of snakes as we ran alongside a cargo. I quickly reefed his hand to the side of the cargo, placing my hands together so he could raise himself on top of it. Instead he swept me off my feet and easily placed me onto his shoulders so I could reach the top.

My hands shuffled around the edge of it and I found a secure place where my fingers could grip, and raised myself up. I braced myself as I grabbed at Ashley's hands, pulling him up as one of the snakes wrapped around his leg, squeezing at it. Surprisingly the snakes were alarmingly heavy and I struggled to lift his weight. With determination I was eventually able to do so. When he rose, I grabbed Aeisha, Misfeata's Immortal Blades, from my side and sliced at the first snake that plunged its fangs into my leg, cutting its head off.

Still unsure as to what these creatures were or how they materialized, we had no other choice but to fight to reunite with the others. *I must find Paul. He will be safe until I reach him,* I told myself.

I hovered over Ashley, slicing the snakes that bit and strangled at him, cutting at them like the others I had sliced before. Ashley's face froze and I followed his gaze to see that the snakes we had cut down somehow reproduced. They burst to life from within a white shell. One leapt for my chest and a scream emerged from the depths of my throat, only to be smothered by a snake wrapping itself around my mouth. In so long I had not screamed. In so long I had not been this frightened. What was happening?

I heard another scream, but this time the high-pitched squeal belonged to Scott. Ashley cut the snake from my mouth, accidentally grazing the blade down the side of my cheek. I reefed the other snake away from my chest only to have it bite into my arm and wrap its limbless body around me. Ashley went to cut it, but another snake plunged for the same arm and wrapped itself around his hand that held the knife. A snake coiled itself around my waist. The crushing around my stomach reopened my wound, making me hunch over in pain.

I projected my Shield so the snakes that entangled me were thrown over the edge of the cargo. I searched through my dark-brown ripples, gasping at how many of the vile creatures were attacking us. Many lunged and struck at my Shield, only to be diverted elsewhere. I quickly scampered over to Ashley, who was on his knees still trying to fight with his one hand. They swarmed his body for warmth.

I couldn't send a huge pulse of my projected Shield over them because it would send Ashley over the edge as well or even worse, crush him. Thinking of no other way, I quickly jumped on Ashley's shoulders like a cat, plunging him into the ground, shoulders first. I sent my projected Shield across the cargo, bringing it quickly back in as I turned him over. He struck out at the snakes that still layered on him, tormenting, biting, and strangling his body.

I sliced at them all with Aeisha, quickly throwing their carcasses over the edge before they could reproduce over us. I let my Shield fall, finally catching my breath. Ashley tried slowly raising himself as I searched over his more severe wounds. I recoiled at his mangled hand that had been broken from the constriction of one of the snakes.

"I'm okay," he choked, putting his hand to my stomach and holding it in front of him so he could see the blood from my reopened wound. "Thought so." He leaned slightly on me for support.

"We don't have long," he stated simply. "We need to get out of here."

"Not without Paul and Scott," I said raising myself over the cargo to see thousands of snakes building up across the ground that was once empty. What was this? How was this even possible? I saw in the corner of my eye Ashley looking at me calculatingly, but he said nothing. I continued searching over the grounds, finding no one else in sight.

"Look there," I pointed at the manmade tunnels I had seen before. "They may have gone in there. The snakes are surrounding themselves around the cargos and us; they could have escaped in there. If we can get in there quickly, we may slip past these creatures."

"Karla, we should just go, maybe they made it out already," Ashley said bluntly.

"That is our best option," I said ignoring his comment. There was an awkward pause. I cared what happened to Paul and couldn't take a chance with his life.

"And how do we get to those tunnels? Considering they might be a dead end," he asked, agitating me even more. Was he only like this because of this uncertain danger we were in? Was it because we didn't know how these creatures had manifested or was there more behind his spiteful tone?

As if hearing our questions, and breaking the tension between Ashley and me, an elephant burst from one of the tunnels, stomping on the snakes that lay in front of it, pounding its way toward us. As it neared the edge of our cargo, it stretched forth its trunk and laid an unconscious and bloodied Paul into my arms. The elephant shrunk and flapped up to us in pigeon form, and then turned into a human. Scott stood and readjusted himself in his red suit. He was also bloodied, although he still somehow looked in better shape than the rest of us.

"What happened?" I raged at him, looking down at Paul's face.

"They seem to be building up to reach this height, as if replicating the cargo's mass. Their numbers are vast; we do not have much time to waste here. We need to leave now!" Scott focused on me unsteadily.

To my surprise, he had not yet abandoned us when he could've simply flown away. I heard the piercing of metal beside me and found an arrow with white rope strapped to it, which stretched down to the manmade tunnels. Lucas's companion waved to us, suggesting for us to climb down it. Ashley and I looked at one another and then at Scott, who was already adjusting himself to swing down it.

"Can't you get us out of here, Scott? Turn into an elephant or something again?" I questioned, not wanting to accept the help of the enemy, especially a companion of Lucas's.

"There is only so much I can handle," he explained, pointing at his arms and legs, which I hadn't noticed before. Blood oozed out of many little holes, causing his suit to stick to his skin. "I need to heal."

Scott took the rope, and, using the material from his suit, glided down to the young girl who tugged at the rope to give the 'OK'. I looked at Ashley with uncertainty and then at Paul. Looking between Paul's unconscious face and Ashley's broken hand, I realized they would never make it down in such a state.

The snakes had not yet detected Scott and the unfamiliar girl. They continued to pile up, trying to get to us on top of the cargo. Lucas now stood next to them as well, tugging on the rope for support. After some hesitation, he quickly began climbing up the rope, showing that although his exterior had seemed to wither slightly in time, his strength had not left him. Within moments he was by our side, like me, the first thing he looked at was Ashley's broken hand and Paul's unconscious face.

"I would rather die than accept your help," Ashley scolded and then spat on Lucas's shoes. Lucas swiftly glided behind Ashley, hitting him in the back of the neck with the handle of his blade. Alarmed, I raised my Shield in front of both Ashley and Paul while Lucas and I pushed for dominance over one another's Shield. They pushed and grated over one another's edges as I felt his familiar projection touch mine. I intensely kept pushing it as much as I could, starting to lose my breath as he did, his stance edging closer and closer to the edge. We did not fight beyond this, surprisingly. We just stood there staring into one another's foreign eyes. All I could recall was the heavy betrayal he burdened me with.

"It's the only way Ashley will let me help," Lucas gasped.

"You? Help? What an odd thing for a traitor to do. I told you the next time we meet, we fight. You have come to me and I can do nothing but make that happen." I swung myself around, focusing my Shield to pinpoint on one section of his Shield so I could break through. I used Aeisha to cut through Lucas's shirt as he shuffled back, and I plunged both sais down. Using his own sword he blocked both of my separate blades, looking at me hopelessly. I felt Misfeata stir again but ignored her, edging my blades closer to his throat.

"Would you really choose to kill me instead of protecting them?" he questioned. I stared at him coldly and continued pushing my Shield as well as my blade near him.

"Answer me, Karla!"

I lost all focus as I noticed the snakes that piled around us. I was instantly thrown off by Lucas's projected Shield. I shuffled myself over to Paul, cutting at the snakes that tried to pour over him. Lucas had Ashley over his shoulders firmly and grabbed Paul from my hold as well.

"Get behind me. We need to tuck them in-between us so we don't lose either of them."

Listening to him, I grabbed both of them as Lucas threw himself onto the rope and swung his legs toward me. I had no choice but to agree with him for now. *I must keep Ashley and Paul safe.* And Lucas was right. This was the only way Ashley would have come down the rope if he had to accept their help.

"Entangle your legs into mine and we will place both of them between us."

I did as he said in one swift movement, throwing myself down and catching them between our legs just in time. We both projected our Shields into our palms and slid down the rope with immaculate speed. Scott and Lucas's companion caught Ashley and Paul between us as we awkwardly collected ourselves on the ground.

"They need healing," she said briefly. "I can do that now if I can exit out of these grounds."

"You do so. I, however, am going in there," Lucas nodded toward the tunnel.

"As you wish." She nodded with a slight courtesy, making me question the relationship they had. She rose to her feet and threw both full-grown men over her shoulders as if they were only flour bags. My mouth opened in astonishment as she quickly ran away with them. I stood to run after them but Lucas grabbed my hand instead. I tore my hand from his, catching him off guard and cutting his cheek with Aeisha.

"Don't you ever touch me!" I roared.

Lucas dabbed his cheek and stared at the blood in front of him with sad eyes. Although it had been two months since we had last seen one another nothing has changed of my feelings toward him.

"She will look after them. I—... " Lucas tried to reason before I cut him off.

"You what? You 'promise?' Your words are like acid to me!" I said, almost fearful at the amount of angst I held toward him.

He ducked his head. "I simply mean to question... Wouldn't you wish to at least accompany me? You do want to know what it is that has created such monsters, don't you, Karla? After all, you would have been here in search of Starkorfs, right? Not these creatures that have clearly put us all near death. Don't you want to know where they came from?" He gestured toward the pile of snakes that now covered where we once stood. "A normal snake would have not taken that long to register we were down here. In fact they would've noticed straight away, these are not normal snakes."

"Karla." Scott was still with us, looking at me questioningly. "I would like to see the reason behind what has happened today, but if you wish me to follow the other young lady that took Paul and Ashley, I will do so. But in saying that, you know either of them would not want me to leave your side. Paul's disapproval would be more apparent than Ashley's, but on this I can conclude with confidence." I was surprised to hear Scott talk with such formality and strength of tone.

"Do as you please," I answered coldly.

My anger was not directed at Scott, but I spoke with frustration as I had lost all power over the past few minutes as these new creatures came for us. I was scared of these snakes, and even more terrified that I was unable to protect Ashley and Paul. I didn't want to go with Lucas, and yet I had to find out what had put Paul in such danger. I dipped my head in shame for my weakness and stormed toward the direction of the tunnel, readjusting my keen sight as I disappeared further into darkness.

Chapter Three- Puppet

*M*y hands fumbled against the walls of the huge tunnel and I squinted, the darkness forcing me to rely upon my exceptional sight. I put one hand to my stomach as my reopened wound introduced itself to me once again. I focused on Lucas who walked in front of me with ease through the eerie tunnel.

He is trying to make me trust him and have some sense of security around him. I refuse to let him get the better of me. He already tricked me once, making me regret my judgment of him and the feelings I thought I had for him. What if this is an ambush, what if his brother and he are working together and they only wanted me, the last descendant of Misfeata, and they now have exactly what they want? I have walked straight into this trap. What do I do then? I can hardly see anything in here.

Lucas's shoulders tensed and his pace slowed, forcing me to retract Aeisha, preparing for an attack. "I'm sorry." His words punched me in the stomach, making me lose any breath I had in my lungs and for a second, my eyes went out of focus. *I have walked into an ambush.* Regaining my strength quickly after the stupidity of losing focus over two words, I spat back the only words that could escape through my lips.

"I wish you were dead."

And yet, after my spiteful words, he only looked away pained, and nothing eventuated from it. *Does this mean this is not an ambush?* I searched around, waiting for attacks, but nothing came. *Is it really only Lucas and I here? Then what is he apologizing for? For his betrayal, the lies he fed me months ago?*

As if the walls themselves heard me, a crackling noise rang out from all around us. Squinting into the darkness behind us, I saw small flickers of shadows, which I assumed to be the snakes following us. I started to run, forgetting the sharp pain in my stomach and the noise that came from the front. A sharp turn in the tunnel forced bright light into my eyes. I raised my hand. I ran for it quickly, still hearing the crackling from ahead.

"Stop," Lucas forcefully said, keeping with my pace. "Something is not right, let me go first." With that I ran faster, trying to forget he existed in the same tunnel that I did. Lucas was the last person I would accept help from. I continued running. *I am strong and will not be manipulated with easy words*.

I burst into an open space that had five exits: two to my left, two in front and one on my right. Quickly scoping the circular room, I paused, mesmerized. Large colored eggs sat on slim black carved pedestals.

I hesitantly walked toward the first one, hovering over it in awe. *What is this?* I looked at the finely detailed pedestals; on them were carvings of what I thought to be war: tiny figures with swords and knives, arms and legs — death and life. All were ornately and neatly scratched into the black wood. I searched over the blue egg that nestled upon the wood. My hands drifted over it in amazement before what felt to be a pulse from the egg stabbed into my hand and threw me away from it.

"Karla, what is it?" Lucas came to my side, looking over my hand as I did.

It is alive. The egg has something in it. But... it feels like death.

"Don't touch, little Shielder," commanded an unfamiliar voice. A woman approached from the third tunnel. A glimpse of the black hair reminded me of someone. *Raven*. Having another quick glance at her, I realized it was not Raven, although she had very similar features.

Raven was the first Starkorf to ever attack me, but now she was dead by my very own hands. I watched her die. And although she always appeared as a twelve-year-old child, this was what I imagined her form would be if she had reached adulthood.

Still feeling threatened by the woman and the stirring feeling of danger that rose within me, I knew I had to throw Aeisha at her. The woman was evil. On my journey, one thing I have learned is to never deny my instincts.

Before I could throw Aeisha toward her my blade was taken from me, and it stabbed into my hand, pinning me to the ground. I looked up at Lucas, not giving him the satisfaction of a scream. I looked into Lucas's deep-brown eyes. He looked down on me with an expression of mortification.

Traitor, you stabbed me in the hand.

The woman laughed to herself, clapping a small round of applause. "Dance for me, Puppet. Dance." With that, Lucas started to move oddly, disjointedly, into what appeared to be a dance. I could see no strings pulling him into the strange moves, but he danced as if he were a puppet.

But, Raven... No. Raven is dead.

I glanced back at the woman, who had the thickest of black hair, which came down to her waist, wavy and freshly brushed. I glared into the blue eyes that reminded me far too much of Raven's, eventually looking away in disgust. I glanced over the long deep-purple dress that flowed to the floor, trailing behind her into the tunnel she had entered from. It was a very distinct material. *Elemental Breather*. Her face was very narrow and pale; if I hadn't known her to be a threat I would say she was radiant. She was tall, with an hourglass figure. Her stern glare was a mixture of hatred and boredom.

I grabbed the hilt of Aeisha in my hand and tore it out, trying to express little pain. I glared at the woman, slowly rising. *I was right — she is an enemy. Is she the woman behind all of these bizarre creatures?* I projected my red-rippled Shield, watching the woman for any sudden movement. I didn't yet understand her Element. Her laughing stopped abruptly and she twisted her lips in disgust.

"You killed my wolf," she spoke harshly. "Now I'm going to kill your hound."

Lucas struck at me with his knife in a bizarre manner — a weapon that I hadn't noticed him carrying before — forcing me to jump back. *Is she referring to Lucas as my hound?* I paced around the edges near the walls, staring into Lucas's tortured deep-brown eyes as he continuously attacked me, strike after strike.

I ran toward the wall, jumping onto its hard edge and pushing myself off it with an extra boost from my Shield. I landed in the middle of the room. As I landed I bumped into one of the eggs. It rocked back and forth before falling. A heavy scrape ran across my stomach because for some reason I was hitting the floor to save the egg. I caught it in time. But why? Something had taken control of my body and yet Misfeata was still dormant.

"How dare you try to break my egg!" the woman shouted, infuriated. My body erected; every fiber in my being changed. "Dance for me, Puppet, dance!"

Her previous comment to Lucas rang through my head. *Is she somehow able to control my body, and Lucas's too?* My movement was not of my own will. Slowly my chin started to lift and I put Aeisha to my collarbone, slowly cutting strips into myself. My Shield wouldn't project, it was nonexistent; I had no control of my body nor my ability. I tried staring into the woman's eyes, trying to understand how she had control over both my body and ability — was this her Element?

Lucas tried plunging his blade into her, but when she easily avoided it he only had time to barge her. He was fast, and the tunnel she had come from swallowed her. My body dropped instantly. I was released from her hold, and the weight of my body was my own. *What just happened?*

I stared at the ground, dismayed. *Who is this woman?* Lucas helped me to my feet as I became competent once again. We knew that to get away we would have to run into the same tunnel we had come from. Projecting our Shields, we prepared ourselves to swim through the snakes that had backed us into this very hole. But no snakes were seen, allowing us to run through the dark without challenge.

We finally broke out into the moonlit grounds once again. We were alone and the snakes had somehow simply vanished, as if none of it were ever real. Was it an illusion? Looking at the blood that dripped down my neck and the snake bites that had started to heal on my skin, I thought not.

We kept running, away from whatever or wherever that woman was. Finally we hit the main street of the town. Only a few pubs were still open but it gave us a chance to slow our pace and walk; try to collect ourselves, clean ourselves up a little. I used my hair to cover the cuts down my collarbone that I knew would be healed soon enough. I clung to my stomach with my other hand so nobody raised eyebrows to a young girl walking down the main street with a bleeding stomach. Surely the woman would not follow us into such a public, open place. Lucas combed through his dirtied hair, straightening it and then his long black shirt. Only a cut was evident on his jawline.

"Are you alright?" Lucas asked, slowly catching his breath.

"Don't pity me. Where are the others?" I scowled, searching over the few drunken men that wavered toward our direction with filthy whistles.

"Not far out of this town. We have made camp for tonight. They will be there. Harmony will be healing them," he said, ignoring the acid in my tone.

I grunted with distaste, thinking of the young girl that had once stood before me, Harmony. *How could I have let Paul and Ashley go with her?*

"You felt it, didn't you? That woman back there — she changed us. She controlled us. You felt that, didn't you?" he inquired quietly.

I was all too familiar with the feeling of having no control over my body because of Misfeata. But this foreign Elemental Breather was an external danger and not the same kind that I had to fight from within.

"Yes."

My limbs did not work around that woman, nor did my Shield. I was utterly defenseless around that all-consuming creature.

Chapter Four- Dreary Night

*W*e walked about thirty minutes out of the town, cautiously making sure we were not being followed. Not only did I have that to contend with, but my ever evolving suspicion of Lucas. We walked in utter silence with a tension so thick between us that I didn't even dare heavily breathe. The silence only enhanced my dizziness and I clutched at my hand. It was now almost healed, as was my stomach wound. Slowly but assuredly, they were healing.

When having Lucas so near to me became almost unbearable, I thankfully noticed a small dim light flickering in the distance. I ran to it gratefully, knowing exactly who would be lying near those flames in such a cold and dreary night. I noted the small tent close by.

I searched around the fire, finding no one. I then burst into the tent, catching my breath while scanning the scene that lay before me. My eyes fell upon Paul. "How are they?" I demanded of Scott, searching over Paul's bruised and cut face.

"They are fine, Karla," Scott said in a low tone, suggesting that perhaps I should follow suit.

"And Ashley?" I examined his bruised and cut face as well, finding a reflection that mirrored Paul's: bloodied and bruised.

"They are fine, dear girl. The way you are pining would make one think you have lost an army... or a lover," Scott taunted.

I stared at the cheap-looking blankets. "Is this really enough to keep them warm?" I fumbled at their feet, trying to tuck them in for warmth. I straightened as I noticed Lucas's companion. Harmony, if I remembered correctly. Her eyes were staring into mine as if they were searching for something. Her eyes antagonized me as they narrowed. She glowed with an unassuming innocence and yet I couldn't help but feel something vile radiated from her.

"You're being a bit over the top," Ashley dismissed, following this with a coarse splutter as he woke. Embarrassed by my performance, I looked away as I had broken my composure.

"I am not," I forced out, leaving the tent in defiance.

I sat on a log near the fire, examining my hands and wondering how

I could have shown such weakness. Finally, I mustered the courage to look up at the sky. The night air had a stillness that only highlighted how my mind was racing. My mind poured over every humiliating detail of the last few hours.

I could not feel Lucas's presence anywhere close-by, giving me time to breath in relief that Paul and Ashley were okay and safe. We had to be on our defense at all times around Lucas. There was a small rustling behind me and as it silenced, Scott sat down beside me, staring with me at the moon.

"What happened?" he urged.

I sat silently with my hands pressed behind my back, leaning into the wood I sat on. Such hard wood, so grounded and stable, feelings I so wished I could have for myself. "You care about them and you're scared too. I don't know why you don't admit it. It is no crime."

"I am not scared," I said flustered, embarrassed by my own state. "I cannot afford to be scared because every part of my own being is against me. How can I let others in if I am fighting myself? I need strength. Or I—..." I lost my words.

I need strength, I reminded myself. *It is the only way I can fight and protect them.*

"I have no choice. Not only does my mind have to be strong — so I don't get taken over by an avenging Elder — but my body fights against me as well. I am, and can only be, strong."

"Such pretty words, aren't they?" Scott scorned. His sharp words were punctuated by a loud crack of the firewood. "Whether you accept that your arrogance is your weakness and your cold heartedness is fake, or not, you still have two people lying in that very tent right now that you instinctively protect. Now, if you aren't going to show your inclination toward protecting them, then I will. Tell me what you saw."

I pondered over it for a while. Was I feeling obliged to protect them because I was afraid to take steps further into the darkness by myself? Was it not selfish to continue dragging Paul with me into uncertain danger? Was I really protecting them or was I being selfish by keeping them close to my heart still?

"Scott..." I paused for a moment, trying to find the correct words to broach the subject. "How does your Element work?"

"Ah." He sighed to himself. "Well you see, neither my father nor my sister much understood it either. I was, well, I was different from the start. They both believe in certain Elements, such as their own, but not one as unpredictable as mine. Unlike my father, who can call upon lightning, and my sister who can spit flames, I... well, my Elements are every Element. My power is contained in the body of course. Anything in my body I can change:

I can adjust any of my cells into almost anything physical. I can condense myself into a cricket and enlarge myself into a killer whale with gills. Everything in my genes, I can alter. *Anything.*

Ultimately, I could probably be anything I want or maybe even anyone I want. But I have never tried turning into another because I am too damn perfect already. When they abandoned the cottage though, it made me wonder about the outside world and the last person I had seen since all that time was you, so I came in search of you. Anything must be more enjoyable than being in that dusty old cottage. I remember how lonely you were when you stroked through my fur when I was in wolf form. You were nice, no matter what my appearance, so I want to be of some help and enjoy the fun."

Scott was very different to when he was in his wolf form. There was so much inconsistency within his character. At times he would burst with fabulousness, and then at other times, he was serious and could be seen as a powerful threat. As I looked at him through the corner of my eye, I questioned whether one was a fake persona, or perhaps we had not yet fully understood Scott at all.

"Could you turn yourself into a dragon?" I questioned idly.

A large cackle pierced my ears and scraped down my spine, lifting every hair on my body. Scott finally calmed his screeching rage of a laugh and answered modestly. "Well I have never tried, but I suppose anything is possible."

Anything is possible: like a strange woman controlling your very existence, your body, your soul... A woman was locked in my body, an immortal entity. *Anything is possible.*

"A woman," I quietly said.

"Pardon?" he asked absentmindedly.

"You asked what I saw tonight. It was a woman."

Cradling my knees under my chin, I stared into the flames of the night, explaining to Scott the woman I saw, and what power she held over me. I told him the finery of every detail and in the end I concluded that, yes, anything was possible.

We stayed in the small camp for four days, ready to go at any point if anyone came across us. With Lucas and Harmony gone to scope out the tunnels where the woman had confronted us in, Scott and I hovered around the tent closely, in case of an ambush. Paul and Ashley's wounds slowly got better. It was almost miraculous how Scott understood the wounds; he was a fantastic healer.

I stood by the door of the tent one afternoon, watching him hover over Ashley. He was holding his broken hand with an odd look of concentration on his face. Ashley looked up at me with furious eyes as Scott fumbled with his hand. I couldn't help but give him a small smile. A look of concentration was such a bizarre thing to see on Scott. I expected at any moment for him to burst at the seams in laughter, shaking the whole tent as he swirled in it like a lady of the night at a ball, or a tornado. Now that I thought about it, more like a tornado.

A large crack was heard and Ashley forcefully tried to retrieve his hand back with a bellowing yell. Ashley's roar had broken Paul's sleep, and he sprung up and winced, holding his stomach. He searched around him for signs of attack, finding me instead by his side. I started damping the cloth with the water bottle. He looked at me with eyes that said *'really?'* I gave up on the cloth and gave him the bottle of water to guzzle down while I continued watching Scott's 'Miraculous Medical Healing', as he called it. Then he stopped and let go of Ashley's hand.

Ashley stared at it in amazement, and then as quick as his gawking had stopped he started to move his hand back and forth, circling it in disbelief. What a valuable ally indeed. Scott continued to do this for the four days that we lived amongst the little camp, slowly but surely fixing any scratch or bruise that was on anyone's skin, not to mention all the punctured holes from snakes everyone had all over their bodies. Mine, however, healed within the first night, although my wounds from my fight with Tyran still disturbed my every move. When would these wounds heal?

It was on the fourth day that we decided everyone was in perfect shape to leave the area before Lucas and Harmony got back. As we started to take our leave, they walked out from the trees. Out of habit both Ashley and I already had weapons out in front of us.

Harmony lifted her bow, ready for any kind of confrontation that was waiting to unfold. Lucas flicked his fingers, addressing her to slowly drop the bow.

"I have information about that woman. We found some if you're willing to hear," Lucas offered gently.

"We want nothing from you, filthy mutt," Ashley spat, glaring at Lucas in disgust.

Then Lucas's eyes found mine and he looked into them, as if trying to look into my soul to find something there.

"Karla, please," Lucas then searched over all four of us quickly. "You need information, at least on this woman. You don't know how much of a threat she is."

"There is no way in hell your information is the truth, you

murderer." Ashley's fist trembled. The knife he held was clamped firmly in what was once his broken hand.

"Paul." Lucas's eyes flicked to him instantly. Following his eyes, I searched over Paul as well, watching his body tense as Lucas began to speak to him. Paul's grip slowly tightened around the backpack he held. "Did Karla tell you that woman almost killed her? She's a threat. And as loathed as you are to speak with me, I know you will stand for reason."

I hadn't told him. I paused beside Paul, somehow losing my voice in the process. I went to object but suddenly Paul stopped grinding his teeth.

"Then tell your important story," Paul seethed.

We all stood around the ashes that framed the remains of the fire, arms crossed, and yet at the same time, all on guard. Except Scott of course, who had taken his seat quite quickly as if someone had challenged him for that exact spot. He glanced around and then crossed his arms with a mean look on his face.

"She has already started moving. There were a few companions with her, from what we have gathered, there are two prisoners. By the looks of it, a male and a female, we weren't too sure. We could only manage a quick glance at them before they were forced into the carriage. Her mode of transport was a large carriage with horses, which had slight defects. They had paws instead of hooves and some bizarre green stripes across them, like a tiger."

Lucas glanced around at us, allowing his gaze to linger on mine for far too long. I glanced over to his young companion, feeling nothing but disgust when my eyes fell on her. Something about her unsettled me. Every part of me wanted to jump across the ashes and lay my hands contently around her throat, watching that stupid innocent...

"Karla?" I was nudged out of my daydream by Paul who was looking at me with a confused expression.

"What?"

"We came across a wolf with some defects like that as well. Didn't we?"

"Oh yes. Yes, we did." I remembered the large wolf with all its deformities.

"Well, it's apparent the woman is an Elemental Breather. The only issue we are having is we have never heard of one who can control Shielders and Starkorfs. We don't know if it is only our kind that she can control or humans as well." Lucas focused on my eyes once again.

Starkorf. The name and meaning rolled around my mouth with such distaste I wanted to spit it back in his face as easily and quickly as he was able to conjure up the word.

"Well of course no one knows because no human has made contact with her, well as far as we know," Paul interrupted. "But if you want that issue resolved, I nominate myself to make contact with her, just so we can verify if—…"

"No." I stubbornly said. "We will not follow this woman, none of us." I glanced at Paul, Scott, and then Ashley. Ashley nodded in agreement. He knew how much of a threat this woman was without me even having to explain the details or the severity of the situation. "If there is no reason for us to follow this woman then we will not do so. We had a random run in with her; a situation I will not put myself or anyone else here again." I caught the emotion in my words and rephrased quickly: "I will not push any of these three men toward a fight, when there is no need."

"But we must," Lucas forced. "Karla, I was summoned to that place that night."

"By who?" Ashley spat.

"By you." Lucas pointed at me. Everyone else's eyes locked on mine for the slightest sign of betrayal.

"That is the most ridiculous thing I have ever heard. I never wanted to see you again, not once for the rest of my life and even then, I told you if we did make contact I would kill you then and there."

"Well doesn't that say something? If they sent me a letter to meet at that place that very night. The same night you turn up—…"

"We were on a personal task. We had no invite nor—…"

"Then doesn't that say something? Don't be so stupid and stubborn. The woman played us. Meaning she must have had some form of knowledge this whole time of where we were, who we were with... We walked into her trap."

I stared at Lucas as everyone went quiet, digesting this new theory. We had investigated that location that very same night because we thought there was Starkorf activity. Was it possible that the newspaper was a fake? How could we have fallen for such a trap?

The only thing that was heard was the rustling of leaves around us, and a bird whistling. There was a light shuffle from Scott, and then Ashley spoke very cautiously: "I don't see why we should attempt to involve ourselves, Karla. If the woman is searching for us for some reason, shouldn't we find out why first, instead of running into a situation we have no idea about? We need background information... a proper understanding of how her Element works. She's an Elemental Breather, she could potentially destroy us all."

I was surprised by Ashley's quick rationality of the situation, especially as he had been so keen to fight before now.

"You're bleeding," the young girl pointed out. I looked to where she pointed, finding that blood was seeping through my gray sleeveless shirt over my stomach.

"So you are." Lucas's eyebrows lowered over his eyes as he too stared at my bleeding wound.

I still held my ground. I waved Paul over, even though he was not that far from my side already. "Paul, will you please redo my bandages?"

He tried taking my weight under his but I waved him off as we started to walk toward the trees. We pulled through a tightly packed bag for bandages.

"A parting gift from your father," I heard Ashley spit at Lucas.

Scott and Ashley followed. We worked in silence as we mulled over this new information, and how best to proceed — if at all.

"My dear girl. You never told me you had such terrible wounds. I don't understand, was this the outcome of your fight with Tyran? May I look at them and see if my ability could perhaps increase the speed of its healing?" Scott looked over my body, confused.

Before he could ask the remainder of his question, I answered it for him. "It has been almost two months now and my body has not healed. Misfeata has inflicted this wound upon my body, and her blood will not fix it." I smiled weakly as I sat myself up against a tree, slightly lifting my shirt for Paul to remove my soaked bandage. Ashley stood in front of us, looking over in agitation at Lucas and Harmony.

"But still, perhaps I could try." Scott quietly leaned over my stomach, assessing the wound as a small gash widened.

"Maybe later. For now, we need to discuss what to make of all this. Ashley?" I asked.

He turned, looking at my stomach and then slightly smiling to himself. "How odd for you not to just run into a situation all by yourself... for once you are considering what we want."

"As if you are one to talk, sounding strategic and cautious just then over there. I thought you hadn't a concern in the world; you wanted to throw yourself in any fight. So, why all of a sudden the caution?"

Ashley simply smiled and I heard a small laugh shake next to me. Paul laughed to himself, finishing with my stomach and wiping over his hands with another clean cloth. I looked at him questioningly. He smiled cheekily.

"What? You're cute," he said under his breath, wiping away a piece of hair I hadn't noticed fall into my eyes. Scott broke out into a monstrous laugh making us all flinch and cringe in sync.

"No, you are," Scott shoved Paul, nudging him enough to make him fall against a tree. Paul all of a sudden wasn't smiling. Somehow I managed one instead. Somehow I was still able to smile. How, I didn't know. But no matter how much I smiled, I knew there were still decisions to be made.

"So, what did you have in mind?" Paul interjected.

Chapter Five- Fatal Blow

"*We* need to find as much information on this woman as we can before we get involved. I mean the fact is, she can definitely muster control over at least Karla." Ashley pointed out. "On top of that, we don't even know if we would be of any value because we don't know if she can do the same thing to us... whatever it is she actually does."

"You've never heard of another Elemental Breather like this, Scott?" I asked.

Scott drew his concentrated gaze away from his nails, looking up at us with his iridescent pink eyes as if he had only just walked into the conversation. "No, I haven't, sorry. But in saying that, my father had a lot of journals about other Elemental Breathers, of anyone or anything he encountered actually, so maybe he left those behind at the cottage. I permit you all to join me in my abode." Scott gestured as if he were the most noble of kings sparing some bread for peasants.

"That sounds like an alright plan, Karlz," Paul nodded. "I mean, even if he wrote something down about her or maybe if she is really good friends with Scott's dad she might—..."

Scott giggled to himself and then allowed a large roar of hysterics to rip through the sound of the rustling leaves around us. "My father had no friends, dear boy. Oh, I do cherish my time with you. You are so cute," he spluttered through giggles.

Ashley and I gave one another an unsure glance, recalling the last time we were at that old cottage. We were dragged there and betrayed. The memory flashed before both our eyes. A betrayal not only from Trish, Lucas, and Max Jacket, but from Scott as well.

Scott interjected quickly as if remembering the same thing. "I was forced to do it. Now that my father has vanished, I am now my own person. But back then when you last visited, I was not. Also, I have just given you permission to enter my home, which no one else resides in at the moment. You are safe."

"Well, that sounds fantastic on paper. But what will we do with the other two?" Ashley asked, looking over in the direction of Lucas and Harmony. "Kill them or just leave?" Ashley directed this question at me. My eyes strained above, through to the sun that peered through certain leaves. "I mean, we can't trust them, and on top of that, we know nothing of the girl and we definitely know who Lucas is. Remember he is practically the prince to everything we despise and he has already betrayed us once."

His manner seemed too well composed. Seth has been killed by Lucas's brother. For some unknown reason, Ashley didn't seem as self-destructive right now as he had been after his father's passing. For some reason, he was being rational once more, instead of jumping into any dangerous situation. *Is this his way of finding a purpose and start living again?*

"I know, Ashley," I stated, as if the reminder of Lucas's betrayal was directed at me. "I know."

"Well, the girl means no harm," Paul quickly summarized. "She looked after me for a little bit in the tent. I don't think she is here to harm us. She reckons she's just a follower of the Divine, sent to Lucas's side. She's been there faithfully ever since."

"You two were alone? Talking?" I asked, my eyebrows narrowing on him. I quickly regained my composure. Surprised at my flustered expression, I peered through the leaves once again, hoping that the wind would send the answer we needed to heed. "And the bow with no arrows?"

"She said it's a gift from the Divine. I think she said something like: 'If I ever need a bow, the Divine sends me one, usually to defend Lucas or myself.'"

"Sure, of course. Why not?" Ashley spat in sarcasm. "I'm sorry man, but after the things that this so-called Divine has dragged me into, it's either a lie, or we're really hated," Ashley said angrily, his hatred of the world coming to the surface once again.

I often questioned whether Ashley's hostility toward Paul was because he felt that in some way I was obliged to stay with the others, to continue fighting. I wondered if he blamed Paul for my leaving, even though he was aware of my search for my parents. It might have been my imagination, after all Ashley was hostile to everyone now.

"There's no need to preach to me, I was just saying. No matter how much self-pity you put on yourself it doesn't give us the answer we need," Paul dismissed.

Before Ashley could spit his comeback to Paul's simple yet correct snipe, I pulsated my Shield slightly toward Ashley's direction, so he could feel the small nudge and find my narrowed eyes, which he knew simply meant: *enough.*

"This follower of the divine — Harmony — is she another Elemental Breather as well, Scott?" All of a sudden I felt like I was contending with a room full of Elemental Breathers and with them their endless abilities. A Starkorf I could fight with no doubt I would be the victor with Misfeata's strength residing in me, but with Elemental Breathers so much caution was needed in their presence.

"No, I couldn't sense that of her. My Element also allows me to partially encase myself in another's body, so I can sense or assess their physical state, helping me to get a sort of vibe from them." As he said it, it made sense to me as to how he was able to help heal Ashley and Paul so quickly. He explained that he could change the fiber within himself, did that mean he could have influence on other people's bodies as well, not only his own? Was that how he was able to help speed the healing process?

"We will go," I finalized. "We need to, no matter who it is she is targeting or even who is involved with her." I glanced over in the direction of where Lucas and Harmony sat near the logs, still suspicious of their involvement. "We need information about her; if she crosses our path again we must be prepared."

"So what do we do with them?" Scott questioned. We all gazed over at Lucas and Harmony, all wondering the same thing.

"I don't want them in my sight," I said, aggravated. We all felt the same, none of us wanting Lucas in our sights, as if he physically hurt our eyes.

"Whether you want them in your sight or not," Scott said passively, "They could follow us anyway and if—..."

"Then let's just kill him now!" Ashley erupted.

"Well, that was rude," Scott calmly said, as he brushed his knees with his hands. "I'm not saying who is what but I've always stuck by the good old motto: 'keep your friends close, but keep your enemies closer'. Worst-case scenario, they are in cahoots with this unfamiliar woman. Perhaps we could figure it out before hand, before any serious ambush or something draws itself to our attention. The way I see it, we either be followed or play the host. Either way they are near."

"So why don't we kill them?" Ashley nudged, irritated. "He's a Starkorf, Karla." Ashley started waving his hands around forcefully. "And better yet, he's the descendant of Tyran. You said you'd kill him and if you won't then I sure as hell will." Determination evident across his face, Ashley began to pull out the small blade he always had sealed away in his back pocket, aiming in the direction of where Lucas and Harmony sat.

I shoved Ashley to the side just in time. A white arrow snapped in front of my eyes as my Shield pulsated around me. *She shot at Ashley. She tried to hit Ashley.* My hands turned into fuming fists as I touched the ground in a cat-like crouch. I looked toward the bow and the woman that shot the arrow at my companion. *Harmony. I do not like the presence of this girl. She is mine.*

My heel dove into the dirt beneath me and pulsated with enough pressure from my Shield to give me a thriving start as I ran for her. *If she is going to try and kill Ashley then I have no choice but to silence her, they are the enemy after all.* Within seconds I had reached for Aeisha, ready to attack. I folded the handle of Aeisha around my knuckles and found a firm grip around it. I pointed the blade down, ready to strike this intruder down.

It was a guaranteed strike, or so I thought. My blade crashed into another, causing a screech of metal. I looked to the hand, the wrist, the arm, the collarbone and then up to Lucas's eyes, his deep enticing dark-brown eyes were staring back at me with the same intensity I imagined to be in my own. He fought me to protect her, like he had once with Raven.

Our Shields collided and pulsated from one another's as we forcefully drove into each other's shoulders; arm raised high with our weapons, trying to find an opening, any opening, for that fatal blow. My feet were dancing with his; his would move right and mine would follow. I would forcefully pounce forward as his legs buckled back. Our blades continued to crash into one another as his one sword held off my two — my darling, partnered blades: Aeisha.

I kicked my right leg into his left shin, finding that he had already stepped back. I rolled forward, landing myself onto my back and kicking my feet into his shins, this time connecting and knocking him into a fall. Before I could roll to the side to avoid his defensive attack, he hovered over me as our Shields fought for dominancy. He hovered in the air as he balanced on top of my Shield. Between our Shields, our blades fought for control. *I will not lose to you.* A small drop of sweat dripped off Lucas's face and stayed suspended above me as our Shields continued to fight.

Such pressure of another Shield on top of my body helped to build the pressure within me before I created a huge bomb from my Shield. Instead of feeling that pulse, I felt the familiar stir within my body. I clutched at my chest. Instantly, my Shield vanished and dropped, and Lucas and his heavy Shield fell on top of me.

I felt his weapon pin my shoulder into the ground and I clasped my hands over my chest, trying to control my body as it thrashed around. I couldn't take any breaths. My body was now my own enemy. *Misfeata can't come, this is my body.* I felt her stir within me like a snake sliding over water, creating ripples over the areas she touched, but making her presence echo all the way through to the edges of my body. *You can't have this. I won't let you.*

I slowly released the pressure I had built into myself. Feeling her presence leave me, I finally found my breath again. My eyes fixated on Lucas, who still lay on top of me; panicked eyes searching over the knife he had just embedded into my shoulder. I looked between him and the blade. I could see it through the corner of my eye sticking out of my body.

"Get off her!" Paul was quickly by my side, throwing Lucas off my body forcefully. After nearly being possessed, pain and discomfort were trailing through my body.

"No, I can make it better!" Lucas barged Paul off me as I fell into a deeper state of despair. My human blood and Misfeata's immortal blood now fought. *I am dying.* My body stopped taking in the air it needed and now left me out of breath. *My body, it's shutting down.* I lay there, numbly gazing at Lucas and Paul who fought over my dying body.

"I can make this go away. I can!"

These were the last words I heard as Lucas's hand found my face. The indescribable burn was all I could focus on as he held my cheeks, draining me. But as he drained me, the pain began to drift as well. It was not only Lucas who drew me deeper into darkness, but the pull of an all-familiar being residing within myself. *Misfeata.*

I lay in the darkness, listening to the sound of dripping water. Drop by drop, the sound rang through my head as it vibrated the ground beneath me. I placed my hand on my ribs. My head lay in liquid. I coughed into the floor beneath me, which was soaked with the itchy substance. My eyes began to register light as I slowly raised myself to my knees, taking in my surroundings.

Bricks enclosed me. Large strips of sun pierced at my eyes through stained glass. The figures that were etched on the glass stared back at me impassively. I stared up at them, understanding after a few moments that with the number of seats, candles, and stained glassed windows, I was in some form of church.

I raised one knee up, stretching to get up. Beneath me, I saw liquid. A dark red surrounded me, and a puddle of blood stained my skin.

"Don't get up." My eyes flew from the blood to Misfeata, who stood calmly amongst the trickling and dripping of blood. Her green dress was saturated with red that oozed from her shoulder. I gazed at her shoulder, and then looked to mine. Both shoulders glistened with red where Lucas embedded his blade. "You recoiled from my help."

"I didn't need it," I said in disgust, trying to stand.

Within an instant Misfeata wrapped her hand around my throat, growling at me like a beast. "I said don't get up!"

As I scratched at the hands that tightened around my throat, I stared into her eyes. They resembled the orange glow of a flame. I focused my mind as I choked on her hand, trying to find some sort of pressure to project my Shield.

My throat was crushed harder as Misfeata stared at me, infuriated. "How dare you try to use that against me!"

Misfeata pulsated a tumbling Shield. It threw me from the grasp of her hand across the echoing room, smashing me into the bricks that supported the building. I coughed into the liquid on the ground that almost drowned me as I fell into it.

"What's it like?" I choked, wiping away at my mouth for no reason as blood covered every inch of my body. "To be just like your brother?"

A green shard pierced into my stomach, pinning me onto the brick wall behind. I spluttered more liquid into the lake of blood that now surrounded me up to the hips. I could only just focus on her eyes as I lifted my head, my vision going blurry.

"I am no Starkorf!" Tears welled up in Misfeata's eyes and green gems fell instead of teardrops, dropping into the pool of blood that had now risen to my chest. "And I am nothing like him!"

Her voice broke through my ears as it echoed through the church, cracking the perfectly stained glass windows. They shattered into the room, letting more blood pour into the sacred ground. I spluttered on the poison as it took away my last breath. I found myself still pinned to the wall drowning, as the blood rose over my mouth and nose. My sight darkened and I continued to choke in the filthy liquid as I begged for breath.

My eyes burst open to the purity of white, and I realized it was clothing that inhibited my sight. I was on top of Harmony with my hand around her throat, pinning her to the ground inside the tent.

"Karla! Let go!" Paul pulled at my arm that was high in the air, catching it before I plunged my fisted Shield into the girl's face. I resigned my position in confusion until I remembered this girl tried to kill Ashley. Before I could lunge at the girl again, Paul tugged on my arm. He had a hold of my body, and I had no way to escape. My head pounded in disorientation as I gathered my thoughts.

Misfeata isn't here. It wasn't real. Harmony tried to kill Ashley. I was fighting Lucas. Lucas stabbed me. My body tensed as all the memories gathered at once, making Paul's hold irrelevant, until his hand cupped my face and his thumb started stroking across my cheek slowly. I tried to focus on Paul's deep-green eyes. I felt his touch again stroking past my left cheek

45

now, and I continued to stare into his eyes, mesmerized. His dark-brown, almost black, hair had grown a lot longer during our time together. He regularly held me this way now after I had terrible nightmares. I only slept now and then, avoiding it as every time I did so, it let Misfeata into my mind, where she tortured me. I had much to thank Paul for as he was the only reassurance I had that I was still a part of the human world.

"Stop crying. It's ok." Paul wiped across my cheek again as tears welled up in my eyes. "It was just a dream." He pulled me in more, placing my face softly into his hard chest. His left arm wrapped around me and the other stroked the top of my head. "It's ok." I fell into the comfort of his grip, catching my breath and letting everything just stop for one moment. I calmed myself.

After a couple of minutes composing myself, I placed my hands between Paul and myself and put some distance between us. I stared back at where Harmony had sat, noticing that no one else was in the tent but Paul and I. The wind tugged at the exit of the small tent, sending the material back and forth and revealing the outside to be dark. I lifted the green flap above my head and I looked to the sky, finding no shine from the moon, only the burn of an open flame.

Scott, Harmony, and Lucas sat around the fire, sitting awkwardly and quietly on the logs that surrounded it. Paul lifted the tent door as well, seeing the same awkward image in front of us. I said nothing, not knowing what to say. Lucas shot up from his seat, his eyes burning as wildly as the dancing fire.

"Can we talk?" Lucas demanded over the howling wind, his sandy-blonde hair looking like flames themselves in the golden light. Scott stared between Paul and me, for once he said nothing turning back to the fire. Harmony sat beside him, coldly prodding a stick at the fire.

I looked at Lucas as I rubbed my hand on my shoulder, remembering the wound he inflicted on me. It was gone. Of course it was gone. He drained me to take the pain away; but at no point would I thank him for doing such a despicable thing. Remembering how casually he did it, I wondered how many times he had done it to me before. I had died numerous times when they first found me. Was it he who continued to bring me back from the dead by draining me?

"You stabbed me," I spat almost sleepily, regaining the image of Lucas plunging into me with his knife.

"It was an accident." He stood tall, straightening himself as if he were a businessman. "I am sorry," he then mumbled, looking to the ground. He walked over to me fidgeting, gesturing with his eyes to a tree that stood near the tent a distance away from everyone else near the campfire. I looked at Paul, whose fist was clenched around mine. Lucas stared at Paul's hand over mine, before looking away and walking toward the tree.

"He hurt you. I don't want you near him. I don't want us around him anymore." Paul held his eyes on mine with determination and squeezed my hand protectively.

"I know." I took my hand out of his and ruffled it through his hair. "Everything will be fine," I tried to convince myself; uncertain of what was to come. Paul had always told me everything would be fine, but now it was my turn to reassure him. He continued to stand where I had left him as I walked away with Lucas.

Lucas looked forlorn. "I didn't mean to stab you, but you dropped your Shield and I had no time to move it. I was only protecting Harmony and myself." Lucas ruffled his hair, recalling what had happened. "If I left my Shield projected I would have crushed you."

"She shot at Ashley," I accused. I kept my guarded stance, flicking my eyes from one direction to another in search of Ashley. *Where is Ashley?*

"Ashley's fine. He just simply left the camp. And Harmony only did that to protect me." All I could think about was hitting him, beating him, making him hurt, destroying him. "But that isn't the point here. Scott told us about going back to his cottage to get information about—…"

"No."

"But we—…"

"We? There is no 'we.' You are a Starkorf. I'm a Shielder. On top of that, I know you can feel his influence on you. I know Tyran is already affecting you, even if he isn't in your body yet. To be around you is insufferable. And I hate you." I coldly brushed back my hair and tucked it behind my ear as the wind tore at it with ferocity. Lucas was silent.

And that was it; nothing else was to be said. *I will not let him follow us or join us. I hate him.*

Chapter Six- Distraction

$\mathscr{I}$ had no interest in staying in the presence of Lucas, nor did my companions, so we left Harmony and Lucas at their campsite with no further invitation to talk. We had agreed that Max Jacket's cottage was somewhere we had to go to try and find information on this unknown woman. For now she posed a threat toward us and it was not an uneducated fight I wanted to dive into with Paul by my side to protect. For some unknown reason this woman had purposefully made sure of our meeting. She made known her interest in hurting me. I had to find out why before she tricked us again.

I had for a very long time tried to distance my thoughts of Lucas, tried to contain them. But my thoughts now raged only on Lucas even though I have said what I needed to. Lucas could apologize to me no more; if he tried, it would only fall on deaf ears. I had no time for his apologies. His treachery was far too deep. Besides, we were on different sides of this contentious war.

If I were to be challenged by Lucas's brother, Nathanial, and defeated him like I had his father, Praytar, then Lucas and I were destined to fight. My feelings were still so raw for him that his very presence made me sick. In some way his presence was familiar, he was once my protector and seemingly a lot more to me as I depended on him heavily. Without trust we had nothing. And what he did now, I did not care to hear of. As long as he had no intention of going in the same direction as us, I did not care.

And then I had Paul. I wanted to protect him. He was so stubborn, squashing any doubts I may have had so far. We often trained when we could. His hand-to-hand fighting was already superb from his years of boxing. Even though he was a fast learner and seemed to be a natural, his blade handling was not as strong. Or perhaps he knew he had no choice, it was, after all, life or death if we were ambushed.

Paul regularly took care of my wounds that still opened on a regular basis. Never did he let me think I was by all alone. In every way he was the very last string I had attached to the reality of the old world I once lived in. Although we have both drastically changed, he made me believe that in his presence, everything would be alright and that I would be okay. He lifted my head if I felt the need to drop it in doubt or fear. Paul was my everything, even if I avoided showing it. I had already pulled him too deep into this parallel world.

After our battle in the Starkorf hideout, Ashley and I had a rare relationship; one I couldn't even label, but we knew we could depend on one another, and in some way I felt responsible for him as well. He didn't mention much of his mother, Helena's progress, but from what he had expressed, she was still in great despair after losing Seth. Suzumiya and Chris continued to hunt and fight Starkofs, although not as easily or well equipped as they once did under the guidance of Kurt, who had suddenly vanished as well. After my arrival and the awakening of Misfeata, everything had changed for them too.

And now in search for my parents, Paul and I decided to head east of our hometown, Roperia; finding comfort as we distanced ourselves further and further away from all that had happened. We were blind in our search. I had found no hint of my parents as we drove from town to town. I asked strangers if they had seen them, showing them recent photos, but with no success. Asking the police was not an option; if anyone had taken them, I was sure it was the Starkorfs. Paul never let me believe something bad had happened to them.

Although avoiding contact with any groups of Starkorfs to protect Paul as much as I could, I monitored them as well, noticing if there were any nearby, but so far found none. My own feet, unsure as to where they would take me, only guided me now. All I knew was right now I had Paul and Ashley by my side, as well as my somewhat new acquaintance, Scott. Although sometimes annoying, he was invaluable because of his bizarre abilities, knowledge, and healing powers. And if going back to his cottage could gather any information, whether about the new unknown woman who attacked us or about my parents, I could not resist. For in my heart I knew they were still alive and I had now the ability to protect them. But first, I would have to find them.

"Yes, well I saw your car and I can assure you there is no way I will be affiliated with it." Scott pranced onward, waving his hand around as we walked toward the motel Paul and I have stayed at only a few nights ago.

"Who cares what it looks like? It's just a car," Paul growled, closing his eyes and rubbing his forehead in annoyance. "How did we get involved with this again? Why does he have to come? And him for that matter?" Paul demanded, throwing his hand toward Ashley.

"Well, I might be of some actual use to her," Ashley antagonized coldly. "But it's a perk you can cook and clean, right? That's what pulled you over, wasn't it, Karla?"

"If you want to do this right now," Paul exclaimed, holding his gaze on Ashley.

"Boys, boys, don't fight over me," Scott giggled. "My goodness, are they always like this?" Scott questioned. I could only imagine it to be some sick fantasy of his if I said yes.

"Let's just grab the car." I found a pace ahead of them before stopping and staring at the empty car space. "Which isn't here." I slapped my hand against my leg in defeat.

"Well, what did you think would happen?" Ashley found his way to my side, folding his arms. "You did forget to pay your nights in advance, didn't you? So they probably impounded your car."

"I'll go speak to the receptionist," Paul said with hesitation, looking between Ashley and me before making his way toward the main building.

"I will come with you, my darling." Scott beamed with joy as he skipped beside Paul. "I will make her forget this whole incident with the snap of my fingers."

"You have the ability to do that?" Paul questioned. I didn't know if it was hope or simple interest that made him ask.

Scott let his high-pitched laugh break out from where he had clamped his hand over his mouth wickedly. "Oh dear boy, no! I am an Elemental Breather, not a hypnotist. But for you I would try almost anything." He pouted with a questioning eyebrow.

Paul flinched uncomfortably under Scott's dazzling eyes, looking back at me with innocent eyes of concern. With a last look in my direction, Paul and Scott entered the reception.

"Get rid of him," Ashley demanded, speaking of Paul.

"No sooner than I would dispose of you," I said, annoyed by his indifference toward Paul. "You both have the choice as to whether you wish to follow me. I won't take either away."

"I don't know what you see in him. He gives you no advantage whatsoever in this war."

"He does not view me as someone at war. He does not see me as an enemy and he is helping me find my parents. I have no reason to explain any of my actions to you. This is the longest we have spoken in months. And another thing…" My eyes exchanged a harsh look with his. "This is not my war. And if you were smart you would stop following it as well."

"It is so easy for you to try and deny it. And yet you are the living, breathing focus of this war. I am honestly surprised you made it this far with how many are tracking you. And somehow you've managed to keep him alive as well," Ashley nodded toward Paul, who stormed out with Scott

50

watching him from behind.

"What?" Scott exclaimed dramatically as if they were a couple. "I had no choice. She was boring and wouldn't shut up."

"Karla," Paul flashed angrily. "He did something to the receptionist."

"Don't be so dramatic," Scott shushed, "I just put her to sleep."

"You knocked the receptionist out?" I questioned, a small stir reacted inside of me.

"Well, somewhat, I just... She was rude, okay?" Scott raised his hands in a quick flash. "You would have understood, Karla, she was rude. Girl to girl, you would have understood."

Misfeata slightly stirred within me, making me look into the distance and focus my Shield at the bottom of my feet that touched the graveled ground. I sensed Starkorfs were nearby. We had made it two months unnoticed, I guess now our luck had run out.

I raised my finger to him, forcing him to focus and turn into the same direction that I was focusing on.

"In the middle of a town in broad daylight," I said, pulling Aeisha out from my side pockets, hidden underneath my brown jacket.

Scott took the form of a pigeon and flew off quickly. I stared after him in bewilderment as he flew away. "Truly?" I spat under my breath. He still ran at the mention of Starkorfs. And after our last encounter, I had thought him better and braver then that. "Pathetic."

"Karla, we have to take this out of public view," Ashley ordered, his blue eyes flashing through thick eyelashes. He was right. We shouldn't involve innocents. *This is not their fight, nor should they know of it.*

"Like I've said..." I raised one blade of Aeisha in front of my face and the other in front of my stomach. "This is your war, not mine." There was no time to divert them anywhere else and the motel seemed barren anyway. Luckily I could sense no one else in the rooms. Snarls and screeching began as I projected my Shield around me, flashing orange ripples. Was it because Ashley had been around me the last few days that they found Paul and me? Or had Lucas told them?

Two figures came running from between two of the motel rooms. I began running at them at a much quicker pace than their own. I threw the left blade of Aeisha into the first woman, who screeched mortifyingly as she dropped and rolled a few times along the gravel in the car park. Ashley ripped Aeisha from her corpse, then ran behind me throwing it toward me to catch as I was ahead of him. An arrow shot and knocked Aeisha out of my hand and I searched in the direction the arrow had come from, finding nothing. The second Starkorf was already grabbing Aeisha from the graveled ground as I outstretched my Shield while running toward him. He rebounded off my Shield, hitting hard into the brick wall of the motel behind him. Aeisha dropped from his hand as he attempted to stand using the wall for support.

Another arrow shot into my Shield, distracting me. A Starkorf screamed as Paul cut her down with the long knife I made sure he carried with him at all times. Another three surrounded him as I ran to his side in time to slice past one of their chests, jumping around Paul to kick another one away from him. I was confronted by the next, who punched into Paul's stomach, ignoring the deep cut that sliced into its shoulder. A small girl jumped over him swiftly, trying to grab for Aeisha who was held firmly in my left hand. Her hand was thrown back from my Shield and in Aeisha's stead, she grabbed the handle of Paul's knife and took it with her as she flung herself over Paul and began to run in the other direction.

I found my hands around the neck of the male who had just forced Paul to the ground. I drove my knee into his stomach, knocking the back of his neck. He fell unconscious and I kicked him away from Paul and me. *They are all killers.*

They're after the blades, I realized, searching for where Aeisha once was. I looked down at her paired blade in my hand, summoning the energy it possessed. I could sense her partnered blade — it was not that far from here. Was the girl a distraction?

As if hearing my annoyance, Ashley ran over to me as the Starkorfs all began to flee behind the small girl that took Paul's knife, which held no significant power to it, why run away with it? Plus, they had Aeisha's other blade.

"They're here for the Immortal Blades. Chase them and find that girl, find out who sent them," I shouted.

I felt Aeisha's pulse once more from whoever held it and ran with my blade. The girl that had taken Paul's knife must have been a distraction. I ran into the direction where Aeisha called to me. It didn't take me long to run past only eight houses until I found the four Starkorfs that ran from me. The one in front was holding Aeisha.

They quickly turned to face me as another arrow shot at me, this time breaking through my Shield and into my shoulder. I winced at it, holding my hand firmly to the injury. *How did it get through my Shield?* I felt the pulse of Tyran and then the shiver of Misfeata coming to the surface. *But how is Tyran close? Does that mean Nathanial is behind this ambush and close by? Have they been following us this whole time or is Lucas working with him, telling him of our location?*

"Get out!" I screamed, ripping at the arrow and tearing it from my shoulder. Pain stirred in my wound more than usual. *What does this mean?*

Is Nathanial absent, but still leading this ambush?

I projected my Shield once again as orange ripples swirled around me, only to be broken by another arrow that shot into my leg. I screamed once more in anger as I felt my face twist, trying to compose Misfeata. *Where are these arrows coming from and how are they penetrating my Shield?*

Anger swelled within me as I faced the Starkorfs, still running for them.

"Give me Aeisha!" I raged, angered by my attackers, annoyed they thought they could successfully steal Aeisha from me.

I cut the first Starkorf's stomach quickly, catching it as it fell forward and using its body as a shield, noticing another arrow coming at me. The arrow pierced into the Starkorf's body as I dropped it, leaping for the other. I caught its wrist and swung him in front of me as another arrow shot for me. Another Starkorf's burnt face caught the corner of my eye as it tried to use Aeisha against me, trying to strike me down with her.

I crouched quickly, using the Starkorf I had a hold of as the shield to my back. I elbowed the oncoming attacker in the stomach and quickly slashed Aeisha across his knees. He staggered and dropped as I pierced his leg, catching Aeisha's partnered blade as his grotesque figure screamed on the ground.

I jumped over a fence and hid against the side of a house, pinning my back to the wall to hide from the archer. I searched for the archer, noticing the other Starkorf who now ran in the opposite direction, away from me. An arrow hit her back and she dropped to the ground as another caved into the side of her head. *The archer is killing his or her own kind.*

Perhaps the archer was no ally of the Starkorfs either? Or maybe because they hadn't killed me or stolen Aeisha, and the archer was displeased. I stared for a little longer, hearing a sob behind me. I turned with blades in hand ready to confront my attacker, only to find a small child in front of me with tears running down her face.

My eyes widened. *Is she human? Or is it a trick?* I briefly searched behind: a trampoline, a few toys on the ground, and a vegetable garden at the back. No hiding places for any others to attack from. I stared back into the child's face as emptiness filled it and shock echoed through such innocent eyes. *There is no evil in this girl. She is only a mere human child.* I looked away in disbelief. *She would have seen everything.* The reality of this other world made me nostalgic. *I have taken the innocence of this girl away, opening such a horrific nightmare in front of her.*

I will now be the memory of her greatest fear.

"Lucy?" A woman's voice yelled as the back door swung open.

53

"Lucy, where are you, it's almost dinner time."

I ran in the other direction as swiftly as I could, back toward where I had last spotted Ashley and Paul. I ran not only from the child, but the guilt that lay heavy on my back. Jumping fences and crouching low over each one, I registered the settling of Misfeata. I found she was a lot more determined to fix the wound instead of fighting against me.

Ashley and Paul were not that far from where I had last left them. They now fought in the back car park. Paul's face had cuts all across it and Ashley seemed to be standing unsteadily. Another arrow shot for me, preventing me from running into the fight before me. I saw the flicker of a curtain as I realized a bystander was watching from their window.

The curtain closed quickly. I ran for the window and dove into the glass. I jumped onto a small girl inside who cut at my face with her nails; the same girl who had stolen Paul's large knife. *No, not a girl, a Starkorf.*

The rattle of a bell caught my attention as another arrow was shot into my shoulder. The intensity of it burned like acid as I searched around for where the archer was. A long sword hovered over my back. Before I could project my Shield, the sword found its way to the girl through my back, causing her to drop to the floor. I kicked the Starkorf who had pushed the sword through me, trying to gather my feet as quickly as I could. Another arrow shot at me. Using my enhanced hearing, I dodged it, feeling it slice past my arm.

I rolled myself out of the window, coughing at the pressure of the sword still inside of me. I looked up to see a gray car with no roof screech into the car park, wiping out four of the Starkorfs that were surrounding Ashley and Paul.

I rested my hand on Aeisha, finding no strength to pull myself up as the sword still ached in my back. Ashley and Paul ran over to me before gathering me and pulling me toward the car. Although I was still mortal, Misfeata's blood ran through me, which made me believe that I could only be killed by Tyran, or Misfeata herself. But I still felt pain. And being struck through was an unbearable feeling. Even if Misfeata's power could censor most of the pain, I still felt this human pain.

Scott leapt over us, changing himself into a wolf. A yelp was heard behind as Scott fended off any followers. I was placed carefully but quickly into the back seat. Ashley took the driver's seat as Paul jumped on the back seat, covering me. The great big wolf jumped into the front as Ashley accelerated, and the car quickly sped away.

"Get it out," I spluttered to Paul, gesturing to the sword as I fumbled my hand over the blade, trying to reach for the handle myself. Paul tensed, looking at me with pained eyes, not wanting to do it.

"Oh for goodness sake," Scott flushed. Scott reefed the sword out of my back as the feeling of relief washed over me, allowing me to breathe properly.

This is all so impossible; I should be dead by now. *So many times. So many times have I been in so much pain and near death, and yet I can keep walking, I can keep fighting as long as Misfeata resides within me. How does this keep happening? I am meant to have all this power and yet... I seem useless. I am able to project a Shield, and yet I keep letting my guard down.*

Paul slowly helped me into a sitting position in the back seat as I winced at the injury, knowing that soon it would heal. "It will heal in no time," I judged, as Paul looked over me with sad eyes. I looked at Scott from behind, looking at the two arrows that had pierced him in the side and shoulder.

The arrows began pushing back out, dropping out of him as his wounds began to heal, before being covered by skin. It was as if the wound had never been there. I watched in amazement as his ability enabled his body to recoup in such a way.

"Smells like Nathanial, does it not?" Scott questioned with a bitter taste to his words. "They wanted you dead and were not so willing for us to take you. Perhaps Lucas's brother is closer than you think."

"I thought you had left us for dead," I dryly prodded.

"Oh, me?" he cheekily smiled. "I just had to go out and get a nice ride."

Chapter Seven- To Simply Be

*N*ight had fallen. I thought of all those we have encountered, and how they had fallen to their deaths at my hands. Only a few of those Starkorfs had a human form. My thoughts dwelt on the young girl who I crossed paths with, and I felt remorse for the sight she must have seen. I was angry at the monster I had become and sad for the time I now spent fighting. It was so easy for me to take another life. And yet, I could not help my mind from charging on, trying to think rationally as to our next step and challenge. *We must move forward.*

"Did you notice?" Ashley broke at the heavy silence that hung over all of us for the last few hours as we continued the drive toward Scott's home, back to the direction Paul and I have been running away from.

"I did," I sighed heavily. "Almost all of them."

"What was almost all of them?" Paul interjected.

"Few of them that we fought today still had a human form, they all had severe physical mutations," I remarked to Paul.

That large group of Starkorfs who dispersed after Praytar's death, where did they all go? Who did they follow? After that day, had their eating patterns lessened if they had no one of a higher rank to lead them? Was this how they were born? Where did all of them go with no leader? Had they been reunited with Nathanial?

"What I am most interested in knowing is how their archers were able to break my Shield, and whether it had anything to do with Nathanial's command," I said, voicing my thoughts. *But why would Nathanial make it so obvious? And why all of a sudden are there attacks in that small town in broad daylight? Have Paul and I been followed this whole time without realizing it? Was it Lucas who told him of our whereabouts?*

"Right now it seems irrelevant and you are missing the objective: whatever their methods were, they were after one thing, and that was Aeisha," Scott said, looking back at me, his pink eyes seeming a deeper red in the moon's light. He was right. They were after Aeisha.

I pushed aside my brown jacket, looking down on one of the sais, reassuring myself that they were there. *Why is Nathanial after my Immortal Blades?*

56

"Do you think he might have thought we had Borac and was hoping for that instead?" I asked. After I had killed Praytar, my deal was to give Max Jacket Borac, Tyran's Immortal Blade, in exchange for saving Paul's life. Perhaps that was what Nathanial was in search of. After all, he was entitled to it now. But allowing him to have that blade would have been a fatal mistake; coming into contact with him after that would only strengthen him and give Tyran full control to turn Nathanial's body into any beast he wished. Now Borac was the property of Max Jacket, who I would never be able to obtain it back from. I couldn't imagine anything else that Max would bargain for or that would be any more valuable than that. But I must believe in his and Trish's ability, knowing that they would not let anyone steal something from them, especially the invaluable Borac.

"Maybe," Scott said simply as he looked back toward the road, leaving us all to sit silently as we continued to drive. The wind whipped nastily at my long light-brown hair. I looked to the side of the road, watching the trees vanish across my eyes, in deep thought once again. I dared not sleep.

Paul's gentle hand rubbed my back. I looked at him; he gave me a small smile for comfort. There were a few scratches on his face, and a small cut on his arm. Other than that, we were safe. *When we stop, I will ask Scott to heal it, although I doubt I would have to ask. Scott has taken quite the liking to Paul.*

I gave Paul a small smile back, looking into his moss-green eyes that could hardly be seen in the dark night. He shifted slightly, holding me gently around my shoulder and rubbing my brown leather jacket with a light touch. Accepting his embrace, I rested my head on his shoulder, exhausted by today's events. I was happy to know that Paul was so easily able to take the burden of my thoughts away with his gentle touch and small comforting smile.

Embracing him and his masculinity, I inhaled all of him, simply being. I did not sleep nor did I think too much. For this moment I simply just wanted to be, and be in the embrace of Paul's comforting arms.

Paul did not push his affection on me, although for the past two months we had been alone a lot. He had once made his feelings for me very clear, before this war had begun for the both of us. I trembled at the thought of a romantic relationship. It would only complicate our situation. I was already far too dependent on him, and would I not be taking away his opportunity to leave me even more?

I should be encouraging him to leave, and yet I can't. My feelings for Paul are undeniable and yet I must restrain myself, because one day I risk the chance of this body not being my own. It is my first fight at hand. And I cannot fight that if I am fighting for a love I may never have the right to own. I promised to protect Paul at all costs, even though it is me who has endangered him. And I will stay true to that promise. But for now I will embrace this moment and simply be.

For many days we continued to drive with nothing more eventful to entertain us than Scott's high-pitched laughs, small talk of the Starkorfs that attacked us, and trivial conversation over what fuel station food we wanted to eat at. We simply drove. Scott, Paul, and Ashley took turns driving. The suspense was gripping as we got closer to Max Jacket's home.

    I wanted to go back to Roperia to see if my parents had miraculously appeared, but I knew within me that was not the case. Right now I had to research any danger this unknown Elemental Breather might bring to us before I can have a reunion with my parents. I might possibly put them in harm's way if that woman followed us.

    After driving on a dirt road for hours, we reached the point where we had once been ambushed by many Starkorfs as we ran away from Max Jacket's cottage. That was the first time Misfeata had taken over my body completely and used her horrific strength and power with every intention of killing Trish. It was the first time I had become completely transparent and she used my body to her will. Something I now fought on a regular occurrence.

    Looking over the dirt of where we were once parked, I couldn't help but feel helpless as the memories flickered by. Paul and I had not yet been reunited then. It was Lucas who looked after me: pulling my hand toward the safety of his bike as he drove us away from such dangerous attackers, protecting me. The thought left a bitter taste as I remembered his leather-gloved hand holding mine. I clutched at my own hand now, feeling stupid. He wore leather gloves and long shirts all the time so if anyone touched him, his bare skin wouldn't drain them. So why didn't I not notice it sooner? Why was I a victim of his lies, believing him to once be my protector and close to my heart?

    "Karla!" Paul exclaimed, breaking me away from my conflicting thoughts. "Are you coming?" he said, shrugging his backpack on. Ashley was already walking ahead.

    "Yes," I replied, no longer dazed. I fell in line with the others as we paced toward the cottage. This time the pace wasn't as harsh as last time and we could comfortably walk, reaching there in an hour.

There was a large open space in front of the abandoned cottage. I reflected on how much had changed since I last looked at it. But this time, it was with Paul by my side.

As Scott ventured toward the cottage, I couldn't help but wrap my arms around myself, feeling on edge by the thick eeriness surrounding me. I didn't sense Max Jacket or Trish, but their disappearance seemed very strange. Why would they leave their home? Very little made sense to me at this point and I needed to remind myself that we were there to go through all the books that Max Jacket had kept. Perhaps we would find some information on this Elemental Breather woman who could control both Shielders and Starkorfs.

Following Scott into the cottage with Ashley and Paul, I looked around in dismay just like I had the first time I looked at the large room covered in books. The dozen couches and large coffee table next to the fireplace were dusty. The large chandeliers that were once so brightly lit were now still and dusty, a shadow of the beauty they once radiated.

Circling the room, Scott lit them all so we could properly see. Paul looked around in dismay like I had once, and Ashley was standing on the coffee table to reach the chandelier to light it.

"Get down!" Scott angrily commanded, standing tall and threatening. I clutched for Aeisha at my side, startled by his outburst. Ashley stared at him, still stretching up with a lighter in hand, just as surprised.

Scott closed his eyes, his pink eyes no longer claimed by black in the threatening manner all Elemental Breathers had. "Please get down, my father may not be here but I will not let you place your dirty feet on our furniture or disrespect my home," he rambled. "Granted, I came in search of your group, thus why I have not yet requested you change your clothing. But do not push me to my limits." He regained his composure.

Ashley slowly crept off and accepted the long silver candle holder that Scott offered. Walking over to us, he gave Paul and me a candle, looking at me oddly. Within seconds Trish would have had every candle in this room lit, but now we had to hold our candles against the edges of the dusty bookshelves, hoping to find something on their binds.

Looking at Scott's suit, I recalled the formality that Elemental Breathers demanded of others in their presence. Last time I had come to this cottage I was forced to change into a red, tight dress as did the others. We had to change into such clothing so we were deemed presentable in front of Max Jacket, Trish, and Scott. I wondered how hard it would have been to be Scott in wolf form. When I spoke to him, did he have the urge to answer back Or was he so used to being hidden as a wolf that he stayed silent?

"Well. I will start from this end," Paul said, grabbing hold of the long ladder to the left, closest to the door. On our right was the hallway that we had once been chased down when ambushed by Lucas's brother, Nathanial. *The night when Lucas and I spoke of our childhood, or perhaps that was all a lie too?*

As Paul climbed a few steps, I watched over his broad shoulders shifting through his shirt as he reached the fourth step, feeling the presence of someone staring behind me.

Scott's pink eyes were fixated on Paul's back, as he noticed me he quickly glanced the other way toward Ashley as he too began to search.

A small smile pressed on my lips as I felt amused by Scott's fascination with Paul. I stepped in front of the large bookshelf, looking up and reading over the thick spines, fighting tiredness and hurriedly getting to work. *We will find something on this woman — we must.*

Chapter Eight- A Place To Go

*A*fter hours of endless searching through the vast book collection and handwritten texts through sunken eyes, Ashley gave a loud sigh of frustration, placing the book back where he grabbed it. As I rested my back against the bookshelf, I felt the same frustration that he did. We could be here for weeks going through all these books.

"I will see if I can find some tea," Scott offered. He was sitting around the coffee table across from Paul. Paul closed his book as well while everyone decided to take a break. Scott closed his book and left it on the coffee table, walking toward the kitchen. Feeling fatigue hang over my eyes heavily, I decided to go outside for some fresh air. After the constant and active effort of not falling asleep, exhaustion lay heavily on my body. I couldn't understand how my mind was still able to run through various thoughts. I worried that the tiredness of my body could easily show cracks in my inner guard against Misfeata, giving her enough advantage to take possession of my body.

But I cannot sleep; she will only torture me there. I heavily sighed into the dark, chilled night, looking up at the dim moon with its surrounding dark clouds. *Will we find anything on this woman?* I was tortured by how close we were to my hometown. *What if my parents are waiting there for me to come home?*

I crossed my arms in exhausted exasperation. So many things to decide and find, yet I felt as though things only became more tiring and useless.

"Karla," Ashley said as he approached me, looking at the sky as I did. "How long do we plan on staying here if we can't find anything? It is a known spot of Nathanial's... staying here too long may endanger us."

"How far away is your mother, Suzumiya, and Chris from here?" I asked, avoiding his question. I didn't want such a heavy decision placed on my shoulders. I knew by being here we were in danger, but everywhere we went may turn out dangerous. There was no longer a safe place to be. Not for myself or for Ashley: the leading fighters who wiped out the Starkorfs' hideout and killed their leader, Praytar. There were many that chased us for that.

Since then Helena, Suzumiya, and Chris, went into hiding after

Kurt's disappearance. Kurt had been missing since his departure from the old warehouse where Seth had been killed. Ashley hardly spoke of them. Whether it was because I left their organization or because I brought more risk to them as the last descendant of Misfeata, I did not know. Ashley and I have been through a lot as we went through our inner transformations. It made us stronger, and understood one another amidst our own suffering.

"I can't tell you that, sorry Karla. My mother didn't want me to tell you where they are. She actually gets really infuriated when I come in search of you to let you know what we have found out. When Scott came to us, she forbade me to come and see you," he said heavily. "I guess she knew I would only want to join your cause. Since the death of Dad and the disappearance of Kurt, they have been left scattered. Suzumiya and Chris still venture out, but it isn't the same. For me though, I couldn't waste away what it was my father raised me to become and that was a fighter, to hunt and kill the Starkorfs. My mother feared to lose me as we did Dad, but I know this is what I want to do with myself, whether it does condemn me to death. I realized that after you left," he concluded.

Was this the feeling I felt radiate from him only days ago? Because the Starkorfs are after me, does he find himself to be most helpful to his cause by fighting by my side? Does Ashley truly believe this to be his purpose?

"If I had the choice…" I said, putting myself in his shoes. "I would not choose this life. And if you only wish to stay because you want to fight, then I suggest you go back to Helena because this fighting is nothing but a void. There is no winning in this battle, only death."

A loud crack came from the left, grabbing both of our attentions and breaking us away from our heavy conversation. I projected my Shield beneath my feet, quickly absorbing the ground's energy to obtain information of what surrounded us: two Starkorfs. My body was so fatigued I didn't sense them sooner.

Ushering Ashley back —much to his annoyance of being told what to do — I ran into the direction that the noise had come from and projected my Shield, ready to quickly dispose of them. *How long have they been following us for and whom do they report to?*

Irritated, Ashley followed, pulling out his long knife that he always carried with him. I grabbed Aeisha. Reaching closer to the noises, we jumped over a freshly fallen tree, *was that the noise we heard? The crashing of this tree?*

Leaping over it, we stopped searching for the two Starkorfs, who now lay dead on the ground. A small woman was hunched over them, pulling a small black knife out of one of their eyes. Still crouching, she looked up at me. She had big gray eyes; a small face well portioned to her small frame; black hair that was cut short at the back of her neck and long toward the front; and tanned olive skin. She looked no older than twenty.

As she reefed the knife out, she wiped it over a small black sheath of the same size as the knife that was strapped over her small chest and leathered sleeveless shirt, uninterested in our arrival. If I could sense the two Starkorfs then why could I not sense her?

"Who are you?" I asked, raising both of Aeisha defensively.

Still unfazed, she let a small crooked smile appear as she stood up and dusted her hands. "I am the person who just killed these feral creatures, all whilst minding my own business." She crossed her arms across her chest before continuing rudely: "You have an attitude problem."

I was agitated at her antagonizing remark. "I beg your pardon?" I asked, annoyed.

"Are you camping somewhere close by? I was going to but it's cold tonight and I don't want to contend with the chill of tonight's air," she said, disregarding my comment to ask Ashley directly.

"What are you?" I demanded of her, as Ashley looked between us, unsure of how to react. "A Shielder?" I didn't detect a Shield on her — perhaps she didn't have the ability. "An Elemental Breather?" But even if she were, I should have been able to sense her presence. And normal humans had a presence as well. *What is she?*

"Ew, no," she muttered, not without sass. "So can I join you or not?" She flicked her hand out toward Ashley in demand of his answer.

She was deliberately still ignoring me and I flushed in annoyance. *She thinks I have the attitude problem?*

"Look I am not an enemy. Obviously, if you came after these Starkorfs you're on the same team as I am. Unless it was me you came to fight?" She narrowed her gray eyes on me.

"We were here for the Starkorfs," Ashley uttered, interrupting the contentious stare between the foreign woman and me. "You can come back with us. Karla, right now, anyone who kills Starkorfs is a friend of mine."

"Great. I'm Paige by the way," she said with a bright smile. "Oh and another bone to pick with you…" She pointed her finger at me, aggravating me even more. "I don't like cleaning up your mess either. Remember, I don't know, a dozen or so Starkorf carcasses you left lying around in a small town called Darby? Yea, I didn't appreciate being left to clean that before the humans saw it." She was walking between Ashley and me, unfazed by the tension between us.

I regained my composure, not allowing myself to get flustered. It would only stir Misfeata more. Closing my eyes in agitation and hoping to open them to her absence, I was greatly disappointed as she looked back at me with eyebrows raised.

"Well, are you showing me to your camp?" she challenged patronizingly. I gave Ashley a harsh glare, annoyed that he would let her join us. I was extremely against another joining us, out of caution. With all these creatures and Elemental Breathers chasing us, I had to know if Scott could sense anything ominous emanating from her. Anything supernatural could be the key to discovering the disappearance of my parents.

Ashley walked ahead as I bore my eyes into the back of the small woman. Although I saw the logic in the decision, I didn't like her any more because of it. This woman has an attitude problem.

Walking back to the cottage, Paige stopped, looked over it calculatingly, shrugging her shoulders as if to say 'it will do', and let herself in. A smile stretched my mouth as Scott in wolf form lunged at her territorially. This was his home and he was an Elemental Breather. She couldn't just invite herself in. She flushed red; taking a few steps back and clutching at her black knife, ready to fight Scott. He growled at her from the front of the door, watching her carefully.

Paul came out, leaning against the doorframe, confused as to what was happening.

"She is with us," Ashley said, stepping forward.

Scott's form changed back to normal as he looked at her angrily. "You cannot invite whomever you wish into my home," he lectured, his piercing black eyes threatening.

"She has been following us for a while. She cleaned up the mess we left in that town before. And she just killed two Starkorfs that were near here. The least we can offer is a warm fireplace," Ashley said, crossing his arms as he steadily watched Scott.

"On my way here I encountered some ape-looking creatures with deformities," Paige said, grabbing my attention. "I may have damaged them a little. I got in their way but decided to retreat. They were really strong. Oh, one more thing," she paused, looking directly at me, no longer alarmed with Scott's presence. "They weren't after me. They were following you. One cut my arm, you owe me a bandage."

"So why follow us?" Paul interjected.

"I'm here for the same reason as him," Paige said, pointing her blade to Ashley. "And her," she continued, pointing yet again at me. "I want the Starkorfs dead. And my best advice to you all is to leave this place. You may have only just arrived, but I say this with great caution: those things out there are chasing you, those creatures are after you. And on my way here, so were those Starkorfs."

64

The Starkorfs seemed irrelevant in comparison to these creatures that were said to be following us. But who is this woman and why is she following us? *I don't believe for a moment Paige wants to genuinely help us. And my goal is not to fight the Starkorfs but to find my parents.*

"I think for the time being we should seek rest," Scott said. "If we are in no immediate danger then I will pour everyone a cup of tea before we have a few hours of rest." He raised his eyebrow at me, insinuating that I too needed sleep. "She is welcome to come in, but tomorrow is when we will decide where to go."

Paige quickly followed him, as did Ashley, giving me an uncertain look but leaving me to my own peace. Paul leaned against the doorframe waiting for me to join them.

"I will not be sleeping tonight, Paul, but you should rest too. I will keep watch tonight," I said with a small smile out of politeness, wanting privacy.

We had to leave again and we had neither a lead nor a place to go; we were constantly running with no destination. *Is there any hope for us or will we forever be running in search of my parents with no lead?*

After a few minutes, Paul came back outside with a small red blanket. He brushed it over my shoulder where I cradled it with one hand, feeling the thick silk material. The moon still rose over us beautifully, only a few hours of night was left until the sun was to rise.

"Please don't stay out here all night," he pleaded, rubbing my shoulder. "It will all work out." I wanted to argue; why does he have so much belief that all would be well?

Instead of debating, I accepted his encouragement, agreeing with him. He left a warm kiss on my forehead, walking back inside and leaving me to my own thoughts. *I must believe in Paul's words. If there is no hope, then what will I have to drive me; something will come and my questions will be answered. All will be well — because it must. Our very lives depend on it.*

As if answering my questions, an arrow shot past my face and into the side of the cottage. Startled, I dropped the blanket, holding Aeisha firmly, feeling no presence of anyone surrounding me. The arrow had a small piece of paper attached, wrapped in blue ribbon to keep it secure. A message? As I cautiously searched the trees looking for the archer, I slowly opened the handwritten letter.

Karla,

I know you do not trust me, and I do not blame you. The one thing that will never change for me is that in every way I will always watch over and protect you. Much has happened over the last few months that has become very clear and true to me. I do not expect you to ever trust me, but please do believe I will protect you when I can. For some reason, I think this Elemental Breather is following you specifically and I do not know why. Harmony has found the possible hideout of the woman who attacked us. I will wait for you tomorrow at dusk in a small park in an old town East of Max Jacket's home. The town is called Caloor.

With no name scribed on the bottom, I knew it could only be from one person: Lucas. Crumpling it in my hands as his words stung at my chest, I prevented myself from shredding the letter into tiny pieces. Was this my message? Was this the sign I was after? No longer scrunching it, I loosened my grip. We came here to see if we could retrieve information about this woman and this may be our lead.

I had to tell the others instead of letting my own selfish thoughts cloud my judgment.

Paige sat cross-legged on one of the couches, drinking tea. Ashley, Paul, and Scott, were still searching through the books. Before I could tell them of the letter, Paul exclaimed loudly, breaking everyone's heavy concentration as they searched over the books.

"Karlz, is this image similar to the eggs you were talking about?" Paul asked, piquing my interest. He handed me the heavy leather-bound book and I opened it to the page he gestured at, while Scott and Ashley looked over my shoulder. The eggs had an odd green tinge to it, obviously hand-drawn with a thumb mark painted across the edge of the egg. It stood on a pedestal.

"Thy who creates beast can manipulate one's soul and appearance. She is ever changing — her creatures and the biological fundamentals of everyone around her. Thy murderer and creator — she calls herself *Mother*," I read, confused by its meaning. I looked back at Scott as he stared blankly at the page, sickly white.

"That is my father's writing," he said faintly. I flicked through to the next page where an image of a large blue beast was sketched viciously. There were ice shards protruding from the larger beast's skin. Scott's skin was no longer porcelain but sickly white, as all color seemed to have vanished. Scott ran for the door, vomiting suddenly. I searched over the bizarre image, looking back over Scott's hunched back, surprised by his demeanor.

"What did you see?" I asked of Scott, still not comprehending his sudden illness. Was it because of this book? The words made no sense to me. Was there any other writing to follow?

"We need to leave now," Scott said, hurriedly pulling a handkerchief out of his pocket and wiping his mouth. "We're not safe here. I think I know why father and Trish vanished." He looked over me seriously and then at Paige, who, only moments ago warned us to leave. I narrowed my eyes on him, slightly tilting my head as a darker eeriness filled the atmosphere. I allowed my Shield to connect with the ground, finding an odd pace of footsteps approaching.

"We need to get to the car before they get here," Scott said, wiping over his white hair, arranging it. *Are the footsteps that approach the beasts Paige spoke of previously that are following us?* "Whoever that woman is, she will follow us. I didn't realize at the time who she was but I have encountered her ability before," he explained, stricken. "I didn't know she was who we were contending with, but we need to leave now."

"Who are you talking about?" I asked in a frustrated tone; his words were like riddles. He was beside himself. I had never seen him so frightened.

"She is the Elemental Breather who killed my mother. Her ability, it is the same," he said, flushed and frantic. "And no two Elemental Breathers have the same abilities, so it must be her. Whatever you can sense coming toward us will be no different to those creatures that attacked us at those cargo ships. She will kill us all." His chest was rising and falling rapidly. "We can only hope that she wants to kill us because if she traps us, we are worse off." He looked over us frantically. "We need to go."

Scott was slicking his hair back vigorously. I looked at Ashley and Paul steadily. We had come all this way only to leave hours after. I was scared to ask Scott any more questions on the matter, as he seemed to be falling apart. His words were so rushed and his meaning was so vague. He didn't make any sense. But what I did know was that something was quickly approaching and if we didn't want a confrontation, then we had to leave. This much truth shone through his scattered logic.

"Well," Ashley said heavily, walking toward Scott, who seemed taken aback that Ashley was the first to follow him, despite their differences. "If we have what we need and Scott can tell us more on this woman, then perhaps we should leave before whatever it is attacks us."

I was surprised by Ashley's quick judgment of Scott and his compliance. Had the last few fights made him value his life? Or had he found a reason to live? *I thought he said he only came to fight...*

Paige finished her tea, placing the small plate on the coffee table with the cup on top. She walked over to us and waited alongside Ashley and Scott.

Paul didn't move until I took a few unsettled steps forward, tiring of the constant run. *Why has the usual composed and flamboyant Scott shattered at the thought of this woman? And why is she chasing us?* I gave them all a certain nod, ready to run to the car and disappear from this place. Not only must we contend with the Starkorfs who were after Aeisha, but this woman as well. What happened to Scott's mother for him to be so distant and fidgety?

As the book had no more pages, I left it in the bookshelf where Paul had found it. We found what we were searching for. And as always, my priority was to keep Paul safe.

"You guys, I think I know where we need to go after this," I said flicking the letter that was sent to me by arrow in between my fingers.

Right now we had to leave, but we at least had a clue as to who she was.

Chapter Nine- Hateful Eyes

$\mathcal{I}$ awkwardly sat between Paige and Paul. The atmosphere between us all was subdued; everyone was preoccupied by their own thoughts on how to best move forward. Paul was peering outside of the car, arms crossed. He was annoyed to hear that a message had been delivered to me on behalf of Lucas and that the place we ventured to next was to meet with him. Ashley was also distant; he hated Lucas and wanted to avenge his father, Seth.

Scott didn't want to be any closer to this Elemental Breather; he was still staying quiet after revealing that his mother had been killed by the very same woman. He said no more, avoiding anyone who tried to broach the topic. He was hidden in memories of an event that he could not yet share. As much as I wanted to reach my hand out to him and ask him what had happened all those years ago, I didn't. When I went to ask him before, his hurt eyes had avoided me before he walked away. For now, Scott was very silent on his mother's death. Was this because he was an Elemental Breather? Perhaps he was unable to tell us.

Paige, however, clearly didn't care. She just hopped in the car with us, looking away bored. Her chin was sitting on her hand and she was sighing loudly to herself.

We were all extremely tired after very little rest from the previous night of travel. I couldn't help but peer over Scott as he looked forward, feigning concentration on the road as Ashley drove. I wonder what happened to his mother? Max Jacket had never mentioned a wife. What had this Elemental Breather done to her to disturb him so much?

With only a few stops we continued driving until we arrived in the small town Lucas had described in his letter. It was now tucked within the pocket of my dark-colored jeans. Should I go to the location by myself, keeping the others from harm's way? We were only there to investigate. *I will not actively try to involve myself with that woman. But if she is following me I have to know why.*

Timing was perfect as we arrived in the small town and found the park almost immediately. We parked the car across the road from it. It was almost dusk. There was no sign of Lucas, or his companion Harmony. In the park there was a small child's play area with a swing, slide, seesaw, and little monkey bars. Next to it were a few dark cemented homes that looked like they were once a long set of units turned into some sort of office buildings. It was clear that no one was currently residing in them. The scene before us held a very abandoned atmosphere as only a faint breeze swept through it, making the old swing creak.

I could sense the presence of two people in the old office buildings, assuming it to be Lucas and Harmony, but I was always wary. "There are two in those old buildings over there," I said to them all, indicating toward the long, connected building. "But I can't be sure if it's them." I couldn't sense if it was definitely them or not.

"I would usually enter a part of myself within them to see who it was, but it is too far from here," Scott admitted quietly, looking down at his hands. We all looked over at the buildings, evaluating the danger. Paige suddenly jumped over the door of the car and began walking toward it.

"What are you doing?" I hissed in a hushed tone. She looked back at me as she continued walking across the road. It was very evident what she was doing.

I opened the door quickly, pacing behind her. We had to see if it was them; after all, it was Lucas who said this place at this time, and we were being cautious. Following her pace, I crept behind her as she walked toward the large metal door that had padlocks on it.

Pulling her small black knife out of her sheath, she made a clean break over to the padlock. Within seconds she was opening it and looking into the dark empty room. Without further hesitation she walked in. I looked behind me to find that the others have decided to follow. Scott changed into a glow-bug the size of my fist, lighting our path as we walked.

We squinted into the darkness. We were getting closer to the presence we sensed. I already knew that if it were Lucas and Harmony, they would have made their presence known by now. Unsure, we continued to follow Paige, who heroically continued forward.

She abruptly leaned against a wall, and Scott changed into his usual self. Light no longer shone around us. I heard his heavy breaths as we looked back over to the entrance. If this were Lucas and Harmony, they would have revealed themselves by now.

There is something dark in here.

While we took a moment to contain ourselves, I projected my Shield, shuffling past Scott over to Paige. She looked back at me, her gray eyes dull in the darkness. No noise was heard and nothing approached. Scott transformed himself after a moment's silence back into the glow-bug he had been before.

As he flickered on, we turned to look around the corner. A hairless face with no eyes and big nostrils edged toward us. Its figure was ape-like, with large front arms; its nostrils enormous slits down half its face; it had no eyes, and sharp green feathers traced down its back into some form of tail.

Realizing we were staring into a hideous creature's face, Paige struck at it with her small black knife, causing it to squeal in a high-pitched tone. Another cry rang out from behind, indicating that there were two. Paige ran back and out for the door, and we all followed. I turned behind, forcing my Shield into the second creature that burst from the darkness. As it ran at my Shield I was pushed back and outside of the building.

It followed me quickly. Paige prepared herself behind me and lunged for it, cutting at its arm as my feet still slipped beneath the gravel from being pushed back from such strength. The creature blocked the path to the others as they were chased further into the other end of the building.

I must get to them. With Aeisha in both hands I ran for the creature, its large tail slamming into the side of my Shield and throwing me into the monkey bars. I fell under the creature's strength and it shattered my Shield. I fell to the ground, coughing and clutching at my back as it ran toward me. Paige lunged for it with both feet kicking it in the side of the face, enough to disorient it. I held my back uncomfortably, looking back at the creature carefully.

This monster has such powerful strength? Is this the very same creature that Paige had spoken of that followed us? Did it know we would be here? Was this a set up? A large scream that sounded like Scott's echoed through the empty building, piquing my sense of alarm once again. *I must get in there. I must protect Paul.*

I ran for the door again as the creature quickly diverted its attention onto me once again. Its shard-like tail swooped past my wrist as I jumped back. It crept behind me, grabbing at Aeisha with its human hands. A long sword stabbed into its hands; forcing it to pull back its hand in a screeching wail. My eyes fell upon Lucas. He was still holding the handle of the sword, which was embedded deeply. In a split second he was flung over the monster's shoulder. Letting his sword go, he reached out his hands and pushed against the ground forcefully before falling harshly into it. He was suddenly flipping over into a stance, looking back at us.

I ran for the creature while it focused on Lucas. Paige ran from the other side and we both swung our blades over the creature. Its speed made it hard to follow as it quickly dodged our attacks. The creature backhanded Paige across the graveled ground, and followed me. I almost tripped over the seesaw jumping over it, but fortunately, the creature itself tripped over it. Quickly regaining its composure, sniffing and snorting heavily into the air, it pushed itself up with its large arms, roaring and swiping at me. I jumped up on top of the monkey bars, looking down on it.

"It can't see!" I shouted so everyone else knew its vulnerability. Paige clutched her ribs as Harmony helped her stand. I looked at Lucas who had no weapon as the sword was still embedded into the large creature's hand. *If it cannot see then we can use that to our advantage. Does it only go by smell or hearing as well?* Looking over the creature I could see no evidence of ears.

It flung its large tail up toward me as I jumped off and advanced toward Lucas, Paige, and Harmony. With one clean cut the beast's tail sliced through the monkey bars and it shattered.

"We need to attack its blind side," Lucas spoke out. "We need to ambush it from behind at an angle where it cannot directly smell us." So close to Lucas, I could feel his Shield tickle on the edges of my own as he prepared himself. Stepping back so I could no longer feel his shield, I looked over at Paige, who held herself straight, giving the beast a wicked smile.

"My pleasure," she sneered, agreeing to the plan.

As the beast ran toward us, Lucas quickly ran toward it as a distraction. If he could project his Shield heavily enough, he could handle the force of the creature's strength head-on while Paige and I attacked from behind. As if hearing my thoughts, Paige's wicked smile widened as she ran around the beast. I mirrored her.

As Lucas took the creature head-on, it swung at him, dragging Lucas back only slightly as he strained to keep his projected Shield strong enough to compete with its might. As he kept the creature there momentarily, Paige and I jumped upon it at the same time, bringing our weapons down on it. Its nostrils flared at me as I bore Aeisha firmly into both sides of its neck; Paige's black knife plunging into the top of its head.

Lucas jumped back. It felt like gravity itself was defying us. Paige and I appeared to hover in the air as we eyed the monster for signs of life. This one moment struck me as surreal, condemning me to my new reality of this unknown world: a world full of monsters. As it had no eyes to stare into, I could not see the beast's soul, whether it feared death, or whether it was dead.

My shallow breaths caught up with time and everything became surreal. The large creature crumbled to the ground, Lucas dodging its large body to keep it from falling on him. It felt like a gust of wind brushing past. The other creature came from behind, barging me, its tail grazing the side of my stomach as its hands glided past Aeisha, stealing her from me. The creature stopped and tried to take hold of her partnered blade, but I held her firmly, projecting my Shield so the creature was pushed off.

Instead of it coming back at me to fight, it ran. Instinctively I was chasing it as it had just taken Aeisha's partnered blade. As I ran down the street where lights brightened the dusk of day, its figure grew smaller in the distance. It had escaped with one of my blades even when I ran at my exceptional speed; even with Misfeata's heightened stamina and endurance.

They were after Aeisha the whole time?

Infuriated and unsure of what to do, I looked over my empty hand, annoyed with myself for letting my guard down. *How could I not have known? Does this somehow mean that the attack carried out by the Starkorfs only days ago was in alignment with these creatures, with that Elemental Breather woman controlling them from behind, or is this a mere coincidence?*

As many thoughts rushed over me I remembered Paul. The other creature was contained in the same building as Paul and the others. *Does that mean—...* I rejected the thought running back for Paul. *He cannot be dead.*

I burst into the dark room where Lucas, Paige, and Harmony waited. Harmony held a torch, allowing me to clearly see. Scott was hunched under Paul's angered frame. Paul was holding him up as Scott had collapsed into him, his back swollen and lashed with cuts. He bled onto the floor.

"He blocked the creature from getting to us," Ashley explained quietly as I looked over him mortified. Ashley was now standing beside Paige, who looked over the scene, all unconcerned. They were backed into a small corner where I imagined Scott to have changed into some creature in front of them, blocking the way. Scott had saved them.

Paul searched my eyes angrily and looked away as Ashley and Paige tried to lift Scott up. The anger on Paul's face stung me. They helped the unconscious Scott away from the darkness of the room and into the outside air. I stared after them, hurt by his harsh stare. *He hated me. This was too much for him. Does he blame me for what had happened?*

Paul had made his opinion very known that he had no interest to meet here. I didn't listen and it led to Scott's attack. Already the burden of not protecting Paul weighed heavily on me. Is he angry because he felt like perhaps he couldn't do anything? *Does he hate himself or me? But that is not what Paul is here for; I should be the one protecting him, no matter what.* I tormented myself with so many thoughts.

Tonight I realized my own reality. He was regretting his decision to be by my side. He would have seen Scott's face scrunched in pain, no matter what form he had taken. Screaming as he protected them from a creature they could not possibly have fought.

And where was I? Chasing Aeisha, a blade that was not even mine, and yet, the other part of my entity. I mourned my broken vow to protect Paul.

Paul hates me.

A cold leather glove touched my wrist, grabbing my attention. Lucas let his fingers hover over my wrist, his sandy-blonde hair tinted golden by the light that Harmony held as she slowly walked behind us toward the door.

"We must go now, Karla," he said softly.

I didn't move. His touch became firmer around my wrist and he lightly pulled me toward the door. "We must go." I slowly pulled my wrist out of his hand and dropped my gaze to the ground.

My guilt lay heavy within. Paul's stare broke me in two. *How can I look him dead in the eye knowing how much he hates this world?* As I looked down at Aeisha I could not explain the pull of her, the desire and need to have her partnered blade back. I could not defy such an intoxicating need. I needed Aeisha. *I must follow that beast to find her.* I was torn by my true desire. *I do not want this world and yet I cannot get myself out. I am so heavily enticed by it.*

Lucas's shoulder muscles rolled as he walked. My eyes battered in disbelief and I choked on the realization that I looked at him in that moment, not in hatred, but as someone who truly accepted what I was.

I hid my face behind my long hair as he looked back at me, his eyebrows knitted in confusion as he too hadn't known what that look meant.

I pushed past him and out into the night. I let the warm air sweep through my body as I inhaled deeply, trying to purify all the toxins that resided within me. Scott was sitting upright on a bench assuring Paul that he no longer needed his assistance. He was bare-chested, as his beautiful red suit had been torn to shreds. He looked over his red pants evenly.

I approached slowly, trying to avoid Paul's eyes. As I looked over his back I noticed it to be already healing, his skin slowly knitting itself together like it had once before when it pushed out the arrows.

"I have thought about it," Scott croaked coarsely, still sounding like a broken man. "I want to follow you to find this woman... to find the Elemental Breather who killed my mother."

Chapter Ten- Loneliness

"*We* need to keep our distance from those creatures," Paul said bleakly, looking down at Scott. A normal human would have died. Paul's words lashed at my chest. I knew he was right; after the battle with Praytar, we were to avoid fighting as much as possible. And now I was actively chasing it. But everything has changed — they had the partnered Immortal Blade of Aeisha. *I have no choice but to go.*

Paul was always by my side, telling me it would be okay, caressing me when I doubted our motives. Now watching him despise our mission made my chest ache. If he no longer believed in our safety and future, then who would?

"No," Scott said bitterly. "This is a score my family has been meaning to settle for a very long time. I wish to no longer be scared of her. I will avenge my mother, and the childhood that woman took away from me." His eyes dulled into black, his black pupils engulfing his irises as he recalled a memory. I wanted to ask why and what had happened, but he excreted a very toxic atmosphere around him. No one dared to ask anymore, only looking at one another with uncertainty.

"I agree with Paul," Harmony said in a low silky voice. "We should stay away; I think we should retreat to a camp."

"And when did you earn the right to start deciding what is best for everyone?" Paige countered harshly, her gray eyes narrowing on the young girl who glimmered in white clothing.

"Don't speak to her like that," Paul interjected angrily. "We all have a right to speak here."

"Paige is right," I remarked, although her help would have been appreciated. She had proven herself already to be able to fight when we were in the cargo ship grounds and were being attacked by the snakes. But for some reason, now she had hidden. I did not like her and something about her flustered and angered me.

"No, Paul is right. Paige shouldn't speak to her like that," Lucas added, taking a step forward in front of her to push my raging gaze from the girl to him. I flushed red, as did Paul. Harmony's very presence unsettled me. Paige obviously felt the same as she began throwing her arms around argumentatively as she explained her distaste for Harmony.

Looking at Lucas, I was annoyed to have him so quickly jump to the defense of this girl, just as he had once for me. Pushing away that unreasonable justification, I angered at a different thought. It was not because he had done the same for me but because he would so quickly stand against me. He had described in his letter how he wanted to gain my trust once again. I flushed red as my irrational thoughts submerged. *I cannot be hurt by his indifference. I hate Lucas,* I reminded myself.

I diverted my eyes in shame as Paul looked over at me accusingly. Never had I seen him apply such harsh stares toward me. I didn't know what he was thinking. I didn't know if he was ready to leave. My heart clenched at the thought.

"Lucas," Scott interjected, urging everyone to be quiet, much to Paige's dissatisfaction, as she seemed to be enjoying the argument. She crossed her arms, snorting in aggravation as the noise ceased. "We came here to collect details from you. Please pass that onto us now so I can go, whether anyone wishes to join me is their own choice. I will apply no pressure. I feel as if this is a fight I must personally deal with but as she has now harmed all of you in some way it is your right to join me. I will not stop you but I will not encourage you either," he said softly, looking at Paul.

"We should leave in a few days then," Harmony suggested. I resented her eagerness to slow our progress down.

"No. I will leave now to wherever that beast has retreated too. Taskatae is her name; that is all my father could learn of her identity. They will not be expecting us so soon. We can gather much more information that way; I have my own details I want to gather about her before I confront her. I may even search for my father and sister first so they know of her location. They too would want the opportunity to be able to kill her," Scott lamented, his jaw clenching.

"I am going, Harmony," Lucas whispered to her and she looked up at him disappointed. Still avoiding Paul's stare, I said I was also going, as did Paige.

"I refuse to work with him," Ashley stated angrily. "What are you thinking, Karla?!"

I flinched under his words, ashamed that my recent thoughts of Lucas had begun to change. I felt I had betrayed Paul in a different way. Much as I wanted a life with Paul — though I tried often to deny my feelings for him — I could only notice our differences right now, as it was Lucas who agreed to be by my side and help me give chase to retrieve Aeisha. He understood that I needed my blade back but Paul didn't. Ashley didn't understand either, but Lucas did.

"I need to get Aeisha back. I will be going no matter who accompanies me," I announced, lifting my gaze to Paul's hurt face before he looked away. I was no longer confident of the journey we would continue to share. I began quickly walking toward the car before I cried at the pain within my chest that Paul so easily inflicted. "Let's go."

Paige smiled. Despite what seemed like a serious injury earlier, she was beaming with excitement for yet another confrontation. Scott too walked beside us, reaching into his boot and quickly putting on a purple suit, covering his masculine frame.

So quickly we were all divided. I needed to find this woman and her creatures to obtain Aeisha's partnered blade, her pull far too strong to deny. It was not only Misfeata who needed the Immortal Blades, I too was influenced by the strong connection I had with them. No weapon could ever be of the same quality. Aeisha were my blades and I needed the partnered one back.

For some reason Scott now gained the needed courage against the woman he was so scared of only hours ago. After protecting Paul, was he after revenge because he couldn't protect his mother? Whenever Scott seriously spoke of something, I still couldn't help but feel as if behind each word he still had a silent motive, and one which I had not yet understood.

Lucas was enthralled by this woman, needing to know why she was after him. It made me seriously question if he only came on such a journey because he no longer had a place to return to after betraying all those who raised him from a young age. He could never look Helena in the eyes again. He fought against his father to help me sever the bond of Tyran who possessed Praytar's body, turning him into a beast. Did he regret making that decision? He was no longer welcome there after helping me kill his own father, who was also leader of that Starkorf clan. Was this his way to try and search for a purpose, because this woman was chasing him?

Although I still didn't know much of Paige — who had become an unlikely member of our group — I realized she enjoyed fighting. It made me question for how long she had hated Starkorfs, and why she wanted to hunt them all. Without knowing any of us, she had become attached to our mission despite her obvious lack of social skills. Looking over her curiously, I questioned as to what motive she herself might have.

Ashley had little interest in working with Lucas or following this woman; if he were not interested he would not be a part of it. And as for Harmony, it put me on edge to know she were to stay by Paul's side. Her motives were still unclear to me; all I knew was I did not like her or trust her. But I trusted Ashley and Paul's judgment that she would not jeopardize them in anyway.

But where will they go when we leave? Will they stay close to this town? Will I find them easily after we part ways? I have no right to ask where they are going or why they will not come. They have made it clear they do not want to follow us. And for the first time in what felt like a very long time, I felt truly alone.

Lucas sat in the driver's seat, waiting for us to gather in the car as we looked back at those who we left behind. To my disappointment, we were the only ones to come; the others' minds firmly made up to not follow. Ashley, Paul, and Harmony looked over at us with their own hurt expressions. *Am I selfishly leaving Paul behind? But I had to obtain my partnered blade, without it I already feel unbalanced.*

They had every right to be mad: not only had I betrayed their trust, but my own as well. Looking at Lucas's sandy blonde hair, I questioned whether I pushed him away so many times because deep within me, without my own knowing, I still deeply cared for him. If that was the truth of my heart then what did I feel for Paul?

Lucas drove us for only a few hours then came to a stop alongside bush land within a deserted location. He had previously mentioned that Harmony had found this place. Harmony had told Lucas that she saw odd creatures coming from a certain cave as they had camped one night; she had been hunting for meat so they could eat that night. When hunting that is what she had found: the two creatures we were attacked by were hovering around the edges. As they were outside, she expected them to be guarding something precious or even the Elemental Breather who had attacked Lucas and me. She thought it most pertinent to attack during the day, as when she had a second look during the morning, there were no guards.

Scott raged with the thought of the woman who had killed his mother being close by, as I did over my stolen Immortal Blade. Paige only because, well, I think Paige just enjoyed fighting, and Lucas had his own reasons, she was following both him and me.

Turning the car off and getting out, we followed Lucas, who brushed aside numerous bushes for us, clearing a path. After half an hour of walking into a hidden area surrounded by trees, we saw some flames on sticks, revealing the cave that had been described to us.

There was no creature on guard like Harmony had described. Did the woman only have the two creatures? We had killed one, so then where was the other? Paige as quickly as always looked at her surroundings and irrationally stepped out, running alongside the cave and then leaning against its wall, looking around. She gave me a queer look, as if I was taking too long to reach her side. Scott changed into a small bug which I could hardly see as he flew over to her. Lucas followed with his long sword and I shuffled behind. We all stood outside the cave entrance.

Scott flew in the cave, coming back minutes later. We had waited for him to return to give us a report. When he did, he appeared in front of us as his usual self, looking at me gravely.

"What is it?" I whispered, uncomfortable under his stare.

"Karla. I sensed a human deeper within the cave, alongside a few others, as well as Taskatae. I didn't venture in further because I partially entered the human to find who it was. She is a prisoner in there." With an awkward sigh Scott looked at the floor, seeming unsure how to proceed with the information. "She was the same as you." His eyes were looking at me directly, captivating my attention. I held my breath, eager for what I thought he might say next. "Karla, it's your mother."

Chapter Eleven- Reunion

*L*ucas held me firmly from behind as I tried to run for the entrance, covering my mouth as I gasped angrily at him. I tugged away from him. I projected my Shield against his desperately, but they were too evenly matched. Step by step however I was able to drag him behind me as adrenaline pumped through my body to reach my mother.

Paige tried grabbing at me to no avail as her hand bounced away from my Shield. I was engulfed by blind desperation. *I must reach my mother.*

As Scott stood in front of me he suddenly vanished and a shudder ran through my Shield, causing it to ripple. My legs could no longer move, though they were in no pain. I looked down to see a worm like organism strapped over my legs coming from beneath the ground.

The sensation was an intense feeling. My own energy within my legs was suppressed, and somehow I knew it was Scott. It felt like his presence. I knew he was able to change himself and enter other living people.

I projected my Shield even more harshly. Red ripples pulsated consecutively. I had hoped to push Scott away from me to no avail. He was attached to me and I could no longer move of my own will. I needed to get inside— this was no longer about Aeisha, but my mother.

"Karla. You must be calm," Lucas said, standing in front of me and cupping my face, forcing me to look into his dark-brown eyes. My heart raced as I was fueled by angst. *If I am to retrieve my mother, I must think rationally and use my wits. This woman is not a weak opponent. With the help of the others I will be able to set my mother free and we'll be reunited.* My heart slowed its beating and I felt Scott detach himself from my legs.

I took a step forward with control of my legs once again. I looked at Scott differently as he appeared in front of me, unsure as to how I should react after he had reached within my body. I never knew that he could be able to slip past my Shield so easily. If Scott were ever to be my opponent, he would be a very strong one indeed.

Scott pressed his finger to his lips reminding me to be quiet as Paige walked behind him, slipping into the dark cave. Lucas detached his soft-leathered hand from my face, startled that he touched me so. As he slipped into the darkness behind Scott, I did the same.

It was very dark inside the cave. There were a few torches to light in certain areas of the rocky walls. Somewhere close there was the noise of water dripping. Scott overtook Paige, turning left into a narrow crevasse that we could only just fit in. It seemed that the cave might have been a hideout for some time now as it was well structured and much larger inside than it had appeared from the outside. It had small gaps everywhere that either led deeper into another area, or suddenly ends.

A few times we had gone in the wrong direction as Scott led us deeper into the cave. We stayed wary of any sudden movement, just in case any beasts or the woman heard us. As we crept further in, Scott suddenly stopped. Paige looked behind him and then at me. I held my breath as they both let me slip past them to view my malnourished mother; hands and feet tied as she rested against a rock. Long thick black bars jutted from the ground to the ceiling, creating a prison. A locked door kept her contained.

She hasn't yet noticed us and I took in the surrounding area, finding her to be unguarded. Although in her state she would not pose much of a threat. I tried to contain myself, trying not to do anything rash or cry at the scene.

Lucas brushed past my shoulder as he ran toward my mother's cell. He projected a small Shield within the lock, breaking it so that it quietly creaked open. She looked up at him weakly, scared but making no sound. Her lips were dry and her face was smudged with dirt.

I ran over to the door, holding myself up using the frame as I was so frightened by what I saw. My poor mother seemed at first incapable of recognizing me. Her dry mouth continued to widen and close in shock and despair. Tears trailed down her face as her eyes widened before me and a glimmer of the mother I remembered shone through: my beautiful mother.

Her arms opened wide for me and I rushed past Lucas, collapsing into her and holding her tightly. Despite her frailness, she held me just as firmly. Brushing my hair and sobbing, she touched my face gently with her shaking hands.

"I'm real, Mum," I said my voice low, pushing past the lump in my throat. I grabbed her hands, raising her frail and battered hands to my lips, kissing her knuckles. "I'm real," I reinforced as tears spilled over my face. Her usual vibrant wavy hair was tattered and her hallow eyes were looking at me ghost-like as slowly my touch seemed to awaken her.

"We must get her out," I pleaded of Lucas, desperate for my mother to be safe.

Lucas cautiously lifted her to her feet, making sure not to scare her as she stared at him in dismay. She then looked to me and I signaled it was okay. He lifted her onto his back as I continued holding her hand. She began to sob when our hands were almost separated.

I cried at the unexpected reunion with the frail woman in front of my very eyes; this was not the reunion I was expecting. I was expecting my mother; who always smiled at me for comfort; who was beautiful, vibrant, and funny; who always made me feel safe. I now stared back at hollow eyes. This world no longer affected only me, but it had also destroyed the closest thing to me and that was my mother.

What of my father? I looked around at the other two single cells, but I couldn't see him. I projected my Shield past my feet into the ground, absorbing what information I could. I could only sense dark creatures and one that hurriedly ran towards us. I looked into the direction of where I felt the presence of the beast. Paige threw her black knife and a ghastly noise that sounded like a bird squawking came to us; she has obviously hit her target. Paige ran for the creature as I felt another come at us from another tunnel. The creature that Paige had killed was loud and it had alarmed all others that we currently positioned within the belly of the enemy's cave.

Was it too easy for us to get in? Was this a trap, to have no creature on guard? We were strategically being surrounded as the cells were in the middle of all connected tunnels, where the creatures were now running to. Another creature I could not yet see began squawking from the darkness. Scott lunged for it, changing into his wolf self. I watched his fur fade into the dark as growling, tearing, and barbaric squawking was heard. My mother began to cry and held onto Lucas tightly as he tried his hardest to breathe. She wrapped her arms around his throat, scared.

"Mum," I whispered, tapping her arm as I looked into the darkness that surrounded us. Where had the flames gone? "Mum, it is going to be okay." The remaining flames that flickered within were extinguished, leaving us in pitch-dark. Underneath my mother's disorientated sobs I could hear creatures approaching. I could not both project my Shield and drain from the ground as well. I could still hear Scott growling in wolf form, attacking other creatures that created spine-tingling noises. I heard Paige's heavy breathing from a distance as she continued to fight the same beasts. *I must get my mother out of here.*

Deciding I would rather know where I was, I projected my Shield at the bottom of my feet so I could sense my surroundings. I grabbed Lucas's hand so he could follow me and I could lead my mother out safely. Lucas held her tightly to his back.

As I scurried through the small crevasses hurriedly avoiding the creatures I heard come from behind, I also looked for my father, whom I could not sense. To my surprise the closest thing I found to humans were a few Starkorfs within the cave. *Why are there Starkorfs here? Are they under Taskatae's command?*

As we entered a larger area with a small flame lighting the room, I saw five eggs on the same dark wooden pedestals I saw the first time I was attacked by Taskatae. Within the eggs there were living beings, their form unknown to me.

Something was living inside of them. My mind was quickly distracted as a creature hurriedly approached the same room. A beak crept out from the shadows and a sliver of light revealed its face. Scales framed large orange owl eyes. It stood upright onto two back legs like a human would, its two thin arms trailing into long claws.

I held the only blade I had, Aeisha, ready to protect mum with my life. Feeling unbalanced by the disappearance of Aeisha's partnered blade, I prepared myself for battle. Slowly Lucas and I walked back toward the other crevasse.

I now felt the presence of the Elemental Breather, Taskatae, and another beast that waited for us outside. Behind this one creature who now confronted us, a build-up of other creatures followed from behind. We must escape now and prepare for the confrontation with Taskatae. *I must protect my mother.*

The ugly creature's scales lifted slightly and they began to quiver and rattle as it opened its beak and let out an excruciating squeal. The sound lingered down my spine as it charged for me. As its eyes were set on me, I rolled to the side, distracting it from going toward Lucas and my mother. As it turned its long neck to where I was, I jumped toward it, cutting its left eye.

The creature screamed even more horrifically as its limbs flung from side to side, hitting me in the stomach as it lunged for me once again. Its scale-like skin was cutting into my already injured stomach. Thrown to the wall, I hit it hard, dropping to my feet and rolling against the wall as the creature once again tried to plunge its head into my stomach. The part of the cave it just collided with began to crack.

As it threw its head toward me once again I projected my Shield so it collided forcefully under the pressure of its own strength. As it stood slightly disorientated for a moment, I ran toward the wall, jumping onto it so I could plunge my blade into the creature. I wrapped my single Aeisha over the back of its neck but there was no damage because of its scaly skin. It thrashed around at the graze Aeisha left. I instinctively grabbed the back of its neck before being thrown over.

Misfeata began to stir within me as the creature's thrashing loosened my grip on Aeisha and I almost let her slip. Although forcefully

83

keeping my grip on my blade, Misfeata still stirred within, irritating me; my mind feeling as if it were slowly slipping as her presence crept forward. *I mustn't let her in.* I heard her disgruntled snarl as she heard that thought before I quickly concentrated on forbidding her access to my body, forcefully pushing her back down within me.

As I held the creature firmly between my hands I projected my Shield between my palms, crushing down on the creature's neck. A loud crack was heard and it dropped to the ground heavily. I jumped off quickly collecting my stance and dropping my Shield so I could yet again press it into the ground so I could feel what was surrounding us. I was startled to discover other creatures were following us from deep within the cave; Scott and Paige still fighting them off. I collected Lucas's hand, once again leading him into the dark whilst trying to ignore my mother's disorientated cries.

Everything will be okay. I must get her out and then everything will be okay, I tried to convince myself, before tears spilled from my eyes. I looked at my quivering mother; my guardian was falling apart in front of my very eyes.

Preparing myself for the fight to come, I took in flames from the entrance of the cave. I faded my Shield within my feet and projected as strongly as I could around myself, as Taskatae stood not too far from the outside of the cave. As I did this, I felt the tickle of Lucas's do the same as he would have known a threat would be approaching for me to do so.

Our Shields tickled over our hands and I looked at our hands entwined. I was scared for the fight were about to face, knowing that his Shield didn't fully cover him as my mother lay on his back. And my mother was completely unprotected. *We must get her away safely.*

I let go of his hand, bursting out of the cave where instantly the control of my body was taken from me, as Taskatae stood in front of me, her hand held in front of her. A giant beast two times her height hovered behind her, making her look insignificant in comparison.

I looked in horror as it had the resemblance of some sort of reptile creature with wings. I looked into its blue, wide eyes. Terrified, my mother screamed and thrashed, ripping at Lucas's hair and throwing him to the ground before fleeing into the bushes. Because of her sudden outburst of energy, the creature took an interest in her. Swinging its large head toward her, it began to run.

Chapter Twelve- Broken

$\mathscr{L}$ucas scampered onto his feet, and then instinctively he was running to reach my mother in time as I was held against my will. Taskatae dropped the control she had over my body and settled her focus on Lucas. To my despair he stood awkwardly under her control.

As soon as her hold of me dropped, I ran for my mother. Taskatae directed her power between Lucas and I. She continued to alternate between the both of us as we tried our hardest to reach my mother. She ran blindly, frightened of the giant beast that rapidly followed her. Taskatae had control of both Lucas and me; it was futile. I tried my hardest to reach her to no avail. My eyes widened as I realized I was about to witness my own mother's death.

I tried summoning Misfeata, pulling her from the tight lock I once had of her, hoping that within these few pivotal seconds she could do something. *If anyone has the strength to save my mother and fight with Taskatae, it is Misfeata.* She stirred within and happily reached within my skin, taking possession of my body and jumping toward the giant beast with rapid speed. My head was pulled down by Taskatae's invisible strings, plunging me into the ground face first. I rolled over my own body, the pain excruciating as I had no control of my body.

Fear struck me, as I realized not only did my Shield against Taskatae not work, but neither did Misfeata's. As we breathed heavily into the ground, Misfeata looked up from beneath my thick eyelashes to watch my mother scream as the dragon-like creature's hand swiped at her. I could only watch in horror.

A large black snake burst from the ground using its forehead's strength to push against the beast's open hand. The snake had two iridescent pink eyes. He looked at me before throwing the creature off and using his tail to swipe the beast heavily across the ground. It was thrown into surrounding bushes.

Scott.

My mother wailed, coughed, and spluttered into the dirt, clutching at her chest and fainting. I felt the restraints lift from my body as Misfeata lunged for Taskatae, angered by her attack on us. *I wonder if Misfeata has ever had someone else take control of her, just as she does to others.*

Taskatae tried to concentrate on controlling Scott in his snake form, quickly being distracted by Misfeata who jumped for her now, taking hold of her and throwing us into the ground once again.

Lucas did the same before being thrown just as we had. Taskatae was beginning to become infuriated as she had to continuously throw us off instead of attacking her target, Scott, as he wavered in front of my mother protectively. The beast regained its stance, angered by being attacked.

Paige ran from the cave, running for my mother. She helped her to safety as Lucas and Misfeata continued to distract Taskatae. She had very little time to control someone else, especially Scott or Paige.

This was Scott's chance to fight the woman he claimed to have killed his mother and his pink eyes radiated with the glow of death. *He wants to kill Taskatae today; this is his revenge and his motive, driven by hatred and bloodlust.* His pink eyes flashed with black as they were absorbed by the raging spirit inherent in an Elemental Breather.

Taskatae flushed with anger, whistling loudly as she no longer had hold of Lucas or Misfeata. The ground shook beneath us as more of the same creatures we once fought piled from the cave entrance and toward us, lunging at Scott. Their beaks ripped at his scaled skin while he thrashed around irritated, and he changed himself into something so small that my keen eye could not see clearly where he disappeared to, away from the piling creatures.

Upon his disappearance the creatures took a moment to understand that they were only attacking one another wildly. Taskatae clapped angrily, dispersing the creatures that fought amongst themselves. She could now focus on Lucas and me, and we held our weapons before us, projecting our Shields.

Taskatae held her hand out toward the giant dragon-like beast, pulling it forward as if strings were attached. It roared in angst and she narrowed her eyes on the beast that was obviously trying to resist her. *Does Taskatae not have complete control of it?* As if hearing me, she pointed toward me. The beast followed her command on its thick legs. It came pounding towards me. I braced myself as the enormity of its being increased as it approached.

Misfeata pulled my lips into a smile. She took a perverse pleasure in the fight at hand. *Fighting is all that Misfeata knows. And now I have allowed Misfeata to awaken within me for the sake of my mother.*

Misfeata jumped for the dragon, projecting her Shield and holding Aeisha. It seemed to throw Misfeata off balance only having the one Immortal Blade instead of two. The dragon forced down its hand as Misfeata tested her strength. The creature pushed harshly down over her head as she held her arms up, placing most of her energy into the top of her Shield and therefore protecting herself against the beast's might. Another smile crept past my lips. She was pleased to find her Shield alone matched the beast's strength.

Her hands seeped through her Shield where she forcefully pushed the beast off of her, jumping between its hands and cutting between its fingers as she jumped onto the creatures arm, trailing Aeisha alongside it. The effect was insignificant on such scaled and hard skin.

One of the owl-like creatures jumped, trying to bite at our stomach. Misfeata jumped off, standing and re-evaluating the situation in the dark. Taskatae controlled the other beasts, drawing attention to them and commanding them to focus.

'If I kill her, they cannot be controlled by her,' Misfeata thought to herself, ignoring my outstretched hand. She was trying to gain eternal control of my body once again.

Have I lost my own inner battle? Has she locked me away forever? Am I now trapped completely?

Misfeata ran for Taskatae as Lucas continued fighting the creatures behind us, blocking their view of me as I ran toward their master. Taskatae already knew we approached, and was looking at us with annoyed eyes. Her hand outstretched to us, taking control, and dragging us along the ground to her feet.

Taskatae's blue eyes stared at Misfeata with disgust but as her eyes continued to search in what seemed to be my soul, I realized she was in search of me. She was looking deeper than Misfeata as her lips curled in hatred and a small snarl ripped from her lips, reminding me too much of Raven, as the little girl had once done the same to me. The first Starkorf I had chosen to kill. They looked so similar and yet it must be only coincidence that I must face another enemy that looked like the first I had met.

"I can create as many artificial children as I please," she said angrily her voice unentertained and cold. "And yet you kill the only child I bore from my own body." She grabbed my chin, as Misfeata flushed angrily at having her body controlled against her will. She thrashed from beneath Taskatae's control.

I killed her only child?

A small knife slipped under Taskatae's long flowing dark-blue sleeve as she stared at me with hatred. She had every intention of slitting my throat.

A large wolf lunged for Taskatae and she was forced to take a few steps back. Scott had reappeared and now tore viciously at her arm. She held her arms out to him, instantly changing him to human form. He frowned at the sudden change. She continued clenching her fist, flustered as Scott's fingers began to tremble and his shoulders began to roll awkwardly.

Her arm was heavily bleeding and her blue eyes focused on Scott as he stared at her just as narrowly. Slowly he took one step forward and then another; each seemed to be less awkward. *Is Scott able to evade her control? Is he immune to her Element?*

Scott changed back into his wolf form, confirming my suspicions. Now that Taskatae no longer had control of Misfeata as she was distracted by Scott, we jumped for Taskatae, plunging Aeisha deep into her stomach. Misfeata froze with Aeisha deep in her stomach, watching as Taskatae smiled. She dropped to the ground on her knees, letting a whimper of a laugh pass through her before she coughed a patch of blood on my face, Misfeata smiling in response at her victory.

Before fully projecting her Shield, Misfeata was thrown across the dirt, slightly knocking her from consciousness. I seized the moment, taking control of my body and locking her away once again. As she came to consciousness she was furious to find I had regained control of my body once again. I could now feel how I was aching everywhere in my battered body and especially in my bleeding stomach.

The dragon beast ran for me after throwing Misfeata so forcefully away from Taskatae, whom it was protecting. Lucas cut it from behind, dodging the other creatures that flustered behind, trying to attack him. His large sword cut deeper than what Aeisha was capable of.

As heavily injured as Taskatae was, she still fought against Scott, who was immune to her control. But it didn't stop her from controlling her creatures as she summoned them to fight against him and he continued changing into different forms according to what best suited his situation. He dodged and then attacked in various forms.

Lucas circled the beast as I did the same, slightly hobbling at first with an injury I hadn't acquired myself. I jumped for the creature, slashing at its face as it roared, infuriated, and crushed its hands down on Lucas's projected Shield. Taking advantage of the situation, I leapt for it. I was knocked off my feet and thrown into the bushes with such a forceful blow from the creature's quick reflexes that a ringing in my ear created a disorientated dizziness.

My mother looked over me, her hands clutched together at her chest. She was crying. I rose to my knees so I could look at her evenly. I tried my hardest to center myself as the world around me seemed to swirl.

"That beast," my mother said, pointing into the direction of the dragon-like creature, her mouth opening and closing as she could say nothing else.

"It's okay, Mum," I said trying to reassure her as Paige came to my side. I was reassured by Paige's presence. She made her intentions very clear as she held her knife in a defensive stance in case any creatures followed. Much to my surprise, Paige was protecting my mother. I now knew I could believe in her and trust her judgment. She knew that we were fighting today to protect my mother and to deter the creature's infatuation with her. Paige had acknowledged that objective and I was grateful. I had now learned I could rely on Paige and I was thankful to her for fighting alongside me, instead of only opposing the enemy.

Today, she fights with me.

The beast had followed me into the bushes, its eyes widening at the sight of my mother who wailed loudly behind me, hands still clutched together pitifully. Lucas jumped from behind onto the beast, dodging as it tried to fling him against a tree. Paige jumped for it, throwing her black blade into the creature's blue eye. It wailed and thrashed its head back and forth wildly.

I must protect my mother.

I ran toward it with Aeisha, ready to place all my force into it. I aimed for its chest, projecting my Shield at the end of my blade's handle, feeling the bond and connection between us as it took to my power and Shield smoothly. I pressed as much force, strength, and energy as I could into its chest. Lucas threw me his long sword. Catching it, I knew I could take no chances despite having forced Aeisha into the beast. I stabbed Lucas's long blade into the same spot, taking no chances. His blade ran along my own and pierced the beast's chest.

My mother screamed, her noise piercing my ears as she screamed out "No!" Scott ran from the bushes, bloodied and eyes wide as he looked back at me. I dropped to the ground, prepared for the creature to lash out once again. Instead it stayed frozen like a statue and slowly its scales began to quiver with a piercing noise, sounding like shattering glass. The scales dropped and beneath it the creature's core shrunk down toward me.

I choked on my own breath, realizing what I had done. The creature was not a beast at all but a human. I held my arms out wide for him, clinging to him desperately, his blue eyes staring back at me, blind. His red hair was sticking to his face with dirt.

Dad.

I dropped to my knees beneath him, holding him up as Aeisha and Lucas's blade stuck out from his chest. I frantically searched over the blades, my eyes blurred with the tears that came from my eyes.

"Dad!" I croaked in a broken voice, numb to all that surrounded me. Never had anything been so surreal. *This cannot be real*. "Dad!" I screamed, desperately trying to fathom how the beast I just killed could be my father. "Dad!" I screamed again, wailing as I clung to his filthy, cold body. I was desperately pulling him closer as I cried into his neck. I scratched at his back trying to pull him closer, nursing him as if he were sick.

Only sick, I tried to convince myself.

I could no longer breathe as I felt my own life being swept away. But it was not my body that was breaking, I was not dying myself. My heart now broke; my family was shattered. I just killed my own father.

"Dad!" I whispered into his ear with futile hope that it would wake him. *It must wake him*, I frantically thought. My mother hugged me from behind, making my mistake so much more monstrous. *I am a murderer. I love my Dad. I killed my Dad. I am a monster.*

I screamed into the dark night.

I don't want this torture. I can't have killed him. I love my Dad.

The image of his smile continued flashing in my memory: his dad jokes, his kindness; my dear father. I have just killed the man I have loved so much. Darkness surrounded me, as finally I was broken. After everything that has happened, this was what broke me.

I love you Dad.

Chapter Thirteen- Break of Dawn

I held his lifeless body, crying into his cold neck. I begged repeatedly for him to come back and return to me. How could this have happened? How could I have killed my own father? My mother held her cold hands over mine as we hugged my father. We had no time to say goodbye; there was no farewell in such circumstances.

The night edged into coldness as we cried until we could release no more tears. There were no more attackers. Lucas, Scott, and Paige, left my mother and me to our grief. Night passed over and the sun slowly came up. My mother now slept behind me, cradling me as she lightly snored against my back. She had cried herself to sleep.

I wondered if she had she known this whole time that the beast was Dad, perhaps that was why she was so frightened of him and ran away. *Did Taskatae do this to him? What happened to my dear mother?* My mind ran over so many thoughts and questions as I numbly tried to evade the reality of my father's death.

I could feel something within me had instantly changed. I felt a darkness sweep over me. This world has brought darkness into my life and in that moment I would let the darkness consume me. *I will look after my mother and make sure she is safe by finding her a place to stay. And then by my own hands, I will kill Taskatae, as I am sure it is her who has done this.*

"Karla."

Lucas's soft voice broke my concentration and at his soft tone I couldn't help but cling tighter to my father, fearful that Lucas had come to take him away. I never wanted to be parted with my father. *Not again.* Paul wouldn't take him away. Paul had been with me for so long now looking for them, and now that I've found them, it was death I faced, not happiness.

This is not real, this is a nightmare, and Paul will wake me up soon. After looking so long for him, I do not want this to be the end. So many beings with abilities... someone can help him. Someone can heal him so I am no longer feeling this brokenness, it can be fixed.

I looked at Scott with determination as he sat on a fallen tree, now fully healed from any of the injuries he has acquired. *Did Scott know about the beast's true identity? Is that why he looked at me remorsefully after plunging Aeisha into him? He can heal him. Of course he can, he is an*

Elemental Breather, and he can heal himself within moments and then enter others bodies as well. Scott can make this better.

"You can fix this," I said in a much lower tone toward Scott than I had thought I would. I ignored Lucas who had his hand outstretched to me. I looked at Scott through dried eyes as he cringed under my tone. No matter how low it was, he could hear me. "Scott," I said, angry now with him for I knew he heard me.

"Karla, I cannot heal one who is already dead," he spoke gently, looking toward the ground.

"That is a lie," I rejected, tears finding their way down my face once again. "You can do it." I raised myself with my father's weight underneath me, trying to lift him so Scott could heal him. "I believe in you." Shock had still consumed my body and I choked once again on my words. Scott shook his head at me, still staring at the ground.

What will I do?

As my legs buckled beneath me, Lucas caught me from behind. Paige grabbed my father, who still had the two blades sticking out from his chest, and slowly took him away. I tried my hardest to cling onto him again, reaching out for him desperately as Lucas held me from behind.

Under Lucas's touch I crumbled, my knees completely buckling as I turned myself into his chest, crying at the evilness that I now felt consumed me. *What will I do?* For a long time Lucas embraced me as we awkwardly sat on the ground, Lucas rocking me back and forth and brushing through my long hair. I felt so vulnerable as if I had nowhere to go other than Lucas's arms.

"Karla." My mother's voice broke my grief and I looked back into her concerned face. I thought she would hate me, be repulsed by what I had turned into and all I had done. Instead, she gave me a fake smile, a smile for comfort like she always did. My mother now looked like herself, the mother I remembered, not the one who was so traumatized in the cave. "Karla, let us bury your father," she said as a tear slipped from her eye. She looked at Lucas for a moment analytically, and then at me.

"But I—..." I tried to interject but she pressed her finger to my lips, instructing me to be quiet.

"I watched your father be turned into that beast. And in no way could I help him. What that woman did to him was monstrous. But what you gave him was freedom, Karla. He would have been trapped within that beastly form forever. You saved your father. He couldn't have been any more proud. I am only ashamed of myself for being so weak," she admitted, dropping her gaze.

I was shocked to hear her say such things, pardoning what I had done. Before I could say anything Lucas had loosened his grip on me, reminding me that it was he who gave me comfort. I looked up into his deep brown eyes, surprised as I still clung onto his shirt desperately. I dropped my hands, unsure of why I had clung to him so tightly. I looked back at my mother who began to walk behind Paige and Scott upon dawn's break as they carried my father with them.

Lucas held his hand out to me, offering to help me up as I still awkwardly sat on the ground. Hesitantly I took it, accepting his help no matter how much I had claimed to hate him. I so desperately clung to him now.

After a long walk deeper into the forest, a ceremony of sorts had already been organized. Was this what they had done last night as my mother and I cried? I didn't even noticed any of them leave. The ceremony site was upon a hill in an open field where one beautiful tree stood alone. Next to it was a river that continued further than what my eye could see. The colors of the rising sun glistened across the land, making the leaves appear to be a beautiful orange in an autumn glow.

As we approached, the others were already waiting for us. The others have followed. Ashley, Paul, and Harmony were present, even though we were separated for only a short period of time. I let go of Lucas's hand, confused as I quickened my pace toward Paul, who did the same toward me. As I found him he held me tightly, hugging me, and whispering into my ear as he embraced me.

"I am so sorry," Paul gushed as he kissed my forehead, making me want to cry once more. I closed my eyes inhaling his smell, ashamed that I had let anything come between us. Paul was right, we should have never come, but if I hadn't, I wouldn't have found my parents. I have learned much, yet at a very expensive cost. Paige and Scott kept my father hidden from me. My mother was now approaching me and holding my hand as she greeted Paul, sad under the circumstances.

Ashley and Harmony also stood near the tree, their heads dipped in respect. Had Scott or Lucas contacted them telling them to come? As Lucas approached them, Ashley only shuffled slightly, saying nothing as he paid his respects.

We approached my father who was on a wooden plank. The swords were now taken out and replaced with numerous beautiful flowers that covered his wound. He looked so peaceful; there was even a hint of a smile on his face. His face was now cleaner as someone had wiped away the filth; his radiant red hair framed his pale white skin. Looking at him, I couldn't believe this was our goodbye. I tried to be the strong woman he raised me to be, yet I could not help but let the tears run down my face. I kissed his forehead, touching his cold hands where they were entwined over his chest.

I was too late to prevent this from happening, and as much as I ached to see my father dead, I couldn't help but be pulled by the hatred that resided within me for revenge. *I want to kill Taskatae for what she has done to my family.*

Silence echoed in the wind that brushed through us, giving me a chill. I stared at my loving father; my mother holding my hand tightly as she stared at him as well. She gave Scott a small nod as he dipped his head in respect and slowly slid my father into the water.

Miraculously, the pile of wood my father drifted down the river on burst into a small flame, which soon covered him entirely. Without looking away from him I felt the presence of another two people approach. I knew the fire could have only come from one Elemental Breather and that was Trish. A low squeak was heard as Max Jacket's wheelchair stopped by my side. I continued to watch after my father, distraught to see him go.

I could no longer see the flames of my father as he was carried down the river. The sun glistened in my eyes. Still holding my mother's hand, I looked away from my father and down at Max Jacket's milky blind eyes, unsurprised at his arrival. Max's knowledge of certain things ceased to amaze me. It made me question as to why now he decided to reveal himself after hiding for so many months and whether it was Scott who had told them of our location.

Trish looked no different; her short red hair was placed in a bun and her black dress was of the Elemental Breather's exotic material. She stared at Scott as if disappointed. Hesitantly he approached them, somewhat hiding behind me as he did so. Perhaps he was not over his fearfulness of his family as he had once insinuated.

Paige and Harmony came to collect my mother. "Come with us, Dear," Paige said gently, grabbing her hand slowly as my mother stared at me. I ushered her away, reassuring her everything would be alright. I had to make sure it was, as angering Max Jacket and Trish for any reason could be a huge gamble and one I could not risk now.

Paul, Ashley, and Lucas followed me. Max Jacket smiled to himself and grabbed my hand slowly, kissing it, much to my disgust.

"My condolences, Karla. No one should have to experience losing a family member while still at such a young age," Max lamented, looking saddened.

"I too am disheartened to have received word of such a tragedy. I would also like to offer my condolences," Trish said, giving me a small curtsy.

"Why are you here?" I asked bluntly, looking at Borac who was strapped to Trish's back. They have been in hiding to protect this sword, so why reveal themselves now? Why come to me after all that had happened?

"My, you have changed much since we last spoke," Max said, smiling to himself.

"I do not have time for your riddles today, Max," I spat harshly, infuriated by his insincere smile.

"I came because my son requested I do so," he clarified, his milky eyes flashing black as his pupils became engulfed at the mention of his name. Lucas, Ashley, and Paul, readied their defenses. I didn't interpret his anger as a threat toward us but as an expression of disapproval of his son, Scott, who was now hiding behind me. "And also, I believe we have a common enemy. Taskatae." he said seriously, no longer smiling. "Where is she?"

I did not know where she went or if she survived. The only one who would know that was Scott, who was fighting her before I was thrown into the trees. All the creatures disappeared after my father's death. I turned my back to Max, looking at Scott questioningly.

"The Taskatae we fought..." Scott began, his voice quivering in his father's presence. "It was not the real one; she created a duplicate of herself. However, her ability was still in use, so Taskatae must have been close by to control her creatures. After I realized this, I swept the area for her but couldn't find her. She vanished together with her creatures. The Taskatae we fought and Misfeata wounded shattered into nothing after—...." Scott stopped himself; he didn't need to say the words. We all stood still in the silence of his unspoken words. I had killed the beast that was actually my father.

"It was a set-up," Scott continued. All eyes jumped to Lucas and I fought the nauseating feeling of betrayal from him once again. This time the cost was my own father's life.

"I didn't know," Lucas protested firmly and defensively. "This is all I knew, I wasn't forcing you all to come. You chose to. If I had known it to be a set up, I wouldn't have suggested it." He paused angrily. "Karla, you must believe me," he said, seeking redemption.

It was as if his words crept beneath my skin and I looked from his hurt eyes to Paul who now looked at me differently. He looked away as if he too could sense the different feelings I now held toward Lucas, despite my spoken words of hatred.

How can I know if Lucas is speaking the truth? How do I know whom to believe? I can't even trust myself, so how can I trust anyone else?

"No matter, I believe she will return," Max surmised, staring blindly over my handle of Aeisha. Taskatae still had the partnered blade. "We have been recently ambushed for Borac by Starkorfs who were obviously no match for us. Coincidence, wouldn't you say? Not only have we been attacked for the Immortal Blade, Borac, that we carry but for your Immortal Blades, Aeisha, as well, By Starkorf and Taskatae creatures alike. Either they have gone to her for her power and protection after Praytar's death or his sons are in alliance with Taskatae."

Lucas flinched under the accusation, looking at everyone defensively once again. "I haven't spoken to Nathanial since my father's death and don't you think if I was after your blades, Karla, I would have tried to take them by now." As much doubt as I had of his innocence I believed him.

"Then I guess we put up camp and wait for them," I suggested, determined to be the one to kill Taskatae with my own hands. *She destroyed my father and for that I will demand answers before killing her.* She is now not only Misfeata's enemy but my own. And I will not allow us to be defeated.

This I will never forgive.

Chapter Fourteen- Safety

$\mathcal{S}$hortly after my brief discussion with Max Jacket, I found my mother once again. Paige and Harmony left us quietly and I heard the others talk of setting up a tent that they had inside the car that was a fair walk from here.

"Come here, sweetie," my mother said, grabbing my hand. She held it firmly and motioned for me to sit with her. "A lot has changed, hasn't it?" she said gently, watching the gray clouds take over the bright sky; no doubt that was because of Max Jacket's presence.

"Are you disappointed in me?" I asked, upset at what I had become and the monster that lay within me.

"I am not disappointed in you, nor should you ever think that. Your father and I were only disappointed in ourselves for not protecting you. We never wanted you to see this part of life. We had thought for so many years that you wouldn't be involved. Until that day we had to call you, scared out of our minds," she confessed, sounding disheartened. "Your father and I only ever wanted to protect you."

"I am safe," I soothed, trying to convince myself in the process.

"I can see you have surrounded yourself with those who will protect you," she agreed reassuringly. "That young man with the blonde hair; and I am most surprised to see Paul Stuart here amongst the chaos."

"Yea," I confirmed, ashamed that I was the reason why he was involved. "It's a long story."

As much as I wanted this reunion, I felt a distance between us as there was much I didn't want her to know of my journey. There were so many evil things that I had done that I couldn't bear for her to know about. I couldn't speak of Misfeata to her, what would she say? How frightened would she be? She would only blame herself because I was still in her belly when I contracted Misfeata's blood. There was much I wanted to do to protect them yet I have failed in so many ways. I endlessly searched for them for months with Paul's help, and now to have my mother so close within my grasp, I have never felt such distance between us.

"I know you have been through a lot since it seemed we abandoned you," she said, tears sliding down her face. "But there was not one day that we didn't try to fight to come back to you. I am so surprised to see that you have found us; and you can fight?" she hesitantly asked, clearly frightened of my answer.

I made no answer, unsure of how to explain.

"Have you turned into one of them?" she breathed in. Was she hoping that I have been in school all this time in Roperia, working hard and waiting for their return?

"I don't know what I am," I answered honestly. "I didn't have the chance to go back home straight away, Mum. I was taken to another place for a long time. I was taught some things. I've changed a lot. I went home to find you, but you had been taken, and I've searched for you ever since alongside Paul. He has helped me a lot."

"And the other boy?" she asked.

I paused. What was Lucas to me? He had betrayed me, kept many truths from me, but he had also trained me and protected me once. I had once seen his kind side. I was reluctant to acknowledge it again in case he betrayed me the same.

"He has taught me much. I have seen many things I wish I never had, too." A tear slid down my face as I thought of Dad, of my mother watching me as I stabbed him. "I am murderous, I have killed so many," I admitted, choking out the words. I expected my mother's disappointment, even her rejection. But I could not lie to her, not after what she had seen and after what I've done. Misfeata she doesn't need to know of, but my own hands murdering others, she must. She must know that — she must know what her own daughter has become.

After a long pause she held my hands tighter, her blue eyes looked at me, saddened. "I learned a long time ago that there are creatures in this world that should not exist and if these are the creatures you speak of being murderous toward, then kill them all," she said surprising me. "I watched them kill a small town, your Uncle Kyle's wife, and now my husband. I don't want you to be of this world; we must go home together and fix everything. But I believe that my daughter would only do such a thing if she had to."

Mortified by her justification, I felt even more ashamed. My mother was the kindest woman I had ever known and yet her heart had been blackened too by all that the Starkorfs and Elemental Breathers created. Was there no good in any of them? If she knew that Misfeata resided in me, she would be ashamed of me for being consumed by such darkness.

"I don't know if I can go back with you now, Mum," I said, disheartened as her eyes looked back desperately and emptily.

"You don't have to be a part of this anymore. You said you were looking for us, Karla. You have found us. I don't want you to be in any danger and most of all, I don't want you going near that woman."

"If we leave together she will only follow us. The only way I can protect you is by finding her first," I said, with Taskatae in mind.

"It is not your job to look after me, Karla. It is my job as the parent to look after you. I already failed once; please let me look after you. I can't lose you too," she begged.

The sun now reached the tops of the trees and I looked into my mother's eyes, searching for an understanding that I would not find. *I know my mother loves me and I her, but so much has changed within us in only a few months*. We were now divided by two separate worlds. That truth was now hitting me hard and pained my chest. How do I tell my mother that I have the ability to Shield? It was something she despised most and was disgusted by. How can I return with her, knowing that if she knew she would hate me?

"I must," I said, the words sticking within my throat.

"No, not that woman... she is able to change any living creature she wants, like your father, when they are fertile."

"What are you talking about?" I asked, confused by what she meant.

"That woman, she has some sort of capability and she calls herself 'Mother'. Anything fertile, such as the eggs she carries around, or even a human being, she can change them. Modify them even. That was how she turned your father into a beast. I am no longer fertile; I cannot produce children so she couldn't hurt me. But your father she turned into a ghastly beast. Inside his cage beside me she slowly turned him into an animal. I watched him deteriorate and loose his humanity. She would carry colored eggs around with her, doing something to them; and when they hatched, creatures would come from them and quickly grow. She then threw them into the cage your father was contained in and made them fight, enraging your father even more, until he was completely taken over.

Your father was lost and gone. She could make my body do anything she wanted to, like I was some form of puppet. She is somehow able to manipulate anything in another's body and although she couldn't change me, she hurt me," she finished, closing her eyes at the memories and trying to calm herself as she took in her shaking hands. "I can't have that happen to you. I love you, Karla," she added, raising her hand to my cheek and stroking it. Her gentle touch made me crumble at the love I had for my parents.

The hatred within me was building. I had now learned of what Taskatae has done to them and how. I wondered if the others knew of this truth. As much as my mother wanted to protect me, I could not put her in any more danger. I couldn't let her risk her life against Taskatae or any of the Starkorfs, as they searched for me.

As my hand tightened around my mother's, my chest clenched and my lungs froze painfully. I cried out in pain, clutching at them. *Not now, I cannot die now. Not in front of my mother.* It felt as if daggers swept up my body, giving me a spine tingling chill as my body dropped to the side. I attempted to gasp for air to no avail. *My body is shutting down.*

My hearing quickly vanished as my mother screamed over me, screaming into the direction of the others as she frantically cried over me. I wanted to cup her face to tell her it would be okay. But there was much to this that was not okay and I couldn't move my hand to reassure her, even if I wanted to.

I was dragged further beneath my consciousness with a pain that broke into every part of my body. In front of my mother my body lost control and I spluttered blood onto her clothes, wishing for the pain to go away. It happened so much more quickly now and I was unable to scream or release any of the pain as it built up within me.

I so desperately wanted Paul to hurry with the syringe of adrenaline to help me awake and ultimately keep me alive. I could not risk falling unconscious, where Misfeata would be waiting. I called out for Paul desperately, but it was not him who first arrived by my side. Lucas tore off his leather glove frantically to cup my face. I could not feel the burning sensation as he drained me.

As my eyesight weaved in and out on Lucas who frantically yelled at me and Paige who now reassured my mother from behind, I was pulled under by Misfeata's grabbing hands as she reefed me from within, not giving me the chance to awake under the pain of my body. *Am I really dying now? Is this it?*

Frantically, I tried to pull against Misfeata's will but as Lucas drained me, my eyes drooped and I was taken back within myself. Misfeata was greedily waiting.

Chapter Fifteen- Purpose

$\mathcal{I}$was in a barren woodland, spinning in circles as darkness crept from everywhere. I could sense Misfeata but she has not yet revealed herself. I feared what surprise she had in store for me, or what kind of approach she would take. All I knew was I could not let my Shield down and become vulnerable to her. If I was in a state of vulnerability she would engulf my body and push me away as she possessed it for her own madness.

A twig snapped from behind me as her green long dress trailed along the broken shrubbery. Although it was day, there was a chill in the air and the creatures that lurked within the woodland were silent. Her moss-green eyes stared at me for a moment's contemplation as I watched her cautiously, ready for any attack.

She gave an uncertain smile under sad eyes. She sat on a fallen log close by. I burrowed my eyebrows in confusion, unsure about her tactics. What kind of approach is this? After a moment of thick silence she finally spoke.

"I am sorry for your loss and the pain your loved one has left behind. I had never heard of Taskatae's Element in all my years, but I do believe you did the right thing."

Looking at her for much longer than I anticipated I would, I couldn't say anything. I searched my surroundings, trying to be sure that this was the true Misfeata who had attacked me so many times before.

"I know I have mistreated you, child, but I will not interrupt one's mourning. I too once had a family and know what it is like to have that stripped bare, to have one savagely taken from you. But I do think that you freed him. I do not think you should reflect on your actions as one of grotesqueness. You were protecting your mother and there was no coming back for your father. He would have forever been in the form and mindset of that beast. You might as well have thought of him as already dead.

He could never come back; it was not he who existed. He could not have returned from such a form. I know much about the repercussions of such a transformation. You saved him from such a fate."

Broken by her words, but still on guard, I struggled to understand why she showed me kindness in a time such as this. She had done much harm to me and hurt me in more ways than just physically. I was disposable to her and yet she was entrapped within me — I was the last to hold her bloodline. Neither of us enjoyed this conditioning, so why show me kindness now?

"You always forget I can hear what you are thinking and we are of the same entity. I know I have done terrible things to you but you have no idea how infuriating it is to be locked away for so long, constantly being able to watch, yet forced to be inactive," Misfeata explained, watching after a crow that flew by.

I inhaled sharply. "I have no sympathy for you. This is my body. I will not give you my body for a stupid war. Of all the people to lose to, I will not lose to you."

"I already know all that you tell me. Naturally, I know as you resist me all the time," she said with a slight smile before straightening her expression and looking at me seriously. I could not believe how civilized she was being. "I don't like the new threat of that Elemental Breather, Taskatae. Never have I had the issue of having no control of my own body. I do not like it and such a threat must be disposed of. I don't like her interest in Aeisha and now we have to find the real Taskatae to obtain my partnered Immortal Blade. I will not let my invaluable Aeisha be kept as some trophy by such a woman," she growled.

Unsure of what to say, I stared at her for a long moment cautiously; still frightened she would attack at any moment. I saw the irony in her displeasure of someone controlling her, just like she always did to me.

"Please," she said, listening to my thoughts. "I need you to heal your body properly. There is only so much strength within you because of your old wounds." She gestured to my bleeding stomach. It was the very wound she put there months ago as she tried to transform my body into part beast as we fought Praytar, Lucas's dad and descendant of Tyran.

"It is you who put these wounds here," I reminded her forcefully. I suffered everyday as my healing ability could only slightly glaze over it, constantly reopening because of the slightest awkward movement.

"So I did. But even I cannot heal those wounds. Upon observation I think I have found your hero, someone who can heal such devastating wounds."

I questioned inwardly if someone could truly heal such awful wounds and at that thought, it dawned on me: Scott could heal me.

"That is correct. That Elemental Breather has a rare ability and one that can benefit us for our preparation for the next confrontation with Taskatae. You need rest; and then after your body is fully healed we will find her and retrieve Aeisha and you can have your revenge."

"But where do we go from here?" I asked, for once agreeing with her scheme.

"When we ventured into the cave there were Starkorfs present. Your Starkorf lover, Lucas, has found them already."

"He's not my lover!" I exclaimed.

"You may be able to ignore your own feelings but you cannot blind me of the obvious. It is irrelevant. He has gone to retrieve information from them. After all, he is like a prince to them; he is the enemy and next to inherit Tyran. Although you don't seem to mind any longer about his Starkorf position, I will still enjoy taking his life when he is last to receive Tryan. My brother will no longer have a body to possess."

I was surprised to find my fists clenched and I took a step toward Misfeata threateningly. A crooked smile spread across her lips as she looked at my clenched fists.

"It differs not how you feel about it, enjoy what little time you have. Now you fight the realization that the belonging you once had with your old life and family is not one you can return to. Enjoy what you can now because I will take your body when the time permits me to do so and you will have no other option than to call for my strength again."

With her final words spoken, the trees around me started to bend inward, wrapping rubber branches around my body, quickly restraining me. They trapped my movement as I struggled, Misfeata disappearing amongst them.

The branches dragged me to the ground, my legs crushed as they merged with the center of the Earth. I stirred beneath the dirt that swallowed my cries for help. My hand stretched out for the surface and I cried as pain engulfed me.

At my calling, a bright light pulled me from the sunken darkness. Someone from the outside helped me recover my consciousness, away from Misfeata's influence.

"Karla," Paul exhaled, pressing his hand firmly on my shoulder to hold me down. I gasped for air, perspiration on my face. At the sight of him I sat up and took in my surroundings, gasping as I realized I was okay and alive.

I remembered my last conscious realization: I was dying and Lucas tried to save me.

Paul and I were within a small tent alone, his long dark-brown hair slightly stuck to his face in the warmer weather. His beautiful green eyes glistened because of the small candle he held. His heavy breathing seemed intoxicating. It seemed to be the first I had inhaled since Misfeata had me choking on dirt beneath the ground.

"Paul," I breathed. I feared I had lost too much time since my body shut down on me. Paul had been too late to inject the adrenaline into me.

"Where's my mother?" I demanded, remembering her pained face as she watched me die for the first time. She had once heard me over the phone the first time it had happened to me. I wondered if she had known back then what was happening.

"She is safe. She is retrieving water from the river and boiling it to purify it for drinking. Harmony is hunting food for us alongside Paige and the others have gone into those caves, expecting to find some information. They mentioned something of other captives but Paige mentioned to me that Starkorfs were also within the cave. They are going in there to find where Taskatae may have next moved to," he explained, aiding me as I raised myself, wincing at my bandaged stomach.

"Now that you have found your mother, what will you do?" Paul asked me heavily, his eyes looking back at me distantly. I knew I had to face that he may no longer have the intention to follow me.

"I don't know," I honestly said.

Thinking of it for a moment, I felt ashamed for the response I was about to give him. For so long now we had ventured together as I had claimed to only be interested in finding my parents. Now, after finding them already, I could not give him the answer I think he most wanted. I could not yet return to a place to call home with him. "I think I will go after Taskatae with the others."

Paul's hand slowly dropped. He twisted the tips of my light-brown hair as he searched through it evenly, his eyes sad. "Karla, you owe them nothing."

Someone entered the small tent before I could respond and I looked up. Lucas stood strong in front of us. Paul dropped my hair, agitated, and shuffled slightly away from me. Lucas lowly grunted beneath his breath, breaking the awkward silence as he too searched the tent for no other reason than to not make uncomfortable eye contact.

"We have found where to look next," Lucas said carefully, as if already knowing I would follow. "The Starkorfs from within were gifts to Taskatae, only two were still mentally human, although physical manipulation was obvious. It appears they were gifts for her to do with as she pleased."

"Gifts from who?" I asked, looking at Paul. He sat stiffly, his shoulders hunched as he looked away from the both of us, listening.

"From my brother, Nathanial," Lucas admitted sternly. "I know where to find him."

"Why, because you're going to betray her again and it's a trap?" Paul accused angrily.

Lucas's jaw clenched as his fists tightened, his chest slightly rising as Paul stood in front of him tall. They measured one another with no words, hatred sparking between them. Paul nudged past Lucas, escaping into the darkness of night. I felt the pull to follow him.

"Paul..." I called out. I tried to get up, wincing as my stomach pulled me back into my sheets.

"Don't move," Lucas instructed, quickly aiding me and kneeling by my side. I pushed his hands away from me, remembering his touch alone had the ability to drain me. Although he had leather gloves on, I didn't want his touch to linger. Since his return I had been so confused, and amidst my own confusion I had hurt the person who I once claimed I would protect the most: Paul.

"Please, don't," I begged, sad with confusion. "Why did you have to come back?" His dark brown eyes stared back at me hurt, speechless as his shoulders slumped. "Please, just go," I said, closing my eyes and wishing for him to disappear.

A shudder of cold air brushed past me as the tent was opened and Lucas left. As I was now alone in the tent and looking at my bloodied stomach I could only sag in despair. *What am I doing?*

Chapter Sixteen- Fighting Ones Demons

A small mouse crept into my tent, squeaking as its pink eyes stared back at me. *Scott*. He materialized in front of me, changing from his tiny animal form to his human form. He straightened his blue suit and combed through the side of his white hair.

"Hiding from your father still, I see," I remarked bluntly.

"Hiding from your conflicting emotions still, I see," he responded sharply.

I dropped my façade of strength, knowing he was right. "Is it truly that obvious?" I sighed to myself grimly, realizing it was. *Is this why Paul is so hurt?* Apart from the fact that I was no longer willing to follow him back home, did he know that I no longer hated Lucas? My hatred was merely the sting of betrayal.

"Yes, my dear it is. May I suggest instead of letting your thoughts run over you like a roller coaster, you simply let your body react. You are always so analytical in every situation, although I can understand what persuaded you to be so tactful. But you are pushing both away," he explained, looking toward the tent that both had left from.

"Maybe it is for the best," I said, thinking out loud.

"You say that and yet you are still reluctant to tell them to leave," Scott said firmly. "You need to follow your instincts just this once, instead of your mind. You will hurt one or the other but it will save the wasted time involved with eventually hurting both."

"But I can't decide," I said honestly, surprised I was gushing my true feelings to Scott. "Paul is a part of my old life and he has followed me into my new one; he has supported me and helped me and done everything to be by my side, trying to protect me from all of this. Whereas Lucas understands what it is I am now. He accepts me for my curse and even my fate. One day we are fated to fight, and yet instead of fighting against me, he chooses to fight alongside me. He accepts this part of me, darkness and all, something I doubt even my own mother could accept."

"Perhaps you need to stop splitting yourself in two separate worlds. You are deeming yourself unfit for both because you do not yet know what it is you desire or what you are. You need to stop thinking of yourself as two different entities, even if you do have another person completely residing within you," he said with an awkward glance toward the tent roof, thinking over the situation.

"What will you do about your father?" I asked, accepting his advice but finding it to be somewhat of a contradiction when compared with his own situation.

"Well, my situation is entirely different. I know what I am and I am fabulous in doing so," he said with a sly smile. "My father, however, does not accept that and at a young age, I was shunned from revealing myself to others."

After a long moment of hesitation as we reflected on our respective situations, he insisted I lift my shirt to look at my stomach. As Misfeata once said, his healing was unworldly. His hands seemed to melt underneath the bandage. The warmth of his touch literally rose beneath my skin as he pressed firmly into it. After a long moment of concentration Scott finally spoke again, breaking the silence.

"What happened to your father..." he began, broaching the subject carefully, "also happened to my mother. That is how I know of Taskatae." He gave me an awkward glance before concentrating back on the wound and continuing. "My mother was a great Elemental Breather. My father and she met during the time of the Great Wall that contained all those with ability in one alternative world. When it was broken, they helped Elisabeth for many years, killing Starkorfs, as that too was once their responsibility.

Many years later they had me, and then Trish. My mother often played with me more, she always told me I was special, much to my father's disgust. He hated my Element. Trish, who was only two years younger than me, had already started to show promise with her fire Element. I still didn't know what mine was. My father often called me a 'dud.' But my mother always defended me, not believing it to be so.

She was an amazing woman and was able to produce ice from anything. In the kitchen she had no use for knives." He smiled at the memory. "And her fingers turned to sharp blades; she would cut our food and allow me to help her prepare dinner.

One day she vanished. It was on my sixth birthday, and she said she wanted to collect me something nice. But for days, weeks, and then months, she did not return. My father was sure she left us because of the 'dysfunction' in me. We Elemental Breathers are proud beings, and to have a son such as me, well, father thought she left even if she said she loved me. I was a disappointment.

One day we were attacked by some form of ice beast, like you had seen in that image back at our cottage, behind it was a woman who seemed to be controlling the monster. That was the first day we saw Taskatae as she controlled the beast that destroyed our home.

Not all Elemental Breathers are the same, although we are all proud there are few who always want more, they feel godlier. My father did not accept allegiance with that woman and she was furious.

I tried my very hardest to protect my sister, Trish; she was only four and scared to see such a beast. Yet she had more courage within her than I had and I crumbled in fear away from the creature, cowering away from it against our ruined home. As I scampered petrified, Taskatae approached me. My father was distracted by the beast that constantly attacked with ice. It was then revealed to me what my Element was.

I scurried away in tiny mouse form, petrified of Taskatae, who had taken a sudden interest in me. In that time, Trish came to defend me as my father fought the large ice beast off. Her little fireballs burned the woman's face.

She somehow gained control of Trish and a violent rage tore over me. For the first time I understood the quick temper of an Elemental Breather: the blackness that shrouds our eyesight... all we are guided by is hate and murderous intent.

I turned into a wolf, tearing at the woman's leg. She quickly grabbed me by the neck and threw me against a piece of wood from my ruined home, piercing my shoulder. I was mortified to watch the ice beast sweep ice up my father's legs and across his face.

I recall to this day the breaking noise of his legs snapping and then his eyesight being taken away from him. He was in so much agony he was able to strike a bolt of electricity through the beast's heart.

As the sound of shattering glass rang out, the appearance of the beast dispersed, and my mother dropped into the ruins of our home. My own mother had been turned into some sort of ice beast," Scott said, a tear sliding down his face. He wiped it away with his other hand, seeming surprised at the sight.

"I unhinged myself, dropping to the ground as a boy, my black eyes no longer clouded with hatred. Taskatae fled. My father is now crippled and blind, my sister has no memory of my beautiful mother and I lost forever the one person who believed in me and loved me. I still wear that scar on my shoulder. I could have healed myself even back then, but I refused. It is in honor of my mother: a scar to permanently remind me that she is always looking over my shoulder. It is the only imperfection I will allow on my body — because she saw nothing imperfect about me.

I let her die; I did nothing to save her. My imperfections began that very day. My father grew to hate me even more. His own healing abilities and remedies were insufficient to restore his sight or the use of his legs. I offered to heal him but he would not let me touch him. In his words: *'I would not let such a grotesque creature touch me.'* Scott spread a small smile across his face, disheartened, before continuing.

"My father has always blamed me for all that happened because on the day of being caught, my mother had wasted her time fetching me a present for my birthday. Taskatae turned my mother into an unrecognizable beast. We all contributed to her death. I was forced to live my life in secrecy and became accustomed to my wolf form.

Trish began to hate me, feeling the same toward me as my father did, as he fed her stories of how I had taken away her mother, as well as his sight and legs.

My mother showed me kindness and I try to follow that example as much as I can but being an Elemental Breather, with such heightened rage, is hard, even for me. I turned that rage into fear and began to become very frightened of the world around me.

They abandoned me at the cottage, and that was the first time I walked out into the world. That is why I came to find you, although you thought me a wolf back then when you first visited our cottage, you reminded me much of my mother's kindness. My father was so bothered by my presence that when we had guests I was to return to my wolf form, and as I enjoyed our time spent together when you were last at my home, I couldn't reveal myself to you. Although you thought me only a pet then, I was listening and I felt your tears on my fur."

I thought of the time I had spent with him in Max Jacket's home. It was the first time I had been introduced to Max Jacket even though the others didn't want to take the risk of meeting him just for my sake. I had no control of my Shielding ability; my body was shutting down on me and I had hurt everyone, throwing them across the room in my confusion of my new world.

When I had first come to Max Jacket, I had given up on all hope. I didn't know who I was or what I had to live for. I knew nothing. And it was in Scott, in the familiarity of a pet, that I could enjoy comfort. Much had changed since then, I now know more and searched for certain answers, but I felt just as lost as ever. It only seemed fitting that Scott was here once again, comforting me. There was something about Scott that reassured me that I could confide in him; perhaps it was because we were both very different and others who saw us were disgusted by our ability. Perhaps we bonded over that.

He raised his hand, revealing that the healing was done for the time being, as more time was required for such a heavy injury. Scott stared at me seriously. "Perhaps instead of being what everyone else wants you to be, you should discover what you truly want to be yourself. You should come to terms with what has happened and have no doubt about your next decision. You may have been lost in a dark world but it is up to you to shine a light within it so bright you can see properly.

You are kind and warm, and everyone has their own demons and darkness to contend with. No one person has two white angelic wings. We are all confronted one day with the reality of having blackened our morals. Instead of trying to figure out what others are in search of within you, focus on yourself and no longer be inactive. They too are facing their own demons, so let them do so by themselves. You can help them but you cannot choose for them."

I was speechless at his wise words. My mouth was open at all that he had said. I was saddened by his story of his childhood and of his mother's death. He had revealed everything so openly to me. He raised his soft hands to my cheek, pinching it and smiling.

"You are fabulous; it is only your own realization of that which will truly give you peace. Now rest," he commanded, tucking me in. I did so obediently as if under a spell, noticing how relaxed and tired I was, and not wanting to fight the urge to sleep.

"You have done something to my body," I said, realizing why grogginess had taken over.

"Misfeata cannot hurt you within your sleep tonight, Karla. I will watch over you and invade if she tries to do so. I will do the same for your mother tonight when she comes. I will watch over the both of you. Just rest."

Surprised by his kindness and soft words, I slid into slumber. Not one of darkness, but one of peace and nothingness. My body relaxed enough to rest.

Chapter Seventeen- Conditioning

$\mathcal{M}$y sleep was a long and peaceful one, a gift that could have been given by no other than Scott. He gave me a small smile when I awoke to my mother snoring softly next to me, dark circles appearing under her eyes. I was so grateful to have Scott look over us while we slept, mostly for being able to have a proper sleep without Misfeata waiting for me.

He reassessed my stomach wound, healing it for a moment longer. I already felt the difference. The skin that I could not heal on my own had now seemed to strengthen. Every time Scott approached my stomach he thickened the skin somehow, fixing the wound with his outstanding ability.

Afterwards, he walked out into the early morning air and I did the same, still irritated slightly by my stomach but I was no longer wincing in pain, at least. Before following him, I looked back at my mother, sad to know I could not return with her. I had not spoken to her since my body shut down on me in front of her. How would I summon the strength to tell her?

As Scott suggested, I tried pushing that thought away. *Instead of thinking of everyone else's reactions, I should truly consider my own actions and what I want.* The sun was extremely bright as it shone on my face. Ashley, Paige, Max, and Trish, sat around a fire.

Lucas, Paul, and Harmony, weren't around as I sat down next to Ashley, ignoring the flirtatious looks Trish was throwing him. Ashley sat uncomfortably avoiding eye contact with her. She scowled as he turned his focus on me. No matter what happened in the past, I still disliked her greatly.

"How are you feeling?" Ashley asked, relieved that when I sat down I blocked Trish's sight. Paige was sitting next to us looking bored and uninterested in conversation.

"Much better," I answered truthfully. I haven't had a proper night's sleep for such a long time. "Ashley, I need to ask a favor of you."

"What is it?" he asked, fiddling with his eyebrow piercing. He hunched over his knees as if we were speaking in secrecy.

"I fear for my mother going back to her normal life."

"You're not going back with her…" he realized. I couldn't decipher whether he was relieved or disappointed. His expression was unreadable.

"No, I'm not; she won't be safe if I'm with her. Especially not until Taskatae has been dealt with. I was wondering if you could take her back to where your mother, Suzumiya, and Chris are. I know your mother is still grieving and now mine is too. I was hoping they could help each other out, both being widowed. I need someone I can trust to protect my mother in my absence. I know Suzumiya hated me but she lived by a code and did everything to protect humans."

"I don't know, Karla. Her protection isn't guaranteed."

"I know, but nothing is now. I have learned that much to be true. But it is more protection than I can offer her. There are many enemies I must overcome before I can present myself to my mother again. As much as I fought so hard to have her back, I realize now I cannot be so selfish."

"You know, if Taskatae and Nathanial are working together, you are no use to them, continuing on with the others. I don't like who we have aligned with, Karla, and I don't know what you're thinking. We were doing fine on our own. We always have, but now you have allowed the very people we hate most and can't trust be involved with our business. You can't go with them. Unless you want the same outcome as your battle with Praytar. As soon as you get close to Nathanial, you will lose control to Misfeata, and Nathanial and you will only be a mere shell to the Elders."

"I will not lose control to her," I said angrily, knowing him to be right. He had witnessed firsthand the beast I had begun to turn into under the influence of Misfeata. "I will avoid making contact with Nathanial. I will stay a distance away as the others investigate. I am only after Taskatae. I won't put myself into a bad situation."

"It's not worth the risk," he evaluated, grunting as I looked behind me. My mother came out nestled in a thick cardigan; her face and hair now washed.

She uncomfortably walked toward me. "Honey?"

"Ashley is going to take you somewhere you'll be safe, Mum. I have to go for a little while, but I will come back for you. After everything is done and safe I will find you again," I promised, holding tears at bay, and trying to sound strong. Although I knew this was the right decision, it pained me as she began to argue with me.

"No. I won't let you put yourself in any more danger. I cannot lose you too. Your father and I only ever wanted to protect you. I cannot allow it. We will go back home," she said, delusional as she hugged me into a tight embrace. I closed my arms around her tightly, knowing it was the only way I could protect her. Holding her firmly and letting it be my goodbye, Scott crept up behind my mother, nodding as he knew what I wanted him to do. His hand vanished within my mother, through her skin. A small sigh escaped from her mouth and she dropped heavily into my arms, now asleep.

"It will only last a few days but that should be enough for you to get to the location you seek," Scott said to Ashley. I held my mother firmly, ashamed that I had used such a trick on her, especially as she had announced she hated all us creatures alike.

Max made a disgusted groan as he witnessed his son's 'dysfunctional' Element. I mouthed a 'thank you' to Scott, and he returned a small smile before leaving. Ashley gave me a hurt expression as we hadn't yet fully agreed he would take her. But it was the only way I knew to keep her safe.

"Paige, are you able to go with Ashley?" I asked, grabbing her attention as she now looked over my mother bored, her head resting in her hand.

"No. I am not a babysitter," she said, annoyed. "I am going to go where the action is, this is your problem not mine."

I pushed back my agitation; her attitude was as repulsive as ever. I felt delusional forever thinking her to have a good nature. How had she situated herself within our group so easily? What was it she was really after? Was it my own paranoia that made me think the worst in people or was she really here for another agenda? And yet, I couldn't help but feel if my mother were the center of a fight, Paige would agree to go. *Is it the fighting she is following or is it us?*

As all these thoughts rattled in my mind, I cautiously eyed Paige, not willing to demand anything from her until I knew how dangerous she really was. I could not openly blab my thoughts any longer; everything had to be cautiously said and done.

"I can do it myself, Karla. I just really hope you know what you're doing this time," Ashley said to me as Lucas approached us. Ashley's face tore in anger and hatred. "I will leave now. I will find you again, just please still be alive." His blue eyes looked long into my face.

I gave him a small smile, still holding my mother awkwardly. "You too. Thank you Ashley." I knew I could rely on Ashley and that she would get there safely under his protection. He took my mother with no effort, walking toward the direction of the car.

My heart ached at how quickly I was able to let go of my mother, but I had to believe I was doing the right thing. I was sure I was.

"I think we should start packing up and leave. As the Starkorf described, it is only a few days walk from here," Lucas suggested as he too looked toward my mother.

"Where are Paul and Harmony?" I asked, noticing everyone else was ready.

"They're awake, I am sure, but in their tent."

"*Their* tent?" I repeated, embarrassed by my acid tone.

Why are they sharing a tent together? Is he trying to avoid me that much? Perhaps he just wanted to be alone with her. I thought of the sudden fondness Harmony had for Paul and I held down the lump in my throat. I thought of the possible things they could've done without my knowing. It isn't merely convenient for them to share a tent, was it because he wanted to?

"Yes, Karla," Lucas said, as if not noticing my discomfort about the situation.

I still don't trust her. There is something about her that I cannot believe or trust. And I do not want her spending time with Paul or looking at him like she does.

"I will call Harmony out and then we should leave. But Karla, I don't know how far you can come if Nathanial—…"

"I know," I said quickly, cutting him off. "I know."

Chapter Eighteen- Lies From the Start

*W*e all swiftly gathered our belongings, packing as much as we could in our backpacks. Lucas, Scott, and Paul carried the three small tents that were neatly packed. We had organized for Max and Trish to meet us in seven days in a nearby town. We all needed to figure out where Taskatae's location was but for various reasons. Not only did we need to find Taskatae, but we needed to establish what Lucas's brother, Nathanial, was trying to achieve.

Max couldn't be maneuvered through the forest, as bloodthirsty as he was at the chance to confront Taskatae for taking his wife's life. He was unable to join us and Trish would not leave her father's side.

We began walking in the chilled day as sun streaked through the large trees. Paige often flustered at our slow pace; she was too eager to march into the enemy's belly.

Annoyed, I watched from behind as Harmony often spoke to Paul, laughing at a few of his comments. Lucas walked a few steps behind, unfazed. I didn't know how Lucas came across this girl but she radiated with something that infuriated me. Her long blond hair was always perfectly braided, her skin hadn't a smudge on it and her white clothes didn't have the slightest mark of dirt on them although we all walked on the same dirty ground.

The sight of her crossbow still agitated me as somehow she could conjure arrows on demand. Paul once defended her, explaining that she could only do so because the 'Divine' gifted her so. Not only had Lucas so quickly taken her in and now so had Paul, trusting her just within a few days of knowing her.

Not only was I suspicious, but so was Paige, who had no trust for the girl, questioning her true motives. Suggestion of treachery boiled beneath my skin, as at the loss of my father it was Harmony who tipped Lucas off. *Is she a liar? Is she a traitor? And if so, how do I find the evidence to prove it when Paul and Lucas trust her so dearly already?*

Scott too was baffled, as he had not sensed her to be an Elemental Breather. What was I supposed to believe? But as Scott had said, in this world he was no longer surprised by the possibilities of creatures and their abilities. So he passed no judgment over her, ignoring my interrogating eyes as I threw figurative daggers at her back. I had to prove her ulterior motives.

Wary on our walk for Starkorfs or any of Taskatae's creatures, we were relieved when nothing out of the ordinary happened and we had much time to reflect — at the awkward expense of silence amongst ourselves. We had two nights to discuss our plan. It was highly stressed that I was not to become involved. I was to stay at our camp as they ventured toward the area which was described to Lucas. I was not to risk a run in with Nathanial if he also occupied the hideout. If we were to meet or draw close to one another, it would be disastrous as Misfeata and Tyran would once again try to fight.

Under all circumstances I was to avoid contact with Nathanial. If I failed at this, I may not step out as the victor just as I did after the battle against Praytar. Misfeata and Tyran were too unpredictable; the only thing that we all knew for certain was that they would aim for bloodshed, and that blood was mine.

But if I wasn't there, then I wouldn't allow Paul to go any further either. And to my displeasure, Lucas wanted Harmony to stay as well. The sleeping arrangements only infuriated me more as Paul and Harmony shared a tent together both nights. She claimed to be attending to a few wounds he had from the many nights ago on our ambush. And although we all knew Scott could heal him within minutes, Paul didn't request it, agitating me more.

I refused to share with Paige. The only thing we had in common was that we were both in agreement that Harmony was untrustworthy. Even so, Paige's attitude scratched at my every nerve. Inconsiderate, she simply said and did whatever she wanted.

Scott stayed in my tent, watching over me as I slept so I could have a proper sleep. Not much was said between us. We were a bizarre group; no one was able to fully trust or rely on each other.

Despite Paul staying with us and continuing on the same journey as me, he had not yet spoken to me, avoiding me as I approached. After the first day I gave up trying to approach him, ashamed that I had put such distance between us.

After a short night's sleep, everyone awoke, and after extinguishing the fire, Scott resumed healing my stomach once again. We ate the rabbit that Harmony had hunted for us while assessing our weapons.

"Lucas," I said seriously to him, knowing if anyone could relate to my urgency, it was him. "If you find Aeisha, please retrieve her for me." I still longed for my partnered Immortal Blade, my strength slowly seeming to deplete without her.

"If I find it I will bring it back," he promised understandingly, his dark brown eyes appearing orange in the reflection of the sun as he looked back at me. Our eyes lingered for too long. I hesitated to watch Scott and him leave.

They vanished further into the trees leaving Paul, Harmony, and me, to watch over the camp in the small gully we rested in. I felt useless and disheartened as they left. Paul would still not look at me, walking away with Harmony into the woods where they claimed to be hunting.

For hours I worried about Paul, pacing back and forth as they have not yet returned. I embedded my Shield into the ground regularly in search for him, as it seemed he was gone for far too long with her. I sensed someone close by. As I walked into that direction, I sensed the presence of a Shield residing in who I thought was Paul. Is there a Starkorf approaching?

Quietly, I hid amongst the shrubbery, hiding behind a tree as the intruder's pace quickened toward me. I held my lone blade, Aeisha, to my side, prepared for the Starkorf, but it walked past me.

I kicked at the intruder's shins, hoping to drop them to the ground, but instead my leg was rebounded as a Shield reflected it, already prepared for my attack. I projected my Shield and looked into a familiar face. I was looking into Kurt's gray eyes steadily, my eyes widening in surprise.

He was the first who had attempted to help me learn to control my Shield. His Shield was not as weak as he had once claimed. He was the one who ordered for me to be brought back to him and then hesitated to allow me to go back to my family in my hometown, Roperia, to make sure my family was safe. But they had already been kidnapped.

Shortly after Seth's death — and the revelation that Lucas was not what he claimed to be — Kurt vanished. But what would he be doing out here?

"Karla," he called out, seeming surprised. He wore a navy-blue turtleneck sweater with a long black leather coat, a long sword mostly covered by it, with his fingertips gently resting on the handle. He looked at me cautiously. "What are you doing out here?"

"I could ask you the same." I said, uncertain of his motives. He was coming from the direction that the others had walked into. Was he also trying to find the Starkorfs hideout?

"Well, haven't you changed since we last saw one another. All grown up now, I see," he observed, his words making me feel uncomfortable.

117

"I went looking for my parents…" I began. I was cautious because I still didn't know why he had abandoned the others after Seth's death.

"I heard that. Only one of Aeisha, I see. It appears you did know where the Immortal Blades were all along, after all," he remarked, annoyed. "Well, you see, I have a dilemma as I would like that blade."

With confusion I stood silently, looking over Kurt thoughtfully. I had lost Aeisha's partnered Immortal Blade, but why would that be of interest to Kurt? His eyes seemed to strip me of any strength I had. He was once a mentor to me, no matter how little time we spent together; he was the first to attempt to teach me how to use my Shielding ability.

My mouth tightened in horror as I realized why so much interest was taken in me then, and why he looked at me so. I said nothing, regaining my defensive stance now, realizing Kurt to be a threat, an enemy, and a traitor. Kurt too has turned against me.

"You knew the whole time my parents had been taken, didn't you," I accused cautiously. Instead of carefully choosing his words like I remembered him to, he slowly dragged his sword out from its sheath, confirming my suspicions.

"Well I may have had partial influence in it," he admitted with no remorse. Anger built within me; he was working with Nathanial. He must have known of my parents' disappearance. He knew Nathanial when he had attacked us at the old warehouse. He knew all that would happen. Everyone trusted Kurt and was led by him. He was involved with giving Taskatae my parents as a 'gift.' My father was tortured and turned into a beast, and he was involved.

"You knew of Lucas," I said, understanding that Kurt's betrayal was from the very start.

"No, actually, that too I was surprised by. Nathanial never mentioned it," he said purposefully, once again confirming my assumptions. "Karla, I don't want to fight you, but I do want that blade. Do you know, for many years of my life I fought for no reason, never able to reach such strength that the Elders were capable of passing down? I was loyal once. Until I realized there was nothing in it for me other than death. After many years of research I realized that I too could try and find immortality."

"It is impossible," I said alarmed at his madness. This foolish man has fooled me. How did I not know? How were the others fooled as well?

"Or is it? Sebastian disappeared with his Immortal Blade, Sheliste; that power can't simply vanish. I believe I can find his grave and take that power for myself. I believe we could swap our strengths, Karla, with the help of Nathanial. I could offer my body for Misfeata to claim instead of yours, isn't that what you want?"

Unsettled, I took a step back, overwhelmed by all the madness he voiced. *It isn't possible, there is no grave of Sebastian's; he vanished somewhere not even Misfeata and Tyran knew where.*

"You are crazy," I said, ashamed that I had let such a man get close enough to me to take my parents, using them as some kind of bargaining chip.

I jumped at Kurt, projecting my Shield. Our Shields were evenly matched, and before long, my single Aeisha blade was forcing down on him as he pushed me away. He looked longingly at Aeisha, his gray eyes wild.

"Then I will have to take it from you."

He ran for me, his sword hacking at me. I used Aeisha defensively. As he swung his blade down on me once more, I rolled over the ground to the side, finding him to be much slower than me, even if I wasn't at my full strength, and with only one blade.

He traced my steps, trying to hack at me again and I dodged his attack once more trying to tire him out, hoping his age would exhaust him quicker. However, his strength and ability were not what he had claimed them to be; he was a much greater opponent than I had thought.

'He has trained for his whole life,' Misfeata faintly interjected, herself weakened by the disappearance of her partnered Immortal Blade that contained her soul. *'He is not the first I have fought who has babbled such nonsense. There is no such place. I have looked.'*

Kurt swung his sword at me again, gripping the handle of his weapon differently as he tried plunging it into my shoulder. I was able to dodge it. Using Aeisha to deflect his sword, I grated Aeisha up, cutting heavily into his shoulder and spinning back into a defensive crouch as he lunged for me again, unfazed by his injury.

Reaching within his jacket he threw a dagger at me. Using Aeisha to divert it, I dodged his attack, as once again he jumped toward me. Quickly dodging his slow movements, I cut at his leg before jumping away from him again and regaining a strong stance.

I ran at him, sure I could disarm him and tie him up. I needed more answers. He used his weak arm as a decoy, stabbing his sword toward me. I knocked it out of his hand and quickly put up my other arm as he had tried to punch me in the stomach; a move I had anticipated. With a firm grip around his clenched hand, he tried to use his injured arm against me, but I was able to block that as well. Our Shields fought for dominancy and our physical strength matched one another's, but eventually I felt his Shield slightly weaken. Still holding onto him firmly, I kneed him in the stomach, forcing him to stumble back as I spun. I then pushed the back of my foot across his face, knocking him to the ground.

Taking a moment to breath, I watched over him as he stumbled into a fighting stance, but his heavily bleeding leg unbalanced him. *He was right; I am not the woman he remembered me to be*. He was looking at me infuriated, as Paul clumsily broke out of the trees, raising his bow and arrow and shooting it at Kurt. Instantly it deflected from Kurt's Shield. He reached for his leather jacket, pulling out a dagger that he threw at Paul. The dagger pierced his shoulder, forcing Paul to drop his weapon as he fell to the ground.

I ran for Paul too late to stop it from happening. Immediately I tried to tend to his wound, applying pressure tenderly. Harmony broke out from the shrubbery, bow held high. She chased Kurt into the woods.

"I'm sorry," Paul said, trying to sound unfazed by his injury as he pressed my hand. "I'm sorry, Karla. I know you are annoyed when I get involved." He sounded disappointed in himself. "I only meant to help you."

"I know," I reassured him, flustered at his heavily bleeding shoulder. Scott was not around to heal it.

"And I know I have been a fool avoiding you. I just needed to think things over. I am sorry for ditching you," he gushed. I didn't know if he was telling me all this because he was trying to avoid the pain of his shoulder or if he was genuinely sorry he was too stubborn to come and speak what was on his mind to me earlier.

Harmony ran toward us from the forest. "He got away," she said, dropping to her knees next to Paul, her blue eyes concentrating on the injury. "Help me get him to the camp, I can mend him there."

Before I could question how Kurt escaped her in his weakened state, Paul began lifting himself quietly. "Just another casualty I suppose," he said evenly as I tried to help him. He pushed me away, walking on his own. As Harmony helped support him, I looked down at my hand, which was covered in Paul's blood. I wanted to give chase after Kurt but I was hesitant to leave Paul's side once again. Kurt could have killed Paul, but he didn't.

I followed after Paul and Harmony back to the camp, even more wary and on guard as she bandaged him up in their tent. There was nothing I could do to help. I didn't know how to aid another nor did I have the ability to heal someone else. I felt useless and once again was confronted by the fact that my only strength resided in fighting.

I waited impatiently for the others to return, expecting something else to happen. I almost invited opposition just to relieve my rage, but no other enemy came. I was left with my own built anger and mixed emotions; as all I could do was sit around and wait.

Paul rested as Harmony stayed by his side in the tent, irritating me more as I felt like I had no right to check on him. Maybe it was time for me to finally sever the cord between Paul and me. I had dragged him in too far if he thought such an injury was "just another casualty."

My encounter with Kurt today just further reinforced that everything I had learned of this life from the start had been a lie.

2

Warrior

In a lifetime of shattered dreams, and broken hearts,

we fight for those we love, we compete to protect them.
But when our Shield is broken and that barrier is shattered;
Whom can I summon to protect them in my stead?
Is it my strength alone that can protect them or is my death
the valuable lesson needed not to rely on others?
Am I warrior, or am I fighting to my death to find some form
of peace?
And what of my other, would I still aspire to protect them in
the afterlife?

Chapter Nineteen- Hunger

*A*fter a full day's wait, and after relighting the fireplace several times — partly because of my nervous energy and partly to keep myself warm as the cold night edged over me — Scott, Paige, and Lucas returned, finally sweeping my anticipation away.

Depleted, they all collapsed around the fire, Scott questioning where Paul was. I indicated his tent with distaste, ashamed that I still felt jealous of Harmony even though she had just healed Paul's wound, something that I was incapable of doing myself. Scott got up to permanently heal Paul's wound, putting him out of his discomfort.

Paige took her thick leather boots off, clearly relieved to free her toes. I noticed that blood was splattered across her face. She seemed unfazed by her wild appearance and the small cut along her collarbone that still bled slightly. I turned my attention to Lucas.

"What did you find there?" I asked him.

"Very little. My brother was there, but I can only assume Taskatae somehow tipped him off. I am now very certain that they are working together."

"It was still okay, there were other Starkorfs we could slaughter anyway. There were dead bodies everywhere, so we can only assume they've been hiding there for a while and feasting. It was fun." Paige smiled wickedly to herself. Her words sickened me and I tried ignoring them, pretending I didn't hear her.

"While I waited for you I ran into someone who was coming from the same direction. Did you by chance run into Kurt?" I asked, grabbing Lucas's confused attention, his expression enough to tell me he hadn't. "Kurt is a traitor, has been from the very beginning. He had a fascination with Aeisha and rambled about finding the Immortal Blades and Sebastian's grave so he could harness an Elder's strength. He was speaking like a mad man. Lucas, he was part of the reason why my parents were offered to Taskatae as gifts. He aided your brother in that."

Lucas swallowed heavily, speechless. He clenched his hard jaw and stroked his hand through his sandy-blonde hair like he always did when he was thinking.

"I didn't know, Karla," he said, abashed. "I truly didn't know. I am so sorry."

"I could have told you he was a liar years ago," Scott said, coming out from the tent. "His fascination with the Immortal Blades was what turned my father against him. Because my father wanted them for himself, of course," Scott said smirking. "Paul's wound is healed now, lucky for him to be graced with my magical hands, right?" Scott rhetorically asked with a high-pitched laugh. Lucas cringed at the sound and Paige stared at him annoyed before rolling her eyes and walking off.

"I'm going for a walk," I said. After waiting for them for most of the day, my legs needed stretching. The woodland was beautiful and I couldn't let the opportunity slip.

"Do you mind if I come with you?" Lucas asked, already standing. Scott arched his eyebrow at me before walking away whistling. Paige had already left. With no one else around I felt obliged to agree.

As we walked into the woodlands little animals made squealing noises, making it less awkward as we seemed not so alone.

"It's a nice night," Lucas said, admiring the half moon.

I looked up at it in contemplation. "It is," I agreed.

It had been a long time since I could have a brisk walk and admire the moonlight that shone around us. There was a silence, and Lucas shuffled his hands into his pockets. The air surrounding us was giving me an edgy feeling and there was a thickness I felt intoxicated by. Simply walking in silence created an electric atmosphere around us.

I never understood the irrational emotions I had when near him; they were always all over the place. I never knew whether I was angry, sad, or drawn to him. With Lucas, my heart pounded in uncertainty, especially when I looked into the deep-brown eyes that made me feel like I was being sucked into a black vortex of the unknown. Everything around Lucas was uncertain and yet exhilarating at the same time.

When I looked into Paul's certain eyes, the moss-green of them always reminded me of the earth, much like his personality: he was stable and looked after me. He grounded me when I couldn't make sense of my own desires or the world I now had around me. He always drew me close and centered me, making me remember everything it was I wanted to fight for and be.

I realized I felt nervous and not awkward, with Lucas in such proximity. Heaviness exuded around him; there was much to be said. After a few minutes of walking in silence whilst admiring the moon, Lucas finally spoke, his voice firm.

"Karla, every day I wish I could fix how much I have hurt you and betrayed you," he said, looking at the ground. "When I first met you I was a jerk, but because of that you once found me to be a challenge. But I challenged you in a good way; I know you fed off those raw arguments as much as I did." He raised his eyebrow as I recalled the chemistry between us when we argued. I flushed slightly red. "But soon after you joined us, both of us realized we were heavily reliant on each other, and I know it wasn't just me who felt that.

I have tried to change my opinion of you. I have tried to hate you; tried to fight the desperation I feel to have you by my side, but I can't. There is a wickedness inside of me that yearns for you and it isn't the pull of our rivalry. I don't care what descendants we have within us or what fate we have in store. I want to be by your side because I cannot forget that need we had for each other."

My heart raced at his confession. My eyes frantically searched the ground as I didn't know what to say as he conveyed his feelings for me. I too knew of that yearning, the pull I had toward Lucas. I was never sure if it was my own attraction or that of the rivalry in the blood we carried, and yet my heart still pounded. Lucas was intoxicating, when around him it felt like anything was possible and the world we shared could be one of adventure and excitement; not of resentment, pain, and war.

But would it cost me my own morals to be a part of his world, to lose myself to him fully and see the world from his perspective? It is a world where our ability is viewed as magnificent, not a burden. Could this be so much more? Could he be the hand that will fully pull me into the magic of this world without fear, but instead with excitement? Is this a change he could really create for me? An intoxicating, and invigorating life as more than just a human?

Lucas pinned me against a tree. My heart pounded. I couldn't look at him; I was scared to be trapped in his eyes. I was rattled by all the thoughts that rushed over my mind but my skin shivered under his intense glare. How long had I been trapping all these thoughts within me?

"Karla," he growled, his mint breath heating my face. I inhaled it as his lips were so close to my own. "I cannot forget you." His voice was hoarse, raw with desperation. I looked into his dark-brown eyes. His strong masculine jaw was so close. I raised my hand to it, projecting a small Shield onto it so I could touch his skin without being drained. A tingling sensation sparked from my fingertips as it shuddered an electrifying sensation through me.

Slowly his breathing got heavier as mine did the same. My body was aching with urgency as his lips lingered so close to my own. His dark-brown eyes were pooling into me and making me lose sensation in my legs.

He slowly inclined his face toward me; enclosing my small figure with his own as his lips came closer to mine. I felt his projected Shield's presence linger on his lips as I inhaled his hot breath one more time, unable to contain my need for him when he was so close.

Slowly his lips parted my own, hot against mine. His Shield tingled against mine. It sparked on my tongue, making me want more. We could no longer keep such a slow pace as a hunger stirred within me, making me want Lucas entirely. Everything that surrounded us was a blur. I desperately inhaled only him. I followed his lead, pulling at his jacket and pulling him into me as he pushed me harder against the tree.

Our Shields ignited like wild fire on my lips and tongue making me hungry for more; his leathered hand trailing down my body to my hips. He held me tightly; desperately pushing into me. I pulled his leather jacket off, needing more. I was overcome by the heat of our bodies. Lucas did the same to me through desperate kisses, revealing my sleeveless shirt.

My hands fumbled over his hard chest before my hands wrapped around his neck to try to pull him closer. When I touched his bare skin, the back of his neck, collarbone, and arm, I vaguely noticed how a faint trail of flames lingered. Not a painful burn, but one that excited me.

Slowly my kisses became less desperate as my lips took pace with his, my hands slowly dropping against his hard and muscled arms. I noticed my own strength dissipating. Lucas pulled away, his breath heavy as he looked at me, a crooked smile passing his lips.

"I'm sorry," he exhaled as we both realized in unison he had unintentionally begun to drain me. "I can't control myself when I am around you." He pulled back slightly so he no longer had me pinned between his hard body and the tree. I understood his lack of control as my heart still raced and my legs were shaky. I raised my fingers to my lips, remembering the fiery passion. If his draining hadn't intervened, how much hungrier would I have been for him? I looked back into his brown eyes, unsure of what to say. I still felt immersed in his spell; still felt mesmerized by him; still slightly shuddered under his gaze. I pressed my fingers against his chest, pushing him away slightly so I had more room to breathe.

"I'm sorry," I said unsure as to why I was apologizing. Red spread over my cheeks as I noticed the chill of the night air once again. Lucas grabbed both our leather jackets from the ground, offering me mine. I flicked my hair away to put it on. "We've been gone for a long time now," I said, still breathing heavily. I was still shocked by my desperation for Lucas's kiss.

He shook his head, agreeing we should return. He put his own jacket on and stroked his hand through his hair. He slowly entwined his fingers in my own, giving me a cheeky smile as he looked forward. I couldn't help but look back at him longingly. He had always seemed so exotic to me — *untouchable.*

"I don't know what the future holds for us but no matter what; I won't betray your trust again. I will protect you no matter what happens. Whether Misfeata and Tyran intervenes or not. I won't hurt you."

As we approached the camp and the flames from the fire came into view, Lucas let go of my hand, placing his own into his pockets so no one would be suspicious of our outing. I wrapped my hands around my own body self-consciously; unable to explain why I so badly wanted to hold his hand.

Fear prickled as I dreaded how Paul would look at me as we returned to the camp.

Chapter Twenty- Reconsolidation

*M*uch to my despair it was as if Paul knew as he watched us come out of the trees, looking between the two of us before storming into his tent before any words could even be exchanged. I knew Lucas was disappointed to see such a hurt expression on my face, but I couldn't help but feel that I have betrayed Paul, as my chest pined over his hurt and angry eyes. His feelings have always been very clear to me, but I was undecided as I was attracted to both Lucas and Paul. Paul followed me everywhere. My mind still jumbled over many emotions. I went to where Scott was already waiting for me.

Scott watched over me for another night as I slept. He laughed when I voiced my concern about him not getting enough sleep and what repercussions it might have on his body. He said that he didn't really need to sleep, although sometimes it was enjoyable. He was able to refurbish his body whenever he liked, much like he did when he healed himself. So when sleep deprivation, illness, or anything of the sort irritated him, he could simply wipe over it and start afresh.

Scott constantly bombarded me with questions before I slept, claiming to have known something had happened between Lucas and me. Much to my embarrassment I argued that nothing happened but he squealed like a girl, rambling about 'forbidden love.' Not even I understood what happened or how we both were swept over by a hunger of sorts. The fire still danced on my lips when I thought of it.

Once again waking and packing our camping accessories, we headed back to the town where we had to meet with Max Jacket and Trish. We had very little to tell them: there were no leads other than the assumption that Taskatae and Nathanial were definitely working together and it was confirmed that Kurt was a traitor.

Nothing was said as we walked in the still air. Everyone was awkward, unsure of what to say to one another. Paul was unable to look at me. After apologizing and both of us making peace only yesterday, I had yet again betrayed him in such a short amount of time.

Lucas said nothing to me of what happened, but when catching his dark-brown eyes I blushed in embarrassment, unable to find words. Did I like it? I *loved* it. I had never felt such a passionate connection with another.

But I was scared of what it may lead to. What was the possibility of Lucas and I having a future?

Do I want a future with Lucas; is that something I now consider?

My thoughts wandered to my mother and if she had yet reached the destination Ashley was driving her to. I wondered if she hated me for what I have done: taking away her right as a parent so I could justify protecting her.

My eyes bore into the back of Harmony suspiciously as we walked for another day before pitching our tents for another silent night. Paige often wandered off doing her own thing. She had a bad attitude, wanting little interaction with anyone else. Harmony still fluttered around Paul annoyingly. Lucas watched me from afar but made no approach, assuming he was waiting for me to approach him, which I was not comfortable in doing. I was still trying to understand whether the hunger I was consumed by was a good thing. Scott fluttered about by himself, concentrating on his nails for far too long and gazing into the stars above the fire.

I decided to take another walk — by myself — to clear my thoughts, and embrace my own company. It was nice to feel my own entity once again for a short period of time without having to struggle with fighting someone from within.

The night passed quickly and the new day came. We drove to the small town in which Max Jacket told us to meet, and, as Scott predicted, within the small hillbilly-like town they were at the most expensive motel, which was still not up to their standards.

It was daunting as we drove into the car park, but after being crammed within the car for two hours, we all stretched our legs gratefully. Walking up the stairs, Scott pointed to their room, hiding behind everyone.

Before Lucas could knock on the door, Trish opened it, jumping on Lucas in excitement. He projected his Shield, pushing her away from him. Her eyes flashed black and to my own dismay I had to look away. I bit down on my lip so that I did not say anything. *Am I jealous?* Paul watched me very carefully, looking away s I tried to meet his green eyes.

"Where is Max?" Lucas asked firmly, pushing aside Trish's flirtatious greetings.

Her eyes steadied on me as a small smile crossed my lips triumphantly. I couldn't help but feel ashamed of my pettiness; in some way it felt like a win for me, to have Lucas so uninterested in her. I hated Trish, and if she offered I would gladly fight her again.

Trish waltzed to the side, intensely staring at Paul as he walked by her. My own steps were slowing as I waited for him to pass so I could give her another harsh stare. There was no way I would let her filthy hands touch him. Paul, also uninterested, continued walking despite my petty run-in with Trish.

"Ah, Karla," Max said, holding his hand out to me and welcoming me in.

For a motel it was luxurious, but it still could not measure up to their standards. A bright yellow feature wall with a few cracks that stemmed up, a tiny kitchen, a garish bathroom, and two separate rooms where they each had a bed, welcomed me. It was very quiet as all electronics were turned off. I wondered whether they had ever watched television before. We sat around a small wooden coffee table where cups and a pot of tea awaited us.

"What knowledge do you bring me?" Max demanded curtly.

After Lucas and I explained the situation of Nathanial having already escaped; our assumption of Taskatae and Nathanial working together; and my encounter with Kurt — who had also worked with Nathanial and rambled nonsense about acquiring the Elder's ability at Sebastian's grave — Max only shook his head somberly, seemingly unsurprised by the disappointing amount of knowledge we have gathered. We did not yet know where Taskatae was and that took precedence.

"Well, you see much has happened while you have been gone, and if I might be so bold, I wish to invite you, Karla, to attend a most prestigious ball," Max intonated with the elegance of a gentleman. My eyebrows knitted together in confusion.

"You cannot be serious, Father," Scott protested, rising and then quickly sitting down under the harsh black stare of his father and sister.

"Tsk," Trish huffed, looking toward one of the bedrooms angrily with her hands crossed across her short purple dress. Her raunchy attire was completed with high black leather boots.

Paige made a loud noise of contempt while smiling sarcastically at Trish, purposefully agitating her more. For whatever reason Trish was annoyed by Paige, who seemed intent on making it worse, presumably looking for a fight. Trish held herself tightly and her nails dug into her arms while her eyes flickered black as she stared between Paige and me.

"You see us Elemental Breathers have an annual ball," Max elucidated nonchalantly while pouring tea into cups. He handed one out to each of us, except Paige, who rudely declined. None was offered to Scott. "…Only three nights from now, in fact. It is a little bit out of our way and none of us truly enjoy the company of one another. But in terms of establishing the whereabouts of Taskatae, it may very well be the place to be."

"A ball?" I repeated incredulously, thinking of all the Elemental Breathers that would swarm such a place. Anything could happen and I sensed my kind was not entirely welcome. "Is it only for Elemental Breathers?"

"Correct," he confirmed, taking a sip of his tea.

"So why invite us if it will only create uproar?" Lucas probed impatiently.

"Oh, I did not say 'us,'" Max Jacket said looking to Lucas blindly. "You see, to get there, you must go over a short body of water. Considering Trish's and my Element, I am sure you can only imagine why we don't want to be over a large pool of water," he patronized with a firm smile.

"No, you just don't want to go with humans," Paige interjected, crossing her arms over her chest. "You want Scott to go in your stead. An Elemental Breather who takes non Elemental Breathers to the ball. My, I wonder what unimaginable things could happen if the others took notice."

Paige was astute. It was a cowardly act for Max Jacket to place his son in his stead. If the other Elemental Breathers were utterly disgusted in Scott bringing humans then they might turn on him. Elemental Breathers were proud and cunning, believing themselves to be better than humans in every way. Ignoring the perceived hierarchy could ruin Max's reputation.

"Smart girl you are," Max remarked calmly. "It is as she says. Scott, you will take them."

"When you say 'them'…?" I quizzed.

"All of you. There may be some casualties, so the more of you the better. I need to know where Taskatae is," Max stated angrily, recovering his milky-white eyes from their flashing black. "I have looked for her for so very long after she took something valuable from me. Also, Borac is under my protection so I cannot very well go into an open space with other Elemental Breathers who would wish to acquire my Immortal Blade. I will not part with it. It is only safe with me. All of you must go and find what you can because I refuse to be so close to her."

All that he said made sense and for once our motives were aligned. Although I was still cautious that he might have other motives, for now I knew he wouldn't betray me if he needed us to do this task. He wanted Taskatae and so did I. Although apprehensive about the danger it put us in, I accepted. Those who did not want to come didn't have to and I understood why.

I didn't want Paul to come because of the risk it put him in but when Harmony suggested that the two of them stay together to wait for us, I couldn't help but want to tell her 'no'. I didn't like the way she looked at him. My unsettled feeling of her was still very present, and still no one knew what or who she was. Without hesitation he answered that he wanted to go and so we left without hesitation, not wanting to be in the presence of Max Jacket and Trish any longer. It was Scott who was most flustered; he clearly didn't want to attend. But to avoid confrontation with his father he gave up on the thought of fleeing.

"If we go, we must purchase the proper attire. I will hire us out an hour of Mimi's time, which should be enough time."

"Enough time for what?" a familiar voice interjected as he walked up the stairs. Ashley walked toward us. How he always seemed to know where we were surprised even me.

"Great, another one," Scott said dramatically, waving his arm and stroking through his white hair.

"How is my mother?" I gushed worriedly.

"She's okay. Much like you in the sense that she wasn't really happy after she woke up and realized what has been done, but Mum comforted her and I think she came to an understanding. I think you were right: I think they can help each other. Only time will tell, I suppose,"

"Well, that's all sweet and well. But get in the car," Scott answered grumpily. "If we are going to this ball then we had better hurry up and purchase the right attire. It is about a full day's drive from here, then another day to the docks. We will take turns driving," Scott said, walking down the stairs.

Without further farewell we left Max and Trish.

"Wait, where is this ball?" I asked Scott as we descended the stairs, remembering Max mentioning we had to go over water to get there.

"It's on an island."

Lucas and I gave one another a cautious look. *Great, we are about to be stuck on an island with Elemental Breathers — nowhere to run.*

"Wait, what?" Ashley called, eyebrows knitted together in alarm.

Chapter Twenty-One- Alter World

$\mathcal{W}$ithout room for hesitation we speedily followed Scott, Lucas, and Harmony, along the roads. Ashley was driving a new car that they've stolen from when we left them at the park before going to Taskatae's hideout. Ashley tried convincing me that it wasn't stolen and that Harmony had provided it because she said that the Divine offered it to her as a gift. I rolled my eyes. To my cynical ears it sounded like theft.

Ashley looked between Paul and me numerous times, saying nothing. Paige constantly sighed heavily in the back. Her head rested on her palm as she looked out the window, bored.

Like Scott suggested, Lucas, Paul, and Ashley took turns driving. We had no time to sleep with the ball only a few nights from now. Scott was taking us to a well-known tailor amongst his kind. Although we were not Elemental Breathers he said we were to still wear the appropriate attire or it would only antagonize the others more and provoke a fight.

No other being other than an Elemental Breather has been welcomed into the ball, so we were aware of the possible repercussions, but with very little leads as to where Taskatae was, we had no choice. We had to hope that someone would know where she might be. Perhaps we would even go unnoticed.

Eventually, after a very long drive we arrived in a large town, almost like a city. Bright lights illuminated our path despite the night sky as we drove through the unfamiliar surroundings. It was odd to see so many lights in an urban setting and to look up at the tall buildings in awe, after such a long time in small towns and woodland.

I gawked at all that surrounded us, mesmerized as if I had never seen anything like it. The city was called Shorogo, according to the many signs we drove past as we followed Scott. There were many drunken women in short dresses, laughing at one another and jumping on the men's backs. Others were jogging past them, some still out with prams, walking their babies, and we passed several teenagers who carried large shopping bags.

Paul also looked at it all in fascination. It had been a very long time since we had been in such a civilization; and all of this could be on offer for him if he left me now. Paige was unfazed by the bright lights and only looked up at a few of the people, still bored.

After driving longer through the brightly lit streets, Scott parked his car on the side of a street that seemed a little shadier than the beautiful scene we had been viewing only minutes ago. Steam came from the ground and there weren't as many brightly lit street lamps or flashing signs. He straightened his red jacket and combed his white hair through, waiting for all of us to gather as we looked around suspiciously.

"My little darlings," he condescended. "Just don't speak, she isn't the fondest of your kind, and unusually, unlike most of my kind, she can sense what you are straight away," he said before walking down an alleyway where we were to follow. "And don't let anyone know you are the descendant of the Elders, especially that you carry Aeisha," he shouted back as a warning to Lucas and me.

We could hear a beat of music grow louder as we walked. Tall, eroding apartment buildings were surrounding us and narrowly squeezing us into the alleyway. Following Scott and the music, we arrived at the end of the alleyway, where a small open space with a dirty fountain poured. A white naked statue held a vase that poured green water into the base of the fountain. I looked at the color oddly; a flicker of something came from beneath.

Are there fish in there?

I walked closer to it as the others walked ahead, mesmerized by the colored water. Another flicker came from the water caused by some sort of golden-scaled tail. I looked closer, inspecting it, reaching out to tap the water to attract the fish so I could decipher what it was. I had to know what kind of fish it was.

Reaching my hand out closer to touch it, Scott quickly grabbed my hand, snapping me out of my trance. I looked back at him in confusion as he pulled my hand away.

"No, Honey," he said firmly. "We don't touch that." His eyes diverted up and I too looked upward. A man with only one arm stood above us on an iron balcony. His skin was orange scale, with emerald eyes piercing down at us. He simply stared, his eyes consuming me. I looked back down at the large water fountain. It now seemed not to be so milky.

The green water wasn't glazed over like it had appeared to me only moments ago. Beneath I realized it was not a fish at all but an orange-like organism with scaled skin, much like the man's. To my horror it had five fingers; all up the arm and within the scales were tiny cannibal teeth. It swirled with a demented grace within the water.

I looked back up at the man, abashed. *Had he created some kind of illusion? Would that thing in there have attacked me?*

"What is that?" I demanded.

"He is an Elemental Breather," Scott said simply. "And yes, he would have eaten you, if you touched that thing his fingers would've driven deep into your chest, eating you from the inside out."

I looked back at him, mortified. We were no longer in the sparkling and brightly lit city that seemed so enticing. We were in a different area completely.

"Be cautious of where we are," Scott whispered, his pink eyes daunting.

I held my hand, a little shaken as I stared at the thing one more time before following the others who were looking back at me. I looked up to the apartments where many others looked down on us: some intrigued, some grotesque, some bored — all of them appearing to me as Elemental Breathers.

"You are *mostly* safe with me," Scott promised, giving Paul a sly smile.

"Mostly?" Ashley repeated. I assumed everyone else understood we were not in an area of humans.

"Well, I can't guarantee anything. Out of respect, if an Elemental Breather has a guest, you don't trifle with them. But, well, my kind does have a slight temper problem, so please don't annoy anyone. I have no guarantees," Scott continued walking us to a purple-bricked wall. A few paved steps dropped to the door. He sighed to himself, shaking his head and muttering: "This will be the end of our friendship...."

He quietly tapped on the door. After much hesitation a black older woman with purple frizzy hair and small purple eyes opened the door. She had many gold chains wrapped around her neck, arms, and even ankles. The high waist purple pants she wore were of the fine material of Elemental breathers. She wore a sleeveless light purple shirt with ruffles at the front. She was not amused as Scott clasped his hands together with a smile.

"Mimi," he said, opening his arms out wide for a hug. She raised her hands to him while inspecting us.

"You have the audacity to bring humans to my shop?" she asked, her eyes flickering black as the veins within her skin, especially around her eyes and mouth, lit with a radiant purple. As her eyes glimmered black threateningly, Lucas and I slowly felt for our weapons, expecting her imminent rage.

"Put your weapons away," Scott pouted at us, still carefree of the situation. "I only need to look at your attire and then we shall leave!"

"And for what purpose would the likes of humans need Elemental Breathers' material?" she said, reassessing Lucas and me, her fluorescent veins slowly melting within her skin again and her eyes regaining their purple.

Scott somberly dropped his head and shoulders, looking as if he could cry. "Father is forcing me to take them to the ball."

She laughed to herself with hot breath that seemed to take my breath away intoxicatingly. My eyes went funny as if in a daze. She stopped and looked at us, who were all affected the same. *What is this Element of hers that has affected us simply by her heavy breath?*

"Your father truly hates you and wants you dead," she said with a smirk on her face.

"Please Mimi," he said, dropping onto his knees and holding his clasped hands together up to her. What had happened to Scott's famous Elemental Breather pride?

"Very well," she said waving us all in. The room was dark with light purple lanterns decorating it. It smelt dusty and the opening room had very little space for us to move around in as large clumps of material were piled everywhere.

On the left there was a small wooden desk and a large throne chair where a hairless cat sat hissing and growling at us when we walked through. We followed Mimi into another room that was much larger and luxurious. One long white sofa adorned with pillows ran along the wall next to the door we had walked in from. A bright purple chandelier was lighting the whole room. Across from the long sofa were four small rooms with deep purple curtains hiding what was inside. Surrounding us were large mirrors, making the atmosphere even more exquisite.

"Now, what are you after, my love?" Mimi addressed Scott as he sat comfortably on the cushioned seat, crossing his legs.

"Oh Mimi, whatever you find that suits them best," Scott dismissed with a light laugh. "I don't know if much can be done to help their kind, really."

Mimi clearly agreed with him as she appraised us all distastefully. I couldn't help but feel the obvious status difference that the Elemental Breathers were convinced of. Nodding to herself in contemplation, she began selecting clothing for us to wear.

"The girls go in first," Mimi said, pointing us in the direction of the changing rooms. Paige walked in first, unfazed and still bored, followed by Harmony and then myself. Behind the large curtain was a small room with a wooden side table and a purple lantern. A small white cushioned chair sat beside the mirror and along the wall was a high rack where clothes could hang from.

Mimi let herself into my changing room, giving me only one dress to try and nothing else to choose from as she looked me up and down, disgusted. She hung up a long black backless dress, which had a slit on the outer leg. Small green gems trailed down the light silver chain that wrapped around the neck and hung down the back. I instantly recognized the sweeping circled pattern of Elemental Breather material. I looked at it, sighing in disappointment. Must the Elemental Breathers always choose such exotic and revealing dresses for me?

I slowly put it on, finding Mimi's measurements to be almost exact. It was very tight fitting. The slit crept up on my leg and I wished I had clips to pin it. I frantically looked over at my single blade of Aeisha that was still in my belt now on the floor.

My mind raced in panic. *With a dress so tight how will I hide my weapon? Am I able to walk in with it openly showing or will that only annoy them even more? Worse than that, no one can know I am the keeper of Aeisha...*

"Hurry up and come out, girls!" Scott shouted from behind the curtains. A mouse crept underneath my curtain and Scott materialized from it, making me clutch tightly at my exposed skin, embarrassed.

"Well, don't you look ravishing," he said with a smile. "But I know I am not the only one who wishes to see such a sight. "He pushed me out but I caught myself and clumsily fell before Ashley, Lucas, and Paul, who stared at me, eyes widened. I fiddled with the slit self-consciously.

"Where would you put your weapon?" Ashley asked, having the same concern as me.

"Dear boy, women always have accessories, we can hide it in a clutch or bag," Scott said mockingly, turning me to face Harmony and Paige.

Harmony wore a light blue strapless dress that hung heavily to her feet. Paige wore a tight maroon dress. She seemed undisturbed by its shortness. The material crept above her knees, and with her chunky leather boots she reminded me a lot of Trish. The shoulders seemed padded. A light see-through material covered her collarbones and then faded into the thicker material covering her chest. She swept a look over the mirror before lifting her lips in what sounded to be a growl. With that, she meandered back into the changing room.

"Perhaps you should purchase some masks as well, Scott. I have already assembled some for your consideration," Mimi said as she walked in with colored suits. "Most Elemental Breathers rely heavily on their sight still. Not all of us can simply 'sense' the familiarity of someone, like your father can. Perhaps you should blind the others of their identity if you are serious about taking them to the ball."

"Always up-selling," he said, waggling his finger at her. "Very well, but nothing tacky, and I will take whatever shoes and accessories you find fitting for them, just make sure—..." Scott paused, looking toward the door. "Mimi, I think we may have brought some unwanted guests here..."

"Besides those who are already here?" she smirked. "How far away are they?"

"Not very far. Mimi, let us deal with this, we have already asked too much of you," Scott offered. As they spoke, I projected my Shield into the ground, sensing what it was Scott noticed. As I did I began choking and gasping for air as I instantly felt poisoned from the ground.

Lucas and Paul ran for me as I stumbled back against the curtain, using it to hold me up. I grasped for my throat, coughing coarsely. My sight was being taken over by a purple mist. Mimi came toward me, shaking her head in disapproval. She pushed Lucas and Paul away and grabbed both sides of my cheeks.

She inhaled my gasping breath, and as she did I felt that whatever was consuming me and poisoning me was being drawn out of my body. Her small purple eyes stared back at me, annoyed.

"What did you do to me?" I gasped.

"Who are you?" she replied angrily. "She is not like the others," she spoke directly to Scott.

I must hide my identity and Aeisha.

"Well, let us be honest, we are all a *little* different. That isn't really the problem here," he said once again, motioning toward the door.

"Let me go to them, I haven't had fun for a while," she said gravely, before giving me a suspicious side-glance once more and leaving. *Does every Elemental Breather simply enjoy bathing in darkness, never giving the chance of a fight to pass up? Was she truly more interested in the fight at hand than my identity?*

"What was that?" I said as I looked at the ground, which was unmarked. Lucas and Paul looked over me with concern as I gathered myself, startled by the poison that spread through my body.

"Mimi can poison anything or anyone. She has poisoned her shop and can activate it at any time against intruders or unwelcome guests. You, however, must've triggered it yourself, absorbing the poison when your Shield made contact with the ground. She can obviously extract it from whatever was poisoned as well. That was what she was inhaling, but by doing so she now knows that you are different. We shouldn't be here for much longer in case she becomes curious. If she finds out who you really are and that you carry one of the Immortal Blades it will become problematic," Scott warned as he ushered me back into the changing room to change my clothes and hide Aeisha. "Grab the suits. The rest will be at the counter with your shoes, masks, and everything else needed to make you look fabulous."

Just as Scott said, everything else was already piled on the wooden table when we emerged from the changing rooms. He grabbed the black bags stuffed with suits and dresses.

"Harmony, sweetie," he called, "Can you hold these?" He handed her the other large silver bag of items.

"I can carry those," Ashley said, trying to grab them.

"No. Mimi might be having fun with our guests outside but she won't step out any further than that alleyway away from her shop, then we will have to fight on our own. And I refuse, after spending so much money on all of this, for these to be damaged."

"What's out there?" I inquired, still unable to sense anything from the poisoned walls and flooring.

"Starkorfs," Scott said simply, leaving a small bag of gold on the table as we left.

Chapter Twenty-Two- Her Darkness

As Scott led us outside, a Starkorf came running for us. Before I could react, Scott forcefully threw his hand over mine to stop me from revealing Aeisha. The others quickly drew their blades, uncertain as the Starkorf stopped, choked, and gasped horrifically. Mimi crept from the darkness with a cracked smile as she stepped over another Starkorf carcass. The wounded male Starkorf stared at us pleadingly, his eyes fixated on Lucas.

"Leaving so soon?" she called out joyfully as another ran for her. The Starkorf quickly dropped to his knees as well, choking on what I assumed to be her poisoned breath. Mimi's eyes were engulfed by black and her veins glowed with bright purple. The edges of her eyes and lips now paled into a light purple too.

"I have left you a very generous bag of gold on your desk, Mimi, and now we must leave for our cars before they light them on fire," he laughed to her as he walked past, still carrying the large bags of clothing. She looked at him steadily and then to me, her eyes resting on Aeisha, which was still hidden beneath my jacket.

Mimi was quickly distracted from her fixation on me as a female Starkorf dropped from above. Mimi simply took a step to the side and the woman heavily fell to the cement ground, gasping. The Starkorf's face was melted horrifically on one side. I turned to leave, desensitized to such sights.

I quickly followed the others as Lucas and Ashley stood behind me wearily, making sure Mimi did not once again pry about my hidden weapon. As we ran toward our car, I noticed a dead Starkorf at the edge of the water fountain, his hand dipped in the water. I looked away, wondering about the horrific ending he had. I glanced up at the Elemental Breather, who now rocked back and forth on a chair, comfortable and well fed.

I focused on Paul's back, preparing for the few Starkorfs surrounding our cars. I now felt their presence without Mimi's poisoned barrier. We pressed through the narrow alleyway and broke out into the street. The dim light of the street lamps illuminated several Starkorfs as they screeched and jumped at me.

I instantly projected my Shield, pulling Aeisha out at the same time. They could not compete with my Shield and a few were instantly forced to retreat. I drove Aeisha deep into one's stomach, pulling her out and slicing across another's knees.

I must get to Paul.

I focused on Paul who was beside Harmony. Strangely, she did not shoot arrows but used her bow instead to hit them away forcefully. I couldn't rely on her to protect Paul. He swung his knife at one Starkorf who persisted in reaching him. It ducked as Paul swung his knife.

As the Starkorf was distracted, I ran at it from behind, stopping as Ashley had already plunged his sword into the side of it before grabbing it and flinging it away from Harmony and Paul. I bumped into something behind me but stopped myself from swiping as I recognized that it was Lucas's Shield that rubbed up against my own.

We panted, exhausted by the confrontation. We looked around at the few dead Starkorfs on the ground. To my surprise it seemed as if those who attacked us were the last of the ambush. Many had already gone into the alleyway and had been taken care of by Mimi.

Ashley went to pick one of the bodies up out of habit, needing to rid the scene of the evidence. It would be so much more convenient if they simply vanished after their deaths. As heartless as I felt thinking it, I could no longer see them as humans. The ones that attacked us hardly resembled that, and their nature was too wild. I knew from past experience that they have killed so many people simply to try and stay youthful.

"Don't worry about that," Scott old Ashley, neatly placing the bagged clothes in the boot of the car and dusting his hands off. He had evaded all attackers to neatly put away the clothes. At some point he even somehow managed to take the bags Harmony carried as they were already in the boot. Our priorities were clearly different as my first instinct was to defend us, in comparison to Scott, who believed the clothes, shoes, and accessories must be saved first.

"What do you mean 'don't worry about that?'" Ashley questioned, only hesitating for a moment before picking up the Starkorf's body.

"We can leave it here," Scott explained, walking around the side of the car. "There are a lot of Elemental Breathers within these buildings. One might say some of them will be grateful if we left them behind," he insinuated.

I tried to hide my disgust, as my mind ran over the numerous reasons for which an Elemental Breather might want a Starkorf's body. *Will they experiment? Are they trying to learn more? Will they indulge some cult-like dance in celebration? Will they... eat them?*

I realized now how much they all varied and, looking at Scott, it appeared that he and his family were much more civilized. *Do they differ much from the Starkorfs if they hurt humans?* I thought about the Elemental Breather with scaled skin who mystically enchanted people with his water fountain. If touched, the creature beneath would eat the person from the inside out. I shuddered.

Although I knew the threat inherent in the Elemental Breather kind, I didn't realize how vast their abilities and personalities stretched. I was surprised as to how many Elemental Breathers we now came across on this journey with Scott. So many of them resided within these buildings, yet Kurt and Lucas had once claimed them to be so rare that it was only Max, Trish, and Scott that they knew of. *Were they misinformed, scared of meeting more, or could they simply not find where they hid?*

As I became increasingly enlightened about the species of Elemental Breathers, I began to dread the ball even more.

We drove for hours. The time slowly crept to when we had to be at the docks. Scott wanted to avoid the large masses as most took their own boats and yachts. Few took the standard free boat, which would later help us to avoid attention.

He said some wore masks, as they didn't want others to know their true identity for whatever reason, giving us the perfect excuse to all wear one. Most, however, didn't do it, as their kind was always proud, so we still had to exercise caution at all times. We were to later approach the ship differently and make very little contact with one another so others wouldn't be suspicious.

We first stopped at a nearby motel. Scott persuaded the staff to accept a gold coin instead of the value in actual cash. We changed into our respective formal wear in nervous silence. Lucas, Ashley, and Paul, were in another room getting changed.

As I self-consciously straightened my own black dress, Scott came in wearing a white long-tailed suit with a red tie, his white hair slicked back. I noticed the appearance of foundation on his already perfectly unblemished skin.

He insisted on doing our hair and makeup. Much to my horror I had to comply. When I looked over everyone else, it was clear none of us had much of an idea how to apply makeup. He straightened Harmony's hair and then applied natural colors to her face with lipstick and eye shadow.

Paige snapped one of the blush brushes in front of Scott, warning him not to touch her or she would stab him with his own tool. He giggled and then evaporated just as Paige passed out. He left her body after putting her to sleep, but then he stared at her for a long moment, confused.

"What is it?" I said, intrigued.

"Within her I can feel no presence. It's utter darkness within her. I've never made contact with someone like that," he admitted haltingly. "She's empty."

I looked over Paige with him. *Well, if she isn't human, then what could she be?*

Scott inspected her for a moment longer and then proceeded to do her hair as she slept. I looked away. I was already worried about the terrible things she would say and do when she woke. Paige became resplendent with bold black lipstick, smoky eye shadow and a smoothed black bob. Scott smiled down at his handy work.

He then turned his attention to me. Arranging my long light-brown hair into loose curls, and pinning them to the side. I sighed heavily, feeling the same sort of resentment as Paige did. However, compared to the night ahead, the makeup and hair process was relatively painless.

He painted my lips red, applied blush and then a light shade of green powder across my eyelids, highlighting my brown eyes. Scott was just as impressed with my transformation. We turned as we heard Paige wake. With a smile he grabbed his things quickly and fled.

After listening to Paige rant for several minutes as she threatened to kill him, we finished getting ready. I was not yet sure whether she was serious or not, but she seemed over it. I watched as she fixed her black knife in her sheath at her chest where no one could see it. As Scott had said, the only place I could hide my own blade was within my black, glittering clutch, which I held onto firmly even while putting my matching sparkly heels on.

We were instructed to put on petite masks that were the same color as our dresses. They were very fine masks, which hid our identity with lacy material. I had a fondness for it, feeling as I put it on I was truly hiding myself behind a mask — that I could be anyone I wanted without Misfeata's influence. I haven't heard from her for days now.

The whole process of getting ready reminded me of when my best friend, Sarah, recently wanted me to go to a ball that was being organized by our school. I said no, but to have that moment reincarnated in front of me once again brought on nostalgia. I couldn't help but feel warmth remembering a simple invite from a much-loved friend.

Still thinking of school and my old life, I looked across the room at Paul. The others came to our door, waiting for us. As I looked at him, I could only question how different everything might have been if none of this had happened. Would Paul have asked me to that ball? Would I have accepted? What kind of life could I have had with Paul?

His green eyes looked back at me intently through his white mask. His hair was slicked back and he was wearing a white suit that seemed very similar to Scott's. I grinned as I noticed the 'coincidence.' I couldn't look away from him. I felt as if I were hidden behind the mask and that my feelings were no longer conflicted. In this mask I felt like I was just being, with no hardship or expectations. I could be whoever I wanted to be.

I blinked numerous times, pulling myself back to reality and breaking my intense gaze on Paul. I have stared at him for so long and now I was embarrassed and still conflicted as I felt Lucas's heavy eyes on me. I wanted to run away. I wanted to run away from the both of them. But in such a situation I could only stand in front of them, exposed.

"Karla," Paul said taking a step toward me. "You look beautiful."

"Eh," Lucas smirked coldly. "I think you would look better with less on."

He turned abruptly, following the others and leaving me to the tense atmosphere. Harmony was looking sympathetically at Paul who was flushed with infuriation. I too was slightly abashed by Lucas's comment, surprised he would say such a thing so openly. I didn't know if I was embarrassed or angry.

Paul held the door open for me while I made sure I still had Aeisha in my clutch. "Do you have yours?" I asked, concerned that we were about to arrive on an island of Elemental Breathers. He tapped his ribs lightly, indicating where he hid his knife.

"I do," he said, placing his hand on my back as he walked me out. We followed the others toward the nearby docks, which held an air of abandonment.

I took in a long hard breath, preparing myself for the night to come. I looked up at the half-moon which was obscured by a gray, ominous-looking cloud. *I must do this to find where Taskatae hides — I must find the truth of Nathanial's alliance with Kurt. I must find out where Aeisha is, as without her I can feel my ability depleting.* I've already relied on her heavily. *I must do this.*

Chapter Twenty-Three- Performance

$\mathcal{W}$e agreed to go forward in smaller groups. It was too suspicious if all of us gathered together. From how Scott had described Elemental Breathers, they didn't exactly have many friends. The purpose of their annual ball sounded more like an excuse to exchange information and gossip. If they didn't all get along, why else hold such an event? Scott compared it to a royal gathering so that we could understand. They all wanted one another's land or information so they all played nice. The high standards he saw in his own kind were wearing thin on my nerves.

Scott organized for Paige and Ashley to go together. Harmony and Lucas went as another team, as did Paul, Scott, and I. We did so slowly under his instructions, walking to the docks at separate intervals. It was daunting to walk to the docks where we knew Elemental Breathers waited. Like Scott had said, there weren't too many, and we only spotted six in the dull night. One small lamppost shone over their heads as they waited on the wooden pier. None of them looked abnormal and if I hadn't known better by their Elemental Breather clothing I would have suspected them to be humans.

Ashley and Paige walked past a male, whose shoulder bumped into Paige. She looked back at him tense, her fist slightly raised. They stared at one another angrily before Ashley grabbed Paige's shoulders and ushered her away. The Elemental Breather continued walking and his black flashing eyes were engulfed by blue. Out of all of us I thought it was Paige, ironically, who would fit in most: her temperament being that of an Elemental Breather's. She was always quickly angered and willing to fight. It only impressed on me further what Scott had said about her seeming empty.

Paul, Scott, and I, sat on the clean wooden chairs as I looked over the vast amount of water we ventured over. Scott constantly smoothed his hair and suit, looking at Paul wickedly from the corner of his eyes. I noticed a flickering light in the distance and wondered if that was the island we would travel to.

"Are you okay with this?" Paul asked, deep in thought. I wasn't sure. I was quite nervous, but knew I had to go. My only regret being that Paul was once again in danger. *I will not let anything happen to him.*

"Yes," I said after long contemplation. *I must if I am already here.* He stretched backward, his enormity reminding me of the school chairs that seemed so small in comparison to his large frame. He reached into the bushes behind us before revealing his hand to me, which had a small purple flower in it. Offering it to me, I took it, embarrassed and yet grateful for the gesture.

"You do look beautiful tonight," he whispered heavily, looking away as a blush streaked across his cheeks. "Well, you always do."

Scott stretched out his hand to Paul for a flower too, but Paul cowered from his demanding hand. Across from us on another long wooden bench sat someone in heavy black Elemental Breather clothes, but not like ours. It was a cloak with a hood and they also had a green mask on. By their frame I couldn't tell if it were male or female. But as I looked at the other Elemental Breathers who were alone, this Elemental Breather was the only one that was fully covered, their identity completely concealed.

A loud horn blared, breaking me from my intense trance. I questioned if this was the kind of Elemental Breather Scott was earlier describing, that didn't want their identity to be known.

We rose steadily, looking over the others. Paige and Ashley stood near the edge of the dock. Paige was impatiently waiting for the boat while she tapped her foot, arms crossed. Lucas rested against the lamppost, his hands in the pockets of his black pants. He hadn't bothered to button the sleeves of his white shirt. He was looking far too comfortable and casual to be an Elemental Breather, making me question if he was at all going to try to act like one. I dropped my gaze away from Lucas's dark-brown eyes as he looked over me intently even though Scott had specifically told us to avoid showing recognition.

Harmony stood straight, her hands clasped elegantly in front of her. Scott had purchased for her a sophisticated fur coat, which covered her back and shoulders, concealing the bow that was strapped on her back.

The Elemental Breather in the heavy cloaks boarded after us, just before Harmony and Lucas. Although small, the boat was very luxurious, with fine lacquered wood and a large white chandelier. I admired the white walls and nicely polished wooden floors. There were tables with gold-trimmed cloths and petite wooden chairs with ornate carvings very similar to the pattern on the Elemental Breathers' material.

We took a seat as a woman who had glazed eyes came to us in what seemed to be an unconscious state, offering us wine. I looked into her eyes and saw no spirit. When we declined, she smiled without feeling and walked away, her long black hair swishing side to side. I looked at Scott, who made a sighing noise as he explained.

"The shipmaster can harness people's minds, and once they can't think for themselves only their body remains, so he uses them as servants. He only usually does it to the humans who have jumped on his boat but he takes them for the rest of their lives," he explained in an inappropriately carefree manner before greeting a man who walked past. I looked at Paul, regretting that I had brought him. I tried to keep my obvious concern and fear from my expression, just as he did the same. *Everything will be okay. We will not be noticed.*

After exchanging unsettled looks, we tried to forget the servants. They were already doomed to their fate. We reached where the large light flickered. From afar you could see the bricked steps that crept from the wooden dock. They had lights streaming up the sides. The stairs lead to enormous open wooden doors. We stared in awe; it looked like a castle. Through large windows you could see many lights shining from inside.

Paul grabbed my hand firmly as my heart pumped nervously. I could tell by the firm pressing of his thumb as it stroked my hand that he too was nervous. I held it firmly, still trying to look unfazed as the dazed servants walked past. I couldn't calm my nerves as my chest rose and fell uncomfortably and I began to slightly panic, despite Paul's best efforts to comfort me.

My panic must have started to show on my face. Pauls' grip tightened around my hand as he gestured that I should calm myself. *How can we get out of this? What other Elements are in here and what can they do to us?* Starkorfs seemed like no challenge in comparison to these creatures we were about to face.

Their nature was to savor pain and suffering. My mind appraised our enemies comparatively. Starkorfs had a wildness about them; even from birth most had no control of themselves. They probably never recognized themselves as humans. In comparison, the Elemental Breathers had control of their ability, but chose to use it for pain and suffering. They always allowed themselves to be overcome by a murderous rage. *Who was this world's true enemy? Who is it that I fear the most now?*

Scott grabbed my other hand, giving me a small smile. I felt calmness sweep over me as he etched slightly into my fingertips and calmed my nerves. My heavy breathing subsided and within seconds, I could look back at him steadily. In the castle I knew I had to be cautious and calm. I had to be brave for all our sakes. I wanted to push my hand through Paul's slicked brown hair to tell him it would be okay. But I knew I was only trying to convince myself.

As the boat hit the edge of the pier I felt as if my stomach had been pulled out. We waited for everyone else to leave before we stood up. I tried to suppress the sudden trembling I felt, as a sharp pain shot through the left side of my body, forcing me to straighten. I felt Misfeata stir. I could no longer breathe and I tried my hardest not to choke on the blood I felt rising in my throat.

My body is shutting down on me again.

My chair made a conspicuous scrapping noise across the wooden floor as my body flung forward. I gasped into the floor, grabbing the hooded Elemental Breather's attention. *I am drawing attention to us.* My sight became glassy. I tried my hardest to contain the acid that rose in my throat. My unsteady state tormented my consciousness. My body was breaking apart. My legs were shot with a fiery burn that I wished I could dampen.

I cannot make a scene in front of all of them, they will know...

Paul quickly scurried for the needle he had in his pocket. I lost my grip on him and began to fall into a daze. I spluttered into the floor, no longer able to control it. I winced in pain, trying to contain my screams. Scott's foot extended into a seal flipper so that the blood I coughed dropped onto him and left no evidence on the floor.

A cold burning sensation wrapped around my neck as slowly I felt the burden lift from me, and my sight came into focus. Lucas had a firm grip around the back of my neck as he looked down at me with determined eyes. "I'd appreciate it if you got off the ship now, love," he said with authority, his personality now transitioning into an Elemental Breather's demeanor.

"You will not be telling her such a thing unless you want to die," Scott spat back, his eyes convulsing black. He had quickly jumped into his role. An African-American man came out who looked over us oddly. He was wearing all white and a captain's hat. He somehow created a terrible atmosphere. *Is he the one that takes control of these people?*

As Scott and Lucas acted furious at one another, I gasped loudly for my first breath. I felt Lucas's burning touch relieve all my torture. The poisoned blood still lingered in my throat with a despicable taste, but my body was already recouping from the pain.

I no longer felt alone as I fought Misfeata's presence within me. If my body continued shutting down for a bit longer, she might have taken advantage and possessed my body, but even then if I had no cure, what would she have done in such circumstance? I knew I would have survived with the adrenaline shot that Paul always carried with him. But looking at Paul sadly I knew it was the last one we had for now and I was grateful for Lucas being able to take away my pain.

Lucas coughed into his hand before covering it with his leather glove, but I caught sight of the blotches of blood on it. His face had begun sweating slightly and I realized by draining me in such a predicament that Lucas was hurting himself.

"I won't tolerate this distraction any longer," Scott dismissed dramatically, picking me up by my arm. My legs trembled to stand. His firm grip on me heightened my spirits as I could feel him within me, quickly repairing the injuries I had taken.

He began pulling me toward the door with Paul but the shipmaster stepped in front of us, his dark-green eyes weighing heavy on me. The humans under his control began surrounding us, entrapping us as he stepped closer.

"You will wait here," he said, inspecting me as the mindless humans continued to surround us, their movement slow and unstable.

"I don't want to," Scott retaliated angrily, his black eyes mirroring the shipmasters. All other guests were now off the ship. The cloaked Elemental Breather watched us intently from the docks. *I cannot fight these people, even if they are no longer in control of themselves, I cannot hurt them. Could we attack the shipmaster? How long did it take for him to take someone's mind?* If anything is to happen right now, at least we will not be seen by other Elemental Breathers or give ourselves away.

The shipmaster took another step forward threateningly. A low thud was heard and his mouth instantly dropped open as his eyes glazed white and he dropped to his knees. As he fell, we glimpsed Paige's black knife protruding from the back of his head.

I looked up shocked as Paige jumped over from the dock she had thrown it from and reefed it out wildly. I looked away, disgusted. I had thought they were already near the castle. Was she waiting for this moment the whole time?

"You can't just kill them," Ashley hissed.

"No one will really care," Scott promised, stepping over the Elemental Breather's dead body. "You'd be surprised how many casualties there are at this ball."

I looked back at Paul, whose eyes reflected my own. *Fear.* I was scared.

Lucas coughed heavily into his leather glove before pushing past Paul and walking out with Harmony. As Paul went to take a step toward Lucas, angered by the harsh nudge, I grabbed his hand and pulled him back from creating a scene.

"We must split up again," Scott said, distracted by the low moans of the humans around us. Slowly they rubbed their heads and looked at one another as the color of their eyes returned. Some were over fifty but some were as young as I was.

"Now my little loves," Scott called out, clapping his hands together at the humans who crept out of their daze. "You will wait here until I return or I will hunt you all down and kill you all," he said, startling them. I grew angry at his threat toward people who had done nothing wrong. "Paige and Ashley, you can stay and make sure they don't leave," he added.

Paige made a noise of disgruntlement.

"You're a liability," he spat, dismissing her. In many ways he was right, her temper was far too great to keep us inconspicuous.

Scott looked at me, rolling his eyes at my angry stare. "This is our only way off this island, Love," he explained. Now that Paige had carelessly killed the shipmaster there was no one else who would wait for us. He was right. But since when did I condone threatening innocent people for my own benefit?

Chapter Twenty-Four- Distasteful Match

$\mathscr{P}$aige did as she was told after Ashley sternly spoke with her. Somehow he had control over her. She listened, although not happy about being left out of a fight, she stayed, her arms folded across her chest while pouting.

Ashley reassured me that he would look after the humans and explain to them what happened. He would try to rehabilitate them into their basic sense of humanity before they were freed back on the main land. I didn't know how effective his words would be. If I woke up years later to find my body had aged and I knew nothing of what had happened, I wouldn't comprehend reason.

Scott took the lead, walking up the long staircase. Paul offered his hand out to me, helping me as he nodded elegantly to one of the standing Elemental Breathers who greeted us. Lucas and Harmony had already entered the towering building. It looked even more castle-like up close. The light reflecting off the water's surface made it seem even more mystical. I looked up in amazement, sad that something so beautiful was in a hidden part of the world. *I wonder if this is an Elemental Breather's home, or is it only used for the annual ball?*

Even the large wooden doors that curved at the top were beautifully detailed and carved with the same vine-like spirals of the Elemental Breather's material. Their whole culture evolved around this one design. It made me question what significant purpose it had, if any. I was now even more intrigued by their existence.

Ashley had once described them to me as 'witches' many years ago. But not much more was said on the matter. No one was very educated on their past or their beliefs, as no one other than an Elemental Breather really knew. I was most interested in what period of time the Elemental Breathers begun to believe themselves as god-like and better than any other being. Was it retaliation after all those years of their kind being burned as witches?

Max Jacket had mentioned a few times that he once worked with Elisabeth, the previous Shielder to inherit and contain Misfeata within her. He said that there was once a place that all those who had the ability were locked away called the Great Wall. This included Shielders, Starkorfs, and

Elemental Breathers. For so many years they had co-existed as Shielder and Starkorf alike. We were educated on our ancestry and knew of this, but still had very little knowledge of Elemental Breathers.

I looked at Scott strangely as if he were a completely different creature to me now. I knew nothing of him or of his kind. We walked through the front doors where bright light and classical music streamed in from and before I could gawk at my surroundings in awe, we were instantly made the subject of attention.

"Oh Scott, my goodness," a handsome man in a gray suit with light-brown eyes and golden-blonde hair called out. He made his way over with a proud stride. "Oh, and you have brought little friends too. What ill reputation you carry with you now," he said looking over us. I looked at him angrily, as did Paul. Here we could freely express what annoyance we had and heighten it into anger, much like an Elemental Breather would do.

"Jordy, it has been too long!"

The two approached one another, giving each other an enthusiastic hug and kiss on the cheek. I pressed firmly into Paul's hand, we had to act as Elemental Breathers, and for this my temper had to be hot. I was surprised by my easy performance skills as quickly I felt myself on the edge of anger. Was this only my performance or could I really be this angry inside? I noticed Misfeata's consciousness was now fully awake and stirring within me, wanting to get out. Her rage enhanced my own.

"Although cute..." Jordy judged, his eyes lingering on Paul. "You really should have acquired better company." His pink lips formed a wicked smile.

Scott's smile faded and he shuffled under a woman's intense stare as she approached. The woman had the same golden-blonde hair and light-brown eyes as Jordy. Upon her stare Scott started twisting his face in pain and disorientation.

"You will not be accompanying my brother. Last time you broke his heart," she said elegantly, her eyes beginning to flicker black above her polite smile. Scott tried smiling between his harsh and shallow breathes, but by looking at his face I could tell he was in far too much pain from something this woman was doing to him.

I intervened with her stare, stepping in front of Scott, unsure of what this Elemental Breather was doing to him. She arched her eyebrow at me in challenge, smiling as a still blackness engulfed her eyes. Jordy tugged on her long-sleeved blue dress, begging her to stop.

A ringing noise in my ears began as she fixated on me. A familiar song came to me as it instantly pierced like sirens within my head, forcing me to clutch at them, covering whatever noise it was. I realized it was not the outside of my ears that beat with such a retched noise; it was within my head. The song continued and under the loud screeching I could faintly hear lyrics. It was my father's favorite song that played, causing me anguish as it reminded me of the joy he had listening to it and dancing, much to my dismay when I was younger. The memory still pained me; the song pulled out a most hurtful sensation of pain.

Just like a snap of the fingers, the noise stopped and I felt the release of pressure in my ears. Taking my cupped hands off I looked up at Paul as he stared at me worriedly, his beautiful deep-green eyes engulfing me as I stared for a moment, trying to understand what just happened. The woman looked at me, unfazed; no longer with black eyes as her light-brown eyes flooded with color.

"I will be going," she said sharply, excusing herself. Jordy dipped his head in apology, following his sister as Scott pointedly fixed his suit.

"Her Element is, well, basically one might say, it is like music of the memory," he said, watching after her in distaste. "You might not think it, but it is a powerful tool. It can pierce one's eardrum, making them deaf if too loud; make someone begin to think they are stir-crazy if too low. But most importantly, she can sense the raw emotions or most heightened experiences in one's life. With music she can express that sensation and emotion, heighten it. She can either make someone deliriously happy or extremely suicidal," he said, still looking at them from behind with a grim face.

I retained the tears that threatened to spill, trying to push my father out of my thoughts to focus on the task at hand. The song made me want to curl myself into a ball and once again cry at my sin, no matter how much I tried to push the thought away. She had brought up too raw of an emotion. I swallowed my emotions and forced myself to concentrate.

"Where do we look from here?" I said, looking around at all the Elemental Breathers who were well groomed. They seemed to be all drinking wine. Some were giggling amongst themselves; others were staring at each other awkwardly as if trying to control themselves from causing a scene.

The room was big and within the center of it were long tables of food, which were placed next to a large round bar where a neatly groomed Elemental Breather poured wine into a woman's glass with a sly smile. Large gold chandeliers hung from the ceiling and candles were attached to the walls. The floors were white marble with a large staircase on both sides of the magnificent room, with gold trimming that rose to the second floor.

Some Elemental Breathers were up there looking down at the others. Behind I could see there to be doors, which I assumed to be rooms.

Large windows surrounded, giving an open view of the water outside that reflected the shine from the lights within. Looking over all the various formal wear, I couldn't help but still feel underdressed; they just glowed with the presence of something... otherworldly.

"Well, of course we start with those who like to sell exotic goods," Scott winked confidently.

"Exotic goods?" I parroted.

Scott searched around the room, fixating his eyes on a much shorter Elemental Breather, one about my height. He had wiry long green hair pulled back into a braid and he was speaking with a woman who looked at him with disgust before walking away. He watched her walk off with hideous, hungry eyes. He was a creep. He wore a bright-blue tailed suit with mismatched green shoes. He quickly drank his wine and walked over to the bar again where hesitantly the barman poured another.

"There he is," Scott said pushing me forward. "Now, you need to get him into that room up there away from the eyes of the others and interrogate him." Scott indicated to one of the rooms I had previously glanced over on the second floor.

"But how will I do that?" I asked innocently, not wanting to be in the presence of such a sleazy man. As I asked the question I looked from the Elemental Breather that repulsed me and then into Scott's beaming face. He didn't even have to say it; as I looked into his pink eyes, I understood instantly and I felt my skin crawl as I contemplated the man's insinuating stare and sly smile.

"No, she won't, he's a creep," Paul quickly said, lowering his voice as a few people turned to stare at us. He looked back over at the sleazy Elemental Breather. "Can't you just turn into a woman yourself?"

Scott looked at Paul with a hard glare then wickedly smiled as a thought crossed his mind. "Would that make the difference for you? Would it?" Paul's face was abashed and he took a few steps back. Scott laughed hysterically, covering his mouth with the back of his hand.

"I've never tried changing into another. I have only turned into animals," he said honestly. "And what would you have me do: strip bare in front of all these other Elemental Breathers? Because *that* won't be suspicious at all! Sometimes I just really hesitate to believe you're in it for the cause," he said sarcastically. As the two squabbled between themselves, I eyed the repulsive Elemental Breather, trying to build my own courage.

If he can lead me to, or give me any information on Taskatae, shouldn't I go? I don't have to do anything; all I have to do is lead him to the room. Surely I can do that? Although it's not what I am used to and I have never known how to use womanly charms, surely I can muster the skills.

"I'll do it," I said unconfidently, stopping my hands as they attempted to stretch out the dress, already I felt like his prying eyes were on me. *I must do this. I must find out where Taskatae is hiding, I must. She took everything from me. I can do this.* With a deep breath, and trying to push Paul's negative words away, I began to step toward the Elemental Breather as he watched a woman walk by him with eager eyes.

I came to the bar, taking the seat next to him, unsure how to appear appealing when I felt only like vomiting at the thought of trying to be suggestive toward such a man.

"What will you be having, Miss?" The bartender with lime-green eyes asked with some sort of thick foreign accent. I looked at him awkwardly, unsure as to what to order. *What do Elemental Breathers order? Can I ask without looking suspicious?*

"She'll have one of these babies," the grotesque Elemental Breather next to me said, looking over me hungrily and gesturing to his own drink. I held my fists tight, forcing away my urgency to clutch Aeisha in my hand protectively. I wanted to ward off his lingering eyes. I nodded hesitantly, agreeing with him as the bartender looked at me for permission before pouring me the red wine.

Accepting the glass, I awkwardly tried to keep eye contact with him, humiliated that I was lowering myself to such an extent.

"I'm Skeath," he said abruptly through uneven teeth. "And whom do I thank for bringing such a fine piece to be the apple of my eye?" Holding back the filthy words I wanted to speak, I smiled awkwardly again, pretending to enjoy his sleazy words, but finding no strength to continue the flirtation.

"I usually thank myself," Lucas said coming from behind me and leaning over the counter while waiting for the bartender. The Elemental Breather's eyes flashed black as he sized up Lucas, who casually looked ahead. Out of all the times, why did he have to intervene now? We were to split up so no one suspected us of already knowing one another. Secretly I wanted to thank Lucas for interfering as I flirted with this disgusting man. But this wasn't part of the plan; I had to reach Paul and Scott in the upstairs room. Looking at the area Scott had previously indicated, I noticed Scott pulling Paul in as he looked over me wearily. It had to be a surprise; they couldn't be seen at the door of where I had planned to trap the man.

Lucas contemptuously looked over the Elemental Breather, Skeath, agitating him more as Lucas gave him a sly smile. *If Lucas agitates him anymore there will be a scene and we are supposed to be avoiding that. What do I do?*

"Don't you think you can do a little better than this?" Lucas said to me, nodding toward Skeath. His words crawled up my spine infuriatingly. "My lady," he added sarcastically. I stared into his brown eyes, questioning why he would so happily ruin our plan.

"I don't think your concern is needed," I said truthfully, staring at the soft lips that had once touched my own so passionately. *How can he be like this now, reverting back to his infuriating ways?*

"Well, as bewitching as you obviously are," he continued, pausing and giving me a meaningful look, "I'd hate to think of such a beautiful lady presenting herself this way to such a fool."

Skeath threw his chair back, his eyes engulfed with black. I saw a flicker of movement behind him under his long coat, and I observed it was a green-scaled tail.

They are going to fight; I had to take Skeath away now if I had any chance.

I projected my Shield around my hand, not wanting to touch him. I grabbed around Skeath's wrist, pulling him away from Lucas. "Let's go somewhere more private, Skeath," I said, holding in my repulsion. He obliged although hesitantly, as he measured Lucas.

How many others have noticed us now? Do they know Lucas is not one of them as he kept his cool? Do they know I am not an Elemental Breather? I avoided looking at the others as I pulled Skeath away. I looked back at where Lucas once stood but he already walked away, and I could no longer see him in the crowd.

Pulling Skeath toward the staircase, I was stricken by my actions, appalled at myself for having to insinuate such a thing. Skeath greedily looked over me. Every part of me wanted to project my Shield and pull away from him. Even Misfeata fought against me from within, angered by my contact with such a filthy being. I directed him up the stairs and began to walk toward the door.

'*You are disgusting,*' Misfeata said, echoing my own thoughts. But then I thought of how she would have dealt with such a situation and, just as I thought, she agreed we had to find a way to manipulate an Elemental Breather into telling us what they knew of Taskatae.

I must keep myself calm…

If anything goes wrong I could protect myself from Skeath or any of these Elemental Breathers. They were not like Taskatae or Scott. *They can't penetrate my Shield,* I reminded myself as I reached for the gold knob before leading Skeath into the dark room.

Chapter Twenty-Five- Secrecy to Death

*A*s I walked into the darkness, Paul jumped from behind the door, punching Skeath in the face and knocking him down. Scott hurriedly approached him and held his hand over Skeath's legs. I used my own Shield within my feet to sense what Scott was doing. I could feel his presence entering Skeath's legs and then leaving it. Skeath was still stunned as he sat against the door, dazed. His legs didn't move.

As Scott turned on the lamp across from us, the sudden burst of light revealed a large bed with a gold frame and a white single couch next to the side-table and lamp. Scott sat down, crossing his legs as Skeath came to consciousness frowning as he stared at his legs. He made a move as if to escape, but his movement was restricted.

"Oh no, dear Skeath," Scott said, intertwining his fingers and folding his hands over his knees. "I have taken your rapid speed away from you for the time being," he spoke with pleasure, his beam reminding me too much of the pleasure Max Jacket had when bargaining with someone.

"Are you okay?" Paul asked as he came to my side and rested his hand on my shoulder, dipping his head to look up at me. I hid my face, ashamed of what I had done. He gave me a firm hug, making me feel safe once again. I have exposed myself to such a creature, and although not indecently, I still felt stripped bare. I hugged him back fiercely, comfortable with his protective warmth.

The situation made me realize how comfortable and safe I was with both Paul and Lucas. And like they had both said, they would protect me and I appreciated that tonight. I now understand there were a lot more things in the world that I feared other than these constant fights I was involved in.

"Of course, Scott. I'm surprised it's you and not your father or sister doing the dirty work. Did Daddy let his dog off the chain?" he said, spitting toward Scott's feet.

"That's gross," Scott said, unfazed by his words and pointing toward the spit. "Taskatae. What do you know of her?" He narrowed his pink eyes on Skeath.

In response Skeath cracked a mysterious smile and tried to adjust his seating. So his Element was speed? Were we just lucky that we had caught him off-guard then? Had Scott known the risk Paul was putting himself in if Skeath dodged his attack?

"I don't know a Taskatae," he said, pinching his lips together angrily as he inhaled deeply, his eyes flashing black.

"Ah. You see, that isn't going to work. Now, I know you have dealt with both my father and even my little sister in the past and from the stories I've heard it took you quite a lengthy time to recover. Please don't make me repeat their actions," Scott threatened, his eyes flashing back.

I felt uncomfortable about what was being said. Scott has quickly changed in front of my eyes. He was changing from someone I could trust into a terrible being, threatening others.

'How else would you find out any information, you stupid girl?' Misfeata interjected into my thoughts.

I closed my eyes, trying to block her out. My hand began to tingle as I felt her essence linger. She reached out, trying to take control of my body. I felt as if I were raising my Shield within myself to push her further down and away from my body, coiling and capturing her within — much to her repugnance. I didn't like Misfeata's recent activities. I was well aware that she now was fully awake once again and fighting to possess my body.

"Please, if I knew a Taskatae, I am sure she would be much more terrifying than you," Skeath uttered, smiling wickedly once more. With a fake smile, Scott raised his hand, transforming them into sharp falcon claws.

"Shall I name the places I will cut away at first?" Scott asked as he walked over to Skeath with black eyes. I watched in horror; I couldn't believe the beast Scott had all of a sudden turned into. *Have I been fooled this whole time? I will not be a part of torture.*

"Scott, I don't think that's necessary," Paul said, interjecting as I looked into his beautiful green eyes, reassured that he too wouldn't be a part of such a cruel thing. I was surprised that I haven't said anything. *Do I want Taskatae's location so bad that I wouldn't stand against Scott's methods?*

"My darling, if this is something you don't want to be a part of, then I suggest you leave the room," Scott hissed, his harsh words seeming too similar to the disposition of Max and Trish. "Where did you get the tail from, Skeath? I know Taskatae can change one's appearance. What did you do for her, for her to give you such a gift?" Scott asked angrily, towering over him.

Skeath looked at his legs where presumably the tail lay concealed with an evasive smile. *The tail wasn't from natural birth? Taskatae was able to do that to him?*

Misfeata stirred within me uneasily but I trapped her again, my heart racing as I clutched at it in pain, distracted from the situation as I tried to control her. I pulled away from Paul, trying to calm my feverish heart that pounded as Misfeata tried her hardest to break from her cell.

A smashing noise broke through the room as the windowpane shattered. The heavily cloaked Elemental Breather I saw earlier on the boat broke through the glass, jumped into the room and onto me, throwing me to the wall. I projected my Shield in defense and pulled Aeisha from my clutch, ready to fight.

A swift noise shot through the outside as an arrow darted past my eyes and into Skeath's chest, instantly pinning him to the door and killing him. As I hid away from the window and Scott pulled Paul further away on the opposite side, I looked up at the Elemental Breather who protected me from the arrow. *Was that arrow intended for me? For how long has he been watching? Who is shooting at us?*

He swiftly shifted next to me, standing tall against the wall wearily as I held Aeisha, unsure if the Elemental Breather was protecting me or if he was against me. Scott looked back over toward the window and then Skeath's body, annoyed. Still with my Shield projected, I looked at the fine arrow feathers. They were very similar to the arrows that were able to penetrate my Shield that day we were ambushed by the Starkorfs. *Who is this archer?*

My chest winced once again as Misfeata erupted from beneath. I heavily breathed, trying to contain her. As I dropped to my knees, Paul quickly scurried over to my side; Scott following him in case the archer was lining us up again.

"Karla," an old, crisp male voice belonging to the Elemental Breather said, forcing me to look up at him though I was panting heavily. I recognized the voice despite how it had aged. He revealed his identity, taking my breath away. I searched into the eyes I long ago had known and had been searching for, ever since. So many times now he had come to me in my dreams, warning me. For so many years now I had missed him. *But what is he doing here?*

"Uncle Kyle," I whispered through a coughing spurt as I felt Misfeata's firm grip around my throat. She was reacting to something she wanted to kill so badly, her wild rage spilling within me. *Does this mean Tyran is close? Is Nathanial close? Is Misfeata trying to take my body so she can fight him? She would only react in such a way to attack, fight, and kill him. She has no control near her brother Tyran.*

The door burst open and Lucas looked over us huddled in the corner. "Karla…" he panicked, confirming my suspicions: he would only panic in such a tone if his brother, Nathanial, was here. *What if I lose control? What if Misfeata possesses my body once again? How will I protect Paul?* I thought remorsefully, looking into his beautiful green eyes.

An arrow shot through the window and I felt Lucas's Shield project powerfully as he sensed it coming. But just like it did to me, it pierced him in his shoulder, throwing him against the wall, where he then clutched at the wound.

"Lucas!" I yelled, reaching out to him. As I did, Misfeata's pull gripped me firmly, pulling me deep into myself as she took control with greedy hands. She pulled toward where her brother Tyran's presence was as her blood pulsed with fierceness. She lunged for the door, opening it and dodging the arrow that came for us.

Breaking into the bright light of the ballroom's chandeliers, we looked down on the scene that unfolded before our very eyes. Ghastly Starkorfs broke out into the room and a war began between Starkorfs and Elemental Breathers. Misfeata searched over the fighting crowd, her thoughts chaotic and wild as she finally narrowed her eyes on the same sandy-blonde hair that Lucas had: Nathanial.

He looked up at us, a cracked smile passing over his lips. I knew by his stare that Tyran already had control.

Chapter Twenty-Six- My War

$\mathcal{M}$isfeata's hands flexed over Aeisha. Her left hand felt bare without the partnered blade. Misfeata's true being was contained within both blades, so part of her entity was missing, therefore sparing my body another horrific transformation.

The anguish they held for one another burned me from within as Misfeata stared at Nathanial, the host of her brother Tyran. She jumped over the gold railing and fell to the floor heavily before quickly regaining herself and charging at Nathanial. He did the same, his long black coat hindering his speed.

Gasps and screams surrounded us as the Elemental Breathers fought against the Starkorfs. Some Elemental Breathers fended them off easily, but others were struggling under the number of Starkorfs that still streamed in through the large wooden doors. Screams echoed through the room, as the Starkorfs drained the guests. What a treat this must seem to them. There was very little loyalty; it was every being for themselves. Only few Elemental Breathers fought back to back, protecting one another. Wicked smiles curled the lips of Starkorfs and Elemental Breathers alike as they slaughtered one another with a primal, wild instinct.

I was now consumed with the same savage fierceness. Misfeata jumped toward Tyran with a savage gleam, having clearly missed her time away from battle. She plunged Aeisha toward him but he used a sword to divert it and twist around Misfeata, trying to slash at her back. Her quick reflexes blocked the attack as she skillfully maneuvered my body. Nathanial once again tried to cut across my chest, but again Misfeata jumped back, bumping into another Starkorf. She quickly circled around it, slicing across his throat. She then used his body as a guard against Nathanial who threw down his sword, slicing into the Starkorf's shoulder in his fervor to get to Misfeata.

Although they fought savagely — without Nathanial having Borac, Tyran's Immortal Blade — he could not change into another form and, alas, neither could Misfeata. They could only viciously fight one another in this ornate battlefield of Elemental Breather splendor.

Throwing the dead Starkorf onto Nathanial, Misfeata jumped back, placing her hands on the rounded bar and flipping over it. She once again diverted Nathanial's sword and a loud screeching noise rang out when she pushed it away. She jumped over the smooth surface once again, swaying backward as Nathanial swung his sword at her. She spun onto her tiptoes and crouched low, trying to slash at his ankles as he brought the sword down. Misfeata speedily protected herself as she looked up into the dark-brown eyes of Nathanial — eyes that reminded me too much of Lucas.

Although I knew Misfeata and Tyran were staring at one another, I also understood that I stared into the eyes of Nathanial. *Does he try to fight Tyran? Is he strong enough? Does he approve of Tyran?* The memory of his sword piercing into Seth pained me. Nathanial had killed Ashley's father, Seth, and now I was forced to fight him. Not me: Misfeata. *Is this a fight that Ashley would want? Isn't this the fight that he is entitled to so he can avenge his father? This is why Ashley decides to fight.*

As my body was used as a tool of war, I faced the purpose of the fight. *Am I fighting for myself as I am actively seeking Taskatae to avenge my father's death? Or is this still a fight of another world I should not be involved with?*

A large ball of acidic goo glided between Tyran and Misfeata, forcing us to jump back. It struck the rounded bar and began to melt the solid wood away. Misfeata raised Aeisha to an Elemental Breather who had tried jumping onto her, as she must have recognized the blade of Aeisha. The Elemental Breather jumped away. They stalked each other in a predatory circle, calculating one another, the woman's crystal blue eyes fixated on Aeisha.

The woman jumped again for Misfeata, large wings sprouting from her back. Quickly she swept across the floor, coming straight for us. Misfeata projected her Shield large enough to stop the woman a meter in front of us. She strategically dropped it just in time, so the woman unsteadily flew through after her flight had been drastically slowed. Before she could stop herself coming toward us, Misfeata wrapped her hand around the Elemental Breather's throat and slammed her back into the ground, plunging Aeisha into her with pleasure. The woman cried out like a dying bird.

Quickly regaining herself, Misfeata projected her Shield. Two Starkorfs came at her but were thrown off by her heavy immaculate Shield. She stood tall with eyes fixated on Nathanial once again.

I tried to reach for my body, hungering to take back control of the body which was mine, but Misfeata was too strong. Like the first time it had happened, she raged with bloodlust for her brother, making her thoughts incomprehensible as she fixated on one thing: killing Tyran.

As he pierced an Elemental Breather through the chest and kicked him away, his eyes grew hungry and he ran for Misfeata. Starkorfs behind me fought over the winged Elemental Breather, draining her to death.

On my left, a large clump of Starkorfs dropped to their knees as the woman we had met at the beginning of the night with golden-blonde hair and brown eyes smiled, looking over them, pleased. I imagined her to be destroying their eardrums like she almost did mine. Her brother held the same malicious beam on his face as he walked over to them, one by one dropping some form of acid from his fingertips onto their heads. They screamed and dropped dead. They looked at one another with great satisfaction; Jordy briefly dusting over his stiff suit as his sister slightly lifted her dress before walking toward the large wooden doors through the chaos.

Tyran's Shield amplified against my own, competing for dominancy. Both of them were hoping to have the upper hand, but they were too evenly matched. Misfeata tightened her grip on Aeisha, savagely trying to strike at Nathanial's throat but missing every time as he quickly dodged it and retaliated.

Paul's voice echoed throughout the large room from above on the second floor as he screamed out my name, making me forcefully reach out at Misfeata, trying to pull her back in. *I must get back to Paul.*

For a brief moment I had control of my sight and I looked back at Paul, who was hunched over the railing above staring over me; beside him Starkorfs were attacking. Lucas stood beside Paul, holding his shoulder firmly, his Shield projected. He was unable to defend himself while applying pressure to his wound. No Starkorfs struck at him making me question whether they couldn't compete against his Shield or if they still recognized him as a leader amongst their kind.

Harmony used her bow, producing white arrows, which she shot at Starkorfs who ran up the stairs. One by one they fell over the gold-trim railings into the bloody battlefield. Starkorfs continued running in from the large wooden doors to fight against the Elemental Breathers.

Are Paige and Ashley okay? Did they get through them first? Are they still alive?

My Uncle Kyle had two long blades that he used to slice over the Starkorfs, his hood no longer hiding his face, revealing his long red hair that came to his shoulders. He forcefully struck the Starkorfs down, very skilled with the weapons he held despite his gaunt face and feeble-looking body.

Scott was close to Paul and was pulling him away from the balcony as they had to move on and descend the stairs to reach the wooden doors to escape. Hesitantly, Paul let go, clutching his knife defensively as attackers came toward them. Scott forcefully threw them off the balcony with enlarged ape arms.

Misfeata pushed me back within myself. The harsher she pushed the less I could breathe. A Starkorf jumped at me just as another Elemental Breather jumped out at Nathanial, splitting us apart once again, irritating her even more. *I must get to the second level to protect Paul and Lucas.*

I fought against Misfeata, trying to take a firm grip on my body. She fought against me from within as she simultaneously fought the Starkorfs. Her Shield was too strong and magnificent in comparison to the enemies that challenged her; hers broke through theirs with ease.

Trying to dampen Misfeata's bloodlust for Tyran was impossible. *How will I separate them so I can get to the others and escape? Why are they here? Why are the Starkorfs attacking the Elemental Breathers?*

All at once, under Tyran's instruction, six Starkorfs jumped at me, agitating Misfeata as she thought Tyran cowardly to not fight her with his bare hands. I couldn't detect whether it was Nathanial who commanded the attack or Tyran. *Is Nathanial pulling away? Has he won against Tyran?*

As the six pounced, Misfeata projected a large Shield around her from more than a meter away. It surrounded her and she pulsated the Starkorfs away with a forceful blow. Three of them instantly hit the balcony, dropping to the ground. Misfeata concentrated her Shield one by one on the other three, forcing them to slam hard into her Shield. They too dropped to the ground.

Misfeata tired herself by isolating her Shield into three directions. I quickly took advantage, gripping her firmly and pushing her back within where I could claim my body once more. As much as she fought back I had finally claimed what was rightfully mine: *my body.*

I instantly searched for Paul and the others, running toward the staircase as they tried to run down it whilst still fighting the Starkorfs who attacked them. Dodging two attacks from Starkorfs, I ran for the staircase, looking up and realizing they were surrounded. In search of an escape plan, I looked above the staircase, noticing a large chandelier. If I could drop that above the Starkorfs it would give us enough time to disperse them and make an escape instead of trying to cut through them to the exit of the castle.

Strike after strike, they were defending themselves. Harmony was now holding up Lucas because of the amount of blood he had lost, his face pale. Scott continued to protect Paul as Uncle Kyle fought gallantly, protecting their circle from behind. I couldn't feel the ability of Shielding from any of the Starkorfs attacking, much to my advantage.

I focused on the large chandelier, concentrating on my feet and projecting my Shield under them. If I could pulse my projected Shield, would it give me enough height to reach the railing where I could then jump onto the chandelier?

Misfeata stirred within me as Nathanial ran for me, quickly forcing me to project and pulsate my Shield beneath me, giving me a boost as I jumped. I grabbed the railing and kicked away from the wall, where I could flip myself over it. I kicked a Starkorf away from me as it tried attacking me with elongated nails.

Another ran for me as I projected my Shield and turned my back to them, balancing on the gold railing and looking down at Nathanial, who growled from below in annoyance. I took only a second to observe the war below me: blood of both Starkorfs and Elemental Breathers streaked the white marble floor; clumps of figures attacked one another ruthlessly. Looking at Paul I gathered the courage to jump on the chandelier, unsure if it would work as it hung near the foot of the staircase.

I jumped, no longer hesitant, knowing this may be the only chance we would have to disperse the clump of Starkorfs who tried desperately to drain the others. Pulsating my Shield beneath my feet, I jumped again to gain an extra boost. I swung onto the chandelier slowly, struggling to lift myself.

As I steadily swayed on the large chandelier, I started striking at the chain that held it. As Aeisha happily accepted the challenge, the familiar energy of my Shield helped me to achieve my objective. I struck once more and the chain snapped, dropping me.

I jumped off, quickly projecting my Shield as I dropped toward the others. As the chandelier shattered on the ground and I dropped awkwardly over the staircase, I summoned my Shield, stretching it wide to enclose the others in, as pieces from the light fixture combusted in front of us. My Shield protected them as the Starkorfs tried to jump away.

I hastily focused my Shield on the railing of the staircase, blowing it away so we could escape around the large chandelier before the stunned Starkorfs got to their feet.

Paul, Harmony, Lucas, Scott, and Uncle Kyle ran past me, entering the war that everyone else so happily fought in. I now protected their backs as Scott and Uncle Kyle took the sides as we tried to escape. Much to my surprise, Tyran didn't follow me. I no longer felt his presence, as it was Nathanial who panted heavily and hid behind his men until he regained himself. *So Nathanial can control Tyran as well?*

He looked over me and his brother Lucas, curling his lips angrily as he flicked his hand up, sending a signal to the Starkorfs who followed him.

Snarling noises, growls, and screams, echoed in the large room that was once so elegant but now glistened with red. We ran for the large wooden doors.

Only a few tried attacking us but they were quickly taken over by Scott or other Elemental Breathers who had been previously fighting them. Their eyes were illuminating black as they fought viciously. As we ran into the coldness of the night, the water reflected flames, drawing my attention to the boat, which was now burning in front of us. As we ran down the red carpet, the Elemental Breather who greeted us when we first treaded up them confronted us. He was now purple, with hand imprints wrapped around his throat. His shirt had been torn away; he was drained to his death.

We ran to the boat where the humans who we have saved lay dead. Drained and dead, some floating in the water; flames tearing viciously at the boat in which we were to escape on. Had we caused their deaths? Had we lead the Starkorfs here?

"Karla!" Ashley yelled as he came out of the bushes, startling us. Uncle Kyle swiftly lifted one of his long blades to Ashley's throat. Ashley quickly raised his sword, blocking Uncle Kyle's. They stared at each other evenly. I interjected before they could seriously hurt one another, making them realize we were allies.

"Where is Paige?" I asked, alarmed as a huge explosion came from the castle. The windows blew out and large flames tore at the edges of the building. Ghastly screams echoed into the night as few made it out alive. They screamed at their burnt skin and jumped into the cool water.

A bulky blue snake shot from the water's surface, grabbing a person with its mouth and flinging them further away before it slipped into the water once again to attack another who also jumped in. *This is one of Taskatae's beasts. She knows of this. Is this ambush the result of a collaboration between Taskatae and Nathanial?*

We can't go into the water. How will we leave the island?

Paige crept out of the bushes, ill-looking as she stumbled into Ashley, who kept her standing. "She fought hard, but the Starkorfs got her. I only made it just in time," he gushed, disappointed in himself as she looked faint. She couldn't fight like this; they had drained far too much from her. Lucas also paled a ghastly white, holding his shoulder lightly as his injured shoulder bled heavily. He would bleed out before we could fight them off.

"We must get in the water," Scott articulated. "I can change into something that can take us back to the mainland but I need you and Lucas to project your Shields underneath me, and one to protect me if anything attacks. I can't attack if I am carting you all on my back."

I looked at Lucas, unsure if he could project his Shield for such a long time in such a weak state. He nodded his consent, breathing heavily as Scott jumped toward the water. My hands began shakily projecting my Shield beneath him as he changed into a small whale. Slowly his back turned into harsh scales that we could grip onto. As soon as his stomach neared the water, one of the large snake-like creatures jumped out of the water. Lucas raised his hand, projecting his Shield. The creature was thrust back from it and thrown rapidly into the water further away.

We hurriedly jumped onto Scott's back and I continued to concentrate my Shield beneath him, feeling the harsh knock of creatures from beneath trying to rip at Scott. I strained under the force, holding both hands out as I concentrated on my Shield that was so far away from my body.

Harmony still held Lucas up as another tried raising itself from beneath the water. Lucas tried to defend us but his weakened state forced it to shatter and the creature came for us, its fangs close to Scott's neck.

I raised both hands to it, removing my Shield from beneath and pushing the snake away from Scott's neck. As soon as it was thrown away I resumed my projected Shield beneath Scott, which meant that we could not see the creatures. I was confronted by a creature that tried to attack from beneath, my Shield protecting Scott from it. Dropping to my knees in exhaustion, Scott began to drift in the water.

Paul held my shoulders firmly as I concentrated on my Shield as well as Lucas, who sputtered, his Shield straining, as his shoulder bled out. I felt the presence of other creatures from beneath swim rapidly to keep to our pace. I had to widen my Shield beneath; I couldn't project in two places at once. I crawled to Lucas's side, who was also on his knees panting heavily next to Harmony, still trying to hold himself up.

"Lucas," I croaked, drained as I projected a large Shield underneath, still feeling the creatures creep up next to us. As sweat poured over his face he looked at me, exhausted. "Lucas," I repeated, trying to grab his focus as his eyes rolled around, looking into the night sky incoherently. "I need you to project below," I whispered as I steadied my Shield into one hand, focusing on it. The creatures would attack now.

As I felt his Shield sweep over mine, he buckled toward me, his head landing into my lap as he winced in pain. His face was filled with sweat and his eye bags darkened with the strain of his Shield, his hands firmly clenched onto Scott's back as he projected below us.

Two large snakes jumped out of the water as I projected my Shield against the one on the right, forcing it away, and then the one on my left, exasperated by the strain it left on my body.

167

A third one came from behind, surprising me, as I did not feel its presence. It bit into the back of Scott. Scott screamed in his animal tone and I projected my Shield between the back of Scott and the snake, shattering its teeth with my red rippled Shield.

I looked into the distance behind where the castle that was once so elegant, burned. The screams were now non-existent. Slowly the fangs that were still edged into Scott's back pushed out. My Uncle Kyle looked at them as they slid into the water behind us, his eyes wide as he looked at me, his hood flapping in the cold wind. I looked away from such a questioning expression, unsure of how Uncle Kyle and I reuniting came to be. I recalled my many dreams of his warnings.

Lucas was now unconscious; he looked at peace, and my shoulders slumped in exhaustion. Paul dropped to his knees beside me, placing his hands on my shoulders. I looked up at him, fatigued. I let myself drop my head onto his chest and I closed my eyes heavily, breathing deeply as I tried to focus and calm myself. Listening to his pattering heart, I still projected my Shield beneath us, listening to the water which would inform me if something came close to attack us. But nothing followed.

My Shield sensed Lucas's energy within him begin to falter; his Shield was beginning to falter. I forced my hand on his chest, feeling his heartbeat thump slower and slower, as did his Shield. After his Shield gave one more forceful pulse that tingled against my own, Lucas's heartbeat stopped.

Chapter Twenty-Seven- Death's Shadow

I stared down at Lucas's pale face in shock. *He cannot be dead. He cannot.* I waited for the beating of his heart to throb under my hand once more; for his Shield to pulsate against mine. The water was still and the cool breeze of the chilled night brushed through his sandy-blonde hair.

"Lucas," I whispered urgently, as Harmony and Paul looked at one another helplessly. My long brown hair brushed into my eyes as I tried to understand the sight before me. Although we were drifting through the water at a rapid pace, everything fell silent. Land was so close now, yet seemed so far away.

I took a muffled breath, sucking in the tears that instantly began to shed as I looked down on his closed eyes and peaceful face. His shoulder was still bleeding and the blood spread onto my fingertips. *Lucas's blood is on my hands.*

"Lucas?" I breathed, waiting for his response. *This is not what it seems; it cannot be. He cannot be dead. I must fix his heart. I must have it beating again. Lucas cannot die. I need Lucas.*

As my chest rose and fell heavily, I panicked. I projected my Shield to my hand before compressing it onto his chest. Knocking away Paul's grip of my shoulder, I came to Lucas's side. I pushed Harmony out of my way too. My Shield compressed heavily on his chest, helping me to attempt to restart his heart.

I frantically pushed on his chest harder and harder, unconfident in what I was doing. I was devastated to find it wasn't working. *Why can't I save Lucas?* Scott edged closer to the dock from which we had once departed — all of us were then alive. Paul and Uncle Kyle pushed me away from Lucas, dragging him onto the dock as Ashley helped Paige stumble onto it as well, Harmony watching from behind as she stayed close to Lucas, checking his pulse.

As soon as everyone was off Scott's back, he changed into his human self, placing his hands on my back and pushing me onto the dock as my feet weren't positioned properly, therefore preventing me from falling back into the water. I stared futilely, my body unable to move from shock. After he edged me slightly forward out of his way, he paced to Lucas's side and put his hand on Lucas's chest. I felt Scott's presence enter Lucas and wrap around his heart. After a moment of assessment he looked up at me grimly.

I focused on him; everyone else's eyes were on me sympathetically. Harmony began to sob and held Lucas's hand. I was in despair; confused as to how easily he could leave me. We were seemingly super-human and Lucas was one of the strongest I knew, but now he lay dead; his skin as pale and as silent as the night. *It is not the truth; it is a lie...Lucas is not dead.*

Dropping onto my knees beside him, I shook my head in shock. I couldn't accept such a fate. *This is not how it is meant to be. Lucas cannot be dead.*

I pushed Paul away as I came to Lucas's side, looking down at him frantically. *He will smile at me soon with a taunting joke. He will make fun of me like he always has. He will say, "it's okay, this will heal in no time"... like he always did. He cannot be... He's not...*

As tears blurred my eyes, a deep sigh escaped my mouth. I looked down at him, near faint as I tried pushing on his chest again with my projected Shield, trying to trigger his heartbeat once more. *Lucas, please come back.*

My pounding got even harder, more desperate. I restrained myself from being too forceful in case I hurt him, and yet it wasn't enough. I needed to fix him. After two minutes of desperate pushing, Paul tried to pull my shoulders back so I would give up. *I cannot give up. I cannot give up on Lucas. He protected me, he looks after me, and he accepts me for what I am, even if I have Misfeata within me. Lucas cannot be dead.*

A shudder ran down my spine as I looked at him remorsefully. *I cannot let him go.* As my projected Shield hovered over his chest with gray ripples faintly rolling over one another, I looked at him desperately, contemplating one other option.

Lucas has done it to me in the past. *If I am dying, he will drain it away and take it within his own body to protect me. Couldn't I do that to protect Lucas? Couldn't I reverse my Shield to drain away this suffering and death and take it upon myself so he can come back?*

I focused on projecting my Shield the same way I did on the Earth when I wanted to sense my surroundings. *If I can drain Lucas and draw his pain into me, will this not bring him back?*

Placing my hand on his chest, I tried not to recoil from his cold skin beneath his shirt. *I can do this. I can take this away from him.* A cold shudder ran through me as I began to feel Lucas within me. His dulled life force entered me and I felt like I was being shrouded in his presence. It felt as I drained Lucas...as if I *were* Lucas.

Is this what the Starkorfs feel when they drain people? Their very life force, their being, their soul — and yet they continue to do so. Can they really live with draining a person with whom they have connected with?

As I tried to take away Lucas's death, my lips tingled with the feeling of the passionate kiss we had shared, the raw tension and feeling we shared, unsure of what could possibly become of it. My heart pained as I felt his presence exerting into myself. The blackness of death within him stained me. My breaths became short as my body began to pain. My body was experiencing a different kind of death: one I had not suffered before even at Misfeata's hands. *Lucas's death... this is real.*

As I felt him heavier and heavier within me, I noticed his big dark-brown eyes open and blink at me. I was suddenly thrown off by Harmony onto the wooden docks. I gasped and staggered to my feet. She stood over Lucas protectively.

"How dare you try to use such a sinful act against him to gain power!" she accused as Uncle Kyle and Paul stood in front of me defensively. Harmony took her bow into hand, directing it at me. I choked once more, my body rejecting what it had consumed. I was overcome with the blackened hate I held for her. *How dare she accuse me of such a thing? I am trying to bring him back; I want him to be alive. How dare she try to protect him?*

My eyes narrowed on her as I was consumed with blackness. I projected my Shield and black ripples pulsated around me as I collected Aeisha, the point of her blade dragging along the wood. I held her near my chest, eyes fixated on Harmony. *How dare she stand against me and accuse me of such a thing?*

"Karla, don't," Paul said forcefully, but I rose tall, uninterested in the looks that everyone gave me. Misfeata stirred within me. Not to control me and not to insinuate her own desires, but to fight with me. I felt myself blacken with determination, just as I did when I decided to take Raven's life. *I do not like Harmony, I never have.*

If she raises her bow at me, then is that not a fair fight? Is she not challenging me? Pushing Paul away and jumping for Harmony, I concluded that it was. *I hate her.* She had both her hands on either side of her bow, wrestling against the force of my Shield. I looked over her hungrily; wanting to force her to take her lying words back.

She was able to divert my Shield to the side, making me take a step to the side as she took another toward Lucas protectively, infuriating me more. I wouldn't harm Lucas. I threw Aeisha at her but she quickly swayed her bow over the tip of my blade knocking it to the ground. As I anticipated that, I jumped, dropping my Shield and punching her in the face as I came down, forcing her to stumble back a few steps. I raised my two fists in a defensive stance, no longer projecting my Shield. *I don't need my ability to defeat her.*

She used the end of her bow like a sword, trying to knock it into my stomach, but I was too quick for her, and was able to dodge it and twist around. She tried to swing it to where I now stood beside her. I held the white bow in my hands, my eyes fixated on her angrily. My elbows were pulled back, pinning me behind against a firm chest. I couldn't hold on to her weapon any longer as they pulled me away. I raised my feet in front of me as she tried to drive the tip of her bow deep into my stomach, but Uncle Kyle grabbed her from behind, pulling her back just as someone did the same to me.

I projected my Shield away from the arms that wrapped around me forcefully, pulling away as Paul looked at me with pained eyes. My chest rose and fell quickly; I felt betrayed that Paul would hold me back. He didn't understand. How could he?

"You would do all of this for him," Paul said quietly, pulling me away from my hatred of Harmony.

A loud gasp broke the tension I held with Paul and I looked behind. Lucas's eyes fluttered briefly and closed again, his hand moving to his shoulder. His Shield briefly pulsated against my own but fell with a weak shatter.

I ran to him, calling for Scott who quickly entered him, fixing his wound. Tears welled in my eyes. I grabbed Lucas's hand, relieved to see him alive, feeling his Shield within him as he rested. *He will live. Lucas will survive.* I cried more, realizing how much I wanted Lucas to stay by my side, how scared I was to not have him. *He is the only one who accepts me; I cannot have him leave my side.* I sobbed to myself, saddened at what I had done to give him life. I drained someone — I had the ability of a Starkorf. I could drain the life of someone. I had no regret, I was able to revive Lucas, but the realization was frightful.

My hands fumbled over his and held them firmly as I looked down at his unconscious face. I looked behind to see Paul already walking away. Harmony followed him from behind. Ashley gave me a disappointed and frustrated look as he carried Paige away, who still hobbled beside him using him for support as she walked.

Paul hates me, and he has every right. By choosing Lucas in this one instance have I damned myself even in Ashley's eyes? Uncle Kyle stood strong, looking back at the glow of the island we were once on. His eyes flickered with such wisdom, saddened by such torture and pain. Everyone and everything else that surrounded us had been poisoned, attacked, and now came crumbling down.

Chapter Twenty-Eight- Evasive Emotion

*A*fter silence had fallen upon us, Scott stood and evaluated the wounds I had acquired during the battle. They have already begun to heal. He looked down at Lucas and then to Uncle Kyle suspiciously before speaking.

"He is resting for now, I've healed him and stopped the heavy bleeding but he will be able to recover himself in due time," Scott said, exhausted. "We can't stay here for much longer. We must move on even if it is only a few hours away from here. We must create distance and be careful."

"I will carry him," Uncle Kyle offered, lifting Lucas onto his shoulders and easily walking with him on his back, despite his feeble appearance. Lucas's hand dangled loosely in mine and I looked up at Uncle Kyle in disbelief of our reunion. *What does Uncle Kyle think of me and how has he become involved in this same fight? How did he know to be on that boat tonight? What was he after?*

"Uncle Kyle—..." I began, standing so I could walk alongside Lucas.

"Not now, love," Uncle Kyle said, his eyes uneasy on Scott. Scott raised his eyebrows in challenge, but walked away instead of making an ordeal about the mistrust directed at him. "We will talk soon. For now we must get away from this place because they will follow. They always do."

I dropped my head in defeat, nervous because of everything that has happened. I was unsure as to why I desperately needed Lucas, surprised by my own feelings and desire for him. I winced at the recollection of how Paul looked at me so hauntingly. Did he truly hate me know?

I trailed behind Uncle Kyle and the unconscious Lucas, who lightly jolted beneath Uncle Kyle's strong steps as we approached the motel where we changed before going to the ball. Ashley drove the car next to us and Paul sat in the front, avoiding my eyes. Ashamed, I looked down, unsure as to how all eight of us could fit into the car.

"I'm exhausted," Scott said looking at the car. "But it must be done. You two get on my back," he continued, gesturing to Uncle Kyle and Lucas. Uncle Kyle looked at him for a long time, his blue eyes staring at him hard. It seemed Uncle Kyle could not trust Scott, or perhaps his attitude was just because of his dislike of Elemental Breathers.

Uncle Kyle nodded his head, agreeing to do so. Scott changed his form into a great black horse, breathing heavily as Uncle Kyle threw Lucas over his back and easily jumped onto the back of the horse with no saddle.

I sat in the car next to Paige, who sat in the middle uncomfortably holding her neck while looking faint. Harmony watched over Lucas from afar as she sat on the other side of the backseat. My temper was rising as I wanted to be as far away from her as possible. *I cannot trust her. She doesn't know my intent or desires so how can she possibly stand against me?*

Scott started cantering as Ashley drove alongside him on the road. The streetlamps soon disappeared as we continued on through a narrow road, which had many holes in it. Scott kept the pace of the car within the trees.

The loud wind brushed past my ears, whistling and tangling my hair behind me. The breeze was like a slap to the face in the open-roofed car as I stared out the window, watching Scott carry Lucas and my Uncle Kyle on his back.

After an uncomfortable hour of silence, Ashley parked the car within the trees. We quickly began pitching tents. Lucas was seated comfortably and Harmony sat beside him. Fires were built so we could all rest for the night before planning our next strategy. Although we all needed rest as we were tired from our fight, we needed to focus on our next plan of attack. However, we were all too distant and silent to approach one another. There was much angst and mistrust between us all. Not only were we all individually reflecting on tonight's battle but also on my desperation to bring Lucas back to life. All those whom I had trusted and fought with still despised him, including Paul and Ashley. Would they now despise me?

I sat on a log with a light blanket over my shoulders that attempted to protect me from the cold wind. Uncle Kyle sat beside me, looking into the trees just as I did. No one else was around. Ashley was attending to Paige's wounds, as Scott and Paul were nowhere to be found. The last I had seen of Paul was when he entered the woods to take a walk, but he has not returned. Scott followed shortly behind to find him.

"My dear Karla, it has been too long," Uncle Kyle's crisp voice broke the thick tension between us. I haven't seen my Uncle for so many years, since I was only a little child aged six. The memories of the bright and glowing young man seemed at odds with the man now beside me. What happened to him during all those years?

"Where have you been?" I asked, finding my own voice to also be crisp and coarse. My heartbeat hastened, as I was scared to hear his response. I had thought my Uncle Kyle — who was my best friend and had always stayed close beforehand — had abandoned me.

"I know you must be mad at me for leaving but that was not of my own choice. Your parents didn't want me around you anymore. I saw what the inevitable was; what you would become as a Shielder and that you would be surrounded with this darkness. But your parents were hopeful and thought you would be hidden; thought that nothing would eventuate from that dark night of Elisabeth's approach. Your parents eventually forbade me to see you any longer and so I left, deciding to research more into this very different world so I could be of more help to protect you. Little did I realize the enormity of that task. The things I have seen and the things I have done..." he said, looking down at his hands, disgusted.

"I think this world has made everyone do things we shouldn't have. I too have much regret in such a short time and I am still without answers," I said, looking at my feet in sadness. "What happened all those years ago?" For the first time, despite what Lucas had said of how I had come to be a Shielder, I could ask someone who was there himself: I could ask Uncle Kyle.

"We were attacked by the Starkorfs when your mother was heavily pregnant. They cornered us into a house and Elisabeth shattered the window and broke in like a miracle. At first we thought she had come to protect us as she somehow projected an invisible wall between our attackers and us, protecting us. Unfortunately the circumference of the Shield in front of her was not large enough to protect us all and my sweet Clary..." Uncle Kyle stared for a while, as if recalling the memory of her death, and a tear slid down his face. "My dear wife could not be saved. I tried to protect her but the Shield not only kept them out, but myself in as well. I watched as they drained her. Her screams have always been the drive behind my strength to kill every Starkorf I have met since.

After a while, Elisabeth, who I since have discovered to be the last descendant of the Elder, Misfeata, was withering; for some reason she was willing to save us even at the cost of her own life. Now that I look at it I wonder if this was simply her way out of this war, whether her own death was the only way she could find peace.

She made an agreement with a fair-skinned girl with bright blue eyes called Raven: if they would let us escape, they could follow her out to fight. And so they agreed. Elisabeth cut herself and your mother, mixing your blood. We were unable to reach your mother. Elisabeth had shielded your mother so no one could interfere. Your mother was mortified. The woman quickly bandaged your mother's injury and spoke of your name. She then gently touched your mother's belly and said 'Karla'.

I still don't understand why they honored her and gave you that exact name. This world was something they so much despised. But the woman did save us and I think for respect of that alone, your mother named you that. After the incident, Raven and her followers chased Elisabeth. And then shortly after, you mother went into labor as we made our escape.

For years I warned them you were like no other; that something would develop from the incident. I feared that the same ones who came for us, tried to kill us, would come for you. But as my own fear manifested deeper, they refused to believe it. They didn't want to listen to me, they couldn't accept it."

"Your fear was very accurate, Uncle," I said hesitantly.

"Where is my brother now? And your mother?" He asked quietly, his blue eyes looking up at me earnestly. My heart sunk. I quickly diverted my eyes away from him and back to my feet. How could I tell him what I had done? How could I tell him that I killed my father, his brother? How could I possibly share that openly?

"He is dead," I said honestly. "Mum is in hiding. I thought it was best for her..." My voice trailed into silence. *Have I done the right thing by her? Am I protecting her in the right way?*

"How?" he asked, shocked. His blue eyes filled with tears. *How can I tell him the truth? How do I tell him that I killed my dad?*

"I..." Choking and losing my words, I had to look away as I said it. "I killed him." Tears trailed down my face. "An Elemental Breather changed his form and I didn't know it was him while he attacked us," I gasped painfully, recalling the memory of my father as he dropped dead in my arms. My father whom I loved so much — dead by my own hands. I looked at Uncle Kyle pleadingly, trying to comfort myself. *My father is dead because of me.*

I thought Uncle Kyle might want to strike me, take his hatred and anger out on me, but instead he stared at nothing in particular. Slowly his arms reached out for me, pulling me toward him into an embrace. He hid his face in my hair. His hug, the embrace of my dear Uncle Kyle, did not ease me. Instead it pained my heart, as I now understood how long ago this war had started; affecting my family and tearing us into different directions from the very start. How could my Uncle still love me after what I have done?

"My brother loved you dearly. We all do. I'm sure you have put him at ease if he was turned into something he didn't want to be. Unlike you and I, Karla..." he began to trail. "They did not want any part in this world. You and I were inevitably a part of it, and I will never leave your side again. I will protect you from them, Karla," his embrace tightened on me, comforting me with the familiarity of feeling like a child once again. Here was an adult I could trust and whom I loved. "I will always protect you."

After much silence, Uncle Kyle slowly let me go from his embrace, looking at me evenly and pulling on a strand of my long light-brown hair. "You have grown so much. I am so proud of you, for everything you have done to survive, and I am so sorry I didn't find you sooner."

I smiled at him feebly, never thinking I would ever hear those words. Never did I think someone could be proud of me after the things I have done.

"Uncle Kyle, what were you doing at the Elemental Breather's ball?" I asked, sitting back down on the log. He also shuffled and thought about it with a pause. He looked at me calculatingly, as if thinking whether to tell me or not.

"For many years now I have been following both Starkorfs and Elemental Breathers alike. I have an informant I met many years ago. He has told me of a cure for you. So you will no longer have to be like this, with that woman inside of your head trying to take control of your body."

"How do you know that? And who has been telling you about this madness, there is no way to get rid of Misfeata. I have tried," I said taken aback.

"I went to that ball because he said there may be a lead. He has looked after me for many years and has never been wrong, so I couldn't give up the chance that I might find you a cure. But instead I found you, Karla. It was an even greater gain."

"Who has spoken of this to you?" I asked, almost angry as I recalled my confrontation with Kurt. He had spoken to me of a way to relinquish my ability, therefore taking Misfeata away forever. My senses ached as I felt the presence of an onlooker. I quickly gathered Aeisha in my hand, standing and peering into the direction of where I sensed two people coming toward us.

"Kurt. He has been in allegiance with Kurt," Max Jacket's crisp voice called out as Trish's hand burst into a flame to light their path. She pushed his wheelchair across the rocky ground.

"What are you doing here?" I asked, looking around to see whether Scott was nearby.

"That is not the question here. What part has this man had to play in the scheme of things? That is the true question," Max said seriously. I noticed Borac was strapped to his back.

"You're the Elemental Breather with Borac!" Uncle Kyle said as he quickly stood. A lightning bolt shot from the sky and came close to his feet, forcing Uncle Kyle to step back.

I clumsily tried to stand in front of Uncle Kyle; unsure as to how Max would act. From the other side of the trees Scott came, his eyes fixated on his father and sister disapprovingly.

"Father, surely you don't think one human can—..." A lightning bolt struck Scott down as Max's eyes flickered black. Scott's cry echoed and I took a step forward to help him. Trish's hand was completely engulfed by flames and they extended up her arms. Her eyes flickered black, daring me to take another step.

"Do not speak to me, you disgusting, abnormal creature!" Max shouted angrily. "Still you have gathered nothing of Taskatae. How is it that I alone was not at the ball, yet I have obtained more information than all of you together as to where they have gone?"

Scott whimpered on the ground trying to hold himself up, but his knees curled beneath him. Shortly after his wincing and heavy breathing subsided, I saw the lining of his stomach slowly stitch itself back up, relieving Scott of his wound.

"What do you want?" I asked, still unsteady in front of Uncle Kyle.

"To get this man to take you back to Kurt, to find out where Nathanial is so we can find Taskatae. Honestly, is it that complicated? I watched from afar as all you good-for-nothings could only just protect yourselves. How can I depend on you to find her? How?!" Max Jacket raged. Looking at the blind man, behind the hatred, I saw his pain. He wanted Taskatae, he needed to confront her — she took his wife away from him.

"I do not know of a man named Kurt!" Uncle Kyle exclaimed angrily, almost challenging Max. "He goes by the name of Christopher and I cannot just find him, he has only ever approached me."

Lucas came from the tent, supported by Harmony as she looked between everyone evenly. Lucas clutched at his shoulder, carefully appraising Max. Trish smiled at him and flirtatiously waved with pouted lips. Max steadily looked at Harmony; his black eyes flickered and then returned to his milky glaze before looking at me once again.

"I have found Kurt. He told us everything and where to find them. We will ambush them in the coming days," he declared calmly. I couldn't understand why he was so composed. Before he raged for us to find Kurt and now he claimed to have already found him. *Is he tricking us? Was that his intention the whole time?*

"You found him?" Lucas queried quietly.

Harmony looked between all of us, uneasy. Ashley and Paige slowly crept out of their tent. Ashley held Paige back as she already pulled the knife from near her chest, on guard.

"Yes, little Starkorf. I have, and I will tell you where they are hiding in the morning," Max said assertively. "We will come back; we have more appropriate accommodation nearby." Trish began to push him away in his wheelchair, blowing a kiss to Lucas. Scott looked confused, shaking his head as he didn't understand his father's quick mood change either. "Karla, do not disappoint me twice. It will be costly."

"He is a Starkorf?" Uncle Kyle exclaimed angrily, startled that Max had addressed Lucas as a Starkorf.

I directly looked at Lucas, confused as to what Max Jacket meant. My stomach dropped as I noticed everyone was here but Paul. *Is Paul my cost?* I ran for the trees, my mind scurrying over dark thoughts. *What if he has done something to Paul? What has he done to Paul?*

Chapter Twenty-Nine- Our Separation

A branch scratched my face as I ran through the foliage, frantically absorbing from the ground. I concentrated my Shield onto the ground, trying to source Paul's location. *How long has he been gone now? Is he okay?* Surrounding me were thick trees and branches with spikey plants that surprisingly survived in such a dry state. I felt lost in them as I anxiously ran through all the crisp and dry trees. When I looked back toward the direction of the small open space of where we had set up camp, I saw nothing. I was completely enclosed and lost in the wilderness.

His presence suddenly overwhelmed me and I relished the feeling of his familiar energy. I looked into the direction from where I felt it, increasing my pace and running to him. More dry branches and twigs scratched at my face and pulled at my long hair.

I stopped near a tree as soon as I could see Paul, who sat on the ground next to a dried-out water hole. He sat there fidgeting with a half bitten red apple before throwing it toward the dried-out earth. He sat there staring at the empty water hole before picking up a stick, filing the tip down with his blade to form a spear.

He is safe.

I was hesitant to step out toward him, not knowing what to say. Instead I wanted to leave him in the peace he had in his solitude. He had put this distance between us so he could sit and think. I crouched next to the tree, cradling my knees to my chin, leaning against it for support so that I could watch him from afar.

Very little of the moon's light penetrated through the cloudy sky. Looking up at the moon, which was partially covered in gray clouds, I too enjoyed the serenity, and from here I could still watch over Paul. He would despise me if he knew I still followed him and tried to protect him as he had always tried to be the one to watch over and protect me.

Have I dragged him through too much, will he now break? Is it time for me to tell him to leave? Perhaps now is the time to make that real — to force him to go back home and give him no choice. I cannot give him what he so desperately wants from me. I cannot provide him with anything but danger. My face twisted as I thought of letting Paul go and how to say it.

Paul's figure was unmoving. As the time ticked on and my eyelids grew heavy from the silence of the night, I fought against sleep. I knew Misfeata would be waiting. Already I felt her presence creeping up on me, waiting for the opportunity to take control. And yet I couldn't help my eyes growing heavy as I fought off sleep. A snap of a branch alarmed me. I stood tall with Aeisha in hand. Paul quickly stood as well, inspecting the direction from where the noise came from.

My jaw dropped and I found myself stunned as I watched a replica of myself walk out toward Paul. I tried to yell out to Paul, to tell him it was not me, but my mouth did not move, nor did my feet when I tried to run toward them. Misfeata had gathered enough strength in my weakened and tired state to take partial control of my body. But for some reason it was only partial possession she took, enough to prevent me from moving and warning Paul.

"I've been looking for you," the imposter said, who looked just as I did with long light-brown hair, green eyes, fair skin. Even the same torn dress I wore now. I fought against Misfeata, trying to regain control.

You can watch,' Misfeata whispered from within me. *'I told you no one shall steal my heart. Your affection for this boy is too costly. He must go.'*

I panicked as my eyes widened on the imposter. *I must escape Misfeata's grasp.*

"Karla, what do you want? I think enough has been done. I can see how fond you are of Lucas. Despite the fact that I have been with you all the way... You choose him. It's disgusting," Paul said in a hurt tone, holding his hand toward the imposter in a gesture to not walk closer.

I could still feel the breeze on my body but nothing would move under my control. Misfeata contained me in a determined grip.

Please Misfeata, I begged. *Please let me go. I'll do anything.*

My imposter looked down toward her feet silently, pulling out Aeisha. I panicked to know they would use my own blade against Paul. *Please Paul, see it, I cannot watch. I cannot let her hurt Paul.* I stirred, trying to project my Shield, desperately trying to push Misfeata away but to no avail.

"Paul," the imposter breathed his name longingly in my voice. The intonation startled even Paul as he looked at the imposter, confused by the loving tone. Now my imposter stood directly in front of Paul with Aeisha in hand. *Please see past it Paul.* "I want to go back with you. I don't want this anymore. Let's go home."

"Why?" Paul asked, confused and now examining my imposter, his once angry face now suspicious. My imposter threw the fake Aeisha to the side, which was so close of a duplicate that Paul couldn't have noticed the difference.

"Because, I love you," the imposter simply said, leaning toward Paul. Her lips paused in front of Paul's as she evenly looked into his eyes. As their lips found one another's, I stared blankly. The imposter's hand coiled around Paul's neck as he gently placed his hand on her hip, cupping her face with his other hand. I stared, pained, uncertain as to what I was watching but a raw, grotesque emotion rose within me. *That isn't me he is kissing. It is an imposter.*

The cool breeze swept around me once more, tingling my skin. Misfeata's grip lessened and I felt her withdraw within me in satisfaction. As her firm grip of me broke, my legs scuffled forward on the ground beneath me. It broke the embrace between Paul and the imposter. I felt awkward as if somehow I were intruding.

I was stunned I didn't know what to say, what action to take. I wanted to run away and pretend I had never seen anything. But I had watched Paul gently caress another. I felt betrayed and I could not understand why. I held my hand around my neck, unsure as to what this emotion stuck in my throat was.

"Karla!" Paul said, pushing away the other person. He looked between us confused, standing back as he measured the other person once again.

"Busted," the imposter said shrugging her shoulders. The form of my body changed and Scott appeared, making me wince at the betrayal of our friendship. Why would he do this? He had once implied he had never tried to turn himself into a human, so why would he now? What could possibly drive him to do such a thing?

Paul's eyes widened as he began to wipe at his mouth with the back of his arm, his eyes raging. He looked back at me angrily as I held back tears at what Scott had done. Why would he do this? And why would Misfeata make me watch? I clutched my chest, not wanting to look into the eyes of either man who stood in front of me. When I looked up, Paul's face tore in anger.

"I hate this!" he snapped, his emotions breaking free. "I hate all of this. I only ever did it for you! But I can't anymore. I can't be a part of these games you play."

I took a step forward, wanting to nurse him, but he held out his hand forcefully, warning me to keep away. I rocked back on my heel, hurt that he would not let me close to him.

"I'm done, Karla," he said, his voice quiet but full of anguish. "I can't do this anymore."

His words stuck in my mind and I tried to prepare myself for what he was about to say next. His words were like a punch to the stomach, knocking all wind out of my lungs.

"I'm leaving."

He looked between Scott, who looked down in shame, and then me. I felt my eyes pleading for him to take his words back. And yet I hesitated from asking. This was what Paul wanted. And this was what I should have encouraged from the start. This was the only way I could protect him.

Paul stormed between Scott and I back into the trees as I closed my eyes, cowering away from the scene of him leaving. A tear slid down my face as Paul's presence disappeared amongst the trees and I fell into the tree I had once leaned against for support. I cradled the tree, trying to hold myself up, but instead I dropped to my knees, shaky, my heart in unbearable pain.

I tried to steady my breathing instead of pursuing Scott who had also left. I cradled myself beside the tree, trying to push away the unbearable pain Paul left behind, as I felt lonelier than ever before. *This is what is best for him, isn't it? It has to be. It's the only way I can protect him.*

Staring at the same spot that Paul was once sitting at, my shaky breath eased and puffs of cold air left my mouth in a steady rhythm. The sun slowly rose over the cold ground and small rays of brightness broke through the trees. Ashley and Paige's presence came closer toward me but I hid away from their faces, wanting to be left alone.

"Karla! Paul's gone!" Ashley panicked as he came to my side. I didn't divert my gaze, still staring at the empty water hole. It was probably once beautiful when it was full of water: whole and able to provide for the animals around it, nurturing them, and helping them to survive. Now it was dried up and was a large sunken hole in the ground without purpose. A memory of its former glory; I too felt like a sunken hole.

"I know," I said my mouth dry and my skin chilled.

Paige's skin no longer glowed with an ill tinge and she looked much healthier. The purple marks that were once on her skin from where the Starkorfs drained her were no longer visible. Perhaps Scott had healed her?

"He's gone with Harmony," Ashley said, grabbing my attention. I angrily looked up at him. *So Paul left so he could run away with Harmony?* Ashley took a step back from my gaze which must have conveyed my pain and rage to find out Paul had done such a thing.

"Karla. He didn't go with her," Lucas said, surprising me. "She took him."

I looked at Lucas hesitantly. He too looked healthier after last night's ordeal and his experience with death. He looked at me sympathetically, his eyebrows burrowed in confusion as I tried to understand his words. I was so relieved to see him okay. So much had happened since yesterday.

"Karla," Ashley said more forcefully, trying to make me understand. "Harmony has taken Paul."

"What do you mean she 'took' him?" I asked haltingly, the bitterness I held toward Harmony burning my tongue. I slowly began to register his meaning. She 'took him'. A large white bird swooped at Ashley before he could speak and Scott manifested in front of him, igniting my anger.

"Harmony is a traitor. To be more precise, she was never on our side of this war. She is one of Taskatae's creatures. She took him," Scott explained. I narrowed my eyes on him angrily, realizing why Max Jacket had so easily changed his tone last night. He was extremely angered but then as soon as Harmony came from her tent, he acted calmly and claimed to have known where Taskatae was. Max created a lie that Harmony had fallen for.

Scott purposefully made me watch as he kissed Paul, creating a rift between us. Someone needed to separate Paul and I so Harmony could easily take Paul. It was all a set up. The most upsetting thing to come between Paul and I was created by Scott. By kissing Paul he was so easily able to separate us. Even Misfeata — who held me back from interrupting and even forced me to watch — must have known. Taskatae had Aeisha's partnered blade, and Misfeata needed a way to her location. They all knew and saw the scheme that was being created. Everyone but me.

"You knew," I said, putting it all together. "That's why you did it."

Scott played me for a fool and has endangered Paul. He tore Paul and me apart purposefully.

I swung Aeisha near his chest but he speedily dropped to the ground as a mouse and scampered over to Lucas before standing as his human self, unfazed that I had attacked him. Instead of pursuing him, I breathed heavily, exhausted by all the lies.

"Yes, I knew," Scott admitted. "It was the only way we could trick Harmony. We needed to force her to panic and go warn her master. I am assuming we are not too far away for her to have acted so quickly. She has taken Paul as leverage, but she will lead us to Taskatae."

"She could change him into a beast before we retrieve him," I countered, incensed we had been used at the risk of Paul's life; the very person I wanted to protect the most.

"That could happen," he answered honesty, hiding his own emotions. He was too fond of Paul for his indifference to be real.

Lucas looked pale white as he realized the companion he had roamed with for so long now was not his ally at all but a traitor. The irony was that he had once been the traitor and still was in many eyes.

"Max is tracking her, isn't he?" Ashley asked, confirming the last piece of their unspoken plan. Max could sense people because of the electrolytes in their body. Max Jacket was tracking her now.

"Karla, you can hate me all you want, but this we had to do," Scott said confidently. It sounded mostly like he was trying to justify to himself the betrayal he had forced upon Paul. It may have cost Paul his life. But how did Misfeata know? How could she have guessed?

'I have been amongst the games of war for a very long time,' she responded, unapologetic. She had a part in this. And there was nothing I could do to rid myself of her.

"Karla, we should go," Lucas said lightly. "We need to go and retrieve him now."

"Don't forget that this is not just about getting Paul back," Scott forcefully said to Lucas. "We are there to confront Taskatae."

With no other option but to retrieve Paul, I swallowed my panic and found my will to achieve my goal. *I will rescue Paul. I will obtain Aeisha's partnered Immortal Blade and not allow myself to be controlled by Misfeata. And I will force Taskatae to her knees, repenting at what she has done to my father. I can do this. I will do this.*

Chapter Thirty- Strength

Uncle Kyle had already packed most of the tents and utensils. He cut down the rope of the last tent with his sword and assessed his weapon before folding down the tent material.

As he did, Max Jacket and Trish appeared on the horizon. The sun had still not fully risen and was just edging into dawn. I clenched my fists, infuriated at the tricks they played, using Paul as bait.

"He is not important to me. I gave him a second chance once. Who knows? He might survive again," Max Jacket said with pursed lips as Trish walked him toward us in his wheelchair.

"Doubt it," Trish smiled as she stared at me, her eyes flickering black. I could hardly contain my hatred of Trish anymore and my emotion boiled over. I wanted to put her in her place.

Even as an Elemental Breather, she was no better than us. None of them were. They would use anyone or any methods for the revenge they desired. They had even used me in the same way when they had wanted Borac so badly. They just wanted possessions other Elemental Breathers didn't have. Max had claimed that the Starkorfs betrayed him, so he wanted their treasured item, Borac, Tyran's Immortal Blade. He had forced me to get that, almost destroying me in the process. No matter what it was he was after, he didn't care about the casualties he incurred.

Unable to hold myself back from an eagerness to fight her, I ran for her. She smiled, removing her black lace glove and moving away from her father. She got exactly what she wanted: a fight. I projected my Shield as red curls pulsated around me and then I charged for her. Fire licked my Shield as I held Aeisha firmly to my side, running for her. She waited for me with a bright beam, her pupils swallowing the surrounding iris of her eyes.

As I swung Aeisha at her, she dodged to the left, punching flames into the side of my Shield, trying to weaken it. I swung for her again as she jumped back once more, Aeisha slightly grazing her arm. The flame on her hands strengthened as she realized she was too slow.

A large bolt of lightning struck at me but I dodged it, still following Trish, who encased me in a large ball of flames that she began to squeeze tightly. I looked up, sensing Max Jacket, who had sent another bolt of electricity toward me. I rolled back and out of the flames that encased me, strengthening my Shield and avoiding the lightning.

I balanced onto my heels and crouched, flicking my head up and removing my hair from over my eyesight. Lucas grabbed me gently from behind, and I tried to pull away. As I moved to charge forward toward Trish, his grip clenched down firm and he held me back. I tried projecting my Shield to deflect him but his Shield only compressed against my own, his breath striking down my back as he spoke.

"Not now. We need to find Paul first," he said, forcing me to regain my focus on what was most important to me right now. Max came to Trish's side, giving her a firm gaze. Her black eyes dissolved into her usual green. She then tauntingly smiled at me again, retrieving the patterned black glove out of a pocket on her dress.

"Where are they?" I demanded, ignoring Lucas's warm gloves on my cool skin. He dropped his hands and looked at the others. Ashley narrowed his eyes on me, disgusted. Uncle Kyle was being held back by Paige, who let him go as the tension subsided. As the fight was now resolved, he angrily looked between everyone before sheathing his sword once again and continuing to pack the bags.

"As predicted, they are not too far from here. In fact they themselves have only just reached it now," Max continued. "It's on another island near the Elemental Breathers ball, about four hours in the other direction across the water. However there is a narrow piece of land that you can reach it by. The appearance of its location might indicate she has been planning to make her attack on the Elemental Breathers ball for a while now."

"Well then, lead us there," Lucas said, still his Shield rubbed against mine as his anger wavered.

"And risk my prized Borac and make the same mistake as she did?" Max said snidely, gesturing at me. Aeisha's partnered Immortal Blade was stolen from me. "I do not think so. This is where that useless dog over here comes in use," he said, nodding toward Scott, who said nothing.

"Always cowering from the fight, huh?" Paige said with a mocking smile, provoking Trish.

"There is a difference between blindly and tactfully fighting, Girl," Max said in a crisp tone. "And why should I risk myself on the frontline when Karla must go anyway? I will follow. Taskatae is to be left for me. But in ambushing her hideout, there might be some casualties. I don't want to bother myself with any such burdens."

I bit my words back, knowing him to be right. Whether he came after or not, I would still go there anyway. But despite Max's beliefs, he was not the only one who wanted Taskatae.

"Let's go," I said bitterly as Paige, Ashley, and Uncle Kyle, carried the bags toward the hidden car.

"And Karla?" Max said, making me stop and look back at him bitterly. "When you obtain Aeisha's partnered Immortal Blade, I wish you the best of luck upon your confrontation with Nathanial. Who knows what Misfeata might turn your body into. Even if Tyran cannot do the same without Borac, I wouldn't think Misfeata to have enough strength to let the opportunity pass. So don't lose yourself to her," he said seriously. His serious tone deceived the mockery behind his words.

"Come on," Lucas said, grabbing my shoulders and pulling me away. *There is no time to waste on these two any longer if I must find Paul. No matter what risks it may bestow on me.*

'We are there for Aeisha, I couldn't care less for your lover,' Misfeata spoke within; making me gasp at the breath she had taken. I fought the nausea of her pull. Within me I could feel her resting. *This is what she has been doing these last few days. This is why she has been so quiet and has let me be: so she could rest and rejuvenate herself for this fight today. She knew Nathanial would be a part of this all, she knew she would confront her brother, Tyran.*

Lucas's black leather jacket shifted over his shoulder blades as he walked in front of me; strapping blades to his belt and hiding them under his jacket. *If I must fight Nathanial today and something happens to him... if Nathanial dies... I will then have to fight Lucas.*

As if hearing my thoughts, Lucas looked back at me. I dropped my gaze, not wanting him to guess exactly what I was thinking, but it was too late. He stopped me before we reached the car. He held my arm firmly and tilted my chin up to look into his dark-brown eyes.

"No matter what happens today..." he began, pausing for breath. "I will not fight you; I will protect you no matter what."

My eyes were lost in his, pained at his words. If Nathanial dies, we were fated to fight. We would not be able to control the Elders within us if we were close to one another. Already the connection between us was too strong to deny and that could be the influence of our rival bloods.

But if a confrontation was had and Nathanial lost, then I would die.

"I want you to promise me something," I said as a cool breeze swept past my torn dress. "No matter what, I want you to make sure Paul makes it out alive. No matter where I am. I need you to promise me."

"Karla—..." He cupped my face as I pulled away from his embrace.

"I need you to promise me," I interrupted. After a long hesitation I grabbed his hand and cupped his leather glove to my face. "Please, Lucas."

The wind whistled between us, shifting the leaves on the trees.

"I promise," he said virtuously. I mouthed 'thank you' to him as the words were stuck in my throat. I nestled my face into his hand, comforted to know that he had consented and I could save Paul. With Lucas's word, Paul would be saved.

"Karla?" Ashley intruded.

Startled, I pulled away from Lucas, ashamed by the embrace we were caught in. Pain stirred within my stomach as I caught the disgust in Ashley's eyes. "You need to change." He threw clothes and boots toward my feet. I remained silent and collected them.

"I'm sorry," Lucas said, picking the clothes up for me and holding them out to me. "For everything I have made difficult for you."

I accepted the clothes, looking over my torn dress that was once so beautiful. "Only I am responsible for my actions," I muttered, quietly reflecting on that as I walked over to the trees to change.

My belt was amongst the scattered clothing. Slipping off the dress, I looked over a body that was now muscular and toned from training and fighting. Not only had my mental ability and control of my Shield strengthened, but my body did as well. I had to keep up with the physical demand of the fighting.

I put my black leather boots on over my jeans, and then pulled on a dark-blue sleeveless shirt and my black leather jacket; zipping it up as I felt like I was encasing myself in some kind of protection. I was weary of the fight I was about to enter. I was in search of Taskatae and this was what I wanted, but not at the cost of Paul. I strapped the belt tightly to my waist where Aeisha snugly fitted, my left side bare without her partnered blade.

I lifted my hair, using some strands to tie it back so it would not be in my eyes. Now I was appropriately dressed and ready to go. I looked back at the trees and closed my eyes, smelling the fresh air. *I must fight, but if I don't come back from this...* The thought left a bitter taste in my throat. *If I don't survive, then at least in the end I have found what was worth fighting for. I fight for my family and for Paul. I fight alongside those who have been by my side, no matter for how short a time.*

I have found my Uncle Kyle who had been protecting me for so long now. I have found my parents who lost so much from this war. My mother is now a widow. I have recurring nightmares of murdering my own father. I would fight the things they hated most: Starkorfs. *I hope as my father watches over me he will be at ease as I destroy them. I hope my mother understands I hid her to protect her.*

Ashley and I had bonded over the betrayal of Lucas and over the loss of his father, Seth. We shared the common urge to run into battle recklessly as we had lost ourselves amidst the rage of war.

I was still pained by Scott's betrayal. My pain softened as I thought how little time we might have together after today. He has helped me on many occasions now; helping me sleep to avoid Misfeata's torturous grasp and protecting Paul in my stead. He opened my eyes to the world of Elemental Breathers, something about which I have previously known very little.

Lucas and I would always have a strong bond. He was the one to claim he would protect me no matter what. He taught me to control my ability, showed me how to care once again after such hardship, opening my heart once again.

And Paul — who I have always wanted to protect but never truly been able to let go of, even when I put him in such danger. My own selfishness kept him close and yet I always hesitated to allow myself to become too close, fearful of my own heart's desire and confused as to what I wanted.

These were the people I had fought alongside with, fought for, bonded with over near death experiences. And these were now the people I protected. Not because I had the strength of Misfeata or the ability to Shield, but because I wanted to protect them, with all the strength I could gather.

I will look after my family.

Chapter Thirty-One- A Lost Soul

*A*s Ashley drove and Scott directed him, we sat in silence, uncomfortable in one another's presence. As usual Paige looked outside the window at the trees, bored and impatient for the fight. Her black bob wildly blew in the wind. I sat uncomfortably between Paige and Lucas. Ashley often looked back at me in the rearview mirror and then at Lucas angrily. Lucas looked out of the window, avoiding me.

Uncle Kyle drove behind us on a yellow motorbike. It had been parked not too far away from the docks and he had retrieved it before packing the tents. He didn't let anyone know he was going to retrieve his items and said he was also on the lookout for any Starkorfs or creatures that may have been close by. He didn't own many belongings and firmly believed that the only thing he needed were the weapons on his back and the big bag of clothes he carted around.

My hands tightened and clutched my knees as I tried to calm myself, frightened as to how many other beasts we would have to face. *Could there be even more Elemental Breathers there to confront us? And what do I do if I come into contact with Nathanial, how can I control Misfeata if I have both of Aeisha's Immortal Blades?* I remembered the near death she placed on my body during the fight I had with Tyran in Praytar's body; she shredded my body apart trying to transform me into a beast. How did I control her? How did I claim my body once again before she destroyed me?

As swiftly as the thoughts surrounded me, my hands were warmed by Lucas's leather glove. He still looked out of the window, his hand firmly placed around my own for support. I then noticed how tightly my hands grasped at my knees. I loosened my grip as it had stiffened into such a fierce hold in the cool chill. I twisted my hand beneath his, holding it lightly. It was not only me who risked their soul, but Lucas as well. He must be worried too about Tyran's grasp on him if his brother was killed. He was the last descendant of Tyran. I wonder how heavily that played on his mind?

His sandy-blonde hair flickered like golden flames as the sun grew overhead. I looked between Scott and Ashley into the small narrow road we drove on. We must be close. Looking back over Lucas, my eyes bulged as a large white creature from the forest ran for us. All of us looked at once, attracted to its quick movement as it slammed into the side of the car, spinning us off the road and into the trees.

The impact of hitting the tree front-on whiplashed my neck and smashed the back of my head into my seat. I squinted and sat dazed. Lucas slowly peeled himself off me and I realized he had covered me and projected his Shield, protecting me from the impact. I instantly looked for the beast, observing with horror its large horns across its nose; inflamed nostrils; thick legs and stocky body.

Scott's head bled as he sat there, unmoving. Ashley winced behind the wheel, his forehead bleeding. He turned around to see if Paige was okay. She wasn't in the car. We all panicked and looked around for her. She was warding off the beast that now charged her. She quickly jumped around it, avoiding its attacks and distracting it as she tried cutting at its ankles. When did she jump from the car? Uncle Kyle, also unscathed with his motorbike safely parked a distance away, attacked the creature with his large sword.

"Ashley!" I yelled as another similar creature came charging toward him. I threw myself over his chair, but one of my feet got pinned under the chair when it collapsed on me. I projected my Shield in front of him. The creature pushed my Shield back, dragging the car along the grassy ground. The creature shook its head and charged again, dragging us further back.

Startled, the other creature that Paige and Uncle Kyle had been fighting ran for us from the other side. Lucas projected his Shield, preparing for its attack on the side of the car. As it ran for us Paige jumped on its neck, grabbing its horns from behind and wrapping her arms around it from underneath. She was forcing it to run to another direction.

"Get Scott out!" I yelled at Ashley, wincing as I tried to move my foot, but it was tightly jammed at an awkward angle. Noticing my pain, Lucas lifted the heavy chair swiftly, helping me release my foot. It was clearly broken with cuts all down my leg.

"Grab him!" Ashley said to Lucas, indicating Scott. Ashley's eyebrow piercing was no longer there and blood dripped from the opening. As Ashley handed Scott's unconscious figure over to Lucas who now stood outside of the car, the creature charged my Shield once again, dragging the car back and putting pressure on my Shield. I strengthened the purple ripples.

As the dragging stopped and the creature sized up another angle to attack, Ashley jumped over the seat pulling me along with him as we jumped out of the car together before the beast struck it one more time. Without my Shield against it, the creature dug its horns deep under the car and flung it across the road before looking over us hungrily with red eyes.

My heartbeat raced as I looked at the poor creature. It was so tortured and had nothing but bloodlust in its eyes. Was this a person that Taskatae had done this too? Or was it one of her creatures created from her eggs? Ashley held me firmly at the waist, holding me up as I still hobbled on my ankle. I felt it healing, surprised by my tolerance now of pain, but as I focused on it I realized that Misfeata was fawning on that area, not allowing me to feel the pain as she healed it quickly. *She can't use a damaged body to fight*, I thought bitterly.

'*If I left it to you, we would both be killed by now,*' she shot back, loosening her grasp on my ankle. Pain shot up my leg. She quickly blocked it again, relieving me of the agony. Ashley glanced at me as I whimpered before hurriedly escorting me to the tree where Scott rested. Lucas distracted the creature from us as it charged him and his Shield constantly.

"Scott!" I said, resting my ear and hand to his chest, checking that his heart still beat. As my hand rested on him he gasped loudly, scaring me, and I fell backwards. His pink eyes widened in shock as he looked around him. He pressed tentative fingers to the wound on his head.

"Where am I?" Scott's voiced wobbled. His face became distorted as he panicked. "Who are you?" he cried as he looked at the blood on his fingers.

"He doesn't remember who he is," I said in a panicked voice to Ashley, who could only look back helpless.

"Scott," I said gently. He froze under my voice, his eyes widening as he leaned backward, terrified of me. "It's okay," I whispered, scared of the damage the car accident had inflicted on his brain. "It's me," I continued, my voice catching on my words. I held back my tears at seeing Scott in such a delirious and terrified state. He would never lose his composure like this; his eyes were gleaming with pain and incomprehension.

"Does he automatically heal or does he need to make the decision to?" Ashley asked.

He clutched his long knife as he watched over the other two who fought, still distracting the creatures that attacked them. One of the creatures screamed out loudly as Paige jumped on its neck once again, stabbing into it three times before flinging herself over its horns. As its head wavered from side to side in pain, she struck it another two times in the chest.

Still with the black blade in its chest, the creature knelt and then plummeted to the ground as she reefed her knife out. Its eyes were still red and wide as its body hit the ground. Dead. Paige and Uncle Kyle ran toward Lucas panting harshly. *She enjoyed that*, I realized. Paige loved to fight.

Uncle Kyle's face was hard and determined as he contemplated the second creature.

Scott gasped loudly as his hand firmly grasped around my arm, hurting me.

"Scott, you can heal yourself," I said trying not to make any sudden movement as he looked over me, lost. "Just think of yourself healing yourself." *He must recover from this delirium.* His pink eyes closed as he began to cry and whimper, mumbling words I couldn't make sense of before he broke into a wail. His grip tightened on me and his nails dug deep.

His hand squeezed tighter as his shape changed and each and every scale scratched at my skin. I looked away from the pain it shot in my arm, trying not to scare Scott anymore then I already had. Ashley was instantly at my side, his long knife held near his face as he readied himself to attack Scott. I frowned at him, shaking my head vigorously before Scott saw. *We can get him back.* We must bring him back. After all that we have been through, I would not let him be beaten by a head wound after all the injuries he should've died from in all these years. He could not die from a simple, mundane head wound.

The sound of the second beast crying shook the ground lightly as Scott's eyes widened once again. He screamed at the sight of his arm, trying to crawl away from it, finding it to be a part of him. As his grip loosened little scratch marks were left all over my arm from his unintentional damage.

"Shh, Scott it's okay," I pleaded, my heart breaking to see him not recognize himself or me. He shriveled behind the tree as Paige approached, her face covered with drops of blood. Uncle Kyle and Lucas wiped over their blades as they walked behind.

"What's wrong with him?" Paige asked nonchalantly.

"He can't remember who he is or who we are," I explained, focusing on Lucas. "He can't heal himself, it's his head." I already felt Scott was too far gone. *Has he gone crazy, will he forever be crazy?*

Lucas reefed his leather glove off and barged past Ashley who restrained himself from using his weapon on Lucas. Lucas grabbed Scott's hand, much to his dislike, and he cried out, scared of the man in front of him. Uncle Kyle and I watched intently. Uncle Kyle's face twisted as he watched Lucas use such methods as draining.

Scott cried, screamed, and thrashed in pain as Lucas drained him. *Does Lucas think that will work? Weakening him, how could it work?* I didn't want to hear his screaming any longer. Before I could reach out to Lucas to say stop, Uncle Kyle had reefed Lucas back. Lucas coughed into the ground, squinting as he held his throat and then his head. He was clearly in immense pain in his own body at the exact spot where Scott's injury was.

Scott's cries quelled though he looked dazed. "Scott?" I whispered. I flinched under his glare at me. He sat up contently. *Has he come back to his wits?*

The stitching of his cut began as slowly a small piece of glass protruded out and dropped into his lap, the skin layering over it as if it had never happened.

"What happened?" His smooth voice was demanding as he looked around at the others and then at me.

"You couldn't mend yourself," I explained, pulling myself back calmly. My own injury now healed. "You didn't know who we were; you didn't know who *you* were."

"We don't have time for this," Scott forced back after a moment's hesitation, realizing that he too could be killed at any time. He stood, straightening his purple suit and slicking back his white hair. Cracking his neck he pointed into a direction over my shoulder.

"This way, we aren't that far away," Scott said before quickly walking toward it. Black birds spread over the sky in the same direction in which he pointed. The sky should have been lit with sun but it was dull with black clouds, an indicator that Max Jacket was near.

I helped Lucas off the ground but for a moment he paused, his head spinning. Uncle Kyle and he shared a harsh glare. Although he was a Starkorf, his ability could save lives as well, taking that energy on board himself. He had already done that for me. But what effect did it have on his own body? If Starkorfs could save lives with their ability to drain, then why did they continue to kill?

"How many people have you killed?" I asked curiously, wondering as to whether Lucas had always done this. But he was over ninety years old. How many people had he killed to keep the age that he appeared now?

"Many," he said honestly. "But I haven't since I was a boy, since I was with Kurt and the others. I haven't hurt a human since. I've been maintaining myself on animals."

"But you had the appearance of a young boy for many years?" I accused. Although I wanted the answer I was fearful of the response. Lucas had murdered to maintain his immortality. *For how many more years would he do that? When would he think a lifetime is enough?*

"Too many years," he spoke out.

My throat felt of acid and I wanted to vomit at his confession, disgusted at the answer I already knew I'd hear. *How many was enough?*

Were all Starkorfs the same or was Lucas different? Could there be some that didn't enjoy killing humans?

"Come on, Karla," Uncle Kyle said, who was ahead of me. "We've got to find Paul." His eyes never left Lucas's as he said this. My skin was tingling as I realized Uncle Kyle hated Lucas for everything he was. Uncle Kyle reached his hand out to me, offering for me to take it and follow him. Looking between the stumbling Lucas and my Uncle Kyle, I couldn't leave Lucas to walk on his own in his weakened state — not until he regenerated through his quick healing.

Much to my uncle's disgruntlement, I still helped Lucas as the others walked ahead. I needed Lucas's strength to get Paul out alive. *I want everyone to make it out alive.*

Chapter Thirty-Two- Magnificent Fortress

*L*ucas's walking was strong again after only minutes as his migraine obviously disappeared. We all cautiously walked ahead, waiting for more creatures to attack. We finally reached a small strip of land which had a wide and long dark wooden bridge attached from our side of land to the other side.

When we left the trees and looked over the water, my mouth widened in awe. Over the water on the other side of the large bridge that swept over the grassy plain was an enormous castle: one that epitomized prestige, elegance, and uniqueness. It must have been here for centuries, large and structurally sound.

There were large trees dotted sporadically around the castle. With my keen eyesight I noticed little funnels from the bricked walls leaked water into the wells. There were many stairs leading into the three-story castle. It was enormous and no clear entrance could be seen. Although there were large windows near every staircase, no light came from within the castle's walls, and the inside of the castle vanished into darkness; from where we stood we could not see any doors.

We looked at one another in alarm. I don't think anyone had prepared themselves for how large Taskatae's hideout could be. I wondered how many creatures lived within the mighty walls. Black birds swarmed the trees behind and watched us steadily. Much to my disgust, all the black crows had three eyes and all of them watched us cautiously. They all began flapping their wings and squawking loudly.

"That's creepy," Paige acknowledged before walking toward the bridge. The ominous setting clearly was no deterrent for her. Hesitantly I unwrapped my arms from around my waist. It was a grotesque image, so many disfigured birds watching us.

"Karla, are you sure about this?" Ashley asked me, taking my attention away from the birds. Ashley's eyebrow still bled from where his piercing had been reefed out. His black hair stuck to it as his blue eyes looked back at the birds, also uncertain. We were used to fighting Starkorfs; most took a deformed form, but were still of human lineage. We were not equipped to fight such terrible and unknown beasts. This expanded our world far more than we had ever known; now anything seemed possible and our futures were most uncertain.

"You don't have to, Ashley," I said considerately. He was not one who I wanted to risk. "But I must find Paul." The birds squawking heightened as a sweeping noise crashed from the trees. A breeze of smoke brushed through over the green grass; still the crows cawed on the tree tops. Paige, who now stood in front of the bridge, looked behind her at the trees in curiosity, pulling out her small black knife from the sheath at her chest. The noise went still and all of us pulled our weapons out, preparing ourselves as we watched the smoke sweep over Paige's feet and toward ours. I sensed darkness from the smoke and projected my Shield, which burst into gray ripples.

Paige squinted into the trees further. Something rushed for her and threw her through the smoke. Something lashed out at Uncle Kyle and Ashley, throwing them toward the water so quickly I wasn't able to identify what had thrown them.

My feet dragged back as something pushed heavily on my Shield. I looked in surprise at what pushed me so heavily against the once green grass: a thick vine. Its branch was dead and black, with bright green thorns. As I looked at it stunned, another three branches similar to the first one struck at my Shield, the fifth one breaking through. Its thorns cut across my face and flung me toward the water.

I hit the cold water forcefully and I strained to swim to the top. I felt something within the water drift past me. I projected my Shield from my body, pushing out the water. Although I couldn't breathe in it, I felt safer as I looked into the darkness of the water and at my surroundings. I was reluctant to reach the top but I knew I was not alone in the water.

I began swimming up as strongly as I could, but, letting my Shield down, I felt the trickle of something brush past my waist. I madly swam in the direction where the water was much clearer under the sun's beam. Something grazed past my ankles as I frantically projected my Shield once again. My eyes narrowed on the small fish-like creatures with scaled spines that looked back at me with moss covering their eyes.

A multitude of them surrounded me. The one directly in front of me had its eyes opened; there was only blackness. It sprayed a green mist around my Shield. I could no longer see where the surface was as the creature distorted the color of the water. In the water I could not sense where they were; I could not physically drain water to feel the presence that surrounded me. I was blind in this water and unable to swim as well as project my Shield.

I must get out of the water.

I quickly let my Shield down so I could swim again, stronger than I had ever before. I was swimming to the top before the breath I clung to left me. I was cut everywhere. I coiled myself in a bundle and projected my Shield outward in protection as the overwhelming sting of cuts all over throbbed. Again, with my pulsated Shield projected, the water around me was clear and I looked into the moss green of the fish with spiked spines. Red drifted from its spiny back: my blood from where it had injured me.

I pulsed my Shield, shattering it. It slightly pushed them back and before they could swarm me I projected my Shield again so they won't have the force to penetrate it. They waited again patiently until I was vulnerable. My breath became non-existent and I began to struggle under the desperate need of oxygen. I gathered my energy before projecting a huge shock wave and my Shield combusted, pushing away the water. I frantically swam to the top.

The surface of the water was within my reach as I held out my hand to the sun. I found the edge of the water and grass to reef myself up. My feet were cut everywhere and my surroundings were darkened once more by the dark-green taint of the creatures. My hand firmly planted on the ground on the outside of the water as I projected my Shield again around my whole body where they could not attack. I pulled myself up and gasped loudly for air, opening my eyes wide. Ashley grabbed my hand, pulling me out of the water before he was knocked away by the vine-like creature. Ashley's hand pulled away from mine as he was thrown toward the large wooden bridge by the vines.

I couldn't see Uncle Kyle but a large white bird flew overhead. Lucas and Paige tried getting further into the trees, cutting away as the vines scratched past them. The giant white bird suddenly dropped and then Scott emerged, holding his arm, which bled heavily before quickly healing.

"There is a moss-like organism in the middle. We need to destroy it somehow," he said, panting heavily. The crows that once surrounded flocked back to the castle as the trees moved and grew, and more vines pierced the top of the green treetops.

I dodged the vines that tried attacking; not making the same mistake as I had last time — underestimating the might of their swing. *But how do we destroy it?*

Lucas stood in front of Paige as she had been knocked off her feet and a vine went for her throat, flicking away from Lucas's invisible Shield as it pulsated. I ran toward Paige and Ashley who still struggled to stand from when it last attacked him.

I reached them quickly, relying on my Shield alone to protect me. I looked over the sheer size of the creature, feeling disheartened. *How could we possibly destroy it? What destroys trees and plants?* As it came to me I looked across at Uncle Kyle, who had run back for his bike and was now riding it toward us. *If we can combust his bike into that creature then it should set all of it ablaze.*

"Ashley!" I yelled, trying to grab his attention, but already his face was determined. And somehow we all knew what had to be done. We all worked well together, despite the mistrust we held for one another. Uncle Kyle drove beside us as Paige pierced her small black blade into the fuel sector quickly. Uncle Kyle jumped off the bike but it still drove deep into the tree, leaking fuel as it went.

Ashley held out a lighter to the fuel quickly and it blazed, trailing up to the bike and amongst the trees. Lucas and I both stood in front of everyone, our Shields covering us as the bike exploded and parts flew beside us; objects and flames appeared in front of my eyes but I still looked away on instinct.

The trees groaned and flared quickly, the long branches and vines thrashing back and forth as the flames engulfed them. We all held our breath and watched the creature diminish. We looked back at the wooden bridge that we had to walk across to enter Taskatae's home. Already my legs have healed, but they still shook in fear at the enormity of what was ahead.

If she has creatures like these at the gates of her castle, then what does she hide inside? Not able to think about it any longer, I began walking to that direction. I will not let her create a creature out of Paul. Holding onto Aeisha firmly and with Misfeata within me eagerly awaiting, I appraised the situation. Misfeata was stirring within me. *Is it because Aeisha's partnered Immortal Blade is within or could it be because her brother, Tyran, is also here? Who is exciting her?*

'*Both,*' she hungrily responded.

Chapter Thirty-Three- Starkorf Allegiance

$\mathscr{I}$ looked over the water, looking for the creatures within that have previously attacked me, but none arose. As I took my first step onto the large wooden bridge, I flinched, expecting something to jump out at me. Instead, only a few crows squawked listlessly overhead, making me wonder if Taskatae now welcomed us into her abode.

The surrounding clouds gathered darker and thicker, indicating Max's rage. I speculated inwardly on how far Max Jacket and Trish were from here. Their cowardly actions left a bitter taste in my mouth. But Max carried Borac on his back, and if Nathanial were to obtain it, then who knew what might happen. I hesitated to take my next step so I procrastinated; focusing on one of the windows of the castle. Lucas caught up with me and came to my side.

"You promised me," I said to Lucas, thinking again of Paul. "No matter what."

"Uncle Kyle," I called, grabbing his attention as I looked back confidently. *I cannot have weakness as I walk in, I will not let my fear shine.* "This is the home of the Elemental Breather who changed Dad into a beast. I will do what I feel is necessary. Please respect that. No matter what might happen today."

Before he could say anything I turned and continued walking. *I must be strong in my decisions and quick with my reflexes. If they fight with me then that is their choice. But I must do my best and let my instinct follow its calling. As a Shielder I am here to protect, but also to do what I am best at — and with Misfeata's blood sparring through my veins, that is to fight.*

The sun began to irritate my eyes as it shone brightly through the clouds, suddenly illuminating deformed figures that poured out from the castle. Starkorfs ran for us as we all gave one another a certain glance. We chose to be here and we would fight to the very end. As I mustered my strength and looked at the Starkorfs that swarmed quicker, I firmly held onto Aeisha.

We will fight them front-on, we will get past them and I will find Paul. Paul, I am coming for you. I fight for you. My steps quickened and I ran over the wooden bridge onto the other side as the others followed, giving me strength as I knew I didn't stand alone. We all had something to fight for and something to claim in this day.

I shouldered the first Starkorf with which I came in contact with and it was thrown back. Paige stabbed it in the neck, pushing it away. The others charged forward into the pit of Starkorfs.

I kicked a Starkorf away who tried bringing down an axe onto my left shoulder. I kicked him away and sliced at the stomach of another on my right, pushing it away as its ghastly noise echoed through my ear. As the same male Starkorf with the axe tried swinging at me again, I hid behind another, cutting the back of its legs as it dropped in pain. I twisted behind it and deflected the axe. I pulled the axe out of his hand, pulling him toward me and pulsating my Shield into him. He was flung off and thrown into the water. The same creatures that once attacked me pulled him under.

With axe now in hand I swung savagely, forcing all those who tried to jump on me to stumble back in defense. I was quickly surrounded. I held my breath for a moment, increasing my energy within and shattering my Shield to throw back eight of them.

I felt already overwhelmed by the release. Two tried to jump on me, one's spear almost slicing at my face. I had to lean back, dodging it. I grabbed firmly the spear, pulling it toward me and then throwing it behind as another Starkorf tried to attack. I slashed the first Starkorf who now had no spear or weapon and I cut her across her chest with Aeisha. She savored the blood, and my heartbeat pulsated as one with her energy as we filled with raw hate.

Misfeata aroused within, her hatred boiling within me. I tried to contain her and fight, but I was still not able to kill them. As I had a moment to look around, I saw that Paige savagely attacked them. There were a few purple and blue marks on her where Starkorfs had hit her. Defending her back, Ashley stood hacking at them with such hatred. I watched as he excessively stabbed into some.

Uncle Kyle did not stray far from me; he was cutting through them steadily with skill as he tried to get closer to my position. Lucas was ahead of me, his long sword easily cutting through them as he wrestled amongst them. My alarm heightened as not many of them we fought today had the ability to Shield. I wondered if this was strategic or was it just that they were weakened after the death of their leader, Praytar.

A sword collided with Aeisha and I protected myself before looking into the eyes of the male Starkorf. He had one eye stitched together by his own skin. He was quick and continued hacking at me. My blade was small in comparison to his, and my Shield trickled out from my body. Blue ripples projected around me and I felt the faint touch of his Shield as he exerted more pressure on mine. We stood there, our blades against one another, struggling for dominancy. It surprised me how strong he was.

He was only new to the battlefield. Many Starkorfs had fallen. As I peeked behind him I noticed more trailed from the castle, looking a lot stronger than the last warriors. It was tactical and now we must fight those who could Shield. I panicked, realizing only Lucas and I could protect ourselves from their Shields. The others were defenseless.

Paige's aggravated cry snapped me out of my thoughts. She was held firmly by her throat and was clawing at the invisible Shield that surrounded the man who drained her. She tried stabbing at him but her blade constantly stopped around his Shield.

I pulsated my Shield, pushing the Starkorf that fought me and dragging his feet back. *My Shield can better theirs. I need this strength.* I illuminated my Shield around me, barging through his once again and breaking it as I swung my leg behind me, circling and kicking him in the face before throwing him to the floor.

I ran for the Starkorf who held Paige, jumping on his back as I pinpointed my Shield on the surface of his, shattering it and wrapping my legs around his stomach from behind. I avoided the touch of his skin. As I pulled him back I projected my Shield behind me, rolling over it as I flung him back and away from Paige. I collected myself into a crouching position as my feet now rest on the ground. Ashley jumped on him while the Starkorf's Shield was down, ending his life.

Another ran for Paige but I kicked his shins hard, shattering his Shield and tripping him. Paige pounced wildly, her weakened state no longer apparent as the call of war beckoned her. Her black knife slashed back and forth as quickly as her hair swished as she moved.

Scott screamed, agitated as he was surrounded by twelve Starkorfs. A spear protruded from his stomach. He winced and as the others jumped in with their blades trying to kill him, he changed into a creature that had hard skin. The spear poked out from his shell, slowly pushing out and I knew he was healing himself.

I ran toward Scott. Uncle Kyle joined too, cutting at his attackers. He forcefully brought his sword down on one and was pushed back by their invisible Shield. I hurried to his side as now another four had piqued interest surrounding him, making ghastly and savage noises as they looked over him hungrily. I could feel three of them to have the ability of Shielding, but nothing that could compare to the strength of my own.

I helped Uncle Kyle to his feet, looking behind at Scott who was still being attacked. His hard shell was protecting him as the sphere slowly continued to push out. As purple ripples surrounded me, I could feel theirs project. One by one they circled and ran for me. I allowed them to get closer to me so I could fight them off, trying not to rely on my Shield as it took its toll. If they increased their Shield then I would have to do so with mine but for now we were to simply fight like the warriors we were.

As one cut my arm I grabbed his wrist, twisting it and throwing him over my shoulder. When he fell, I stabbed Aeisha into his stomach; he tried to claw at my face. As a woman tried to scratch at me I flung myself over behind his body, pulling Aeisha out as I stood again quickly. I dodged her attack to the left and holding onto her black torn shirt, I threw her away from me.

I raised my elbow to the next attacker's face and swung myself around to quickly slash Aeisha across his stomach. The fourth's thick wooden stick ploughed into my stomach, it winded me and I took a few steps back, blocking his fist. As my hand was wrapped around his I contained my scream. I quickly pulled away from its burning and draining effects. As I pulled away, he quickly swung the wooden stick across my face, dropping me to the ground. I forcefully projected my Shield stronger so he could not hurt me. He tried plunging the wooden stick into me but it splintered and shattered.

I regained control of myself after taking a breath, rolling onto my back and kicking at his hand to flick his weapon away. As he tried punching me I rolled to my side, collecting myself on my feet and stabbing Aeisha into his stomach. I raised myself as I quickly pulled her out. Unfazed by the injury, he swung for me again. I dodged back, swinging my head back and projecting my Shield to my forehead, head-butting him. He was thrown back meters and slipped into the water where he did not resurface.

My head spun from the forceful blow as I stumbled toward Scott, who now was uninjured. The remaining Starkorfs were on the ground, unmoving. Lucas still powerfully slashed through the fighters as their numbers quickly diminished. Lucas now had two swords slashing at all those who came at him, breaking the few clumps of attackers that still poured out, dispersing them around him.

Ashley and Paige ran toward us, catching their breath before we were forced to fight once again. Blood spurted everywhere as the others savagely cut through the Starkorfs. Again the crows' loud noises were heard as they watched over us, and I focused once more on the castle. *I must get in there.*

An arrow shot through the air and I focused on it and ran for the target, trying to protect Ashley. I projected my Shield but I was already too late and Ashley was pierced in the chest, losing control of his legs as they buckled and stumbled backward toward the edge of the water. I screamed out his name over all the clashing of weapons. My eyesight was caught by a white-tipped feather that resembled Harmony's distinctive arrow.

I dropped to my knees next to him as he looked over it in confusion, gasping and straining to focus on anything at all as he coughed blood. I held his hand firmly, not sure what to do. Scott ran to us, as everyone else heard me scream out his name. Lucas, Uncle Kyle, and Paige stepped back, fighting harder to keep them away as Scott and I sat by Ashley's side.

"Scott, you must heal him!" I cried, as I saw Ashley's life dimming within his blue eyes. *I can't have him die.* Not after watching his father, Seth, die as well. *Ashley cannot.* Scott concentrated on Ashley's chest, pressing his hands on it heavily. Scott's eyes widened as an arrow shot into his back. Another one shot for him and that one pinned him too. Scott still tried to concentrate on Ashley.

I stood in front of them, cutting the tip of the third that shot directly at Scott. Its point was diverted but the wood still splintered, cutting my stomach. I narrowly focused on the arrows that shot at us, projecting my Shield to protect them instead. One pierced straight into my leg, instantly getting through my Shield. The same as when we had fought in the small town and the Starkorfs first came for Aeisha. The archer all this time had been Harmony.

I couldn't protect myself nor the others with my Shield projected. These arrows could pierce through. One by one I cut at the arrows that came, and the splintered wood still scratched past me. With so many coming I missed some, my own body being the only thing to come between the arrows and Scott, who was trying to heal and save Ashley.

Lucas stood in front of me, his long swords far more efficient to cut through them without being scathed. I tiredly dropped to my knees, pained as I pulled two arrows out of my legs. *When did I become accustomed to this?* I crawled to Ashley's side as he still gasped heavily, Misfeata busily repairing my damaged legs.

Ashley was almost crying as I held his hand, his lips tightening as he looked up at me in pain. I held onto his hand as firmly as his held mine, unable to do anything. Small spikes broke through the water's edge as the creatures within swarmed around, expecting Ashley to enter as well.

"Ka—…" Ashley spluttered as he tried to speak my name. I put my finger to his lips, ushering him into silence.

"Let Scott fix you," I said remorsefully, watching the light dim in his eyes as the reality of death was apparent. *I may be able to heal. But others cannot, this is a game of life and death.* "Everything will be okay."

My long light-brown hair brushed in my eyes as the wind picked up, like a wild storm. Thunder began pouring from the sky as only the Starkorfs dropped — all of them being shot down dead by Max Jacket, whom I could not see but knew to be close by.

As they all stilled, the arrows also stopped coming. The others ran over to us, looking over Ashley. *If the arrows have stopped does that mean Max has killed Harmony?* Scott pushed the arrow out, his own still in his back as he exhausted himself trying to heal Ashley. Frowning in concentration, his pink eyes narrowed as slowly Ashley's chest began to stitch and his breathing became shallow.

"Give him a few minutes. I've done what I can," Scott said as the arrows dropped out of his own back.

The few Starkorfs that survived groaned, bringing my attention back to our mission. "Karla. We must go," Lucas said. I knew he was right, while we had no Starkorfs surrounding us, we could get further into the castle before more came.

"Paige. Please look over him," I commanded. She agreed, much to my surprise, as she had always been resistant of looking after others and missing out on 'the fight'.

"Karla..." Ashley whispered. Before he could say anymore I stroked back his black hair out of his eyes, avoiding the injury on his eyebrow. Helena would have never forgiven me to have her husband and son taken away because of this war I fought. I would have never forgiven myself. At least this way I knew he was safe.

"You are safe here," I promised, rising and running toward the castle over a smaller wooden bridge with Lucas, Scott, and Uncle Kyle. We got closer and looked up into the enormity of the castle. All the pipelines flowed with water into small water wells and the staircases were layered with golden bricks. A flicker of a shadow across one of the great big windows on the second level grabbed my attention. Lucas ran toward it, choosing the closest staircase. To our surprise, nothing ran at us — yet.

Chapter Thirty-Four- To Find You

*W*e cautiously took it step by step, anticipating anything. As we reached the top of the stairs, large wooden doors stood tall in our way. They were neatly carved with images of creatures I had never seen before; they were destroying men on horses with swords in hand. It loudly creaked open and we looked at it in suspense, but nothing came.

Lucas carefully placed his hand on the smooth wood, pushing it further open into the dark entrance. But still nothing came. *Is this Taskatae welcoming us in?*

As we all slowly walked in, a strong wind brushed past us, sweeping through the hollow hallway and extinguishing candles that lined the walls. The wind howled down the hall eerily. Very little light shone through the big windows that extended on both our left and right. Flashes of lightning streaked across, giving us very little light as the gray clouds blocked any chance of sun. The thought of splitting up terrified me, but we had very little time to find Paul.

"We stay together," Uncle Kyle said forcefully as he began walking into the hallway on our right. Hesitantly I agreed as I followed him, noticing that Lucas didn't follow and had already started walking the other way, holding his two long swords strongly.

"Lucas," I whispered, his sandy-blonde hair flashing white as another streak of lightning flashed. He gave me a faint smile and continued walking. This was the quickest way we can find where Paul was being kept. *We must split up, the castle is too vast.*

The first room on our left had a large wooden table with twelve chairs; large paintings surrounding of bizarre, disjointed creatures. *Are these images of Taskatae's creatures?* I held my sneeze as another gust of wind blew through, stirring the dust contained in the room and swinging the chandelier back and forth violently.

We checked the second room. There was an old dusty bed with a small bedside table and a painting over the large wooden bedframe. My eyes widened in horror at the painting; it had the resemblance of Raven, in fact it couldn't be anyone *but* Raven with such black hair and blue crystallized eyes. She was smiling as she held firmly onto a small fluffy creature with a tail that extended to spikes.

"Karla," Uncle Kyle whispered, snapping me out of my fascination. I recalled Taskatae's words, she had once said I had killed the only child she bore herself. As I stared at the painting of Raven as a child, much smaller than the age of when I had met her, I shriveled at the thought. Raven was the first Starkorf life I took. She had hurt my parents so long ago and many more people since. Her twisted, elderly soul had been in existence for far more than one lifetime, maintained by draining people and keeping the appearance of a young child.

Could she have been Taskatae's daughter?

Focusing on their resemblance I now realized what Taskatae had meant by her insinuation. I had killed Raven, I killed Taskatae's daughter. Their hair color and eyes were the same. When I first saw Taskatae, I thought she was Raven at first glance. *This is not a hunt for just Aeisha. She is after me.*

I slowly pulled the door closed, my heart racing as Uncle Kyle called out my name. *Taskatae wants to kill me, for a far greater reason than I had ever thought. What she did to my father, was that because of my doing?*

We looked into a large open room with an ostentatious chandelier that creaked as it gently swung back and forth in the wind. The room was at the end of a hallway with five other doors. As we opened the first, we saw it was another hallway. Looking into the second room, we saw that chains hung from the roof and it reeked of death.

As Uncle Kyle opened the third, his shoulders broadened and I could not see past him.

"Not that room," Uncle Kyle said, quickly closing it.

"What's in there?" I asked, barging past him and opening the door myself. I clamped my hand over my mouth, instinctively trying to keep the stench away as tears instantly rolled over my knuckles. Dead bodies rotted the room. Some were chained to the walls, others face first into the ground. As I stood there shocked, Uncle Kyle slowly leaned over me, closing the door. I gasped in horrified disbelief at all the bodies. Man, woman, or child, it did not matter —they were all brought here. What were they here for? For Starkorfs? For Taskatae's tricks? How could something so horrific happen?

"I cried when I first saw that room," a familiar voice said. As I spun around my eyes narrowed on Kurt, who stood in front of me in a long black coat, his hands in his pockets.

"You are meant to save these people," I said, my voice breaking.

"No, I am supposed to save my people — my kind," Kurt said forcefully, his gray eyes flashing white as lightning streaked over the large windows on the left. The chandelier began to swing back and forth more violently as the two great wooden doors rattled open.

"What do you want from this, how could have you done this?" I asked, appalled, remembering the trust everyone once had in him. I thought of the respect he had from Seth who had died for such a cause.

"Because I believe in the exact same thing he does," Kurt said strongly, pointing at Uncle Kyle, who held his sword firmly. "That Misfeata can be extracted from you, and her immortality can become my own. You were never deserving of her skill or gifts. You didn't have to fight all the years I have had to, for a war that I never had the choice to claim as my own. I can restore my people. If I can harness her immortality, I can live forever and watch over that."

"You are no Elder!" Misfeata's voice rung through my throat and distorted my own voice as she savagely spoke.

"Ah, and Misfeata," Kurt said calmly. "You can be rid of her, Karla, you can go back to your schooling days, you can go back home with your mother and Paul and pretend like none of this happened," he cooed.

"Don't you think that this war has taken far too much of me to pretend like nothing ever happened?" I asked strongly, realizing my true ambition in life. The reality he spoke of was now shattered. I understood there was no ending this.

"You are much like what Elisabeth was," Kurt said serenely. "She fought against Misfeata who was lived within her, after so much was taken from her. At first she approved of Misfeata, killing all those who had taken her lover, hunting for Tyran for many, many years. But soon she realized Misfeata was not after a partnership and she fought her from within every day. Eventually, she also sought a way to extract Misfeata. For as long as Misfeata was within her — and Elisabeth as her last descendant — she constantly forced Elisabeth to drain humans. So her body would remain youthful and never deteriorate. You have immortality within you, Karla, it is just not a gift that is bestowed on your body.

Who knows what was running through Elisabeth's mind when she combined Misfeata's blood with yours and ran to her death. Perhaps she finally gave up. Let me take that burden away from you. I want you to live and have the life you've always deserved. Come with me, Karla, we can figure this out together. We will find Sebastian's grave together."

My heart pounded as so many images flickered past as if they were my own memories. *Misfeata had forced Elisabeth to drain people? Would she soon make me do the same? Is Kurt lying? Is there really a way to extract Misfeata?*

"Where is Paul?" I demanded, my mind starting to scatter. I must focus on one thing: Paul.

"He's only in that room there. Remember, Karla, if you want any kind of life with him, you will have to find a way to rid yourself of Misfeata. I can help you," he said, offering his hand out to me. I eyed the fourth door.

"I decline," I said bluntly. Kurt pulled out his sword from the sheath strapped to his side.

"Then I am sorry, Karla, but I cannot let you go," Kurt said calmly. Uncle Kyle stood protectively in front of me with his own weapon.

"Go. He is not the first with the ability to Shield that I have fought." As Uncle Kyle walked toward Kurt, I ran for the fourth door. My shaky steps rattled my sight as the noises of their weapons from behind clashed. As I thrashed at the handle I saw that it was locked. I projected my Shield on the door, blasting it open. Very little light came from within. I used my keen sight to focus on Paul. Two long chains that hung from the ceiling held him up, his arms raised over his head. His feet dangled above the ground as another two chains strapped around his ankles. His shredded shirt hung limply at his sides. There were whip marks around his chest, which still bled lightly.

Paul's dark-brown hair covered his face as his neck drooped and sagged over his chest.

"Paul," I gasped desperately, running to him. His faint whisper of my name registered as tears of joy reached my eyes. *He is alive.*

"Paul, it's me," I said, holding my hand to his face as his glazed green eyes looked down at me. "I've got you."

I slashed Aeisha across the two thick chains that held him up. He fell on top of me and I awkwardly caught all of his weight. I brushed my hand over his hair frantically as his head rested on my chest, near unconsciousness. Desperately I touched his face and hair, so relieved to have found him alive and unscathed.

"Karla—..." he gasped as he tried to lift his face to see me. As his dazed eyes looked over me, I smiled weakly.

"It's me," I said, emotion shaking my voice. I rested my hand on his cheek. "You're safe now." I cut the chains from his legs that slightly bled from the pull of the chains, setting him free.

"I'm sorry," he said, his green eyes sad as a tear slid from them. He looked very dehydrated.

"Please don't speak," I said, struggling under his heavy weight as I lifted him and tried to walk him out. As I walked for the entrance, Harmony appeared, her white loose pants wavering in the wind with a breeze I could not feel. She shot her arrow, but as she released it, aiming for my chest,

Ashley jumped on her, barging on her. The arrow drove deep into my stomach instead. My breath was knocked out of my lungs and my knees dropped.

Quickly Misfeata gathered herself as I heavily panted, struggling under Paul's weight. I watched slowly as it pushed out, Misfeata embracing my stomach as she repaired my body. Or what she thought to be her body. I thought about Kurt's words of immortality. How many people fought for such a thing? The very thing that resided within me. I feared that like Elisabeth, she would force me to drain humans, and every day for the rest of my life from now on would be a fight from within. I had never thought of my future being intertwined so significantly with another person's desires and will.

As the arrow dropped out of my stomach and Misfeata dispersed thoroughly through me once again, I stood up straight. The wound felt like shards of ice and I cried out in pain, dropping to my knees again and throwing Paul off me. He heavily plummeted to the ground. I held my stomach firmly, my head leaning against the ground as my knees coiled beneath me.

My other hand reached for Paul, wanting in every way to protect him. My breath stopped as pain echoed all through my body, a fire rising within as everything stopped. My body began to thrash, yet I still reached out for him. My eyesight became hazy and I needed adrenaline to stop my body from shutting down.

Paul's hand reached out for mine as he looked up at me, his fingertips brushing past mine. I screamed again in pain, turning onto my back where I began to splutter. A huge blackness swept over me and I felt my Shield break from my body pulsating. I fell into certain darkness. The chandelier above shattered, and the glass dropping toward me was the last thing I saw.

Chapter Thirty-Five- To Fight For

My eyes were heavy to lift as my body now felt like it was drifting apart. My eyes felt sticky and unwilling to open. I just drifted; naked, and vulnerable, sinking. I felt my body slowly plummeting.

"Your weak body is a disgrace to offer me," Misfeata said hauntingly. I couldn't see her as my eyes were still closed, but her torturous words were always present when I fell into an unconscious state.

"I don't like this," I said contently, my voice shaky and distant. The drift pulled me under, but it was serene and contemplative. If I don't fight this, if I don't swim up — I will die.

And yet I found my arms and legs unmoving, unmotivated to keep going. "I'm tired," I said honestly. This was such an easy way to rest, to be free from Misfeata, pain, guilt, and grief. I could be free and I could rest. This war could be over.

"Stupid girl. Do you really think it would be that easy? What happened to 'you must always fight'... you fight for Paul. What happened to that strength? Swim, dear child."

"You don't care what happens to me, only what will happen to my body," I said unfazed. A small jolt rocked me as if someone were trying to shake me conscious again. I didn't want to be woken. "I'm just tired — I want to rest."

"It is very simple, really. You lose yourself to unconsciousness forever, that is okay, I will claim your body as mine forever anyway. I won't have to fight you. It will be mine, you will simply be a memory," Misfeata said calmly. "I won't protect that boy."

My eyes opened as I thought of Paul under the manipulating hands of Misfeata. The dark space around me gave me no clarity. I thought of his face; his brilliant green eyes; his dark-brown, almost black hair; his large arms and firm chest; his perfectly pink lips and brilliant skin. I could never let Misfeata hurt him.

My choice was to push away serenity and peace. I choose for the remainder of my life to fight. It was Paul who helped me in that decision, whether he realized it or not. The effect he had played on my heart; he let it beat and patter like rain on a rooftop. Paul was my salvation.

"Paul," I whispered. His name was on my lips before I could even articulate the sound. I felt exhausted and was jolted heavily from beneath. My eyes groggily opened as I winced at my stomach. Paul's dark-brown hair brushed against the side of my face. I looked ahead; Paul was running with me in his arms. I held firmly onto his chest, my arms wrapped around him. He ran for the long wooden bridge which segregated the castle from the land. Behind us ran Uncle Kyle, Scott, Paige, and Ashley. I slowly came to consciousness, taking in the random staircases and waterlines that poured into the wells below.

I frowned in confusion, wondering what happened: *wasn't I dying without adrenaline?*

Ashley ran ahead, pushing the large wooden doors open. It was a circular room with huge bay windows. Above us fluttered little gold birds that idly flew around overhead. They were peaceful and serene. Of all the bizarre creatures Taskatae created, these were beautiful.

They swarmed the room, surrounding us. Gently they landed on the small perches that were set for them, whistling and singing to us peacefully. Slowly I pushed myself off Paul, my legs dangling from our height difference before I could rest them easy on the floor. He looked over me gently, still resting his hand under me as I slightly wobbled. I felt Misfeata quickly renewing my energy.

I assessed the marks on Paul's chest that were now faint. Scott obviously had healed him. As my hand lingered on his chest, I paused in thought intently as I looked into his green eyes. I cared about him more than I had ever realized and more than he would ever know. I could've ended it all, but for him I gave myself a second chance. For better or for worse, there was only one way to see what could come of it. And that was to live.

To my surprise, however, it was Misfeata who encouraged me to live. Quickly I realized her manipulation. She wouldn't have been able to possess my body if I were dead. If I had decided to go, she would have to, too.

'Clever as always,' Misfeata sarcastically spat.

"We must keep going," Ashley yelled from the other side of the large room, the door held open.

"Come on, Karla," Paul said gently, grabbing my hand from his chest and holding it as he pulled me toward the door. My feet froze and Paul looked back at my unmoving body oddly and then behind me, his face changing to white. He stood in front of me protectively.

214

"Well, I finally found you," Taskatae's voice rang out. She had puppet-master control once again over my body.

"More or less, I found you," Scott corrected, walking back into the room, his face hard and his pink eyes flickering over me as he too noticed I couldn't move. He rested his hand on Paul's shoulder and pushed him back behind him, much to Paul's dismay as he tried to lift me and take me away.

He froze, Paul could no longer move as Taskatae has changed her target. I was released.

"Oh, a lover," Taskatae smiled as I looked at her angrily. "They are the best to use — much like your father. Oh, how your mother screamed."

As I went to throw Aeisha at her throat, my hand froze in mid-air. Her blazing blue crystal eyes looked at me. Her long black dress trailed behind her from the entrance of the wooden doors.

"What do you want from her?" Paul asked desperately as the other three gathered behind.

"You see, she took something very precious to me. You took my Raven from me," she said angrily. My assumption was correct: she was Raven's mother. "You took my one child from me that I had spent many, many years loving. You also offer me the chance of immortality. I could alter you in so many ways. I get so tired of constantly having to adjust and exercise my own body to keep alive for so long and to be beautiful at the same time. Well, its time consuming. However, if I possessed the immortality which hides within you... I wouldn't need to do that."

"You have Nathanial so close and yet you never thought of using him. You don't need Karla," Ashley said firmly.

"Nathanial is family," Taskatae snapped. "I couldn't very well do that to him who once was my son-in-law. You took it all away from us; you took his father, Praytar, away from him and you took my baby, Raven. And now you will watch as I do the same to you."

Consumed by her hatred of me, one by one she took control of the others, flinging them out of the room. She attempted to do the same to Scott who evaded her, but she had no control over him. The golden birds flew to the direction of Taskatae's command. Slamming both large wooden doors closed so the others could not enter, they fluttered frantically above in rage. Their once beautiful, serene gold vanished under her manipulation.

As Taskatae had a firm grip of me that I couldn't move, Scott whispered to me, but my ears were not sharp enough to hear what he said. He vanished and as he did, my mouth widened. My body felt heavy and I choked at the sudden shock of having Scott vanish into me. I felt him flutter inside of me; my every individual cell changing as slowly Taskatae's grip of me began to dissipate. I slowly opened my fist and closed it again, noticing that Scott was blanketing me within his own cells so Taskatae could no longer control me.

She raged as I took one heavy step forward. Scott's entirety was within me as I ran at Taskatae in rage. Scott hated her as much as me; this was something we could only accomplish together.

I ran for her with my only blade of Aeisha, charging for her, angry for all that she's done to my father. She commanded the golden birds to attack us as she realized her hold of me was no more. As I cut toward the birds, I frantically covered my face with part of my jacket as their scratching claws dug into me.

My body suddenly felt lighter as Scott's wolf form manifested from my chest, pouring toward the birds and biting at them savagely before jumping for Taskatae and biting her leg.

A wolf with a snake tail jumped from the doors behind her, trailing along her long black dress as it leapt for Scott who then fought it in wolf form. She fixated on me, Misfeata stirring in fury as Taskatae revealed the partnered blade of Aeisha.

"This belonged to my daughter," Taskatae announced savagely.

"They are mine!" Misfeata's growl tore through my lips. My head spun as I felt the familiar trace of Tyran, knowing him to now be too close for Misfeata not to notice. *So he is here.*

I tried to push Misfeata back, queasy as her constant clinging hands tried to possess me. The doors behind us burst open as Max Jacket and Trish entered with black eyes.

"This is my fight!" Max Jacket burst in rage. A bolt of thunder smashed the birds away from me, but so forcefully that the blow rocked the room and pushed me back. As I projected my Shield away from the blast I was pushed back through the window. I screamed as I landed face first into something hard.

A firm claw wrapped itself around me — my fall had been broken. I looked up to see the large white bird form of Scott, who fluttered high, his wingspan wide.

An arrow shot for his wing, plummeting us both to the ground. Once again his form broke my fall as he transformed gracefully. As he changed, I was quickly lost in myself as Misfeata took full control; her eyes fixated on Nathanial whose own eyes gleamed back in malicious joy.

Scott pushed out the arrow from his arm, understanding Harmony had shot him using her bow. His black eyes raged as he ran for her in wolf form, dodging her arrows as she frantically shot them at him.

Misfeata ran for Tyran as he did her, using Nathanial's body. His eyes were raging as I imagined he sensed Borac so close within his grasp.

Aeisha clashed with his long black sword. After he looked over us, Tyran head-butted me and then kicked me, pushing my body back.

Misfeata ran for him, dodging the swing of his sword, and slashing at his wrist. He artfully evaded her, elbowing her in the stomach. As she hunched over, he kneed her in the face, knocking me to the ground.

Thunderous clouds shattered the sky above. She hastily flipped herself over. As he tried to bring his blade down, Misfeata backhanded him across the face, knocking him two steps to the right where she wrapped her legs around his waist, trying to put as much pressure on his neck as possible to snap it.

He grabbed her wrists as he flipped her over, her hands still tight on his wrists. She used them for support to pull herself up and kick him in the face. As he stepped back she once again stood.

"Still, you do not know your place," Nathanial spoke in Tyran's coarse voice.

"I will never fall to silence because of your filthy methods. Sebastian would've hated what you have become," she said, spitting blood toward his feet. "You ruined our family!"

"You tore us apart!" he cursed, trying to drive his black blade in deep. He scathed Misfeata's stomach as she grabbed the handle, pulling it past her and plunging Aeisha into his stomach. As she tried to wildly slash at his throat he pulled his sword back, cutting Misfeata's hand which once had firm hold of his blade.

Their Shield's seemed irrelevant; powerful, yet too equally matched. I feared for when either of them would obtain their blades and turn into monstrous beasts, like the last time such an encounter occurred. A huge bang of thunder rattled the ground as behind us Max Jacket, Trish, and Taskatae fought. Their blades were so close to Tyran and Misfeata's hands.

To our right near more castle doors, with a pipe of water running into a well, Harmony fluttered around Scott, dodging him and shooting arrows. *Harmony too is a creature of Taskatae's.* How many could she create, how many creatures has she created from her eggs and how many people had she tortured and changed — just to claim herself the title of 'Mother'?

My worst fears came to fruition: one of Taskatae's wolf creatures grabbed Borac from Max Jacket's back. Trish quickly set it into flames and a bolt of thunder also stopped it. Another grabbed it, charging for Nathanial.

It was my hand that held it. Misfeata obtained his Immortal Blade, but the gem from it burned her and began to drain Misfeata's hand, making her instinctively pull back. Nathanial grabbed Borac firmly, smiling as he had finally obtained all that he needed to fight Misfeata. Without the partnered blade of Aeisha that Taskatae still held onto, we could not fight equally. Misfeata was so dependent on her blades, which obtained her soul. They were the only things that could enable her to turn into a beast of sorts, to match Tyran's strength.

He threw the black sword toward us, Misfeata deflecting it. His speed had increased. He aimed again. Borac cut deeply into our stomach, the edge of his blade edging up into my body. Misfeata squirmed under the injury, although she seemed to be taking it lightly as she pulled away from him.

"Oh, how this time apart has been miserable without my old friend, Borac," Nathanial said, his eyes gleaming as he admired his sword. "Today is the day I kill you, sister."

As he spoke, Misfeata quickly regained her breath, trying to heal herself as she focused on Taskatae. She was weaving back and forth, dodging Max and Trish as one by one she took control of them, trying to deflect them. She controlled Trish, who now seemed dispensable to Max Jacket who raged and still attacked; blinded by the hatred he had for Taskatae who took his wife.

"Around you, I just cannot contain myself," Nathanial beamed, part of his ear slowly stretching out as a red gem protruded. I watched in horror as he changed Nathanial's form. *Nathanial cannot come back from this. Does he fight him from within like I do Misfeata? Can he control his Elder?*

Borac became a part of him. His hand that wrapped around the handle shone with red gems as it was now an extension of him. Misfeata ran for him, trying to end this before he had completed any transformation. *I cannot let her obtain Aeisha, if she does so around Tyran she won't be able to control herself. She will destroy me.*

She slashed the blade across his ear, but he only laughed in response. Aeisha pulsated out of Misfeata's hand as she began to quiver from a vibration caused by contact with his ear. She ran for Aeisha, unfazed by losing her in the first place. But as she scurried toward the blade, Nathanial had already caught up, kicking Aeisha further away.

Misfeata dodged as he tried to bring Borac down on her right shoulder. He then ploughed into her stomach but she once again dodged him. With speed he charged at her, the tip of Borac aimed toward Misfeata again. She braced herself, using her arms to block the attack before it punctured our chest.

As she diverted it above her head, pain shot through my arms as they were deeply cut into. Blood sprayed: my blood. Something Misfeata so carelessly spared. As his blade was diverted she punched into his stomach twice and kicked him in the face, knocking him off his feet.

She ran for Aeisha quickly, grabbing her from the ground, only to be just as quickly pushed back in defense as Tyran tried to cut her deeply. He missed once again but much to Misfeata's surprise, he punched her hard in the stomach, winding her. He kicked her to the ground. His projected Shield was enhanced onto his foot, shattering our own Shield.

Misfeata was stunned for a moment, wincing into the ground, surprised by the powerful blow. I tried claiming my body. I could fight more tactically; she was too scattered when she fought Tyran. She could not control her rage.

Misfeata, you will kill us! I screamed as I tried to break through her raging thoughts.

Tyran ran for us, kicking us in the stomach and flinging us into the castle wall as he continued to project his Shield more powerfully than our own. Without Aeisha's partnered blade, Misfeata was not at her full strength.

She winced, quickly projecting her Shield as pink ripples appeared around me in protectiveness, Misfeata doing all she could. Tyran quickly penetrated our Shield, punched us in the stomach, and then slammed his blade into our shoulder.

As we were now pinned onto the castle, Misfeata grew dim as slowly the pain reached out to her. My own scream was breaking through my lips as I have gained control of my body.

I had to try to protect myself; Misfeata was killing us. Angrily she fought back. I looked into the eyes of Nathanial who was also too far gone. *Is this what he wanted? Was he happy to give himself as an offering to Tyran?* His dark-brown eyes were far too much of a reminder of Lucas's eyes.

Tyran retrieved his blade, dropping me to the ground as his hand clutched around my throat, raising me and choking me. I couldn't reach the ground. My Shield only tickled against his immaculate one as I tried so hard to throw him away from me. But if Misfeata couldn't reach the same strength as him, how could I?

A small knife pulsated off Nathanial's Shield from the side. He looked over, irritated by Lucas who ran for him with his large sword in hand. Diverting Lucas's attack, Nathanial jumped back. I dropped to the ground, gasping for air and clutching my throat as I felt vomit rise. Misfeata was not helping as she created most of the nauseous feelings within as still she tried to scamper free.

My shoulder and arms bled heavily in repercussion of how careless Misfeata was. Tyran squirmed as he grabbed his head, flinging it back and forth, before his eyes stilled on Lucas.

"Why would you turn on your own brother?" Nathanial yelled, Tyran's voice no longer present. *Nathanial can push back Tyran?* As Nathanial gasped under what I thought to be the same agony Misfeata inflicted on me, he looked over his hand, saddened by the sight. Was he trying to fight Tyran as he changed his form? Is this why he had not yet fully changed?

"You know I can't let you hurt her!" Lucas said with sword in hand. "And let us be honest, any brotherly love we once shared vanished many years before."

Suddenly Harmony screamed as Scott pulled out her heart, his eyes flickering black as he hunched over her, staring into her eyes as they dimmed. Scott had numerous arrows protruding from him. The wind brushed past my eyes as I watched the gruesome image. He threw her into the ground, throwing her heart next to her unfazed.

From the castle doors Uncle Kyle, Ashley, Paige, and Paul ran out. They halted as they took in Scott, who looked at them hauntingly as if he were about to attack. After a pause his pink eyes resumed their color as he contained his rage.

"Then this is how we shall end it all: by your blood, brother," Nathanial said savagely. Taskatae, Trish, and Max Jacket still fought. I clung to the thought of having Aeisha's partnered blade to defend myself with. I felt so uneven without her, only having one. *But if I do that, I risk the chance of Misfeata regaining my body and changing my form completely.*

Nathanial's ear returned to normal and the gems around his hand shattered showing his hand, which wrapped around the handle of Borac. *So we can change back if we haven't fully changed? Unlike his father, Praytar, who had almost completely transformed.*

"I never could bring myself to love you," Nathanial sneered as he ran for Lucas.

Taskatae's malicious grunt snapped me from my daze of watching the two brothers fight as she had been struck in the arm by Max Jacket's thunder. She drew her hand back and I noticed Aeisha still strapped to her waist. *I must obtain her if I want to properly defend myself.*

I cautiously circled her, trying to stay out of her sight as the other two kept her distracted. As I walked behind her I noticed Paul to be mimicking me, obviously realizing what I intended.

She looked at me evilly, noticing me as I reached her from behind. I couldn't move as she resumed using me as a puppet against Max Jacket and Trish. Paul rolled along the ground reaching for Aeisha. He had thrown it toward me. Taskatae grabbed him by his throat, whistling in rage as she began to summon more creatures from her castle.

With both my partnered blades in hand, finally I felt complete and competent enough to fight, no longer feeling unbalanced by the absence of the blades I had longed for my whole lifetime without knowing it.

A large black bird swooped for them but the white bird form of Scott clashed with it in the sky, diverting it so I could run for Paul. As I ran for her, Shield projected, she let go of her firm grip over Paul, flinging him away from her as she held tightly onto me.

I tried my hardest to fight her, but her grip was too strong and she raised Aeisha to my throat with a smile widening across her face. I felt her intention behind it and her fixation on the revenge she had been after for so long, therefore forgetting the reason as to why she once wanted to keep me alive. Scott jumped into my body again, releasing her command of me so I could freely act of my own will.

Strangely, he extracted himself and ran for another creature, leaving me once again vulnerable. She claimed my body again. She forced me to throw myself into the bricks of the castle walls repeatedly. *She is going to kill me*.

Her grasp loosened and I looked over dazed, but Scott had not entered me once again. My body was free. I looked at Taskatae who choked in shock at the knife that was now stuck within her chest. Her hand wavered around her stomach as she looked into Paul's eyes.

As she swiped for him, Scott's bird form swooped and collected him by his shoulders, saving him from the ambush of creatures that now gathered in the spot where Paul had just stood.

She choked, wincing and dropping to her knees. *This is no fake creature of hers now: this is the real Taskatae*. Max Jacket was not too far from her, looking squarely into her dying eyes. She commanded her creatures to attack him, but Trish shot fire at them all, keeping them away from her father.

"You, Taskatae, I have been searching for, for a long time," Max Jacket said, his black eyes not moving from her face. "You killed what was most important to me, and yet all I can do is kill you in return. There is no justice in that. But I will still kill you."

Her hand wavered over him, but I could tell she was now too weak to control him. His face was firm as a lightning bolt struck her, lighting the ground with what seemed like a blue flame. The light lingered in my eyes as if it were in slow motion. Max Jacket continued to watch as the smoke dispersed and Taskatae's body fell to the ground.

"Father!" Trish yelled, setting a wall of flames behind him in defense. Nathanial jumped through them, his Shield keeping him safe. He pierced Borac through the back of Max Jacket's wheelchair, piercing him in the chest.

Lucas grabbed Nathanial from behind, flinging him away as Max Jacket's eyes widened and paled into his creamy white.

"Father!" Trish screamed again, running to her father's side. Scott's white bird form manifested into his human form, dropping Paul as he rolled to a stop. Trish and Scott came together to their father's side, Trish crying and therefore confirming to us that he has already passed. She dropped to her knees, wailing and holding onto his hand.

Scott tried to comfort her, placing his hand softly onto her shoulder.

"Get away from me!" she screamed looking up into her older brother's eyes. Her blue eyes were filled with sorrow. Despite her protestations she cried deeply into her brother's suit.

I cowered against the wall of the castle, trying to push Misfeata away as she still so eagerly wanted to fight her brother. Paul came to my side, holding my shoulder firmly as I struggled to push her away. Her grabbing hands were firmly pushing toward my mind and heart.

"Karla!" Nathanial's voice rang out. He now charged for me, Borac in hand, ready to kill. I raised Aeisha in defense, conflicted as I still tried to push Misfeata down.

Lucas quickly ran beside him, cutting the back of his brother's legs but he continued running through the pain, charging for me. Lucas grabbed his shoulder firmly, spinning him slightly. Lucas now stood in front of me, taking the brunt of Borac, which came down on him. But Lucas had already pierced his sword deep into his brother.

Borac slipped out of Nathanial's hand, as he looked over his brother, shocked.

"She took everything from me," Nathanial spat blood into Lucas's face. "And she will do the same to you. I wish you nothing but suffering and misery."

"I am sorry, brother, I truly am. This is not something I wanted to do," Lucas said heavily. Nathanial's eyes fixated on me as he tried to still grab for me. I cowered behind Lucas, scared of the grabbing hands that so hungrily wanted to drain and kill me.

After one loud more gasp, Nathanial fell backward. Lucas was unable to pull the sword out. He looked at me, blood splattered across his face, his eyes sad.

Looking into his dark-brown eyes I wondered if it were me he fought for or if the hatred he held for his brother was strong enough to force him to do that. Although he hated his brother, he still loved him in a way.

"Karla," he whispered, his black glove rising to my face as he went to cup it. He pulled away, his eyebrows burrowing deep as he looked at me in confusion. He clutched at his chest before taking a few steps backward and crouching as he breathed heavily.

"Lucas," I said reaching out to him, he only pulled away further, breathing loudly.

"It hurts," he gushed, holding his head. Misfeata began stirring within me as I held my own head, pained by her irritating pull. I looked once again into Lucas's scared dark-brown eyes, and he pushed away his sandy-blonde fringe, realizing it as I did: *Tyran is now within Lucas.*

"Lucas," I whispered, my heart now painful as Misfeata so desperately wanted me to take his life while he was in a weakened state.

"It will only get worse, won't it?" he said with worry.

"No, we can get through this," I babbled, reaching out for him again.

"Lucas!" Trish raged, tears still welling over her eyes that had now vanished into black. "Your blood did this to my father!"

A burst of flames trailed along between Lucas and I. I threw Paul behind me, projecting my Shield as I protected him from the flames. I looked back, and when the flames cleared, I saw Lucas crawl toward Borac, grabbing the handle as he looked up at me, his eyes lost.

"I'm sorry, Karla. I don't think I can control him," Lucas's voice quivered. A tear slid down his face as he firmly grabbed Borac and projected his Shield against the flames that attacked. He lost his footing as he began to run away.

Uncle Kyle's hand firmly clung around my arm. I so desperately wanted to run after him. Lucas's run was staggered as he swayed from side to side. Misfeata radiated through me angrily as I felt my body freeze. I watched Lucas run away from me. I coughed into the ground as my body once again shut down on me.

Darkness quickly took over me. My vision of Lucas was fading in and out as he ran away from me.

'Combust your Shield,' Misfeata said angrily from within me. She now had no grip on my body as my life faded in and out. 'Goodness child, it will save you!'

I waved my wrist, flicking it, but despite all my efforts it seemed like more of a spasm. But somehow Uncle Kyle understood, moving Paul away as I tried to do what Misfeata instructed.

Concentrating within, I faded into darkness. I hurriedly projected my Shield from within, letting it break within me to combust outside of my body, throwing one of the nearby golden birds into the side of the castle.

I gasped in a breath, shaking and cold as exhaustedly I looked ahead of me. Lucas was now out of sight.

What happened? I asked Misfeata, surprised that my body was no longer shutting down.

'Combusting your Shield, like last time, creates an organic adrenaline within you. You can now save yourself when your body shuts down,' she explained, exhausted herself as she faded within me.

We have found a way that I can save myself? I can now survive?

Paul helped me up as he looked at me oddly. The others surrounded us.

"Are you okay?" Paul asked, wiping over my face desperately. I smiled faintly, shocked and relieved the fight was now over. I had come for Paul, he was the reason why I so badly wanted to fight.

"Now that you are alright," I confirmed, holding my stomach as I tried to stand. I watched in sympathy as Trish continued to cry over her father's death. Although saddened by another young girl losing her father, I couldn't feel too much sorrow for Max Jacket. He had helped ruin my life. As I looked at all the creatures, the bodies of Taskatae, and Nathanial, I noticed one who had fought us to no longer be here.

"What happened to Kurt?" I asked Uncle Kyle. He dipped his head, the top of his red hair showing blood.

"Although I don't believe the reasons as to why he wants to find Sebastian's grave, I think we should at least look, Karla. If there is a chance to relieve you of this burden—…" he started before Ashley cut him off.

"You let him escape," Ashley angrily accused.

"If he so strongly believed in it too, then I cannot ignore it. Karla, I think there is a chance of this being real," he said pleadingly. "Don't you believe it too, Paul?"

I looked at Paul as he looked back over me. His lips widened as he tried to speak and then silenced, saying nothing. "Paul?" I asked honestly. Was this something he truly wanted, believed in?

"I don't know, Karla. But if there is a chance, shouldn't we try? Don't you want to be rid of Misfeata?" Paul asked innocently.

"It is an outrageous thought. It's not plausible," Paige dismissed.

"I believe it," Scott said as he walked over to us strongly, his purple suit filthy and torn. "I want the Elders gone. This war has gone on for far too long over the stupidity of sibling rivalry."

"Please, Karla, consider it," Uncle Kyle pleaded. I thought of the chance of dispelling Misfeata, ignoring the outrage she spat from within. I rejected the possibility for now. I looked at those within my trusted circle, those with whom I had just fought, risking our lives together, for each other.

If I could make their lives easier and no longer have to fight, then is that not what I should do? Should I not offer that to myself too — the chance of a life without fighting?

I looked into Paul's beautiful green eyes, thinking of a future that would be had in comparison with the one that was to be manipulated by Misfeata. I could reunite with my mother, properly. *If there is a chance of that, no matter how crazy or mad it may sound, should I not take it?*

"Right now..." I said, trying to think of the present only. "I want to rest," I finished, dispelling the heavy conversation amongst us all. *This conversation can be had, but for now I must rest, we all must.*

"Rest sounds nice," Paul said with a small smile. Ashley agreed and began to lead the others toward the wooden bridge. As I walked over the bridge I looked back at what we left behind; remembering Lucas's face as he ran away from me.

"It will all be okay," Paul promised, holding my hand and walking me over one of the dead Starkorfs. I looked at him earnestly, hoping him to be right. I recognized the torture in Lucas's eyes: he was losing control of his own body as the Elder within tried to possess him. I knew that feeling too well. I wondered about his promise. He had sworn he would not harm me or fight me, that he would fight Tyran off. But my belief in that statement dimmed. I had watched him take Borac, his Immortal Blade, and then flee.

Was that Lucas who reached for it, or Tyran?

Chapter One- Ripples

$\mathscr{D}$ays have passed since our confrontation with Taskatae, her creatures, and Lucas's brother, Nathanial, who now lay dead. My thoughts continuously drifted to how Lucas had so quickly run away from me, scared of Tyran's hold over his soul and body. I looked into his dark-brown eyes and saw that he mirrored the emotions I experienced with Misfeata. And that was mostly fear: fear to know that we may not have the ability to contain them within; that the Elder may erode our very soul and take possession of our body; that they would leave what we had of ourselves as a mere memory, a shadow. It would always be a fight, and no matter how much he believed that it would not happen between him and me, it had now become our fate. I had only had two days of rest since that horrific day and images of his pleading eyes still pulled at my chest.

Ashley tapped me over the head, lightly knocking my thoughts away as I focused on him again. "Are you focusing?" he asked, irritated by my eagerness to escape into my thoughts. He raised his hands into fists again, preparing for my attack. I raised mine to his and we bumped fists together, acknowledging it was now fair game as we trained. It was early in the morning and everyone else still rested within the motel room of the seemingly deserted town. Both Ashley and I struggled to sleep after all that had happened, and although Scott was able to heal everyone rapidly, everyone was still exhausted from our battle.

Ashley's wounds were healed except for his eyebrow piercing, which left a small scar. For reasons that he had not yet explained he kept the scar there, perhaps in memory of the day in which we had avenged his father's death by killing Nathanial. We trained behind the motel in a small park which contained only two swings, one slide, and a bench.

He came at me and his large arms punched toward my face. I quickly blocked him and threw him to the left. I jumped into my punch, aiming at his face, but he speedily evaded me. Grabbing my closed fist and holding me beneath my arm, he flipped me over his back. I caught myself, slamming my feet into the ground so I wouldn't jar my back. I then used his arm, wrapping myself around it and flinging myself over it to attempt to lock him in a hold. He hastily let go, releasing me from the hold he had on me.

A piece of my light-brown hair blocked my vision and I blew it away, still cautious of what Ashley was planning next as I pivoted on my feet. I felt Paul's presence and I looked up toward the bench. Ashley took advantage of my distraction, punching into my stomach and brushing past my side to kick at the back of my leg. As I dropped he wrapped his arms around my neck. Not tightly but enough so I was unable to escape. I exhaled in frustration, tapping on his arm to signal that he had me. Although I could easily use my Shield to deflect him, this was a hand-to-hand combat. It was obvious I had lost because I had let myself become side-tracked.

"You need to stop dozing off or I'll start thinking that you are letting me win," Ashley taunted as he rounded on me again. I pulled my fringe over my face and tightened my hair.

"Karla!" Scott shrilly called. Ashley flicked out his hands in agitation at the second interruption. Scott waved over at me flamboyantly before tapping on Paul's shoulder and pointing to Ashley. "Go train. I have to talk to Karla."

Paul looked at him, unimpressed at being told what to do, but he raised his eyebrows at me compliantly and we exchanged places. Ashley swiftly rounded on him, unfazed by the change in opponent. Paul was a close match to Ashley when it came to hand-to-hand after all those years of training to be the best boxer in our small town of Roperia. It was all other elements and paranormal abilities that he lacked in combat.

After everything that had happened, I realized that it was Paul whom I fought for. He had been by my side for so long now that I seemed to have forgotten my appreciation for him. After Taskatae had taken him, threatening to do the same to him as she had to my father, I went into a frenzy to rescue and save him. I had never realized just how dear Paul truly was to me.

"We have a problem," Scott said, now serious as his pink eyes watched Paul and Ashley fight. My heart sank as I once again felt that this was a never-ending run. There was always a problem; there was not a brief moment where we could just rest and think of what to do next.

"What's happened?" I asked, not wanting to hear the answer. I watched Paul and Ashley as they sounded one another out before trying to hit at one another and lock each other in holds.

"I went to see Trish this morning," he admitted, surprising me because of how contentious their relationship was. She hated him. Although you would think the feeling would be mutual, I believed that Scott cared for his younger sister deeply, especially now that their father was killed by Nathanial in front of them both. They were both on their own, but Trish had never strayed far from her father's side, making me wonder where she could now go. Although I despised her as she constantly irritated me and tried to pick fights, my sympathy was with her after losing her father.

I had no pity for Max Jacket, however. He had in so many ways jeopardized Paul's life, as well as my own. No longer would we be manipulated by him just so he could gain power or knowledge.

"I have been watching her closely and monitoring where she's going. At first she was heading back home to our cottage to bury our father, but since then she has had to change her direction. She came across a large group of Starkorfs heading our way," Scott explained, staring at his nails in contemplation.

"And let me guess, they're on their way here?" I sneered in a rhetorical tone, unable to laugh at such absurd circumstances anymore. Of course they were coming toward us. After Ashley and I defeated Praytar we had single-handedly ruined their feasting habits, home, and leader. After that horrific day the Starkorfs fled. When we were searching for Taskatae and Nathanial we learned that some followed Nathanial — the son of Praytar and host of Tyran — but there was still a large amount that were not with him. Who did they follow? Those who followed Nathanial struggled to keep their human form; their feasting habits obviously were affected by the presence of a new leader.

"I'll ignore your queer sense of humor... yes, they are. Toward the castle of Taskatae, in fact, where they will find the remains of their prince and learn that Taskatae has fallen. They will follow us. You have declared war by killing both their leader and his son."

"I know," I said, closing my eyes. How could I have acted in any other way? I looked at Paul, who now sweated through his grey sleeveless shirt, panting heavily as he and Ashley attacked one another more viciously as they were too evenly matched. It was a surprise to Ashley to acknowledge that although Paul did not train as a Shielder, he could fight as well as one.

When I thought of Paul I realized that why I killed Praytar and Nathanial was partially to protect and save him. And although he could have run, and could have escaped this bloodshed and war, he stayed by my side. His courage strengthened me. *I will protect him no matter what, no matter who the enemy may be.*

"Who are they following?" I asked, trying to formulate a plan. First we would have to evacuate, creating some distance between them and us. I would have Ashley return to where my mother, Helena, Suzumiya, and Chris were hiding to confirm they were safe. For precaution they might have to be moved. I couldn't have my mother involved in this fight again, not after it broke her the last time. She despised my kind and all others who were not human. I was forced to take her parental rights away: to shelter me. I allowed her to be put into an unconscious state against her will so that I could protect her from afar.

I now had Uncle Kyle, who had been fighting against the Starkorfs for all these years since I was little, waiting to be reunited with me to help me find a cure to rid me of the Elder Misfeata who resided within me. He had been deluded by lies and false hope. Such a cure could not exist. However, just to have him by my side was a comfort.

"Karla, it's not Lucas," Scott said carefully, surprising me. I looked at him bashfully. Why would he assume I thought it was Lucas who led them? My heart instantly twisted at his name and the thought of him rising against me. I frowned, thinking of the naïve promise he once made to me: that no matter what our fates, he would not fight against me. But as Tyran entered his body and tried to possess him for the first time, I knew that it was a promise neither of us could keep. Despite this, no matter what the circumstance, I did not believe or assume that it was Lucas who led them in the hunt for my head. But now Scott created doubt in my mind. *Are we truly fated to fight and hate one another?*

"Have you ever been in contact with Eden before?" he asked seriously.

I thought of the few Starkorf names I knew and shook my head, not registering the name. "No, who is he?" I asked in anticipation.

"He was second in command in Praytar's time." Scott let the words hang heavy in the air as I thought of the education Lucas once gave me on the Starkorfs structure. He had once mentioned that Raven was daughter to the second-in-command. My stomach squirmed at the realization that it was Raven's father. My eyes widened as I looked up at him, his grim face confirmed my suspicions.

"Raven's father," I whispered with despair, realizing now that his vengeance and hatred of me ran far deeper than those who simply wanted to harness the Elder within me. This was now personal. Raven was the first Starkorf I had decided to kill. Before my birth she hurt my parents and would probably have killed them if the previous host of Misfeata, Elisabeth, hadn't intervened. She had hurt everyone around me; drained and murdered more people than I could imagine just to keep her child-like body. She tried to kill me for the reward of my Immortal Blades, Aeisha. And ever since that day I had decided to end her life — to kill for the first time — I had suffered the consequences.

It had been only days ago that I left in search of her mother, Taskatae, who destroyed my family and turned my father into a beast.

Praytar's son, Nathanial, who was engaged to her daughter, all had a good reason to personally want to kill me and those who were close to me.

And now I had taken Eden's only daughter as well as his lover. I closed my eyes at the thought of the ripple effect I had created. I narrowed my eyes on Paul again, inhaling deeply and thinking only of him as my legs nervously bounced.

"We'll let the others rest for a little while longer and then we must leave. We need to place distance between them and us before we revaluate. We don't know their numbers yet. We just need to make sure we are alive and far away," I said heavily, ignoring the sinking feeling in my stomach.

"Karla, the majority of Praytar's army followed not Nathanial but Eden; he is well known for his years of service and combat, some even deeming him to be one of their best warriors," Scott explained, his pink eyes looking at me earnestly.

The wind blew in my eyes and I blinked several times, digesting this information. I looked at him blankly, trying to muster the courage I knew that would be needed. As much as I wanted to face my new opponent with determination and courage, I couldn't help but dread our next few steps. *When will this war be over? Is it in my death that I can finally be at peace?* I wondered if my death would finally end the war between the Elders.

"Eden is after me and when the time comes I will face him," I said, holding both my hands under my chin and focusing on Paul with determination. My mother also came to my mind, strengthening my resolve. "This is my fight."

About The Author

Kia grew up in the Darling Downs Region in Queensland, Australia. Graduating High School, she pursued a career in freelance journalism. In 2014, having always had a passion for writing fiction, she decided to follow her dream of becoming an accomplished author.

Now living in Edinburgh, Scotland Kia has a can do attitude, a strong will and the touch of kindness that makes it hard not to fall in love with her. Announced 'The Best New Author of 2015' by AusRomToday, and being awarded numerous awards, she has no intentions of stopping. Kia Carrington-Russell is definitely the new author to be looking out for.

Learn more about Kia at www.kiacarrington-russell.com and follow @kia_crystal on Instagram.

Also Available

The Three Immortal Blades
Possession Of My Soul
Possession Of My Heart
Possession Of My Fate

Phantom Wolf Series
Phantom Wolf
Sia
Phantom Eye
Phantom King

Token Huntress Series
Token Huntress
Token Vampire
Token Wolf

The Shadow Minds Journal Series

My Escort Series
My Escort
My Exception
My Expectation

Taming Himself Series
Aroused
Taste

www.ingramcontent.com/pod-product-compliance
Lightning Source LLC
Chambersburg PA
CBHW030641110726
47901CB00002B/534